PENGUIN BOOKS

2922

THE PENGUIN BOOK OF
MODERN EUROPEAN SHORT STORIES

The Penguin Book of
Modern European Short Stories

EDITED BY
ROBERT TAUBMAN

PENGUIN BOOKS

Penguin Books Ltd, Harmondsworth, Middlesex, England
Penguin Books Australia, Ltd, Ringwood, Victoria, Australia

—

First published 1969

—

This selection copyright © Robert Taubman, 1969

—

Made and printed in Great Britain by
Cox & Wyman Ltd,
London, Reading and Fakenham
Set in Monotype Garamond

CONTENTS

INTRODUCTION

GORKY'S 'Twenty-six Men and a Girl' – already famous at the end of the nineteenth century – was an 'advanced' story for its time: not so much because it depends on a point of sexual psychology, which could as well have turned up in Maupassant, as that the point here is one of group psychology, as Gorky insists ('There were twenty-six of us'). The real, almost impersonal subject is the group of workers in the bakery: the proletariat. Sex and the proletariat are two subjects later writers were to develop. Yet Gorky, with his eye for the contradictions of human behaviour, was apt to make out of any subject a mainly psychological point – and in spite of the elaborations that the twentieth century had still to bring to it, psychology as a self-sufficient point for a story was played out by the end of the nineteenth.

I see this story, therefore, as marking the end of something – a nineteenth-century tradition – rather than a new beginning. The starting point I would choose is in the last paragraph of Proust's 'Filial Sentiments' – in the recoil before the horror of life that gives rise to the question:

What joy, what reason for living, what life, can stand up to the impact of such awareness? Which is true, it or the joy of life? Which of them is the Truth?

There is nothing so direct in the whole of *À la Recherche du Temps Perdu*. At the same time, anyone will recognize the tone of Proust's novel in this short piece – it is both freer with its literary allusions and, on the other hand, closer to reality (it was written out of an immediate response to an actual event), yet it belongs no less than the novel to Proust's vision of the uncertainties of living. The vision was peculiar to Proust, but he was like many others in dealing with such uncertainties – and not just for their psychological interest, but fundamentally as questions about values. A concern with values, in conditions where they have been thrown into doubt, if not always so explicitly, seems to me as distinctive a sign as there is of the modern period in literature.

In the light of its final question, much that goes before in Proust's story may seem less like social padding. Van Blarenberghe's manners, 'charming and moderately distinguished', even his neat and exquisite calligraphy, are no doubt those of a society in which such things mattered; but they matter more particularly here in a moral as much as a social sense. 'Playing the social game so sensitively, so loyally' has a moral value precisely because it's not an evasion of uncertainties but supposes a specially acute awareness of them. The abyss that opens at the end reveals just how precarious a social virtue is – and at the same time, in Proust's terms, how admirable.

But the sense of horror became, in other writers, heightened and specialized; and what Proust here calls 'loyalty' already sounds like a farewell gesture to civilized behaviour. Not only the social being but individuals, in anything like the sense once attributed to them, were on their way to losing their meaning. The human situation in Pirandello's 'Destruction of the Man' is a thin one. The one distinction of the hero is that he's more alive than others to the horror of existence; morality itself has become so conventionalized that it's part of the horror; and the only gesture worth making is one of blind destruction. Pirandello anticipated many themes exploited twenty or thirty years later by the Existentialists; but he also already anticipated, in his concise accounts of a situation, so concise that they look more like model situations than real ones, the tendency of a theme to turn into a formula. By the time of Jean-Paul Sartre despair itself had turned into a pretty shallow and perfunctory formula; which was about the time it became widely popular. But the reduction of interest in the human situation went on. Beckett's 'Imagination Dead Imagine' – coming near absolute zero, with both civilization and the natural man translated into a few measurements – is the latest we have on the human situation reduced to a situation report. More than this, though, can be said about Beckett; he is not applying formulas; and the coldness and geometrical lines of this story are less the result of a lack of feeling for the human condition than of a struggle to bring feeling under control.

There is no lack of human interest in Italo Svevo, though the subject of 'Generous Wine', written before 1914 – the loss of confidence came early – is the sickness of bourgeois society. Svevo's heroes are both quick to detect sickness in the society around them, and wonderful examples of it themselves – so that it's not just sickness so much as obsession with sickness that he really deals with: Svevo is an ironist, a healing writer, and his characters – though the hero of this story and of *Confessions of Zeno* are doubtless the same person – are great comic inventions. 'I felt like one of those tiny little dogs that make their way through life wagging their tails' – the moment of self-realization in this story is horrible and diminishing, as in Swift or Kafka. Kafka's hero in 'Metamorphosis' turns into a sort of cockroach, while humiliation in Svevo takes place in the real world; and is no less diminishing for that. But it may be more than just humiliation. Someone, as in this case, may at last see the truth about himself, and learn what he ought to do. To know the worst is not altogether discouraging in Svevo – it comes to the same thing as: know yourself. The point is made in *Confessions of Zeno*, and somewhat crudely at the end of 'Generous Wine', that it's possible, by being thoroughly undeceived, to start putting things in order.

But if pity and terror have found an adequate place in modern fiction – adequate at least to what has happened in fact – it's above all in Kafka. More absorbed in the horror than anyone else, he seems to me, at the same time, the least unfeeling or unbalanced in his attitude to it. 'Metamorphosis' would be included here but for its length; and not just on account of Gregor Samsa and his transformation into an insect but for the wonderful and ironic recovery of normal life at the end – yet a 'normal' life that can only be felt as a defeat, for what it reasserts, once the horror is past, is only indifference and disbelief. As a piece of story-telling, it's one of the great imaginative feats of the century; and what it is cannot be separated from what it says – its penetration into the question of what distinguishes a hideous sickness from a state of health.

'In the Penal Settlement' starts with the apparent disadvantage that, set in a remote and extreme situation, it may seem to offer only too easy, too arbitrary a display of horrors.

But if extreme situations are a favourite subject of modern writers, this is not for the sake of the bizarre and unusual (as in the Romantic movement) so much as because in the twentieth century extreme situations have often come close to ordinary ones. Kafka's story, though set as far as possible from Europe and employing a far-fetched bit of gadgetry as an instrument of torture, in fact closes the distance between us and the penal colony by the very ease with which it domesticates the remote and unlikely. It is a reminder (already in 1914) that all this is absurd but possible and relevant. Since then Auschwitz has entered into everyone's calculations of what is possible; and – though this is incidental – it is unlikely that anyone can read the story today without putting a face to the 'former Commandant' (the story was published in Russia only in 1964). And yet Kafka – the extraordinary calm of Kafka is one of his great and likeable qualities – left 'open' endings to his stories: 'the explorer lifted a heavy knotted rope from the floor-boards, threatened them with it, and so kept them from attempting the leap'. No one knows what will happen next; they might be eternal gestures, repeated for ever.

In Pasternak there is something different – a more positive affirmation than in any of the above writers. It's not an affirmation of the individual. Pasternak, one may feel, takes account of all the doubts about man that were in the air; the difference is that he seizes on them with joy. 'Life', the supreme value he advances, is set in opposition to the individual – 'does not wish to work in his presence and in every way avoids him'. 'The Long Days' is about the growth of a child's mind, and what matters in the interest of growth is not anything that Zhenya or the other children can even know, but what happens to them unawares, 'allowing life to do with them all it thought necessary, essential and beautiful'. This distrust of the individual and individual effort plays an important part in *Doctor Zhivago*. Yet when Pasternak writes of submission to life, it's nothing merely loose and lax that he intends. Very possibly a part of what he had to convey was better said in poetry than in prose, and this accounts for some obscurities in 'The Long Days'. One may compare, however, what he was doing – what he means by 'life' – with what D. H. Lawrence described, in connexion with his own aims, in a well-known letter (also written, like 'The Long Days', during the First World War):

You mustn't look in my novel for the old stable *ego* of the character. There is another *ego*, according to whose action the individual is unrecognizable, and passes through, as it were, allotropic states which it needs a deeper sense than any we've been used to exercise, to discover are states of the same single radically unchanged element.

Something similar – a release from 'the old stable *ego*' – can be seen in the vizier in Andrić's 'The Bridge on the Žepa'. But in Pasternak's Zhenya the dreams, stirrings, moments of inattention that count for more than consciously directed action or thought are still very much a part of her moral history. It's never in doubt that Zhenya's moral history is under our eyes. What the story offers isn't simply a series of impressions on a young mind; it's far more concerned with relating them to the process of growth, and discerning, with a very delicate and unusual feeling for life, what is vital in them, and why it is.

Musil's 'Grigia' takes up more directly the idea of escape from personality ('here one was not, as everywhere else in the world, scrutinized to see what sort of human being one was') and even from personal identity – see the anecdote of the peasant returned from America who finds a wife ready to recognize him in every village. How much could be made of this theme is demonstrated in Musil's novel *The Man Without Qualities*. There is the same sense of release as in Pasternak, or Lawrence; but where, in them, this goes with their special aliveness to the values laid bare, in Musil it goes more with the opposite, a conviction of sickness. Others have shared this interest – Svevo has been mentioned – but what Musil took on himself (like some German writers) was specifically the sickness of Europe. For what this is worth – it strikes me as effective in an impressionistic way – it is well expressed in his paragraph beginning 'It was that standard psychic unit which is Europe . . .', with its shifts between the nostalgias Europe gives rise to and the will to self-destruction.

In 'Grigia' the sensation of allowing 'life' to take charge
is distinctly one of giving way, as if escape from personality
could be a good deal too easy, and the primitive life of the
North Italian valley much too indulgent – in the manner of
the pseudo-primitive cultivated in the twenties. Or of the
beatniks: for Musil looks at things as in a mescalin trance;
substantial flesh-and-blood is reduced to a minimum, replaced
by space, connexions, the infinite number of possible relations between things – the ordering even of villas among
the trees by 'some strange morphological law of which they
themselves knew nothing'. Perception is heightened; but is
it in fact more accurate and truthful? 'Grigia' suggests,
anyway, that its hero is only deceived by the 'new quality'
his life has acquired; he has been engaged in destroying himself.

Of course, if values are omitted altogether, as in Robbe-
Grillet's experiments, there are only objects and perceptions
left. The effect may be simple enough, but even so it cannot be
merely followed with the eye, like a piece of variable geometry.
It challenges the reader to do without values, which is itself
disturbing. We're still not used to such simplicity.

It has been a time of experiment, especially the first quarter
of the century, as if what could be said in fiction demanded a
new set of hypotheses. But I hope a balance has been struck in
this collection between the innovators and those others who
said what they had to say without taking exceptional measures
about it. They include some of the major writers of the time.
And if they had no special need to displace the sensible world
or 'the old stable *ego* of the character', it's not that they were
any less responsive to the experience of their time, with its
peculiar strains and aberrations. They are wary for instance
about happiness. Even in Colette's account of family life, at
once so hard-headed and affectionate, happiness is not a
spontaneous impulse but is assumed out of a 'loyalty' something like Proust's: 'no doubt we looked very happy, since to
look happy was the highest compliment we paid each other'.
Brecht's 'The Unseemly Old Lady' is a concession to kindly
feeling, but the concession has been earned; in his plays – and

they are among the classical achievements of the century –
Brecht is not in the least an indulgent writer.

The typical stories of this kind are realistic: the most ordinary
and recognizable material circumstances are inseparable in
them from the story itself; but however evident and particular
the facts, the story tells more than the facts, and may even tell
something different. Babel and Singer deal with that modern
subject, the disintegration of a community, drawing on their
own experience of Odessa in 1905 or of Poland after the first
war; yet with remarkably little feeling for what is modern and
exceptional about it. One doesn't see only a particular experience, one sees it as prefiguring the future and as age-old and
representative. It's not really paradoxical that writers with a
very live sense of actuality, who rarely depart from the facts
before their eyes, like Colette in her village or Babel in Odessa,
evoke not just the unique temporal fact but a continuity with
the past. And they assume that experience is communicable,
which makes for another continuity – between man and man.
The old Jew's triumph in Singer and the boy's desolation in
Babel are special to them for all sorts of reasons, but not in a
way that isolates them from the experience of any man or any
boy. By keeping open these connexions, realism has been a
great preserver of values in our time.

Not that the Marxist argument about realism would be in
place here. The stories of Bunin, Cora Sandel, Pavese and
Camus are realistic, but they don't depend as stories on what
they say about the state of society. Maybe objectively they
are on the side of progress – since they deal with unstable or
incomplete relationships, and situations that are indeed in
need of repair. But it isn't this fact, or what on the other hand
looks more like affection for the human muddle as it is, that
wants stressing here. Nor is the merely documentary con-
tribution of realism the important point. It is that realism,
if not the main tendency of the time, has still maintained a
living relationship of the writer with what is not unique but
common experience. Common, but not just conventional: for
the point is finally a literary one – the experience may be
ordinary enough; it's the writer, by his response to it, who
gives it value. To set down this or that (Alberta buying peaches;

or Cilia watching her husband in Pavese's story) simply because it oughtn't to be lost, and deserves to be set down faithfully – though it's the writer who has to convince us of that – has always been one of the good reasons for men to write at all. 'Faithful' seems the right word for Cora Sandel or Pavese, who are not highly original writers like Proust or Kafka, but stay close to actual experience and are capable of an exceptionally pure response to it. (And they have a virtue which sometimes looks like carelessness – they surprise their subject, they don't grasp after it.)

'Disorder and Early Sorrow' is the most spacious piece of realism here, but it provides a special case in connexion with values, which are so very ostensibly present that more questions than usual come up about them. Realism, in this vein of affection for turnip greens at dinner and children's games, finds good in everything – or a saving charm anyhow – in spite of unpropitious circumstances, which are those of the bourgeoisie in a German city in the 1920s. It's a complex but rather light story – light for Thomas Mann, who is often more portentous, and light too in what it says; for I think it offers to say more than it does. Clearly it intends a criticism of the prevailing ethos, by means for instance of the connexion the Professor makes between love and history and death – a pretty theoretical point, however. The actual values of the story depend far more on the way it's set, with such ease and intimacy, in a particular family circle which is at the same time a microcosm of bourgeois society. This is a society still apparently solid enough, in terms of furniture and habits, but at the very point of disappearing on the tide of history; and the situation as it's presented bears all the signs of stress and change – the effects of inflation and class struggle and invasion of one generation's territory by another. Yet the story doesn't dwell on disaster. The party at the Corneliuses' is a real teenage party, not a dance of death; and the 'disorder' of the title arises – ironic touch – not just from the state of society but from the most innocent of causes, the instincts of the very young.

A comfortable irony is indeed there throughout, and Mann is known as an ironist; but it may be doubted whether, among conflicting values, he is really holding a balance and honestly testing them. Far from being even-handed, this is an indulgent story, with its benevolence to all sides – a story itself a bit bloated with the sentimentality of the class it describes. Put beside Tolstoy on the subject of family disorder, Mann may be found lacking not so much in sympathy as in detachment. The scene is cluttered with 'life' – much of it well-caught, but exposed to an embarrassing warmth of sympathy such as usually a class reserves for its special totems: sympathy that is no help at all in distinguishing what is particularly fine and what isn't. I call it light, then, by way of suggesting the merits of the story, which are agreeable ones; not many other writers could, without shirking the problems of the times, present such a genial view of human nature. But 'light' also suggests its limits, which are probably the limits of what can be done in the twentieth century in this vein. It is no answer to the question an awareness of tragedy gives rise to. It portrays a dying society, but not with reference to anything that has a better hold on life – only to the values of the dying society itself, or what's left of a last kick in them.

I've referred rather often to other work by these writers, as if the connexion accounts for some at least of the interest of their short stories. And I think this is so; not that the stories depend on the connexion, but that it's useful to see them in relation to a greater work. Proust, Svevo, Pasternak, Musil, Mann, from the early part of the century alone, provide the obvious examples. They all wrote very long novels, which in spite of their length are great acts of concentration: in different ways they are attempts at a synthesis, in which the writer makes one kind of order out of a much-divided world. By force of example, these novels have a considerable effect on our ways of seeing and feeling about the time. And a collection like this, less concerned with the technicalities of what makes a short story than with ways of seeing and feeling, can hardly fail to take such examples into account. I would say, at the same time, that the short pieces have certain advantages: the long major novels are by their nature specialized and limited in a way that hasn't happened – because it hasn't been necessary – in the past; reading one of them, for the length of time that it takes, can be like living with a mania. Some at least of the insights that are valuable in them are brought out more sharply in the stories.

And then, the short story as a form with a life and definition of its own has become rare in this period; I think only the Russians have kept up the tradition. Many writers have published as stories what could as well be called something else – autobiography or experiment; and obviously, to the modern mind, it's the quality of the experience conveyed that matters, not what the form is called. I've taken the liberty of further appropriating to the 'story', in two cases, parts of longer works, as well as Proust's article or essay from *Le Figaro*.

A lot has been written about 'the modern movement' in its various senses, but apparently not many attempts have been made at a collection of modern European stories. I don't know that critical theory – in any case it usually ignores short stories – is much help when it comes to making choices. 'I attach no particular importance to my selection' said Tolstoy about his examples in *What is Art?* and it would be nice to feel so confident, or careless. But it seems to me that a right choice, or near enough right, is the whole point. And this depends on the aim. Given that the aim is to concentrate on significant areas of modern experience – not that this means anything other than what certain writers have found significant in them – the collection couldn't at the same time be generally representative. I find, for instance, that the stories here are all 'in situation'; the 'private worlds' of so many modern writers are not represented; nor on the whole is fantasy. These omissions seemed justified from my point of view, and are largely the reason why not every country has a place.

A collection such as this must try to indicate, among all the possibilities, what is most worth attending to; and if it succeeds I have no doubt that it should have more to say than, for instance, a history of the twentieth century, or any of the other accounts of experience that fall under separate heads, each capable of a certain objectivity and a partial truth. A story escapes the categories devised for systematic inquiry, labelled sociology or psychology or politics. What a writer gives is itself only a selective response, but it's what for him is the needful response, in which his whole being is committed. I would say at least of the writers chosen here that they have been moved or disturbed by life, in a way that only their writing can express – and which it *does* express, beyond any simply aesthetic considerations. Their function is to convey both an experience and why this should be worth doing; for it's not just the experience but the value of the experience that matters. This – the individual, highly selective response – is what they have to communicate; and inevitably, in various ways, it's a response to the time, the place, the age they live in; but still, quite a different thing from a collection of data, or a theory arrived at by a process of abstraction. Writers won't give us that sort of account of the age; but more than anyone else they provide us with our means of understanding it.

R. T.

ACKNOWLEDGEMENTS

For permission to reprint the stories specified we are indebted to Oxford University Press for Svetozar Koljević's translation of Ivo Andrić's 'The Bridge on the Žepa' from *Yugoslav Short Stories*; Methuen & Co. Ltd, for Walter Morison's translation of Isaac Babel's 'The Story of my Dovecot' from *Collected Stories of Isaac Babel*; Calder & Boyars Ltd, for Samuel Beckett's 'Imagination Dead Imagine'; Methuen & Co. Ltd, for Yvonne Kapp's translation of Bertolt Brecht's 'The Unseemly Old Lady' from *Tales from the Calendar*; Hamish Hamilton Ltd, for Justin O'Brien's translation of Albert Camus' 'The Silent Men' from *Exile and the Kingdom*; Martin Secker & Warburg Ltd, for Enid McLeod's translation of Colette's 'The Captain' from *My Mother's House and Sido*; Martin Secker & Warburg Ltd, for Willa and Edwin Muir's translation of Kafka's 'In the Penal Settlement' from *In the Penal Settlement;* Martin Secker & Warburg Ltd, for H. T. Lowe-Porter's translation of Thomas Mann's 'Disorder and Early Sorrow' from *Mann: Stories of a Lifetime*; Martin Secker & Warburg Ltd, for Eithne Wilkins and Ernst Kaiser's translation of Robert Musil's 'Grigia' from *Tonka and Other Stories*; Ernest Benn Ltd, for Nikita Romanoff and Robert Payne's translation of Pasternak's 'The Long Days' from *Pasternak: Prose and Poems*; Peter Owen Ltd, for A. E. Murch's translation of Pavese's 'Wedding Trip' from *Festival Night*; Oxford University Press, the Pirandello Estate, and International Copyright Bureau Ltd, for Frederick May's translation of Luigi Pirandello's 'Destruction of the Man' from *Pirandello: Short Stories*; Paul Hamlyn Ltd, for Gerard Hopkins' translation of Marcel Proust's 'Filial Sentiments of a Parricide' from *Proust: A Selection from his Miscellaneous Writings*; Calder & Boyars Ltd, for Barbara Wright's translation of Alain Robbe-Grillet's 'The Beach' from *Snapshots*; Peter Owen Ltd, for Elizabeth Rokkan's translation of Cora Sandel's 'Alberta' from *Alberta and Freedom*; Martin Secker & Warburg Ltd and Laurence Pollinger Ltd, for

Norbert Guterman and Elaine Gottlieb's translation of Isaac
Bashevis Singer's 'The Old Man' from *Gimpel the Fool and
Other Stories*; Martin Secker & Warburg Ltd, for L. Collison-
Morley's translation of Italo Svevo's 'Generous Wine' from
Short Sentimental Journey and Other Stories.

Michael Glenny's translation of Ivan Bunin's 'Sunstroke' ©
     Michael Glenny, 1969
John Richardson's translation of Maxim Gorky's 'Twenty-six
     Men and a Girl' © John Richardson, 1969.

Maxim Gorky

TWENTY-SIX MEN AND
A GIRL

TRANSLATED BY
JOHN RICHARDSON

MAXIM GORKY

Born at Nizhny Novgorod (now Gorky) 1868; died in Moscow 1936. A leading proletarian writer before the October Revolution and the chief spokesman for literature in the first Soviet period. *My Childhood* and other volumes of autobiography; *The Lower Depths* (play); *Reminiscences of Tolstoy, Chekhov and Andreev*. 'Twenty-six Men and a Girl' (1899), like many of the early stories, stems from his own experience as a casual labourer.

TWENTY-SIX MEN AND A GIRL

THERE were twenty-six of us, twenty-six human machines boxed up in a damp basement, where from morning till night we kneaded dough and made it into pretzels and hard biscuits. The windows of our basement formed one side of a pit that had been hollowed out in front of them and lined with bricks now green from the damp; on the outside the window-frames were barred with a close-mesh iron grating and the light of the sun was unable to force its way in through the glass panes caked with flour dust. Our employer had barricaded the windows with iron to prevent us giving away crusts of his bread to beggars and those of our comrades who, being out of work, went hungry. Our employer used to call us thieves and give us half-rotten offal to eat instead of meat for our midday meal.

It was a stuffy, cramped existence in that stone box with its low, heavy ceiling coated with grime and cobwebs. It was sickening and oppressive inside those thick walls streaked with patches of dirt and mould. We used to rise at five in the morning, without having had a good night's rest, and by six o'clock were seated, dull and apathetic, at the table, forming pretzels from the dough prepared for us by our mates while we were asleep. And the whole day long, from early morning till ten at night, one lot of us would sit at the table stringing out the plastic dough with our hands and rocking to and fro so as not to lose all feeling, while the other lot mixed the flour and water. And the whole day long boiling water burbled sulkily and mournfully in the copper in which the pretzels were boiled, and the baker's shovel made quick and vicious jabs against the floor of the stove, sending up slippery bits of cooked dough on to the heated bricks. From morning till night firewood burned away on one side of the stove, and the red glow of the flames flickered on the wall of the room as though holding us up to silent ridicule. The massive stove resembed the misshapen head of an ogre from some fairy tale jutting up from the floor, its huge gaping jaws ablaze with fire, breathed hot fumes upon us, and stared at our endless toil with the two black ventilation holes above its mouth. These two holes were eyes – the callous and unfeeling eyes of a monster. They always fixed us with the same scowling look as though having tired of watching slaves at work, and, no longer expecting anything human of them, they despised them with the cold contempt of wisdom.

Day in, day out, in the flour dust, in the filth dragged in by our feet from outside, in the thick stale air, we strung out the dough and moulded it into pretzels, wetting them with our sweat. We detested our work with a violent loathing. We never ate anything that our hands produced, preferring black bread to pretzels. Sitting opposite each other – nine either side of the long table – we moved our fingers and hands mechanically for hours on end, and grew so used to the work that we no longer bothered to follow the movements. And we had stared at one another for so long that all of us knew every wrinkle on the faces of our comrades. We had nothing to talk about – a fact we were used to – so we simply kept silent the whole time, except when we swore at one another, for you can always find an excuse to abuse a man, especially a mate. But even the swearing was rare. After all, what can a man do wrong when he is only half-alive, when he is a mere stone statue, when all his emotions have been crushed by the weight of his toil? And silence only terrifies and torments those who have already said everything and have nothing more to add; for people who have never had their say, silence is simple and easy.

Now and then we used to sing, and the song would begin in a certain way. In the midst of our work one of us used suddenly to heave a deep sigh, like a weary horse, and softly break into one of those meandering mournfully sweet melodies which always ease the burden in the singer's heart. Whenever one of us started to sing, we would listen in silence to his lonely song as it faded away and died beneath the heavy basement ceiling, like the light from a tiny bonfire amid the plains on a damp autumn night, when the grey sky is poised above the earth like a leaden roof. Then someone else would join in, and now two voices floated softly and sadly through the stifling atmos-phere of our cramped cell-like room. Then all at once several voices would take up the melody, and it swelled like a wave, gaining strength and volume, till it seemed to push asunder the dank, depressing walls of our stone dungeon. Now all twenty-six of us were singing. Our loud voices, harmonized by long practice, filled the basement; the song strained to escape; it knocked against the walls, moaned, wept and awakened the heart with a dull, prickling ache, opening up old wounds and bringing on a sad yearning. The singers would sigh deeply, heavily; one of us would suddenly break off and listen to his comrades singing, and then again let his voice merge with the wave of sound. Another, with a weary cry of 'Ah me', sang with his eyes closed and perhaps in his mind's eye saw the broad wave of sound as a bright, sunlit road leading far away, and perhaps saw himself wandering along it.

The flames in the stove still flickered, the baker's shovel still rapped against the bricks, and the glow from the fire still shimmered on the wall in silent mirth. And in other men's words we sang away our deadened grief, the deep frustration of human beings deprived of the sun, the anguish of slaves. That is how we lived, all twenty-six of us, in the basement of a large stone building, and our life there was so hard and oppressive that all three floors might have been resting directly on our shoulders.

Besides the singing, however, we had something else that was nice, something we liked very much and which may have been a substitute for the sun. The second floor of the building housed a gold-embroidery atelier, and among the needlegirls living there, was a sixteen-year-old maid called Tanya. Every morning a small rosy-cheeked face with sparkling blue eyes used to press against the glass of the small window cut in the door leading from our basement to the passageway, and a soft, musical voice would call out: 'My captives, give me some of those nice pretzels!'

We all turned round at the clear sound of her voice and gazed delightedly at the pure girlish face smiling at us so sweetly. We liked to see her nose pressed flat against the window, and the small white teeth glistening between rosy lips parted in a smile. We used to run to open the door for her, jostling each other out of the way, and in she came – sweet and happy, holding out her apron, standing in front of us with her head cocked slightly to one side, and smiling all the time. A long, thick braid of chestnut hair fell across her shoulder and lay on her breast. We dirty, primitive, ugly people, we gazed at her from below – the doorway was four steps higher than our floor – gazed at her with our heads raised, and wished her good morning and uttered special words that we kept for her alone. In our conversations with her our voices were softer and our jokes more lighthearted. Everything we had for her was extra special. The baker used to rake out a shovelful of crispy, well-browned pretzels from the oven and toss them deftly into Tanya's apron.

'Watch out the boss doesn't catch you!' we would warn her. She smiled impishly and called out:

'Goodbye, my captives!' and scuttled away like a mouse.

That was all. ... But long after her departure we said pleasant things about her to one another. We always repeated the same things we had said the day before, or the day before that, because she, and we, and everything around us, was exactly the same as it had been the day before, or the day before that. It is very hard and gruelling when a man lives on while nothing around him changes. If that doesn't utterly destroy his soul, then the longer he lives the more gruelling he finds the stagnation of his surroundings. We always talked about women in a way that at times made even us disgusted by our coarse and bawdy comments, and that is not surprising since the women we knew may not have merited any other kind. Yet we never spoke badly of Tanya; never once did any of us take the liberty of touching her, nor did she ever hear any of us make an unseemly joke. That might have been because she never stayed long enough with us – she flashed before our eyes like a falling star, and then vanished. Or it might have been because she was very young and beautiful, and beautiful things arouse admiration, even in uncouth people. And another thing – even though the drudgery of our labour was turning us into bovine creatures, we were still human beings, and like other human beings could not live without worshipping something or other. There was no one as fine as her among us, and nobody else paid any attention to us in the basement, nobody at all, even though dozens of people lived in the building. Furthermore, and this was probably the main thing, we all considered her as our own, as someone who could not survive without our pretzels; we made it our duty to provide her with fresh pretzels and this became our daily offering to our idol; it became a sacred rite and with every day it cemented us to her more firmly. Apart from the pretzels, we gave Tanya a lot of advice – to dress more warmly, not to run up and down stairs, not to carry heavy bundles of wood. She listened to our advice with a smile, responded with a laugh, and heeded not a word of it, but we were not offended – we only wanted to show her we had her welfare at heart.

Often she would come to us for favours. For instance, she might ask us to open the heavy door to the cellar, or to chop firewood. We did this and everything else she requested with pleasure, even with a sort of pride.

But when one of us asked her if she would mend his only shirt, she gave a contemptuous snort and said:

'You've a nerve! Of course I won't!'

We had a good laugh at this clown, and never asked her any favours again. We loved her and there's nothing more to be said. Men always like to lavish their affection on someone or other, although that love has at times a crushing and at times a sullying effect; men may poison the lives of those dear to them with love because in loving they cease to respect the object of their adoration. We had to love Tanya because there was no one else.

Now and then, for no particular reason, one of us would suddenly voice a doubt by saying:

'What are we spoiling the girl for? What's so wonderful about her? We're making much too much fuss of her.'

We promptly and forcefully put down any man who dared to utter such words – we needed to love something. We had found her, and we loved her, and what we loved, all twenty-six of us, had to be sacrosanct to each of us, something sacred, and anyone who opposed us was our enemy. It might be said that we were also loving something that was not really good, but there were, after all, twenty-six of us, and so we always wanted what was dear to us to be sacred to all the others, too.

Our love was just as oppressive as our hatred. And this may be why some of the prouder kind claimed that our hatred was more flattering than our love. Yet if that was so, why did they not run away from us?

Besides the pretzel bakery, our employer also owned another bakery where bread rolls were made; it was located in the same building and separated from our hole-in-the-ground by a wall. But the bakery employees – there were four of them – kept aloof from us, considering their work cleaner than ours, and because they felt themselves above us, never came to see us in the basement and sniggered derisively whenever we encountered them in the yard. We never went near them either; our employer had forbidden us to do so for fear we might steal his bread rolls. We disliked those bakers because we were jealous of them – their work was easier, they earned more than we did, they were given better food, they had a spacious, sunlit bakery, and they were all so clean and healthy-looking. We found them repulsive. We were all sort of yellow and grey – three of us had syphilis, several had scabies, and one was absolutely crippled with rheumatism. On holidays and during time off they dressed in jackets and squeaky boots; two of them had accordions, and they all went strolling in the park, while we wore dirty rags and went about in broken-down leather shoes or bast sandals, and the police refused to allow us in the park. How could we possibly like those fellows?

One day we heard that a baker had taken to drink, that the boss had got rid of him and taken on a new man, and that the new man was an ex-soldier who wore a satin waistcoat and sported a watch with a gold chain. We were curious to see a dandy of that kind, and in the hope of catching a glimpse of him, kept running outside, one after the other.

But he turned up himself in our basement. Opening the door with a kick, he left it as it was, and stood there on the threshold, beaming, and said:

'Hallo, lads! God bless you all!'

Frosty air swept through the door in a thick, misty cloud and swirled around his feet, but he just stood there, looking down at us, and beneath his blond, neatly twirled moustache gleamed large discoloured teeth. The waistcoat he wore really was something out of the ordinary – dark blue and embroidered with flowers, it seemed to glow, and the buttons were made of tiny, red stones. He had the watch, too.

He was handsome was that soldier. Rather tall, solidly built, with ruddy cheeks and large, bright eyes with a clear, friendly gaze. On his head was a white, stiff-starched chef's hat, and from under his spotlessly clean apron peeped the toes of stylish, brightly-polished boots.

Our baker politely requested him to close the door. He complied without hurrying, and then began questioning us about our employer. We told him, all shouting at once, that our employer was a skinflint, a crook, a rascal and a slave-driver; we said all the things that we could and had to say, but which are unprintable here. The soldier listened, wiggled his moustache, and eyed us with a gentle, bright-eyed look.

'You've quite a few girls here, haven't you?' he suddenly asked.

Several of us laughed politely, others leered, and somebody explained to the soldier that in all there were nine girls on the premises.

'Do you use their services?' asked the soldier with a wink.

Again we laughed, but not very loudly, and our laughter was confused. Many of us would have liked to show the soldier they were dashing young fellows like him, but no one dared do so, and no one knew how. Somebody admitted the truth by saying quietly:

'What, us?'

'No, I don't suppose you do!' said the soldier with conviction, staring hard at us. 'You aren't quite the types. . . . You don't have the bearing . . . the right look, I mean. Women, they want a man to look right. They like to see a good build . . . and everything to be neat and tidy. What's more, they go for strength. An arm like this here.'

The soldier pulled his right arm, with his sleeve rolled up to the elbow, out of his pocket and showed it to us. It was pale and muscular, and covered with shiny blond hair.

'Your legs, chest, they've all got to be firm. And then again a fellow has got to dress properly . . . to make himself more attractive. Take me now – women go for me. I don't ask them to, or try to attract them, they come crawling all over me, five at a time.'

He settled himself down on a sack of meal and proceeded to tell us at great length how much women liked him and how gallantly he treated them. Then he left, and when the door squeaked shut behind him we were silent for some time, thinking of him and the stories he had told. Then suddenly we all started talking at once, and it was clear that we all liked him. So simple and unaffected, he came to see us, sat with us, and chatted for a while. No one ever visited us, no one ever spoke to us in that way, so friendly like. And we talked about him and his future conquests among the needlegirls, the ones who stuck their noses in the air when they encountered us in the yard, or else walked straight past as if we weren't there at all. For our part, we had nothing but admiration for them, both outside and whenever they passed our window, dressed in wintertime in their own kind of special fur caps and coats, and in summertime in hats with flowers and with gaily-coloured parasols in their hands. Among ourselves, though, we spoke about these girls in words that would have made them cringe with shame and embarrassment had they heard what we said.

'Suppose he goes and leads our Tanya astray,' our baker suddenly said with concern.

We all lapsed into silence, stunned by the words. We had forgotten Tanya – the soldier, with his large, fine-looking figure, had somehow taken our minds off her. A noisy discussion broke out. Some of us said Tanya wouldn't let herself be taken in by the soldier, others were sure she wouldn't be able to resist him, and a third lot suggested that if he kept pestering her, we should break his head for him. Finally, we all agreed to keep our eyes on both Tanya and the soldier, and to warn the girl to be on her guard. That put an end to the arguments.

About a month passed. The soldier went on baking rolls, going out with the girls from the embroidery atelier, and often came to see us in our basement, but never made mention of his conquests among them. Instead he just twirled his whiskers and licked his lips.

Tanya continued coming each morning to fetch her 'nice little pretzels' and was as charming and sweet as ever. When we tried to broach the subject of the soldier, she called him a 'goggle-eyed calf' and other comic names like that, which made us feel greatly reassured. We were proud of that girl of ours when we saw how the other lassies made up to the soldier. Tanya's attitude towards him raised our spirits, and as though taking our cue from it, we too began to treat the soldier with a certain disdain. And we loved her still more, greeting her still more warmly and affectionately in the mornings.

One day, however, the soldier dropped in to see us while in his cups. He settled himself down, and burst out laughing; and when we asked what he was amused at, he explained:

'Two of the girls had a fight over me ... Lydia and Grusha. You should have seen them going for one another! One got the other by the hair and knocked her down on the floor of the passage, and sat on top of her. They scratched each other's faces, and ripped their clothing. . . . It was killing! Why can't women fight decently, eh? Why do they have to scratch, eh?'

He sat there on the bench, looking healthy, clean and full of life; he sat there and roared with laughter. We said nothing. This time he was objectionable for some reason.

'No, but you've got to admit that I'm lucky with women, eh? It's killing! One wink and they're ready to go! It's the devil!'

The pale arms covered with shiny hair rose and fell on to his thighs with a loud slap. And he kept looking at us with such delighted surprise as though he himself truly couldn't fathom why he was so fortunate in his dealings with women. His broad florid face shone with happy self-satisfaction, and he kept licking his lips.

Our baker angrily rapped the shovel hard against the oven floor and suddenly said with a sneer:

'It doesn't take much strength to fell a fir tree, but you try cutting down a pine!'

'Who do you mean, me?' asked the soldier.

'Yes, you.'

'What's up?'

'Nothing. Forget it!'

'No, I want to know. What's up? Which pine?'

The baker didn't reply as he speedily manipulated the shovel inside the oven, tossing the boiled pretzels, raking out the baked ones, and noisily throwing them on to the floor to the young boys who threaded them on to bast string. He appeared to forget the soldier and the verbal exchange. But the soldier suddenly became restless. He got up and went over to the stove, at the risk of being hit in the chest by the handle of the shovel, which was convulsively weaving about in the air.

'Tell me which one you mean. You've hurt my feelings. Me? There's not one of them that can get away from me. Not one. Those are offensive words you used.'

He really seemed cut to the quick. Most likely he had nothing on which to pride himself but his ability to seduce women; perhaps there wasn't anything else really vital to him except this talent, and it alone made him feel alive.

There are people for whom some malaise of the mind or body is the greatest asset of their lives. They are obsessed with it throughout their lives and it is the only thing that keeps them going. In suffering from it, they feed on it, and they complain about it to others, and in that way make their fellow men take note of them. They extort the sympathy of other people for it, and apart from it have nothing at all. Take away their malaise, or cure them of it, and they'll be unhappy, because they'll be rid of their one means of existence – they'll then be empty. Sometimes a man's life is so lacking in all else that he is obliged, despite himself, to prize a flaw in his character and live on it. It may be said that men are often of bad character from pure boredom.

The soldier, in high dudgeon, advanced upon the baker and roared:

'I'm asking you, who?'

'You really want me to tell you?' The baker suddenly swung round towards him.

'Well?'

'You know Tanya?'

'Well?'

'Well then. Try her!'

'Who, me?'

'Yes, you!'

'Her? Pooh, nothing easier!'

'We'll see!'

'Yes, you will. Huh!'

'She'll . . .'

'Give me a month!'

'You're just bragging, soldier!'

'Two weeks! I'll show you. Who does she think she is, that Tanya! Pooh!'

'Alright, now get out of here. You're in the road!'

'Two weeks and it's done. You . . .'

'I said, get out!'

The baker suddenly flew into a rage and began brandishing the shovel. The soldier jumped back in astonishment, glanced at us, was silent for a moment, then muttering 'alright then' in an ominous tone, stalked out.

Throughout the argument we had been enthralled and had said nothing. But as soon as the soldier had gone, a loud and animated discussion broke out among us.

Someone shouted at the baker:

'Now you've gone and started something, Paul!'

'Get on with your work!' snapped the baker savagely.

We felt the soldier was mortally offended and that Tanya was in danger. We felt this, yet at the same time we were all seized by a burning, titillating curiosity to know what was going to happen. Would Tanya hold out against the soldier? And nearly all of us cried out with confidence:

'Tanya? She'll not give in. He'll have a job with her!'

We wanted terribly to test the strength of our idol; we argued heatedly with one another in attempts to prove that idol was a powerful one and certain to emerge the victor from any clash. Eventually, we began to feel that the soldier had not really been so hurt after all, that he might forget the quarrel and that we should have to pique his pride more thoroughly.

From that day on we began to lead a strange, often nerve-racking life. Never had we lived that way before. For days on end we would argue with one another, our wits grew in some way sharper, and we now talked more cleverly and volubly than before. We seemed to be gambling with the devil with Tanya as our stake. And when we found out from the bakery employees that the soldier had started 'making a play' for our Tanya, life became so wildly interesting that we didn't even notice that our employer, taking advantage of the mood of excitement, had increased our workload by 500 pounds of dough a day. We weren't even tired by the extra work. Tanya's name never left our lips the whole day long. Each morning we waited for her with an odd kind of impatience, and at times we imagined that, when she came in, she wouldn't be the same Tanya as the day before, but someone quite different.

However, we still didn't say anything to her about the dispute. We asked her absolutely no questions and treated her just as as amiably and pleasantly as before. But something new and alien to our former feelings had crept into our relationship with her, and that something was curiosity, as keen and cold as a steel blade.

'Today's the day, mates!' called the baker one morning as he set to work.

We didn't need him to remind us, but we still started up at his words.

'Have a good look at her. She'll be here shortly,' suggested the baker.

Someone said regretfully:

'You don't expect to be able to see any difference, do you?'

And once again there broke out a lively discussion. That day we were to find out at long last how pure and unsullied was the vessel into which we had poured the best in us. That morning we felt for the first time that the test of purity our idol was to undergo might destroy her in our eyes. For some time past we had heard that the soldier was going all out for Tanya and pursuing her persistently, but for some reason nobody had asked her what her feelings were towards him. Meanwhile, she turned up regularly for her pretzels and was just the same as before.

And that day, too, we soon heard her voice:

'My captives! Here I am!'

We hastened to let her in, but when she entered, contrary to our custom, we greeted her with silence. As we stared at her, we had no idea what to say or what questions to ask. We stood there in front of her, a sombre, silent group. She was evidently surprised by this unaccustomed form of greeting, and we suddenly saw her turn pale, grow nervous, begin to fidget, and ask in a fallen voice:

'What are you all like this for?'

'How about you?' retorted the baker sullenly, keeping his eyes fixed on her.

'Why, what about me?'

'Nothing.'

'Then give me the pretzels and be quick.'

Never before had she tried to make us hurry.

'You still have time,' said the baker without shifting or taking his eyes off her face.

She suddenly swung round and disappeared through the door.

The baker took hold of his shovel and said quietly, turning towards the stove:

'That means it's settled. Damn that soldier, the swine!'

Like a herd of sheep we made our way back to the table, jostling each other to make room, and began work in a listless, disinterested way.

'Perhaps she may yet . . .'

'Come on now, talk about something else!' shouted the baker.

We all knew he was a wise man, much wiser than us. And we took his exclamation to mean he was convinced of the soldier's victory. We felt disheartened and ill at ease.

At twelve o'clock, during our midday meal, the soldier came in. He was his usual clean and stylish self, and as usual looked us straight in the eye. We were too embarrassed to return his gaze.

'Well, you honest gentlemen, do you want me to demonstrate my soldierly prowess?' he asked, smirking with pride. 'If so, go out into the passage and peer through the cracks. Have you got that?'

We went out, and piling on top of one another, pressed close to the cracks in the plank wall facing on to the yard. We did not have long to wait. Soon after, through the yard came Tanya, with rapid steps and an anxious look, skipping across the puddles of melted snow and sludge. She disappeared through the door to the cellar. A little later, leisurely whistling a tune, the soldier followed her in. His hands were thrust into his pockets and his moustache bristled.

It was raining and we watched the raindrops falling in the puddles and the puddles rippling under the impact. It was damp and overcast – a very gloomy day. There was still snow on the roofs, but on the ground dark patches of mud had already begun to appear. And the snow on the roofs was also coated with a dirty, browny deposit. The rain fell slowly, with a mournful sound. It was cold and nasty waiting there.

First to emerge from the cellar was the soldier; he walked slowly across the yard, wiggling his moustache, and with his hands in his pockets – just the same as ever.

Then came Tanya. Her eyes . . . her eyes were radiant with happiness, and her lips were smiling. She walked as though in a dream, unsteadily and with faltering steps.

It was more than we could stand. Altogether we leapt to the door, burst out into the yard and began cat-calling and yelling at her in a vicious, savage way.

She gave a shudder when she saw us and stopped, rooted to the spot, in the sludge beneath her feet. We surrounded her and, enjoying her misery, called her dirty names and shouted obscenities at her for all we were worth.

We did it leisurely, and not too loudly, for we saw she couldn't escape, that she was encircled by us, and that we could jeer and deride her to our heart's content. I don't know why, but we didn't hit her. She stood there in the middle of us, turning her head first to one side and then the other as she listened to the insults, while we, more and more vehemently, showered her with the dirt and venom of our words.

The colour had drained from her face. Her blue eyes, a moment before still sparkling, were wide open, her breath came heavily, and her lips quivered.

And we, milling round her, wreaked vengeance on her, for she had stolen from us. She belonged to us; we had given her the finest in ourselves, and although this fineness was no more than beggars' crumbs, there were twenty-six of us, and only one of her. So there was no torment we could inflict worthy of her crime. How we abused her! She just kept silent and stared at us with wild eyes, trembling from head to foot.

We jeered, hooted, snarled. Other people came running over. One of us plucked at the sleeve of her blouse.

Suddenly her eyes flashed. Without hurrying she raised her hands to her head, patted her hair into place, and then said loudly, but calmly, straight to our faces:

'You miserable captives, you!'

And she started to walk right through the circle of us – just as easily as if we hadn't been there at all, just as if we weren't barring her path. And in fact no one stood in her way.

Emerging from the crowd around her, and without looking back, she added, just as loudly, haughtily and with contempt:

'You dirty pigs! You filthy beasts!'

And away she went, erect, beautiful and proud.

We were left standing in the middle of the yard, in the slush, in the rain, under a sunless, leaden sky.

A little while later we returned to our damp stone box. As before the sun never peeped through our windows, and Tanya never came to see us again.

Marcel Proust

FILIAL SENTIMENTS OF A
PARRICIDE

TRANSLATED BY
GERARD HOPKINS

MARCEL PROUST

Born at Auteuil 1871; died in Paris 1922. His life's work was the novel *À la Recherche du Temps Perdu* (published 1913–27) of which the first volume, in the English translation, is *Swann's Way*. 'Filial Sentiments of a Parricide' (1907) appeared, somewhat bizarrely, in the newspaper *Le Figaro* a few days after the events described: though without the last paragraph, which the editor found immoral. The full version is from *Pastiches et Mélanges* (1919).

FILIAL SENTIMENTS OF A PARRICIDE

When, some months ago, Monsieur Van Blarenberghe died, I remembered that my mother had known his wife very well. Ever since the death of my parents, I have become (in a sense which this is not the place to discuss) less myself and more their son. Though I have not turned my back on my own friends, I very much prefer to cultivate theirs, and the letters which I write now are, for the most part, those I think they would have written, those they can no longer write. I write, in their stead, letters of congratulation, letters, especially, of condolence, addressed to friends of theirs whom I scarcely know. When, therefore, Madame Van Blarenberghe lost her husband, I wanted her to receive some small token of the sadness which my parents would have felt. I remembered that, many years before, I had occasionally met her son at the houses of mutual friends. It was to him, now, that I wrote, but in the name, so to speak, of my vanished parents rather than in my own. I received the following reply. It was a beautiful letter, eloquent of filial affection. I feel that such a piece of evidence, in view of the significance which it assumes in the light of the drama which followed so hard upon its heels, and of the light which it throws upon that drama, ought to be made public. Here it is:

> Les Timbrieux, par Josselin
> (Morbihan)
> 24 September 1904

My Dear Sir,
It is a matter of regret to me that I have been so long in thanking you for your sympathy in my great sorrow. I trust that you will forgive me. So crushing has been my loss that, on the advice of my doctors, I have spent the last four months in travelling. It is only now, and with extreme difficulty, that I am beginning to resume my former way of life.

However dilatory I may have been, I should like you to know that I deeply appreciate your remembering our former pleasant relations, and that I am touched by the impulse that led you to

write to me – and to my mother – in the name of those parents who
have been so untimely taken from you. I never had the honour of
knowing them, except very slightly, but I am aware how warmly my
father felt for yours, and how pleased my mother always was to
see Madame Proust. It shows great delicacy and sensibility on your
part thus to convey to me a message from beyond the grave.

I shall shortly be back in Paris, and if, between now and then,
I can overcome that desire to be left to myself which, up to the
present, I have felt as the result of the disappearance of one in whom
my whole life was centred, and who was the source of all my happiness, it will give me much pleasure to shake your hand and talk
with you about the past.

Yours, most sincerely,

H. Van Blarenberghe

I was much touched by this letter. I felt full of pity for a man
who was suffering so acutely – of pity, and of envy. He still
had a mother left to him, and in consoling her could find
consolation for himself. If I could not respond to the efforts
he wished to make to bring about a meeting, it was because of
purely material difficulties. But, more than anything else, his
letter made pleasanter the memories I had of him. The happy
relationship to which he referred had, as a matter of fact, been
the most ordinary of social contacts. I had had few opportunities of talking to him when we had happened to meet one
another at dinners, but the intellectual distinction of our hosts
had been, and still was, a guarantee that Henri Van Blarenberghe, beneath an appearance that was slightly conventional,
and representative more of the circle in which he moved than
of his own personality, concealed an original and lively nature.
Among the strange snapshots of memory which our brains, so
small and yet so vast, collect by the thousand, the one that is
clearest to me when I rummage among those in which Henri
Van Blarenberghe appears, is that of a smiling face, and of the
curious amused look he had, with mouth hanging half open,
when he had discharged a witty repartee. It is thus that I, as one
so rightly says, 'see' him, always charming, always moderately
distinguished.

Our eyes play a greater part than we are prepared to admit
in that active exploration of the past to which we give the
name of memory. If, when someone is scrutinizing an incident

of his past in an endeavour to fix it, to make it once again a living reality, we look at his eyes as he tries to recollect, we see that they are emptied of all consciousness of what is going on around him, of the scene which, but a moment earlier, they reflected. 'You're not there at all,' we say, 'you're far away.' Yet, what we see is but the reverse side of what is going on within his mind. At such moments the loveliest eyes in all the world are powerless to move us by their beauty, are no more – to misinterpret a phrase of Wells – than 'Time Machines', than telescopes focused upon the invisible, which see further the older we grow. When we watch the rusted gaze of old men, wearied by the effort to adapt themselves to the conditions of a time so different from their own, grow blind in an effort to remember, we feel, with extraordinary certainty, that the trajectory of their glance, passing over life's shadowed failures, will come to earth not some few feet in front of them – as they think – but, in reality, fifty or sixty years behind. I remember how the charming eyes of Princesse Mathilde took on a more than ordinary beauty when they became fixed on some image which had come unbidden to the retina when, in memory, she saw this or that great man, this or that great spectacle dating back to the early years of the century. It was *that* she saw: something we shall never see. At such moments, when my glance met hers, I got a vivid impression of the supernatural, because with a curious and mysterious near-sightedness, and as the result of an act of resurrection, she was linking past and present.

Charming and moderately distinguished. Those are the words I used when thinking back to my memories of him. But after his letter had come I put a few added touches to the picture thus preserved, interpreting as evidence of a deeper sensibility, of a less wholly 'social' mentality, certain ways he had of looking, certain characteristics, which might lend themselves to a more interesting, a more generous 'reading' than the one I had at first accorded him.

When, somewhat later, I asked him to tell me about one of the staff of the Eastern Railway (Monsieur Van Blarenberghe was Chairman of the Board) in whom a friend of mine was taking an interest, I received the following reply. It had been written on the 12th of last January, but, in consequence of my having changed my address, unknown to him, did not reach me until the 17th, that is to say, not a fortnight, barely eight days, before the date of the drama.

                                        48, Rue de la Bienfaisance
                                            12 January 1907

Dear Sir,

Thinking it possible that the man X ... might still be employed by the Eastern Railway Company, I have made inquiries at their offices, and have asked them to let me know where he may be found. Nothing is known of him. If you have the name right, its owner has disappeared, leaving no trace. I gather that he was, in any case, only temporarily in their employ, and that he occupied a very subordinate position.

I am much disturbed by the news you give me of the state of your health ever since the premature and cruel death of your parents. If it is any consolation, let me tell you that I, too, have suffered physically as well as emotionally, from the shock of my father's death. But hope springs eternal. ... What the year 1907 may have in store for me I do not know, but it is my dearest wish that it may bring some alleviation to you as well as to me, and that in the course of the next few months we may be able to meet.

I should like you to know how deeply I sympathize with you.

                                        Yours sincerely,
                                        H. Van Blarenberghe

Five or six days after receiving this letter, I remembered, one morning on waking, that I wanted to answer it. One of those unexpected spells of cold had set in which are like the high tides of Heaven, submerging all the dykes raised by great cities between ourselves and Nature, thrusting at our closed windows, creeping into our very rooms, making us realize, when they lay a bracing touch upon our shoulders, that the elements have returned to attack in force. The days were disturbed by sudden changes in the temperature, and by violent barometric shocks. Nor did this display of Nature's powers bring any sense of joy. One bemoaned in advance the snow that was on the way, and even inanimate objects, as in André Rivoire's lovely poem, seemed to be 'waiting for the snow'. A 'depression' has only to 'advance towards the Balearics', as the newspapers put it, Jamaica has only to experience an earthquake tremor, for people in Paris who are subject to headaches, rheumatism and asthma, and probably lunatics as well, to have a crisis – so closely linked are nervous temperaments with the furthest points upon the earth's surface by bonds whose strength they must often wish was less compulsive. If the influence of the stars upon some at least of such cases be ever recognized (see Framery and Pelletean as quoted by Monsieur Brissaud), to whom could the lines of the poet be held to be more applicable:

Et de longs fils l'unissent aux étoiles?

No sooner was I awake then I sat down to answer Henri Van Blarenberghe. But before doing so, I wanted just to glance at *Le Figaro*, to proceed to that abominable and voluptuous act known as *reading the paper*, thanks to which all the miseries and catastrophes of the world during the past twenty-four hours – battles that have cost the lives of fifty-thousand men, crimes, strikes, bankruptcies, fires, poisonings, suicides, divorces, the shattering emotions of statesmen and actors alike – are transmuted for our own particular use, though we are not ourselves involved, into a daily feast that seems to make a peculiarly exciting and stimulating accompaniment to the swallowing of a few mouthfuls of coffee brought in response to our summons. No sooner have we broken the fragile band that wraps *Le Figaro*, and alone separates us from all the miseries of the world, and hastily glanced at the first sensational paragraphs of which the wretchedness of so many human beings 'forms an element', those sensational paragraphs the contents of which we shall later retail to those who have not yet read their papers, than we feel a delightful sense of being once again in contact with that life with which, when we awoke, it seemed so useless to renew acquaintance. And, if from time to time, something like a tear starts from our gorged and glutted eyes, it is only when we come on a passage like this: 'An impressive silence grips all hearts: the drums roll out a salute, the troops present arms, and a great shout goes up – "Vive Fallières!" . . .' At that we weep, though a tragedy nearer home would leave us dry-eyed. Vile actors that we are who can be moved

to tears only by the sorrows of Hercules, or, at a still
lower level, by the State Progresses of the President of the
Republic!

But on this particular morning the reading of *Le Figaro*
moved me to no easy responses. I had just let my fascinated
eyes skim the announcements of volcanic eruptions, ministerial
crises and gang-fights, and was beginning to read a paragraph,
the heading of which, 'Drama of a Lunatic', promised a more
than usually sharp stimulus for my morning faculties, when
I suddenly saw that the victim of this particular episode had
been Madame Van Blarenberghe, that the murderer, who had
later committed suicide, was the man whose letter lay within reach of my hand waiting to be answered. '*Hope springs eternal. . . . What the year 1907 may have in store for me I do not
know, but it is my dearest wish that it may bring some alleviation to
you as well as to me . . .*' etc. 'Hope springs eternal! What the year
1907 may have in store for me I do not know!' Well, life's
answer had not long been delayed. 1907 had not yet dropped
the first of its months into the past, and already it had brought
him his present – a gun, a revolver, a dagger, and that blindness
with which Athene once struck the mind of Ajax, driving him
to slaughter shepherds and flocks alike on the plains of Greece,
not knowing what he did. 'I it was who set lying images before
his eyes. And he rushed forth, striking to right and left, thinking it was the Atrides whom he slew, falling first on one, then
on another. I it was who goaded on this man caught in the toils
of a murderous madness, I who set a snare for his feet, and
even now he is returned, his brow soaked in sweat, his hands
reeking with blood.' Madmen, in the fury of their onslaught,
are without knowledge of what they do, but, the crisis once
past, then comes agony. Tekmessa, the wife of Ajax, said:

His madness is diminished, his fury fallen to stillness like the breath
of Motos. But now that his wits are recovered, he is tormented by
a new misery, for to look on horrors for which no one but oneself
has been responsible, adds bitterness to grief. Ever since he realized
what has happened, he has been howling in a black agony; he
who used to say that tears are unworthy of a man. He sits, not

moving, uttering his cries, and I know well that he is planning against himself some dark design.

But when with Henri Van Blarenberghe the fit had passed, it was no scene of slaughtered flocks and shepherds that he saw before him. Grief does not kill in a moment. He did not fall dead at sight of his murdered mother lying there at his feet. He did not fall dead at the sound of her dying voice, when she said, like Tolstoy's Princesse Andrée: 'Henri, what have you done to me! what have you done to me!' ... 'On reaching the landing of the stairs between the first and second floors, they,' said the *Matin* (the servants, who in this account – which may not have been accurate – are represented as being in a panic, and running down into the hall four steps at a time) 'saw Madame Van Blarenberghe, her face contorted with terror, descending the first few stairs, and heard her cry out: "Henri! Henri! what have you done!". Then the wretched woman, her head streaming with blood, threw up her arms and fell forward on her face. The terrified servants rushed for help. Soon afterwards, four policemen, who had been summoned, forced the locked door of the murderer's room. There were dagger wounds on his body, and the left side of his face had been ripped open by a pistol shot. *One eye was hanging out on the pillow.*' I thought, reading this, not of Ajax. In the 'eye hanging out on the pillow' I saw, remembering that most terrible act which the history of human suffering has ever recorded, the eye of the wretched Oedipus ...

and Oedipus, rushing forth with a great cry, called for a sword. ... With terrible moaning he dashed himself against the double doors, tore them from their sunken hinges, and stormed into the room where he saw Jocasta hanging from the strangling rope. Finding her thus, the wretched man groaned in horror and loosened the cord. His mother's body, no longer supported, fell to the ground. Then he snatched the golden brooches from Jocasta's dress and thrust them into his open eyes, saying that no longer should they look upon the evils he had suffered, the miseries he had caused: and, bellowing curses, he struck his staring eyes again and again, and the bleeding pupils ran down his cheeks in a rain, in a hail, of black blood. Then he cried out, bidding those who stood by to

show the parricide to the race of Cadmus, urging them to drive
him from the land. Ah! thus is ancient felicity given its true name.
But from that day has been no dearth of all the evils that are named
among men; groans and disasters, death and obloquy.

And, thinking of Henri Van Blarenberghe's torment when he
saw his mother lying dead before him, I thought, too, of
another wretched madman, of Lear holding in his arms the
body of his daughter, Cordelia:

> She's dead as earth . . .
> No, no, no life.
> Why should a dog, a horse, a rat have life
> And thou no breath at all? Thou'lt come no more,
> Never, never, never, never, never . . .
> Do you see this? Look on her, look, her lips,
> Look there, look there!

In spite of his terrible wounds, Henri Van Blarenberghe did
not die at once. I cannot but think abominably cruel (though
there may have been purpose in it. Does one really know what
lay behind the drama? Remember the Brothers Karamazov)
the behaviour of the Police Inspector. 'The wretched man was
not dead. The Inspector took him by the shoulders, and spoke
to him "Can you hear me? Answer" . . . The murderer opened
his one remaining eye, blinked a few times, and relapsed into
a coma.' I am tempted to address to that brutal Inspector the
words uttered by Kent in that same scene of *King Lear* from
which I have just quoted, when he stopped Edgar from
bringing Lear round from his fainting fit:

> Vex not his ghost! let him pass: he hates him
> That would upon the rack of this tough world
> Stretch him out longer.

If I have dwelt upon those great names of Tragedy, Ajax and
Oedipus, I wish the reader to understand why, and why, too, I
have published these letters and written this essay. I want to
show in what a pure, in what a religious, atmosphere of moral
beauty this explosion of blood and madness could occur, and
bespatter without soiling. I want to bring into the room of the
crime something of the breath of Heaven, to show that what

this newspaper paragraph recorded was precisely one of those Greek dramas the performance of which was almost a sacred ceremony; that the poor parricide was no criminal brute, no moral leper beyond the pale of humanity, but a noble example, a tender and a loving son whom an ineluctable fate – or, let us say, pathological, and so speak the language of today – had driven to crime, and to its expiation, in a manner that should for ever be illustrious.

'I find it difficult to believe in death,' wrote Michelet in a fine passage. True, he was speaking only of a jelly-fish, about whose death – so little different from its life – there is nothing incredible, so that one is inclined to wonder whether Michelet was not merely making use of one of those hackneyed 'recipes' on which all great writers can lay their hands at need, and so serve to their customers, at short notice, just the dish for which they have asked. But if I find no difficulty in crediting the death of a jelly-fish, I do not find it easy to believe in the death of a person, nor even in the mere eclipse, the mere toppling of his reason. Our sense of the continuity of the human consciousness is too strong. A short while since, and that mind was master of life and death, could move us to a feeling of respect; and now, both life and death have mastered it. It has become feebler than our own, which, for all its weakness, can no longer bow before what so quickly has become almost nothing. For this, madness is to blame, madness which is like an old man's loss of his faculties, like death itself. What, the man who, only yesterday, could write the letter that I have already quoted, so high-minded and so wise is, today . . .? And even – to move for a moment to the lower level of those trivial matters which, nevertheless, are so important – the man who was so moderate and so sober in what he asked of life, who loved the little things of existence, answered a letter with such charm, was so scrupulous in doing what was demanded of him, valued the opinions of others, and wanted to appear in their eyes as someone, if not of influence, at least of easy friendliness, playing the social game so sensitively, so loyally. . . . These things, I say, are very important, and, if I quoted a while back the first part of his second letter, which really concerned only my personal affairs, it was because the practical good sense which it displays seems even more at variance with what afterwards occurred than does the admirable and profound melancholy expressed in its final lines. Often, when a mind has been brought low, it is the main limbs of the tree, its top, that live on, when all the tangle of its lower branches has been eaten away by disease. In the present case, the spiritual core was left intact. I felt, as I was copying those letters, how very much I should have liked to be able to make my readers realize the extreme delicacy, nay, more – the quite incredible firmness of the hand which must have been needed to produce such neat and exquisite calligraphy.

What have you done to me! what have you done to me! If we let ourselves think for a few moments we shall, I believe, agree that there is probably no devoted mother who could not, when her last day dawns, address the same reproach to her son. The truth is that, as we grow older, we kill the heart that loves us by reason of the cares we lay on it, by reason of that uneasy tenderness that we inspire, and keep for ever stretched upon the rack. Could we but see in the beloved body the slow work of destruction that is the product of the painful tenderness which is the mainspring of its being, could we but see the faded eyes, the hair against whose valiant blackness time had so long been powerless, now sharing in the body's general defeat and suddenly turned white; could we but see the hardened arteries, the congested kidneys, the overworked heart; could we but watch courage failing under the blows of life, the slowing movements, the heavy step, the spirit once so tireless and unconquerable, now conscious of hope gone for ever, and that former gaiety, innate and seemingly immortal, so sweet a consort for sad moments, now finally withered – perhaps, seeing all this is a flash of that lucidity now come too late, which even lives spent in a long illusion may sometimes have, as Don Quixote once had his – perhaps, then, like Henri Van Blarenberghe when he stabbed his mother to death, we should recoil before the horror of our lives, and seize the nearest gun, and make an end. In most men these painful moments of vision (even assuming they can gain the heights from which such seeing is possible) soon melt in the early beams of the sun which shines upon the joys of life. But what joy, what reason for living, what life, can stand up to the impact of such awareness? Which is true, it or the joy of life? Which of them is the Truth?

Italo Svevo

GENEROUS WINE

TRANSLATED BY
L. COLLISON-MORLEY

ITALO SVEVO

Born in Trieste 1861; died in a road accident in Italy in 1928.
Novelist of the Trieste business community and bourgeoisie; a
friend of James Joyce, who induced him to write his major novel
Confessions of Zeno. 'Generous Wine' was written before 1914 and
first published in a revised form in Milan in 1927.

GENEROUS WINE

A NIECE of mine was getting married at the age when girls cease to be girls and degenerate into old maids. The poor thing had renounced the world not long before, but family pressure had induced her to return to it, giving up her desire for purity and religion; and she had consented to receive the addresses of a young man chosen by the family because he was a good match. Almost immediately there was an end of religion, an end to dreams of virtuous solitude. The date of the marriage was fixed even sooner than the relations had wished. And now they were seated at the supper for the eve of the wedding.

Being a licentious old fellow, I laughed. What had the young man done to induce her to change her mind so quickly? Probably he had taken her in his arms to make her feel the pleasure of living, and had seduced her instead of convincing her. That is why they needed so many good wishes. All people when they marry need good wishes, but this girl more than anyone. It would be disastrous if one day she had cause to regret having let herself be induced to return to the path which she had instinctively abhorred. And I even accompanied some of the glasses I drained with wishes that I managed to invent for this particular case: 'May you be contented for a year or two, then you will endure the other long years more easily, thanks to your gratitude for having experienced enjoyment. One regrets past joy, and this is a pain, but a pain which numbs the fundamental one, the real pain in life.'

The bride did not appear to feel the need of so many good wishes. Indeed, her face seemed to me to be positively crystallized into an expression of confident abandonment. But it was the same expression she had worn when she announced her desire to retire into a convent. Once again she was making a vow, this time a vow to be happy for her whole life. Some people are always making vows in this way. Would she keep this one better than the other?

Everyone else at that table was thoroughly natural in his

merriment, as onlookers always are. There was a complete lack of naturalness in me. It was a memorable evening for me. My wife had induced Dr Paoli to let me eat and drink like everyone else for this once. Such liberty was all the more precious from the warning that it would be revoked immediately afterwards. And I behaved just like a young man who has been given a latchkey for the first time. I ate and drank, not because I was hungry or thirsty, but from a craving for liberty. Every mouthful, every sip was to be an assertion of my independence. I opened my mouth more widely than necessary to take in each mouthful. The wine passed from the bottle to my glass to overflowing, nor did I leave it there more than a single moment. I felt a longing to move and there, glued to my seat, I had the feeling of running and jumping like a dog slipped from his chain.

My wife made matters worse by telling a neighbour about the diet which I usually had to keep to, while my daughter Emma, aged fifteen, listened to her and put on an air of importance as she supplemented her mother's information. So they would remind me of my chain even now that it had been undone, would they? All my torture was described; how they weighed the little meat I was allowed at midday, taking all taste from it, and how at night there was nothing to weigh, because supper consisted of a roll with a morsel of ham and a glass of hot milk without sugar, which nauseated me. And while they were talking I was criticizing the doctor's science and their affection. If my system was in such a bad way, how did it come about, just because they had brought off their *coup* of making someone marry who would never have done so from choice, that this evening it could suddenly endure so much harmful and indigestible stuff? And as I drank I prepared for rebellion on the morrow. They should see.

The others stuck to champagne, but, after taking a few glasses to drink the various toasts, I had gone back to ordinary wine, a dry and honest Istrian wine, which a friend of the family had sent for the occasion. I liked that wine, as one likes memories, and I felt confidence in it, nor was I surprised when, instead of bringing me gaiety and forgetfulness, it only increased the ire in my heart.

How could I help being angry? They had made part of my
life a burden to me. Frightened and depressed, I had let all my
generous instincts die to make room for pastilles, drops and
powders. No more socialism. What could it matter to me that
the land, contrary to all the most enlightened scientific ideas,
was still private property? What if on that account many people
did not get their daily bread and the modicum of liberty that
should adorn every day of a man's life? Had I either the one or
the other?

That blessed evening I tried to be quite my old self. When my
nephew, Giovanni, a huge man weighing seventeen stone,
began in his stentorian voice to tell stories about his own
smartness and other people's gullibility in business, I felt the
old altruism stir in my heart. 'What will you do,' I cried, 'when
the struggle between men is no longer one for money?'
For a moment Giovanni was dumbfounded by my charged
remark, which arrived quite unexpectedly to upset his world.
He stared fixedly at me with his eyes magnified by his spectacles.
He was looking for explanations in my face to give him his
bearings. Then, while everyone was looking at him, expecting
to be made to laugh by the answer of this ignorant yet clever
materialist, his mind a mixture of simplicity and cunning, a
mind still full of surprises, though it existed even before Sancho
Panza, he gained time by saying that wine alters every man's
outlook on the present, but in my case it was altering the future.
This was something, but then he thought he had found something better and shouted: 'When everyone stops struggling
for money, I shall have it all without struggling, all of it,
all!' There was a long laugh, especially at a frequent gesture
of his huge arms, which he first spread out to their full
extent, then drew in, clenching his fists to give the idea that
he had seized all the money that would flow to him from every
direction.
The discussion went on, and no one noticed that when I was
not talking, I was drinking. And I drank much and said little,
being wholly absorbed in studying my inner self, to see whether
it would overflow with benevolence and altruism. I began to
burn slightly inside, but it was a burning that would afterwards

spread in a gradual glow, in the feeling of youth that wine produces, if only for too brief a moment.

And in expectation of this I shouted to Giovanni: 'If you collar the money the others refuse, they will run you in.'

But Giovanni shouted back readily enough: 'And I will bribe the gaolers and have the people who have not got money to bribe them run in.'

'But money will not bribe anybody any more.'

' Then why not let me have it?'

I grew violently angry: 'We will hang you,' I shouted. 'You don't deserve anything else. A rope round your neck and weights on your feet.'

I paused in astonishment. It seemed to me that I had failed to express my thoughts clearly. Was I really like that? No, certainly not. I reflected: how to recover my love for all living creatures, among whom must be included even Giovanni? I smiled at him at once, making a great effort to master myself and excuse and love him. But he prevented me, because he paid not the slightest attention to my kindly smile, and said, as if resigning himself to acknowledging a monstrosity: 'Yes, in practice all socialists end up calling in the executioner.'

He had scored off me, but I hated him. He had poisoned my whole life, even those years before the intervention of the doctor, upon which I looked back with pride and regret. He had scored off me by raising the very doubt which I had felt so poignantly before he spoke.

And immediately afterwards another punishment was visited upon me. 'How well he looks,' my sister remarked, gazing at me approvingly. The remark was unfortunate, because as soon as my wife heard it she felt the excessive good health that beamed in my face might produce its equivalent in illness. She was as frightened as if someone had just warned her of an approaching danger and attacked me fiercely: 'Stop that,' she shouted. 'Put that glass down.' She appealed to my neighbour for help, a certain Alberi, one of the tallest men in the town, clean, dried up and healthy, but spectacled like Giovanni. 'Please, take that glass out of his hand.' Seeing that Alberi hesitated, she became excited and anxious: 'Signor Alberi, be good enough to take away his glass.'

I tried to laugh, or rather I guessed that a well-bred person ought to laugh, but I couldn't. I had planned my rebellion for the morrow, and it was not my fault if it broke out at once. These quarrels in public were truly shameful. Alberi, who did not care twopence for me or my wife or any of these people who were entertaining him, made things worse by making fun of my plight. He looked over his spectacles at the glass I was clutching, moved his hands towards it as if he were really going to snatch it from me, then ended by drawing them comically back, as if he were afraid of me, when I looked at him. Everybody laughed at me, Giovanni with a peculiarly noisy laugh which left him gasping.

My daughter Emma thought her mother needed help. In tones of exaggerated pleading, as I thought, she said: 'Daddy, don't drink any more.'

And it was on this innocent child that I vented my wrath. I used a hard and threatening word to her, the effect of the resentment of an old man and a father. Her eyes filled with tears, and her mother, engrossed in comforting her, paid no more attention to me.

My son Ottavio, a boy of thirteen, then ran up to his mother. He had noticed nothing, neither his sister's tears, nor the quarrel that had caused them. He wanted to be allowed to go to the pictures with some friends, who had just proposed it, on the following evening. But my wife paid no attention to him, being too busy comforting Emma.

Anxious to recover my self-respect by asserting my authority, I shouted my permission: 'Yes, of course you shall go to the pictures. I give you my permission, and that is enough.' Without waiting for more, Ottavio went back to his friends, saying: 'Thank you, Papa.' A pity he was in such a hurry. If he had stayed with us, his happiness, due to my assertion of authority, would have cheered me up.

Good humour had vanished from the table for a few minutes, and I felt that I had failed in my duty even towards the bride, with whom that good humour stood for good wishes and a good omen. And yet she was the only person who understood my feelings, or so it seemed to me. She looked at me quite maternally, ready to excuse me and be nice to me. That girl had always given an impression of confidence in her own opinions. Just as when she was longing for a cloistered life, so now she regarded herself as superior to everyone else in having renounced it. Now she was looking down upon me, upon my wife, and upon my daughter. She pitied us, and her beautiful grey eyes rested serenely upon us, to see where the fault lay, for, in her opinion, there was no suffering without someone being at fault.

This increased my rancour towards my wife, whose conduct was humiliating me in this way. She was degrading me below everyone, even the meanest, at that table. Down at the end even my sister-in-law's children had stopped talking and were putting their small heads together, discussing what had happened. I seized my glass, wondering whether I should empty it or hurl it at the wall or, better, against the windows opposite. I ended by draining it at a draught. This was the surest proof of energy, being an assertion of my independence. I thought it the best wine I had tasted that evening. I prolonged the action by pouring more wine into my glass and drinking a little of it. But joy refused to come and the whole fierce, too fierce, life flooding my veins took the form of rancour. I was seized with a strange idea. My own rebellion was not enough to put things right. Could not I suggest to the bride that she should join me in rebelling? By good luck at that very moment she smiled sweetly at the man who sat confident by her side. And I thought: 'She does not know yet, and she is convinced that she knows.'

I remember again that Giovanni said: 'Let him drink. Wine is the milk of the old.' I looked at him, wrinkling my face into the semblance of a smile, but I could not like him. I knew that all he cared about was good humour, and he wanted to soothe me like a bad-tempered child who was spoiling a gathering of grown-ups.

After that I drank little, and then only when people were looking at me, nor did I open my mouth. Everyone round me was shouting merrily and this annoyed me. I did not listen, but it was difficult not to hear. Alberi and Giovanni had begun to argue, and everyone enjoyed watching the duel between the fat man and the thin. What they were quarrelling about, I do not know, but I heard pretty aggressive words from both parties. I noticed Alberi on his feet, leaning towards Giovanni and bringing his spectacles almost over the middle of the table, quite close to his opponent. Giovanni, with his seventeen stone stretched comfortably upon an armchair, which had been given him by way of a joke at the end of the meal, was gazing intently at him, like the good fencer he was, as if looking for an opening for his rapier thrust. But Alberi too, cut a good figure, woefully thin, indeed, but healthy, active and serene.

And I remember also the endless good wishes and greetings at the moment of parting. The bride kissed me with a smile that still seemed maternal. I received her kiss absent-mindedly. I was wondering when I should have an opportunity of telling her something about this life of ours.

At that moment a name was mentioned by someone, that of a friend of my wife and an old friend of mine, Anna. I don't know by whom or in what connection, but I know it was the last name I heard before being left in peace by the guests. For years I had been used to seeing her often with my wife, and greeting her with the friendly indifference of people who have no reason to remark on having been born in the same town and about the same time. Now, however, I remembered that many years ago she had been my one backsliding. I had courted her almost up to the moment of marrying my wife. But no one had ever commented on my treacherous behaviour, which had been so brusque I had not even tried to mitigate it by a single word, because she had also married very soon after and had been very happy. She had not been at the supper on account of a slight attack of influenza, which had kept her in bed – nothing serious. But it was strange and serious that I now remembered my offence against love, which came to weigh upon my conscience, already sufficiently troubled. I actually felt that at that moment my former offence was being punished. From her bed, where she was probably convalescent, I heard my victim protest: 'It would not be fair for you to be happy.' I went to my bedroom very depressed. I was rather confused, because it did not seem fair to me that my wife should be commissioned to avenge one whom she had supplanted.

Emma came to wish me good night. She was smiling, rosy and fresh. Her short outbreak of crying had given way to a reaction of joy, as is usual with healthy and youthful systems. I had recently learnt to understand other people's characters, and my daughter was as transparent as glass. My outburst had served to give her importance in the eyes of everyone, and she enjoyed it in all innocence. I gave her a kiss, and I am sure that I thought it was lucky for me that she was so happy and contented. For her own good it would, of course, have been my duty to point out to her that she had not treated me with becoming respect. But I could not find the words and I held my tongue. She went off, and the only lingering result of my attempt to find words was a preoccupation, a confusion, an effort which did not leave me for some time. To quiet myself I thought: 'I will speak to her tomorrow. I will give her my reasons.' But it was useless. I had offended her and she had offended me. But it was a further offence that she had forgotten all about it, whereas I never ceased brooding over it.

Ottavio also came to bid me good night. A strange boy. He said good night to his mother and myself almost without noticing us. He had already left the room when I called after him: 'Are you glad to be going to the pictures?' He stopped and made an effort to remember and before going further said dryly: 'Yes.' He was very sleepy.

My wife handed me the box of pills. 'Are these the ones?' I asked with a mask of ice on my face.

'Yes, of course,' she said gently. She looked inquiringly at me, and, not being able to guess my thoughts in any other way, asked hesitatingly: 'Are you all right?'

'Perfectly all right,' I answered firmly, as I took off one of my boots. And at that very moment my stomach began to burn horribly. 'This is what she wanted,' I thought, with a logic about which I am only now doubtful.

I swallowed the pill with some water and felt a slight relief. I kissed my wife mechanically upon the cheek. It was a kiss such as might go with the pills. I could not have avoided it if I wanted to escape discussions and explanations. But I could not settle down to rest without clearing up my position in the struggle which was not yet over for me, and I said just as I snuggled down in bed: 'I think the pills would have been more effective taken with wine.'

She put out the light, and very soon the regularity of her breathing told me that she had a clear conscience – that is to say, I thought at once, a total indifference to all that concerns me. I had anxiously awaited that moment, and immediately said to myself that I was at last free to breathe noisily, as the condition of my system seemed to demand, or even to sob, as, in my depression, I should have liked to do. But the suffering, the moment I was free, became even more intense. This was no liberty. How was I to vent the anger that raged within me? All I could do was to think over what I should say to my wife and daughter next day. 'You are very anxious about my health, when it comes to nagging me before other people.' It was so true. Here was I raging alone in my bed while they slept in peace. What a burning! A huge tract of it had invaded my system and was trying to vent itself through my throat. There should be a bottle of water on the little table by my bedside. I reached out for it, but knocked against the empty glass, and the slight noise was enough to wake my wife. Yes, she slept with one eye open.

'Are you feeling ill?' she asked in a low voice – she was not certain she had heard correctly, and didn't want to disturb me. I guessed part of this, but had the bizarre idea that she was gloating over my illness, as being the proof that she had been right. I gave up the idea of the water, and settled down once more. At once she fell back into that light slumber of hers, which enabled her to keep watch over me.

Clearly, if I was not to get the worst of it in my quarrel with my wife, I must go to sleep. I shut my eyes and turned over on my side, but I was obliged to change my position at once. However, I was obstinate, and did not open my eyes. But every position meant the sacrifice of a part of my body. I thought: 'With a body like this sleep is out of the question.' I was all movement, all wakefulness. A man running cannot think of sleep. I had the breathlessness of a man running and,

in my ears, the sound of my footsteps, heavily shod. I thought
that perhaps I was turning too gently in my bed to hit upon the
right position for all my limbs at once. It was no good searching
for it. I must let every part of me find the place that suited it.
I flung myself over as violently as possible. At once my wife
whispered. 'Are you feeling ill?' If she had used different
words, I would have answered by asking her to help me. But I
refused to answer those particular words, which referred
offensively to our quarrel.

Yet to lie still should be so easy. What trouble can there be in
lying, just lying, in bed? I went over all the great difficulties that
beset our path in this world and found that really, compared
with any of these, lying still was nothing. Any worn-out old
horse can stand still. In my determination I discovered a position that was complicated, but remarkably tenacious. I dug my
teeth into the top of the pillow and twisted myself in such a way
that my chest also rested on the pillow, while my right leg was
outside the bed and almost touching the ground, and the left
was stiff on the bed, pinning me to it. Yes, I had discovered a
new system. It was not I that held the bed, but the bed that
held me. And this conviction of my own inertness was such
that even when the oppression increased, I refused to relax.
When at last I had to give way, I comforted myself with the
thought that at least a part of that dreadful night was over, and
I was also rewarded by feeling, once I had freed myself from the
bed, as exhilarated as a wrestler who has shaken off his
adversary's hold.

I don't know how long I then kept still. I was tired. To my
surprise I noticed a strange brilliance in my closed eyes, a
whirlwind of flames which I imagined was caused by the fire
I felt inside me. They were not real flames, but colours like
them. Then they diminished and shaped themselves into
circular forms, or rather into drops of a viscous liquid, which
soon became all blue, mild, but surrounded by a glowing red
border. They fell from a point above, grew longer and, becoming detached, disappeared below. It was I who first thought
that these drops could see me. Immediately, to see me better,
they were transformed into so many huge eyes. As they grew

elongated in falling a little circle formed in their centre, which, shedding its blue covering, displayed a real eye, evil and malevolent. I was being followed by a crowd that hated me. I rebelled in my bed, groaning and calling out: 'My God!'

'Are you feeling ill?' asked my wife at once.

Some time must have gone by before I answered. But then it happened that I realized I was not lying in my bed any longer, but was clinging to it, and that it had been transformed into a slope, down which I was slipping. I called out: 'I am ill, very ill.'

My wife had lit a candle and was standing by me in her pink nightdress. The light reassured me, and I even had the clear conviction that I had slept and had only then woken up. The bed had straightened and I was lying on it quite comfortably. I looked at my wife in surprise, because now, realizing that I had been asleep, I was no longer certain that I had called for her help. 'What do you want?' I asked her.

She looked at me, half asleep and tired. My call had been sufficient to make her jump out of bed, but not to rob her of her longing for sleep, which was so great that she did not even care whether she had been in the right or not. Not to waste time she asked: 'Would you like those drops the doctor gave you to make you sleep?'

I hesitated, strong though my desire to feel better was. 'If you like,' I said, trying only to appear resigned. To take the drops was not by any means an admission that I was unwell.

Then there followed a moment during which I enjoyed perfect peace. It lasted while my wife in her pink nightdress, by the frail light of the candle, stood by me counting the drops. The bed was a real horizontal bed and my eyelids, when I closed them, were sufficient to shut out all light from my eyes. From time to time I opened them and that light and the pink of the nightdress gave me as much relief as complete darkness. But she did not want to go on helping me a moment longer than was needed, and I was once again plunged into the night to fight for peace alone.

I remembered that, when I was young, to send myself to sleep, I used to force myself to think of a hideous old woman who helped me to forget the lovely visions that haunted me.

Now, however, I might call up beauty without danger and it would certainly help me. It was an advantage, and the only one, of old age. I thought of several beautiful women, the loves of my young days, of a time when beautiful women had abounded in extraordinary numbers, and called upon them by name. But they did not come. Not even then did they yield themselves. And I called and called them continuously until out of the night there rose up a single lovely face: Anna, yes, she, as she had been many years before, but her face, her beautiful pink-complexioned face, was wearing an expression of pain and reproof. For she meant to bring me not peace, but remorse. That was clear. And as she was there I talked to her. I had jilted her, but she had immediately married someone else, which was only fair. And she had brought into the world a daughter, now fifteen, who was like her in her delicate colouring, her golden hair and blue eyes; but then her face was spoilt by the intervention of the father who had been chosen for her. The gentle wave of the hair had been turned into a mass of tight curls, the cheeks were large, the mouth broad, the lips much too full. The mother's colouring combined with the lines of the father produced the effect of a shameless kiss, in public. What did she want of me now, after she had let me see her so often arm-in-arm with her husband?

It was the first time that evening that I could feel that I had won. Anna became more gentle, almost changing her mind. And then her company was no longer distasteful to me. She might stay. And I fell asleep, admiring her, good and beautiful and won over to my view. I soon fell asleep.

A horrible dream. I was in a complicated building, which I understood at once, as though I had been a part of it. It was a huge cave, rugged, without any of those ornaments which nature amuses herself creating in caves, and therefore certainly the work of man, and it was dark. There I sat on a three-legged stool beside a glass chest, feebly illuminated by a light which I considered must be a quality of itself, the only light there was in the vast structure, though it was strong enough to illuminate myself, a huge wall consisting of great, rough stones and below it a cemented wall. How vivid are the constructions of dreams! You will reply that this is because their architect can easily understand them, but does not remember having done so when awake, and as he turns his thoughts back to the world which he has left, where these constructions sprung up so easily, it may surprise him that everything is understood there without the need of a single word.

I knew at once that the cave had been built by men who were using it for a cure invented by themselves, a cure that would prove fatal to one of those who were imprisoned in it – there must have been a number of people down there in the dark – but highly beneficial to all the others. Yes, a sort of religion which required a victim, and naturally I was not surprised.

It was even more easy to guess that, since they had put me so close to the glass chest in which the victim was to be asphyxiated, I had been chosen to die for the sake of all the others. And already I endured in anticipation the pain of the ugly death in store for me. I breathed with difficulty and my head ached and was heavy, so that I rested it on my hands, my elbows on my knees.

Suddenly everything I already knew was said by a number of people concealed in the darkness. My wife appeared first: 'Be quick, the doctor has said that it is you who must get into the chest.' I thought it painful, but perfectly natural, so I made no protest, but pretended not to hear. And I thought: 'I always considered my wife's love silly.' A number of other voices shouted imperiously: 'Will you make up your mind to obey?' Among them I distinguished clearly that of Dr Paoli. I could not protest, but thought: 'He is doing it for money.'

I raised my head to examine once again the glass chest that was waiting for me. Then I discovered seated on the top of it the bride. Even in that position she kept her perennial air of calm self-possession. I heartily despised the silly woman, but I was suddenly aware that she was very important for me. I should have found this out in real life as well from seeing her seated on the instrument that was to compass my death. And then I looked at her, wagging my tail. I felt like one of those tiny little dogs that make their way through life wagging their tails.

Then the bride spoke. Without any violence, as if it were the most natural thing in the world, she said: 'Uncle, the chest is for you.'

I should have to fight for my life single-handed. That also I guessed. I had the feeling of knowing how to make an enormous effort without anyone being able to realize it. Just as at first I had felt within me an organ that enabled me to win the favour of my judge without opening my mouth, so now I discovered within me another organ, though I do not know what it was, with which I could fight without moving and thus fall upon my enemies when off their guard. And the effort immediately took effect. There was Giovanni, fat Giovanni, seated in the luminous glass chest on a wooden chair like mine and in the same position. He was leaning forward, as the chest was too low, and holding his glasses in his hand to prevent them from falling off his nose. In this attitude he looked as if he were engaged on a business problem and had taken off his glasses to be able to think better without seeing anything. And in fact, though he was bathed in perspiration and already very short of breath, he was not thinking of his approaching death, but was full of mischief, as was clear from his eyes, by which I saw that he meant to make the same effort that I had made a little while previously. Hence I could feel no pity for him, for I was afraid of him.

Giovanni also made the effort successfully. Soon afterwards his place was taken by Alberi, the long, thin and healthy Alberi, in the same position that Giovanni had been in, but he was worse off owing to his height. He was actually bent double and would really have awakened my compassion, if he also, in addition to his suffering, had not displayed the same malice. He looked me up and down with an evil smile, knowing that he could, whenever he chose, escape death in the chest.

Once again the bride spoke from the top of the chest: 'Now, of course, it is your turn, Uncle.' She pronounced each syllable with pedantic distinctness. Her words were accompanied by another sound, very distant, far overhead. From the prolonged noise made by someone hurriedly moving away I learned that the cave ended in a steep passage leading to the surface of the earth. It was only a hiss, but a hiss of consent, and it came from Anna, who once more let me see her hate. She had not the pluck to put it into words, because I had really convinced her that she had been more guilty towards me than I towards her. But this conviction means nothing when it is a question of hate.

I was condemned by everyone. Some way from me, in another part of the cave, my wife and the doctor were walking up and down, waiting, and I knew by intuition that my wife's face wore a resentful expression. She was gesticulating violently as she described my crimes, the wine, the food and my rough treatment of herself and my daughter.

I felt myself drawn towards the chest by the look of triumph Alberi was turning upon me. I drew slowly towards it with my seat, barely an inch at a time, but I knew that when I was within a yard of it – this was the law – I should be carried right up to it at a single bound, gasping.

But there was still a hope of escape. Giovanni, quite recovered from the effects of his hard struggle, had appeared close to the chest, which he could no longer fear, since he had been in it already. This also was the law there. He was standing erect in the full light, looking now at Alberi, who was gasping and threatening, now at me, as I slowly drew near the chest.

I shouted: 'Giovanni, help me to keep him inside. I will pay you.' The whole cave echoed to my cry, and it sounded like a mocking laugh. I understood. It was useless to implore mercy. It was not the first, nor the second who found himself inside the chest who was to die there, but the third. This also was a law of the cave, which, like all the others, was bringing about my undoing. But it was hard that I had to realize it had not been made at that moment deliberately to harm me. This also was a result of that darkness and that light. Giovanni did not even answer and shrugged his shoulders to show his regret at not being able to save me, and at not being able to sell me my safety.

And then I shouted again: 'If there is no other way, take my daughter. She is asleep here close by. It will be easy.' These cries were also sent back to me by a loud echo. Useless though it was, I shouted again to call my daughter: 'Emma, Emma, Emma!'

And from the depths of the cave there actually came Emma's answer, the sound of her voice, still so childish: 'Here I am, Daddy, here I am.'

It seemed to me that she did not answer at once. Then there was a violent convulsion, which I thought was the result of my leap into the chest. Again I thought: 'That girl is always so slow in obeying.' This time her slowness was the cause of my undoing, and I was full of injured bitterness.

I woke up. It was a convulsion, a leap from one world into the other. My head and torso were out of the bed, and I should have fallen out if my wife had not run up to save me. She asked me: 'Have you been dreaming?' And then, moved: 'You were calling for your daughter. You see how you love her.'

At first I was dazzled by reality, where everything seemed to me out of focus and false. And I said to my wife, who also ought to know everything: 'How can we get our children to forgive us for having brought them into the world?'

But she answered, in her simplicity: 'Our children are happy to be alive.'

The world which I then felt to be the real one, the dream-world, was still all around me, and I wanted to proclaim it: 'Because they don't know anything yet.'

Then I stopped and took refuge in silence. The window by my bed was growing light, and in that light I understood at once that I must not describe my dream, because I must conceal the shame of it. But soon, as the sunlight, so soft and bluish, yet commanding, continued to flood the room, I ceased to feel the shame any more.

The dream-world was not my world, nor was I the man who wagged his tail and who was ready to sacrifice his own daughter to save himself.

However, at all costs I must never return to that horrible cave. And that is how I became submissive and ready to obey the doctor's orders. Should it happen that, from no fault of mine, that is, not as a result of excessive potations, but owing to the last fever, I had to go back to the cave, I would jump straight into the glass chest, if it was there, so as not to tail-wag and betray.

Franz Kafka

IN THE PENAL SETTLEMENT

TRANSLATED BY
WILLA AND EDWIN MUIR

FRANZ KAFKA

Born in Prague 1883; died in a sanatorium near Vienna 1924.
Kafka was a Czech writing in German. His longer, incomplete
narratives *The Castle, The Trial* and *America* were published, against
his instructions, after his death. 'In the Penal Settlement', written
in 1914, 'Metamorphosis', which is slightly earlier, and some other
short pieces appeared in his lifetime.

IN THE PENAL SETTLEMENT

'IT'S a remarkable piece of apparatus,' said the officer to the explorer and surveyed with a certain air of admiration the apparatus which was after all quite familiar to him. The explorer seemed to have accepted merely out of politeness the Commandant's invitation to witness the execution of a soldier condemned to death for disobedience and insulting behaviour to a superior. Nor did the colony itself betray much interest in this execution. At least, in the small sandy valley, a deep hollow surrounded on all sides by naked crags, there was no one present save the officer, the explorer, the condemned man, who was a stupid-looking wide-mouthed creature with bewildered hair and face, and the soldier who held the heavy chain controlling the small chains locked on the prisoner's ankles, wrists and neck, chains which were themselves attached to each other by communicating links. In any case, the condemned man looked so like a submissive dog that one might have thought he could be left to run free on the surrounding hills and would only need to be whistled for when the execution was due to begin.

The explorer did not much care about the apparatus and walked up and down behind the prisoner with almost visible indifference, while the officer made the last adjustments, now creeping beneath the structure, which was bedded deep in the earth, now climbing a ladder to inspect its upper parts. These were tasks that might well have been left to a mechanic, but the officer performed them with great zeal, whether because he was a devoted admirer of the apparatus or because for other reasons the work could be entrusted to no one else. 'Ready now!' he called at last and climbed down from the ladder. He looked uncommonly limp, breathed with his mouth wide open and had tucked two fine ladies' handkerchiefs under the collar of his uniform. 'These uniforms are too heavy for the tropics, surely,' said the explorer, instead of making some inquiry about the apparatus, as the officer had expected. 'Of course,' said the officer, washing his oily and greasy hands in a bucket of water that stood ready, 'but they mean home to us; we don't want to forget about home. Now just have a look at this machine,' he added at once, simultaneously drying his hands on a towel and indicating the apparatus. 'Up till now everything has to be set by hand, but from this moment it works all by itself.' The explorer nodded and followed him. The officer, anxious to secure himself against all contingencies, said: 'Things sometimes go wrong, of course; I hope that nothing goes wrong today, but we have to allow for the possibility. The machinery should go on working continuously for twelve hours. But if anything does go wrong it will only be some small matter, and can be set right at once.'

'Won't you take a seat?' he asked finally, drawing a cane chair out from among a heap of them and offering it to the explorer, who could not refuse it. He was now sitting at the edge of a grave, into which he glanced for a fleeting moment. It was not very deep. On one side of the grave the excavated soil had been piled up in a rampart, on the other side of it stood the apparatus.

'I don't know,' said the officer, 'if the Commandant has already explained this apparatus to you.' The explorer waved one hand vaguely; the officer asked for nothing better, since now he could explain the apparatus himself. 'This apparatus,' he said, taking hold of a crank-handle and leaning against it, 'was invented by our former Commandant. I assisted at the very earliest experiments and had a share in all the work until its completion. But the credit of inventing it belongs to him alone. Have you ever heard of our former Commandant? No? Well, it isn't saying too much if I tell you that the organization of the whole penal settlement is his work. We who were his friends knew even before he died that the organization of the colony was so perfect that his successor, even with a thousand new schemes in his head, would find it impossible to alter anything, at least for many years to come. And our prophecy has come true; the new Commandant has had to acknowledge its truth. A pity you never met the old Commandant! But,' the officer interrupted himself, 'I am rambling on, and here stands his apparatus before us. It consists, as you see, of three parts. In the course of time each of these parts has acquired a kind of popular nickname. The lower one is called the "Bed", the upper one the "Designer", and this one here in the middle that moves up and down is called the "Harrow".' 'The Harrow?' asked the explorer. He had not been listening very attentively, the glare of the sun in the shadeless valley was altogether too strong, it was difficult to collect one's thoughts. All the more did he admire the officer, who in spite of his tight-fitting full-dress uniform coat, amply befrogged and weighed down by epaulettes, was pursuing his subject with such enthusiasm and, besides talking, was still tightening a screw here and there with a spanner. As for the soldier, he seemed to be in much the same condition as the explorer. He had wound the prisoner's chain round both his wrists, propped himself on his rifle, let his head hang and was paying no attention to anything. That did not surprise the explorer, for the officer was speaking French, and certainly neither the soldier nor the prisoner understood a word of French. It was all the more remarkable, therefore, that the prisoner was none the less making an effort to follow the officer's explanations. With a kind of drowsy persistence he directed his gaze wherever the officer pointed a finger, and at the interruption of the explorer's question he, too, as well as the officer, looked round.

'Yes, the Harrow,' said the officer, 'a good name for it. The needles are set in like the teeth of a harrow and the whole thing works something like a harrow, although its action is limited to one place and contrived with much more artistic skill. Anyhow, you'll soon understand it. On the Bed here the condemned man is laid – I'm going to describe the apparatus first before I set it in motion. Then you'll be able to follow the proceedings better. Besides, one of the cog-wheels in the Designer is badly worn; it creaks a lot when it's working; you can hardly hear yourself speak; spare parts, unfortunately, are difficult to get here. Well, here is the Bed, as I told you. It is completely covered with a layer of cotton-wool; you'll find out why later. On this cotton-wool the condemned man is laid, face down, quite naked, of course; here are straps for the hands, here for the feet, and here for the neck, to bind him fast. Here at the head of the Bed, where the man, as I said, first lays down his face, is this little gag of felt, which can be easily regulated to go straight into his mouth. It is meant to keep him from screaming and biting his tongue. Of course the man is forced to take the felt into his mouth, for otherwise his neck would be broken by the strap.' 'Is that cotton-wool?' asked the explorer, bending forward. 'Yes, certainly,' said the officer, with a smile, 'feel it for yourself.' He took the explorer's hand and guided it over the Bed. 'It's specially prepared cotton-wool, that's why it looks so different; I'll tell you presently what it's for.' The explorer already felt a dawning interest in the apparatus; he sheltered his eyes from the sun with one hand and gazed up at the structure. It was a huge affair. The Bed and the Designer were of the same size and looked like two dark wooden chests. The Designer hung about two metres above the Bed; each of them was fastened at the corners by four rods of brass that almost flashed out rays in the sunlight. Beneath the chests shuttled the Harrow on a ribbon of steel.

The officer had scarcely noticed the explorer's previous indifference, but he was now well aware of his dawning interest; so he stopped explaining in order to leave a space of time for quiet observation. The condemned man imitated the explorer; since he could not use a hand to shelter his eyes he gazed upwards without shade.

'Well, the man lies down,' said the explorer, leaning back in his chair and crossing his legs.

'Yes,' said the officer, pushing his cap back a little and passing one hand over his heated face, 'now listen! Both the Bed and the Designer have an electric battery each; the Bed needs one for itself, the Designer one for the Harrow. As soon as the man is strapped down, the Bed is set in motion. It quivers in minute, very rapid vibrations, both from side to side and up and down. You will have seen similar apparatus in hospitals; but in our Bed the movements are all precisely calculated; you see, they have to correspond very exactly to the movements of the Harrow. And the Harrow is the instrument for the actual execution of the sentence.'

'And how does the sentence run?' asked the explorer.

'You don't know that either?' said the officer in amazement, and bit his lips. 'Forgive me if my explanations seem rather incoherent. I do beg your pardon. You see, the Commandant always used to do the explaining; but the new Commandant shirks this duty; yet that such an important visitor' – the explorer tried to deprecate the honour with both hands, the officer, however, insisted – 'that such an important visitor should not even be told about the kind of sentence we pass is a new development, which – ' he was just on the point of using strong language but checked himself and said only: 'I was not informed, it is not my fault. In any case, I am certainly the best person to explain our procedure, since I have in here' – he patted his breast-pocket – 'the relevant drawings made by our former Commandant.'

'The Commandant's own drawings?' asked the explorer. 'Did he combine everything in himself, then? Was he soldier, judge, mechanic, chemist, and draughtsman?'

'Indeed he was,' said the officer, nodding assent, with a remote, glassy look. Then he inspected his hands critically; they did not seem clean enough to him for touching the drawings; so he went over to the bucket and washed them again. Then he drew out a small leather brief-case and said: 'Our sentence does not sound severe. Whatever commandment the condemned man has disobeyed is written upon his body by the Harrow. This condemned man, for instance,' – the officer indicated the man – 'will have written on his body: HONOUR THY SUPERIORS!'

The explorer glanced at the man; he stood, as the officer pointed him out, with bent head, apparently listening with all his ears in an effort to catch what was being said. Yet the movement of his blubber lips, closely pressed together, showed clearly that he could not understand a word. Many questions were troubling the explorer, but at the sight of the condemned man he asked only: 'Does he know his sentence?' 'No – ' said the officer, eager to go on with his exposition, but the explorer interrupted him: 'He doesn't know the sentence that has been passed on him?' 'No – ' said the officer again, pausing a moment as if to let the explorer elaborate his question, and then said: 'There would be no point in telling him. He'll learn it corporally, on his person.' The explorer intended to make no answer, but he felt the prisoner's gaze turned on him; it seemed to ask if he approved such goings on. So he bent forward again, having already leaned back in his chair, and put another question: 'But surely he knows that he has been sentenced?' 'Nor that either,' said the officer, smiling at the explorer, as if expecting him to make further surprising remarks. 'No,' said the explorer, wiping his forehead, 'then he cannot know either whether his defence was effective?' 'He has had no chance of putting up a defence,' said the officer, turning his eyes away, as if speaking to himself and so sparing the explorer the shame of hearing self-evident matters explained. 'But he must have had some chance of defending himself,' said the explorer, and rose from his seat.

The officer understood that he was in danger of having his exposition of the apparatus held up for a long time; so he went up to the explorer, took him by the arm, waved a hand towards the condemned man, who was standing very straight now that he had so obviously become the centre of attention – the soldier had also given the chain a jerk – and said: 'This is how the matter stands. I have been appointed judge in this penal settlement, despite my youth, for I was the former Commandant's assistant in all penal matters and know more about the apparatus than anyone. My guiding principle is this: Guilt is never to be doubted. Other courts cannot follow that principle, for they consist of several opinions and have higher courts to scrutinize them. That is not the case here, or at least, it was not the case in the former Commandant's time. The new man has certainly shown some inclination to interfere with my judgements, but so far I have succeeded in fending him off and will go on succeeding. You will like to have the case explained; it is quite simple, like all of them. A captain reported to me this morning that this man, who had been assigned to him as a servant and slept before his door, had been asleep on duty. It is his duty, you see, to get up every time the hour strikes and salute the captain's door. Not an exacting duty, and very necessary, since he has to be a sentry as well as a servant, and must be alert in both functions. Last night the captain wanted to see if the man was doing his duty. He opened the door as the clock struck two and there was his man curled up asleep. He took a riding-whip and lashed him across the face. Instead of getting up and begging pardon, the man caught hold of his master's legs, shook him and cried: 'Throw that whip away or I'll eat you alive.' That's the evidence. The captain came to me an hour ago, I wrote down his statement and appended the sentence to it. Then I had the man put in chains. That was all quite simple. If I had first called the man before me and interrogated him, things would have got into a confused tangle. He would have told lies, and had I exposed these lies he would have backed them up with more lies, and so on and so forth. As it is, I've got him and I won't let him go. Is that quite clear now? But we're wasting our time, the execution should be beginning and I haven't finished explaining the apparatus yet.' He pressed the explorer back into his chair, went up again to the apparatus and began: 'As you see, the shape of the Harrow corresponds to the human form; here is the harrow for the torso, here are the harrows for the legs. For the head there is only this one small spike. Is that quite clear?' he bent amiably forward towards the explorer, eager to provide the most comprehensive explanations.

The explorer considered the Harrow with a frown. Such a version of judicial procedure displeased him. He had to remind himself that this was in any case a penal settlement where extraordinary measures were needed and that military discipline must be enforced to the last. Yet he felt that some hope might be set on the new Commandant, who was apparently of a mind to bring in, although gradually, a new kind of procedure which the officer's narrow mind was incapable of understanding. This train of thought prompted his next question: 'Will the Commandant attend the execution?' 'It is not certain,' said the officer, wincing at the direct question, and his friendly expression darkened. 'That is just why we have to lose no time. Much as I dislike it, I shall have to cut my explanations short. But, of course, tomorrow, when the apparatus has been cleaned – it's one drawback is that it gets so messy – I can recapitulate all the details. For the present, then, only the essentials. When the man lies down on the Bed and it begins to vibrate, the Harrow is lowered on to his body. It regulates itself automatically so that the needles barely touch his skin; once contact is made the steel ribbon stiffens immediately into a rigid band. And then the performance begins. An ignorant onlooker would see no difference between one punishment and another. The Harrow appears to do its work with uniform regularity. As it quivers, its points pierce the skin of the body which is itself quivering from the vibration of the Bed. So that the actual progress of the sentence can be watched, the Harrow is made of glass. Getting the needles fixed in the glass was a technical problem, but after many experiments we overcame the difficulty. No trouble was too great for us to take, you see. And now anyone can look through the glass and watch the inscription taking form on the body. Wouldn't you care to come a little nearer and have a look at the needles?'

The explorer got up slowly, walked across and bent over the Harrow. 'You see,' said the officer, 'there are two kinds of needles arranged in multiple patterns. Each long needle has a short one beside it. The long needle does the writing, and the short needle sprays a jet of water to wash away the blood and keep the inscription clear. Blood and water together are then conducted here through small runnels into this main runnel and down a waste-pipe into the grave.' With his finger the officer traced the exact course taken by the blood and water. To make the picture as vivid as possible he held both hands below the outlet of the waste-pipe as if to catch the outflow, and when he did this the explorer drew back his head and, feeling behind him with one hand, sought to return to his chair. To his horror he found that the condemned man too had obeyed the officer's invitation to examine the Harrow at close quarters and had followed him. He had pulled forward the sleepy soldier with the chain and was bending over the glass. One could see that his uncertain eyes were trying to perceive what the two gentlemen had been looking at, but, since he had not understood the explanation, he could not make head or tail of it. He was peering this way and that way. He kept running his eyes along the glass. The explorer wanted to drive him away, since what he was doing was probably culpable. But the officer firmly restrained the explorer with one hand and with the other took a clod of earth from the rampart and threw it at the soldier. He opened his eyes with a jerk, saw what the condemned man had dared to do, let his rifle fall, dug his heels into the ground, dragged the prisoner back so that he stumbled and fell immediately, and then stood looking down at him, watching him struggling and rattling in his chains. 'Set him on his feet!' yelled the officer, for he noticed that the explorer's attention was being too much distracted by the condemned man. In fact the explorer was even leaning right across the Harrow, without taking any notice of it, intent only in finding out what was happening to the condemned man. 'Be careful with him!' cried the officer again. He ran round the apparatus, himself caught the condemned man under the shoulders and with the soldier's help got him up on his feet, which kept slithering from under him.

'Now I know all about it,' said the explorer, as the officer came back to him. 'All except the most important thing,' the latter said, seizing the explorer's arm and pointing upwards: 'In the Designer are all the cog-wheels that control the movements of the Harrow, and this machinery is regulated according to the inscription demanded by the sentence. I am still using the guiding plans drawn by the former Commandant. Here they are' – he extracted some sheets from the leather brief-case – 'but I'm sorry I can't let you handle them, they are my most precious possessions. Just take a seat and I'll hold them in front of you like this, then you'll be able to see everything quite well.' He spread out the first sheet of paper. The explorer would have liked to say something appreciative, but all he could see was a labyrinth of lines crossing and re-crossing each other, which covered the paper so thickly that it was difficult to discern the blank spaces between them. 'Read it,' said the officer. 'I can't,' said the explorer. 'Yet it's clear enough,' said the officer. 'It's very ingenious,' said the explorer evasively, 'but I can't make it out.' 'Yes,' said the officer with a laugh, putting the paper away again, 'it's no calligraphy for school children. It needs to be studied closely. I'm quite sure that in the end you would understand it too. Of course the script can't be a simple one; it's not supposed to kill a man straight off, but only after an interval of, on an average, twelve hours; the turning-point is reckoned to come at the sixth hour. So there have to be lots and lots of flourishes around the actual script; the script itself runs round the body only in a narrow girdle; the rest of the body is reserved for the embellishments. Can you appreciate now the work accomplished by the Harrow and the whole apparatus? Just watch it!' He ran up the ladder, turned a wheel, called down: 'Look out, keep to one side!' and everything started working. If the wheel had not creaked, it would have been marvellous. The officer, as if surprised by the noise of the wheel, shook his fist at it, then spread out his arms in excuse to the explorer and climbed down rapidly to peer at the working of the machine from below. Something perceptible to no one save himself was still not in order; he clambered up again, groped about with both hands in the interior of the Designer, then slid down one of the rods, instead of using the ladder, so as to get down quicker, and with the full force of his lungs, to make himself heard at all in the noise, yelled in the explorer's ear: 'Can you follow it? The Harrow is beginning to write; when it finishes the first draft of the inscription on the back, the layer of cotton-wool begins to roll and slowly turns the body over, to give the Harrow fresh space for writing. Meanwhile the raw part that has been written on lies on the cotton-wool, which is specially prepared to staunch the bleeding and so makes all ready for a new deepening of the script. Then these teeth at the edge of the Harrow, as the body turns farther round, tear the cotton-wool away from the wounds, throw it into the grave and there is more work for the Harrow. So it keeps on writing deeper and deeper for the whole twelve hours. The first six hours the condemned man stays alive almost as before, he suffers only pain. After two hours the felt gag is taken away, for he has no longer strength to scream. Here, into this electrically heated basin at the head of the Bed, some warm rice-pap is poured, from which the man, if he feels like it, can take as much as his tongue can lap. Not one of them ever misses the chance. I can remember none, and my experience is extensive. Only about the sixth hour does the man lose all desire to eat. I usually kneel down here at that moment and observe this phenomenon. The man rarely swallows his last mouthful, he only rolls it round his mouth and spits it out into the grave. I have to duck just then or he would spit it in my face. But how quiet he grows at just about the sixth hour! Enlightenment comes to the most dull-witted. It begins around the eyes. From there it radiates. A moment that might tempt one to get under the

Harrow with him. Nothing more happens after that, the man only begins to understand the inscription, he purses his mouth as if he were listening. You have seen how difficult it is to decipher the script with one's eyes; but our man deciphers it with his wounds. To be sure, that is a hard task; he needs six hours to accomplish it. By that time the Harrow has pierced him quite through and casts him into the grave, where he pitches down upon the blood and water and the cotton-wool. Then the judgement has been fulfilled, and we, the soldier and I, bury him.'

The explorer had inclined his ear to the officer and, with his hands in his jacket pockets, watched the machine at work. The condemned man watched it too, but uncomprehendingly. He bent forward a little and was intent on the moving needles, when the soldier, at a sign from the officer, slashed through his shirt and trousers from behind with a knife, so that they fell off; he tried to catch at his falling clothes to cover his nakedness, but the soldier lifted him into the air and shook the last remnants from him. The officer stopped the machine, and in the sudden silence the condemned man was laid under the Harrow. The chains were loosened and the straps fastened on instead; in the first moment that seemed almost a relief to the condemned man. And now the Harrow was adjusted a little lower, since he was a thin man. When the needle-points touched him a shudder ran over his skin; while the soldier was busy strapping his right hand, he flung out his left hand blindly; but it happened to be in the direction towards where the explorer was standing. The officer kept watching the explorer sideways, as if seeking to read from his face the impression made on him by the execution, which had been at least cursorily explained to him.

The wrist-strap broke; probably the soldier had drawn it too tight. The officer had to intervene, the soldier held up the broken piece of the strap to show him. So the officer went over to him and said, his face still turned towards the explorer: 'This is a very complex machine, things are always breaking or giving way here and there; but one must not thereby allow oneself to be diverted in one's general judgement. In any case, this strap is easily made good; I shall simply use a chain; the delicacy of the vibrations for the right arm will, of course, be a little impaired.' And while he fastened the chain, he added: 'The resources for maintaining the machine are now very much reduced. Under the former Commandant I had free access to a sum of money set aside entirely for this purpose. There was a store, too, in which spare parts were kept for repairs of all kinds. I confess I have been almost prodigal with them, I mean in the past, not now as the new Commandant pretends, always looking for an excuse to attack our old way of doing things. Now he has taken charge of the machine money himself, and if I send for a new strap they ask for the broken old strap as evidence, and the new strap takes ten days to appear and then is of shoddy material and not much good. But how I am supposed to work the machine without a strap, that's something nobody bothers about.'

The explorer thought to himself: It's always a ticklish matter to intervene decisively in other people's affairs. He was neither a member of the penal colony nor a citizen of the state to which it belonged. Were he to denounce this execution or actually try to stop it, they could say to him: 'You are a stranger, mind your own business.' He could make no answer to that, unless he were to add that he was amazed at himself in this connexion, for he travelled only as an observer, with no intention at all of altering other people's methods of administering justice. Yet here he found himself strongly tempted. The injustice of the procedure and the inhumanity of the execution were undeniable. No one could suppose that he had any selfish interest in the matter, for the condemned man was a complete stranger, not a fellow countryman or even at all sympathetic to him. The explorer himself had recommendations from high quarters, had been received here with great courtesy, and the very fact that he had been invited to attend the execution seemed to suggest that his views would be welcome. And this was all the more likely since the Commandant, as he had heard only too plainly, was no upholder of the procedure and maintained an attitude almost of hostility to the officer.

At that moment the explorer heard the officer cry out in rage. He had just, with considerable difficulty, forced the felt gag into the condemned man's mouth when the man, in an irresistible access of nausea, shut his eyes and vomited. Hastily the officer snatched him away from the gag and tried to hold his head over the grave; but it was too late, the vomit was running all over the machine. 'It's the fault of that Commandant!' cried the officer, senselessly shaking the brass rods in front, 'the machine is befouled like a pig-sty.' With trembling hands he indicated to the explorer what had happened. 'Have I not tried for hours at a time to get the Commandant to understand that the prisoner must fast for a whole day before the execution? But our new, mild doctrine thinks otherwise. The Commandant's ladies stuff the man's mouth with sugar-candy before he's led off. He has lived on stinking fish his whole life long and now he has to guzzle sugar-candy! But it could still be possible, I should have nothing to say against it, but why won't they get me a new felt gag, which I have been begging for the last three months? How should a man not feel sick when he takes a felt gag into his mouth which more than a hundred men have already slobbered and gnawed in their dying moments?'

The condemned man had laid his head down and looked peaceful, the soldier was busy trying to clean the machine with the condemned man's shirt. The officer advanced towards the explorer, who in some vague presentiment fell back a pace, but the officer seized him by the hand, and drew him to one side. 'I should like to exchange a few words with you in confidence,' he said. 'May I?' 'Of course,' said the explorer, and listened with downcast eyes.

'This procedure and method of execution, which you are now having the opportunity to admire, has at the moment no longer any open adherents in our colony. I am its sole advocate, and at the same time the sole advocate of the old Commandant's tradition. I can no longer reckon on any further extension of the method, it takes all my energy to maintain it as it is. During the old Commandant's lifetime the colony was full of his adherents; his strength of conviction I still have in some measure, but not an atom of his power; consequently the adherents have skulked out of sight, there are still many of them but none of them will admit it. If you were to go into the tea-house today, an execution day, and listen to what is being said, you would perhaps hear only ambiguous remarks. These would all be made by adherents, but under the present Commandant and his present doctrines they are of no use to me.

And now I ask you: because of this Commandant and the
women who influence him, is such a piece of work, the work of
a lifetime,' – he pointed to the machine – 'to fall into disuse?
Ought one to let that happen? Even if one has only come as a
stranger to our island for a few days? And yet there's no time
to lose, an attack of some kind is impending on my function as a
judge: conferences are already being held in the Commandant's
office from which I am excluded; even your coming here today
seems to me a significant move; they are cowards and use you
as a screen, you, a stranger. How different an execution was in
the old days! A whole day before the ceremony the valley was
packed with people; they all came only to look on; early in the
morning the Commandant appeared with his ladies; fanfares
roused the whole camp; I reported that everything was in
readiness; the assembled company – no high official dared to
absent himself – arranged itself round the machine; this pile of
cane chairs is a miserable survival from that epoch. The machine
was freshly cleaned and glittering, I got new spare parts for
almost every execution. Before hundreds of spectators – all of
them standing on tip-toe as far as the heights there – the condemned man was laid under the Harrow by the Commandant
himself. What is left today for a common soldier to do was then
my task, the task of the presiding judge, and it was an honour
for me. And then the execution began! No discordant noise
spoilt the working of the machine. Many did not care to watch
it but lay with closed eyes in the sand; they all knew; now
Justice is being done. In the silence one heard nothing but the
condemned man's sighs, half muffled by the felt gag. Nowadays
the machine can no longer wring from anyone a sigh louder
than the felt gag can stifle; but in those days the writing needles
let drop an acid fluid which we're not permitted to use today.
Well, and then came the sixth hour! It was impossible to grant
all the requests to be allowed to watch it from near by. The
Commandant in his wisdom ordained that the children should
have the preference; I, of course, because of my office had the
privilege of always being at hand; often enough I would be
squatting there with a small child in either arm. How we all
absorbed the look of transfiguration on the face of the sufferer,
how we bathed our cheeks in the radiance of that justice,

achieved at last and fading so quickly! What times these were, my comrade!' The officer had obviously forgotten whom he was addressing; he had embraced the explorer and laid his head on his shoulder. The explorer was deeply embarrassed, impatiently he stared over the officer's head. The soldier had finished his cleaning job and was now pouring rice-pap from a pot into the basin. As soon as the condemned man, who seemed to have recovered himself entirely, noticed this action he began to reach for the rice with his tongue. The soldier kept pushing him away, since the rice-pap was certainly meant for a later hour, yet it was just as unfitting that the soldier himself should thrust his dirty hands into the basin and eat out of it before the other's avid face.

The officer quickly pulled himself together. 'I didn't want to upset you,' he said, 'I know it is impossible to make those days credible now. Anyhow, the machine is still working and it is still effective in itself. It is effective in itself even though it stands alone in this valley. And the corpse still falls at the last into the grave with an incomprehensively gentle wafting motion, even although there are no hundreds of people swarming round like flies as formerly. In those days we had to put a strong fence round the grave; it has long since been torn down.'

The explorer wanted to withdraw his face from the officer and looked round him at random. The officer thought he was surveying the valley's desolation; so he seized him by the hands, turned him round to meet his eyes, and asked: 'Do you observe the shame of it?'

But the explorer said nothing. The officer left him alone for a little; with legs apart, hands on hips, he stood very still, gazing at the ground. Then he smiled encouragingly at the explorer and said: 'I was quite near you yesterday when the Command-ant gave you the invitation. I heard him giving it. I know the Commandant. I divined at once what he was after. Although he is powerful enough to take measures against me, he doesn't dare to do it yet, but he certainly means to use your verdict against me, the verdict of an illustrious foreigner. He has calculated it carefully: this is your second day on the island, you did not know the old Commandant and his ways, you are conditioned by European ways of thought, perhaps you object

on principle to capital punishment in general and to such
mechanical instruments of death in particular, besides you will
see that the execution has no support from the public, a shabby
ceremony – carried out with a machine already somewhat old
and worn – now, taking all that into consideration, would it not
be likely (so thinks the Commandant) that you might disapprove of my methods? And if you disapprove, you wouldn't
conceal the fact (I'm still speaking from the Commandant's
point of view), for you are a man to feel confidence in your own
well-tried conclusions? True, you have seen and learned to
appreciate the peculiarities of many peoples, and so you would
not be likely to take a strong line against our proceedings, as
you might do in your own country. But the Commandant has
no need of that. A casual, even an unguarded remark will be
enough. It doesn't even need to represent what you really think
so long as it can be used speciously to serve his purpose. He will
try to prompt you with sly questions, of that I am certain. And
his ladies will sit around you and prick up their ears; you might
be saying something like this: 'In our country we have a
different way of carrying out justice,' or 'In our country the
prisoner has a chance to defend himself before he is sentenced,'
or 'We haven't used torture since the Middle Ages.' All these
statements are as true as they seem natural to you, harmless
remarks that pass no judgements on my methods. But how
would the Commandant react to them? I can see him, our good
Commandant, pushing his chair away immediately and rushing
on to the balcony, I can see his ladies streaming out after him, I
can hear his voice – the ladies call it a voice of thunder – well,
and this is what he says: 'A famous Western investigator, sent
out to study criminal procedure in all the countries of the world,
has just said that our old tradition of administering justice is
inhumane. Such a verdict from such a personality makes it
impossible for me to countenance these methods any longer.
Therefore from this very day I ordain', and so on. You may
want to interpose that you never said any such thing, that you
never called my methods inhumane, on the contrary, your
profound experience leads you to believe they are most humane
and most in consonance with human dignity, and you admire
the machine greatly – but it will be too late; you won't even

get on to the balcony, crowded as it will be with ladies; you may try to draw attention to yourself; you may want to scream out; but a lady's hand will close your lips – and I and the old Commandant will be done for.'

The explorer had to suppress a smile; so easy, then, was the task he had felt to be so difficult. He said evasively: 'You over-estimate my influence; the Commandant has read my letters of recommendation, he knows that I am no expert in criminal procedure. If I were to give an opinion, it would be as a private individual, an opinion no more influential than that of any ordinary person, and in any case much less influential than that of the Commandant, who, I am given to understand, has very extensive powers in this penal settlement. If his attitude to your procedure is as definitely hostile as you believe, then I fear the end of your tradition is at hand, even without any humble assistance from me.'

Had it dawned on the officer at last? No, he still did not understand. He shook his head emphatically, glanced briefly round at the condemned man and the soldier, who both flinched away from the rice, came close up to the explorer and without looking at his face but fixing his eye on some spot on his coat said in a lower voice than before: 'You don't know the Commandant; you feel yourself – forgive the expression – a kind of outsider so far as all of us are concerned; yet, believe me, your influence cannot be rated too highly. I was simply delighted when I heard that you were to attend the execution all by yourself. The Commandant arranged it to aim a blow at me, but I shall turn it to my advantage. Without being distracted by lying whispers and contemptuous glances – which could not have been avoided had a crowd of people attended the execu-tion – you have heard my explanations, seen the machine, and are now in course of watching the execution. You have doubt-less already formed your own judgement; if you still have some small uncertainties, the sight of the execution will resolve them. And now I make this request to you: Help me against the Commandant!' The explorer would not let him go on. 'How could I do that?' he cried, 'it's quite impossible. I can neither help nor hinder you.' 'Yes, you can,' said the officer. With some apprehension the explorer saw that the officer had clenched his fists. 'Yes, you can,' repeated the officer, still more insistently. 'I have a plan that is bound to succeed. You believe your influence is insufficient. I know that it is sufficient. But even granted that you are right, is it not necessary, for the sake of preserving this tradition, to try even what might prove insufficient? Listen to my plan, then. The first thing necessary for you to carry it out is to be as reticent as possible regarding your verdict on these proceedings. Unless you are asked a direct question you must say nothing at all; but what you do say must be brief and general; let it be remarked that you would prefer not to discuss the matter, that you are out of patience with it, that if you were to let yourself go you would use strong language. I don't ask you to tell any lies; by no means; you should give only curt answers, such as: 'Yes, I saw the execution,' or 'Yes, I had it explained to me.' Just that, nothing more. There are grounds enough for any impatience you betray, although not such as will occur to the Commandant. Of course, he will mistake your meaning and interpret it to please himself. That's what my plan depends on. Tomorrow in the Commandant's office there is to be a large conference of all the high administrative officials, the Commandant presiding. Of course the Commandant is the kind of man to have turned these conferences into public spectacles. He has had a gallery built that is always packed with spectators. I am compelled to take part in the conferences, but they make me sick with nausea. Now, whatever happens, you will certainly be invited to this conference; if you behave today as I suggest the invitation will become an urgent request. But if for some mysterious reason you're not invited, you'll have to ask for an invitation: there's no doubt of your getting it then. So tomorrow you're sitting in the Commandant's box with the ladies. He keeps looking up to make sure you're there. After various trivial and ridiculous matters, brought in merely to impress the audience – mostly harbour works, nothing but harbour works! – our judicial procedure comes up for discussion too. If the Commandant doesn't introduce it, or not soon enough, I'll see that it's mentioned. I'll stand up and report that today's execution has taken place. Quite briefly, only a statement. Such a statement is not usual, but I shall make it. The Commandant thanks me, as always, with an amiable smile, and then he can't restrain himself, he seizes the excellent opportunity. 'It has just been reported,' he will say, or words to that effect, 'that an execution has taken place. I should like merely to add that this execution was witnessed by the famous investigator who has, as you all know, honoured our colony so exceptionally by his visit to us. His presence at today's session of our conference also contributes to the importance of this occasion. Should we not now ask the famous investigator to give us his verdict on our traditional mode of execution and the procedure that leads up to it?' Of course there is loud applause, general agreement, I am more insistent than anyone. The Commandant bows to you and says: 'Then in the name of the assembled company, I put the question to you.' And now you advance to the front of the box. Lay your hands where everyone can see them, or the ladies will catch them and press your fingers. And then at last you can speak out. I don't know how I'm going to endure the tension of waiting for that moment. Don't put any restraint on yourself when you make your speech, publish the truth aloud, lean over the front of the box, shout, yes indeed, shout your verdict, your unshakable conviction, at the Commandant. Yet perhaps you wouldn't care to do that, it's not in keeping with your character, in your country perhaps people do these things differently, well, that's all right too, that will be quite as effective, don't even stand up, just say a few words, even in a whisper, so that only the officials beneath you will hear them, that will be quite enough, you don't even need to mention the lack of public support for the execution, the creaking wheel, the broken strap, the filthy stump of felt, no, I'll take all that upon me, and, believe me, if my indictment doesn't drive him out of the conference hall, it will force him to his knees to make the acknowledgement: 'Old Commandant, I humble myself before you.' That is my plan; will you help me to carry it out? But of course you are willing, what is more, you must.' And the officer seized the explorer by both arms and gazed, breathing heavily, into his face. He had shouted the last sentence so loudly that even the soldier and the condemned man were startled into attending; they had not understood a word but they stopped eating and looked over at the explorer, chewing their previous mouthfuls.

From the very beginning the explorer had no doubt about what answer he must give; in his lifetime he had experienced too much to have any uncertainty here; he was fundamentally honourable and unafraid. And yet now, facing the soldier and the condemned man, he did hesitate for as long as it took to draw one breath. At last, however, he said, as he had to: 'No.' The officer blinked several times but did not turn his eyes away. 'Would you like me to explain?' asked the explorer. The officer nodded, mutely. 'I do not approve of your procedure,' said the explorer then, 'even before you took me into your confidence – of course I shall never in any circumstances betray your confidence – I was already wondering whether it would be my duty to intervene and whether my intervention would have the slightest chance of success. I realized to whom I ought to turn: to the Commandant, of course. You have made that fact even clearer, but without having strengthened my resolution, on the contrary, your sincere conviction has touched me, even though it cannot influence my judgement.'

The officer remained mute, turned to the machine, caught hold of a brass rod and then, leaning back a little, gazed at the Designer as if to assure himself that all was in order. The soldier and the condemned man seemed to have come to some understanding; the condemned man was making signs to the soldier, difficult though his movements were because of the tight straps; the soldier was bending down to him; the condemned man whispered something and the soldier nodded.

The explorer followed the officer and said: 'You don't know yet what I mean to do. I shall tell the Commandant what I think of the procedure, certainly, but not at a public conference, only in private; nor shall I stay here long enough to attend any conference; I am going away early tomorrow morning, or at least embarking on my ship.'

It did not look as if the officer had been listening. 'So you did not find the procedure convincing,' he said to himself and smiled, as an old man smiles at childish nonsense and yet pursues his own meditations behind the smile.

'Then the time has come,' he said at last and suddenly looked at the explorer with bright eyes that held some challenge, some appeal for cooperation. 'The time for what?' asked the explorer uneasily, but got no answer.

'You are free,' said the officer to the condemned man in the native tongue. The man did not believe it at first. 'Yes, you are set free,' said the officer. For the first time the condemned man's face woke to real animation. Was it true? Was it only a caprice of the officer's, that might change again? Had the foreign explorer begged him off? What was it? One could read these questions on his face. But not for long. Whatever it might be, he wanted to be really free if he might, and he began to struggle so far as the Harrow permitted him.

'You'll burst my straps,' cried the officer, 'lie still! We'll soon loosen them.' And signing the soldier to help him, he set about doing so. The condemned man laughed wordlessly to himself, now he turned his face left towards the officer, now right towards the soldier, nor did he forget the explorer.

'Draw him out,' ordered the officer. Because of the Harrow this had to be done with some care. The condemned man had already torn himself a little in the back through his impatience.

From now on, however, the officer paid hardly any attention to him. He went up to the explorer, pulled out the small leather brief-case again, turned over the papers in it, found the one he wanted and showed it to the explorer. 'Read it,' he said. 'I can't,' said the explorer, 'I told you before that I can't make out these scripts.' 'Try taking a close look at it,' said the officer and came quite near to the explorer so that they might read it together. But when even that proved useless, he outlined the script with his little finger, holding it high above the paper as if the surface dared not be sullied by touch, in order to help the explorer to follow the script in that way. The explorer did make an effort, meaning to please the officer in this respect at least, but he was quite unable to follow. Now the officer began to spell it, letter by letter, and then read out the words. '"BE JUST!" is what is written there,' he said, 'surely you can read it now.' The explorer bent so close to the paper that the officer feared he might touch it and drew it farther away; the explorer made no remark, yet it was clear that he still could not decipher it. '"Be just!" is what is written there,' said the officer once more. 'Maybe,' said the explorer, 'I am prepared to believe

you.' 'Well, then,' said the officer, at least partly satisfied, and
climbed up the ladder with the paper; very carefully he laid it
inside the Designer and seemed to be changing the disposition
of all the cog-wheels; it was a troublesome piece of work and
must have involved wheels that were extremely small, for
sometimes the officer's head vanished altogether from sight
inside the Designer, so precisely did he have to regulate the
machinery.

The explorer, down below, watched the labour uninter-
ruptedly, his neck grew stiff, and his eyes smarted from the glare
of sunshine over the sky. The soldier and the condemned man
were now busy together. The man's shirt and trousers, which
were already lying in the grave, were fished out by the point
of the soldier's bayonet. The shirt was abominably dirty and its
owner washed it in the bucket of water. When he put on the
shirt and trousers both he and the soldier could not help guffaw-
ing, for the garments were of course slit up behind. Perhaps the
condemned man felt it incumbent on him to amuse the soldier,
he turned round and round in his slashed garments before the
soldier, who squatted on the ground beating his knees with
mirth. All the same, they presently controlled their mirth out of
respect for the gentlemen.

When the officer had at length finished his task aloft, he
surveyed the machinery in all its details once more with a smile,
but this time shut the lid of the Designer, which had stayed
open till now, climbed down, looked into the grave and then
at the condemned man, noting with satisfaction that the clothing had been taken out, then went over to wash his hands in
the water-bucket, perceived too late that it was disgustingly
dirty, was unhappy because he could not wash his hands, in the
end thrust them into the sand – this alternative did not please
him, but he had to put up with it – then stood upright and began to unbutton his uniform jacket. As he did this, the two
ladies' handkerchiefs he had tucked at the back of his collar fell
into his hands. 'Here are your handkerchiefs,' he said, and
threw them to the condemned man. And then to the explorer he
said in explanation: 'A gift from the ladies.'

In spite of the obvious haste with which he was discarding
first his uniform jacket and then all his clothing, he handled

each garment with loving care, he even ran his fingers caress-
ingly over the silver lace on the jacket and shook a tassel into
place. This loving care was certainly out of keeping with the
fact that as soon as he had a garment off he flung it at once
with a kind of unwilling jerk into the grave. The last thing left
to him was his small-sword with the sword-belt. He drew it out
of the scabbard, broke it, then gathered all together, the bits of
the sword, the scabbard and the belt, and flung them so
violently down that they clattered into the grave.

Now he stood naked there. The explorer bit his lips and said
nothing. He knew very well what was going to happen, but he
had no right to obstruct the officer in anything. If the judicial
procedure which the officer cherished were really so near its
end – possibly as a result of the explorer's intervention, to which
he felt himself pledged – then the officer was doing the right
thing; in his place the explorer would not have acted otherwise.

The soldier and the condemned man did not understand at
first what was happening, to begin with they were not even
looking on. The condemned man was gleeful at having got the
handkerchiefs back, but he was not allowed to enjoy them for
long, since the soldier snatched them with a sudden, unexpected grab. Now the condemned man in turn was trying to
twitch them from under the belt where the soldier had tucked
them, but the soldier was on his guard. So they were wrestling,
half in jest. Only when the officer stood quite naked was their
attention caught. The condemned man especially seemed struck
with the notion that a great change of fortune was impending.
What had happened to him was now going to happen to the
officer. Perhaps even to the very end. Apparently the foreign
explorer had given the order for it. So this was revenge.
Although he himself had not suffered to the end, he was to be
revenged to the end. A broad, silent grin now appeared on his
face and stayed there all the rest of the time.

The officer, however, had turned to the machine. It had been
clear enough previously that he understood the machine well,
but now it was almost staggering to see how he managed it and
how it obeyed him. His hand had only to approach the Harrow
for it to rise and sink several times till it was adjusted to the
right position for receiving him; he touched only the edge of

the Bed and already it was vibrating; the felt gag came to meet his mouth, one could see that the officer was really reluctant to take it, but he shrank from it only a moment, soon he submitted and received it. Everything was ready, only the straps hung down at the sides, yet they were obviously unnecessary, the officer did not need to be fastened down. Then the condemned man noticed the loose straps, in his opinion the execution was incomplete unless the straps were buckled, he gestured eagerly to the soldier and they ran together to strap the officer down. The latter had already stretched out one foot to push the lever that started the Designer; he saw the two men coming up, so he drew his foot back and let himself be buckled in. But now he could not reach the lever; neither the soldier nor the condemned man would be able to find it, and the explorer was determined not to lift a finger. It was not necessary; as soon as the straps were fastened the machine began to work; the Bed vibrated, the needles flickered above the skin, the Harrow rose and fell. The explorer had been staring at it quite a while before he remembered that a wheel in the Designer should have been creaking; but everything was quiet, not even the slightest hum could be heard.

Because it was working so silently the machine simply escaped one's attention. The explorer observed the soldier and the condemned man. The latter was the more animated of the two, everything in the machine interested him, now he was bending down and now stretching up on tip-toe, his forefinger was extended all the time pointing out details to the soldier. This annoyed the explorer. He was resolved to stay till the end, but he could not bear the sight of these two. 'Go back home,' he said. The soldier would have been willing enough, but the condemned man took the order as a punishment. With clasped hands he implored to be allowed to stay, and when the explorer shook his head and would not relent, he even went down on his knees. The explorer saw that it was no use merely giving orders, he was on the point of going over and driving them away. At that moment he heard a noise above him in the Designer. He looked up. Was that cog-wheel going to make trouble after all? But it was something quite different. Slowly the lid of the Designer rose up and then clicked wide open. The

teeth of a cog-wheel showed themselves and rose higher, soon
the whole wheel was visible, it was as if some enormous force
were squeezing the Designer so that there was no longer room
for the wheel, the wheel moved up till it came to the very edge
of the Designer, fell down, rolled along the sand a little on its
rim and then lay flat. But a second wheel was already rising
after it, followed by many others, large and small and in-
distinguishably minute, the same thing happened to all of them,
at every moment one imagined the Designer must now really
be empty, but another complex of numerous wheels was
already rising into sight, falling down, trundling along the
sand and lying flat. This phenomenon made the condemned
man completely forget the explorer's command, the cog-wheels
fascinated him, he was always trying to catch one and at the
same time urging the soldier to help, but always drew back his
hand in alarm, for another wheel always came hopping along
which, at least on its first advance, scared him off.

The explorer, on the other hand, felt greatly troubled; the
machine was obviously going to pieces; its silent working was
a delusion; he had a feeling that he must now stand by the
officer since the officer was no longer able to look after himself.
But while tumbling cog-wheels absorbed his whole attention he
had forgotten to keep an eye on the rest of the machine; now
that the last cog-wheel had left the Designer, however, he bent
over the Harrow and had a new and still more unpleasant surprise. The Harrow was not writing, it was only jabbing, and the
Bed was not turning the body over but only bringing it up
quivering against the needles. The explorer wanted to do something, if possible, to bring the whole machine to a standstill, for
this was no exquisite torture such as the officer desired, this was
plain murder. He stretched out his hands. But at that moment
the Harrow rose with the body spitted on it and moved to the
side, as it usually did only when the twelfth hour had come.
Blood was flowing in a hundred streams, not mingled with
water; the water-jets too had failed to function. And now the
last action failed to fulfil itself, the body did not drop off the
long needles, streaming with blood it went on hanging over
the grave without falling into it. The Harrow tried to move
back to its old position, but as if it had itself noticed that it had

not yet got rid of its burden it stuck after all where it was, over the grave. 'Come and help!' cried the explorer to the other two, and himself seized the officer's feet. He wanted to push against the feet while the others seized the head from the opposite side and so the officer might be slowly eased off the needles. But the other two could not make up their minds to come; the condemned man actually turned away; the explorer had to go over to them and force them into position at the officer's head. And here, almost against his will, he had to look at the face of the corpse. It was as it had been in life; no sign was visible of the promised redemption; what the others had found in the machine the officer had not found; the lips were firmly pressed together, the eyes were open, with the same expression as in life, their look was calm and convinced, through the forehead went the point of the great iron spike.

As the explorer, with the soldier and the condemned man behind him, reached the first houses of the settlement, the soldier pointed to one of them and said: 'There is the tea-house.'

In the ground floor of the house was a deep, low, cavernous space, its walls and ceiling blackened with smoke. It was open to the road all along its length. Although this tea-house was very little different from the other houses of the settlement, which were all very dilapidated, even up to the Commandant's palatial headquarters, it made on the explorer the impression of a historic tradition of some kind, and he felt the power of past days. He went near to it, followed by his companions, right up between the empty tables which stood in the road before it, and breathed the cool heavy air that came from the interior. 'The old man's buried here,' said the soldier, 'the priest wouldn't let him lie in the churchyard. Nobody knew where to bury him for a while, but in the end they buried him here. The officer never told you about that, for sure, because of course that's what he was most ashamed of. He even tried several times to dig the old man up by night, but he was always chased away.' 'Where is the grave?' asked the explorer, who found it impossible to believe the soldier. At once both of them, the soldier and the condemned man, ran before him pointing with outstretched hands in the direction where the grave should be. They led the explorer right up to the back wall, where guests were sitting at a few tables. These were apparently dock labourers, strong men with short, glistening, full black beards. None had a jacket, their shirts were torn, they were poor, humble creatures. As the explorer drew near some of them got up, pressed close to the wall, and stared at him. 'It's a stranger,' ran the whisper around him, 'he wants to see the grave.' They pushed one of the tables aside, and under it there was really a gravestone. It was a simple stone, low enough to be covered by a table. There was an inscription on it in very small letters, the explorer had to kneel down to read it. This was what it said: 'Here rests the old Commandant. His adherents, who now must be nameless, have dug this grave and set up this stone. There is a prophecy that after a certain number of years the Commandant will rise again and lead his adherents from this house to recover the colony. Have faith and wait!' When the explorer had read this and risen to his feet he saw all the bystanders around him smiling, as if they too had read the inscription, had found it ridiculous and were expecting him to agree with them. The explorer ignored this, distributed a few coins among them, waited till the table was pushed over the grave again, quitted the tea-house and made for the harbour.

The soldier and the condemned man had found some acquaintances in the tea-house, who detained them. But they must have soon shaken them off, for the explorer was only half-way down the long flight of steps leading to the boats when they came rushing after him. Probably they wanted to force him at the last minute to take them with him. While he was bargaining below with a ferryman to row him to the steamer, the two of them came headlong down the steps, in silence, for they did not dare to shout. But by the time they reached the foot of the steps the explorer was already in the boat, and the ferryman was just casting off from the shore. They could have jumped into the boat, but the explorer lifted a heavy knotted rope from the floor-boards, threatened them with it, and so kept them from attempting the leap.

Boris Pasternak

THE LONG DAYS

TRANSLATED BY
ROBERT PAYNE AND
NIKITA ROMANOFF

BORIS PASTERNAK

Born in Moscow 1890; died at Peredelkino 1960. Russian poet and translator. *Doctor Zhivago*, his only novel, was completed in 1956 and published outside the Soviet Union. 'The Long Days' is the first part of an early experiment in prose, 'The Childhood of Zhenya Luvers' (1918).

THE LONG DAYS

ZHENYA was born and grew up in Perm. As once her boats and dolls, later her memories sank in the shaggy bearskins which filled the house. Her father was the director of the Luniev mineworks and possessed a large clientele among the manufacturers of Chussovaya.

The bearskins were presents, sumptuous and of a dark russet colour. The white she-bear in the child's room was like an immense chrysanthemum shedding its petals. This was the fur acquired for 'Zhenitchka's room' – admired, paid for after long bargaining in the shop, and sent along by messenger.

In summer they lived in a dacha on the farther bank of Kama river. In those days Zhenya was sent to bed early. She could not see the lights of Motovilikha. But once the Angora cat for some reason took fright, stirred sharply in its sleep and woke her up. Then she saw grown-up people on the balcony. The alder hanging over the balustrade was thick and iridescent, like ink. The tea in the glasses was red. Cuffs and cards – yellow; the baize cloth – green. It was like a nightmare, but a nightmare with a name which was known to Zhenya: they were playing cards.

On the other hand it was absolutely impossible to distinguish what was happening on the other bank in the far distance: it had no name, no clearly defined colour or sharp outline: in its motions it was familiar and dear to her and was not the nightmare, it was not whatever rumbled and rolled in clouds of tobacco smoke, throwing fresh and windstrewn shadows on the reddish beams of the balcony. Zhenya began to cry. Her father came in and explained everything. The English governess turned to the wall. Her father's explanation was brief. It was – Motovilikha. You ought to be ashamed. A big girl like you. Sleep. The girl understood nothing and contentedly swallowed a falling tear. She wanted only one thing, to know the name of the incomprehensible – Motovilikha. That night it explained everything, for during the night that name still possessed a complete and reassuring significance for the child.

But in the morning she began to ask questions about what was Motovilikha and what happened there at night, and she learnt that Motovilikha was a factory, a government factory where castings were made, and from castings ... but all this no longer interested her, and she wanted to know whether there were certain countries called 'factories' and who lived in them; but she did not ask these questions and for some reason concealed them on purpose.

And that morning she ceased to be the child she had been the previous night. For the first time in her life it occurred to her that there were things which the phenomenon conceals from people and reveals only to those who know how to shout and punish, smoke and bolt doors. For the first time, as with this new Motovilikha, she did not say everything she thought and concealed for her own use all that was most essential, necessary and disturbing.

Years passed. From birth, the children were so accustomed to their father's absences that in their eyes paternity was endowed with the special property of rarely coming to dinner and never to supper. More and more often they played and quarrelled, drank and ate in completely empty, tenantless rooms, and the tepid lessons of the English governess could not take the place of the presence of a mother who filled the house with the sweet anguish of her vehemence and obstinacy, which was like some familiar electricity. The quiet northern day streamed through the curtains. It did not smile. The oak sideboard seemed grey. The rounded silver looked heavy and severe. The hands of the English governess, washed in lavender water, moved over the tablecloth: she never gave anyone less than his proper share and possessed inexhaustible reserves of patience, and in her the sentiment of equity was natural to her in the same high degree that her room and her books were always clean and well-arranged. The maid servant who had brought one of the courses waited in the dining-room and went to the kitchen only for the next course. Everything was pleasant and agreeable, though terribly sad.

Just as the girl suffered years of suspicion and loneliness, of a sense of guilt and of what I would like to call by the French word *christianisme*, because it is impossible to call it christianity, so it sometimes seemed to her that nothing would or should improve, because of her depravity and impenitence; that it was all deserved. Meanwhile – but this never reached the consciousness of the children – meanwhile, on the contrary, their whole beings quivered and fermented, bewildered by the attitude of their parents towards them when their father and mother were at home; when they entered the house rather than returned home.

Their father's rare jokes generally came to grief and were often irrelevant. He felt this and felt that the children knew it. An expression of mournful confusion never left his face. When he was irritable he became a complete stranger; wholly strange at the moment when he lost control over himself. A stranger rouses no sensations. The children never answered him insolently.

But for some time the criticism which came from the children's room and silently expressed itself in their eyes made no impression on him. He failed to notice it. Invulnerable, unrecognizable, pitiable – *this* father inspired horror, unlike the irritated father – the stranger. In this way he affected the daughter more than the son. But their mother bewildered them both.

She loaded them with caresses and heaped presents on them and spent hours with them when they least desired it, when it crushed their childish consciences, because they felt they were undeserving; and they failed to recognize themselves in the endearing nicknames which her instinct carelessly lavished on them. And often, when a rare and pellucid peace took possession of their souls, when they felt that they were in no way criminals, when all the secrecy which shuns discovery and resembles the fever before the rash had left them, they saw their mother as a stranger who avoided them and became angry without reason. The postman would come. The letter would be taken to the addressee – their mother. She would take it without thanking them. 'Go to your room.' The door banged. They would silently hang their heads and go out, giving way to an interminable and bewildered despair.

At first they would cry; then, after a more than usually brutal fit of temper, they took fright. As years passed, this fear changed into a smouldering animosity which took deeper and deeper root.

Everything that came to the children from their parents came from afar, at the wrong moment, provoked not by them but by causes which were foreign to them; they were coloured with remoteness, as always happens, and mystery, as at night the distant howling when everyone goes to bed.

These were the circumstances of the children's upbringing. They did not perceive this; for there are few, even among grown-ups, who understand what it is that forms, creates and binds them together. Life rarely tells what she is doing with them. She loves her purpose too well, and even while working she speaks only to those who wish her success and admire her instruments. No one can help her; anyone can throw her into confusion. How? In this way. If you entrusted a tree with the care of its own growth, it would become all branch or disappear wholly into its roots or squander itself on a single leaf, forgetting that the universe must be taken as a model; and after producing one thing in a thousand, it would begin to produce one thing a thousand times.

So that there shall be no dead branches in the soul, so that its growth shall not be retarded, so that man shall be incapable of involving his narrow mind in the creation of his immortal essence, there exists a number of things to turn his vulgar curiosity away from life, which does not wish to work in his presence and in every way avoids him.

For this purpose all respectable religions were established, all generalizations, all prejudices and the most diverting and brilliant of them all – *psychology*.

The children were no longer in their primitive stage. Ideas of punishment, retribution, reward and justice had already penetrated into their souls and diverted their senses, allowing life to do with them all it thought necessary, essential and beautiful.

2

Miss Hawthorn would not have done it. But one day, in a fit

of irrational tenderness towards her children, Madame Luvers spoke sharply to the English governess over a matter of no importance at all; and the governess disappeared. Shortly afterwards she was imperceptibly replaced by a consumptive French girl. Later Zhenya remembered only that the French girl resembled a fly and no one loved her. Her name became entirely lost, and Zhenya could not say among what syllables and sounds it would be possible to find the name. All she could remember was that the French girl had scolded her violently, reached for the scissors and cut off the place in the bear's fur which was covered with blood.

It seemed to her that henceforward everyone would scream at her and she must suffer continual headaches and never again be able to understand that page of her favourite book which became so stupidly confused before her eyes, like a lesson-book after dinner.

That day seemed so terribly long. Her mother was away. She was not sorry. She even imagined she was glad her mother was away.

Soon the long day was given over to oblivion among the tenses of *passé* and *futur antérieur*: watering the hyacinths and strolling along the Sibirskaya and Okhanskaya. So well forgotten that during the whole course of another day, the second in her life, she observed and began to feel only towards evening, while reading by the light of a lamp, and the indolent progress of a novel inspired her with a thousand idle thoughts. And when, much later, she would remember the house in the Ossinskaya where they had once lived, she thought of it always as she had seen it on that second long day as it was coming to an end. It was a really long day. Outdoors it was spring. Spring in the Urals, so feeble, so laboriously brought to fruition, then breaking loose wildly and tempestuously in the course of a single night, then flowing in a wide tempestuous stream. The lamps only stressed the insipidity of the evening air. They gave no light but swelled from within, like diseased fruit, from the clear and lustreless dropsy which dilated their swollen shades. They were absent. One came upon them precisely where they should be, in their places on the tables or hanging from the sculptured ceilings of the rooms where the girl was accustomed to see them. Yet the lamps possessed fewer points of contact with the rooms than with the spring sky, to which they seemed to have been brought so close, like a glass of water to the bed of a sick man. Their souls were outdoors, where in the humid earth there stirred the gossip of servant girls and where drops of melting snow, continually thinning out, congealed for the night. It was there that the lamps disappeared for the evening. Her parents were away. But it appeared that her mother was expected that day. That long day or the day afterwards. Probably. Or perhaps she would arrive suddenly, inadvertently. That too was possible.

Zhenya went to bed and saw that the day had been long for the same reason as before, and at first she thought of getting the scissors and cutting away those places on her princess-slip and on the sheets, but later she decided to get the French governess's powder and whiten the stains; and she was holding the powder box in her hands when the governess came in and slapped her. All her guilt was concentrated in the powder.

She powders herself. 'That is the last straw!'

Now she understood everything. She had noticed it long ago. Zhenya burst into tears, because she had been slapped, because she had been scolded, because she was offended and because, knowing that she was innocent of the crime imputed to her by the French governess, she knew she was guilty – she felt it – of something far worse than the governess suspected. It was necessary – she felt this urgently and with a sense of stupefaction – felt it in her temples and in her knees – it was necessary to conceal it, without knowing why but somehow and at whatever the cost. A single hypnotic suggestion moved her aching joints. And this suggestion, agonizing and wearying, was itself the work of that organism which concealed from the girl the significance of what had happened to her, and being itself the criminal, made her see in her bleeding a disgusting and distasteful sin. '*Menteuse!*' She was compelled to content herself with a denial, concealing stubbornly what was worse than anything, standing half-way between the shame of illiteracy and the ignominy of a scandal in the streets. She shivered and clenched her teeth, stifled her sobs, and pressed herself against the wall. She could not throw herself into the Kama because it

was still cold, and the last vestiges of ice were floating down
the river.

Neither the girl nor the French governess heard the bell in
time. The resulting disturbance disappeared in the silence of
the russet-coloured bearskins; and when her mother came in,
it was too late. She found her daughter in tears, the governess –
blushing. She demanded an explanation. The governess
explained brutally that – not Zhenya, but *votre enfant*, she said
– *her child* was powdering herself and she had noticed it and
suspected it long ago – the mother refused to let her finish the
sentence – her terror was unfeigned – the child not yet thirteen.
'Zhenya – you? – my God, what have you come to?' (At that
moment her mother imagined that her words had some meaning, as though she had realized long ago that her daughter was
disgracing herself and becoming depraved, but she had made
no efforts to prevent it – and now her daughter was descending
into the depths.) 'Zhenya, tell me the truth – it will be worse –
what were you doing – with the powder-box?' is probably
what Madame Luvers wanted to say, but instead she said,
'With this thing?' and she seized 'this thing' and brandished
it in the air.

'Mama, don't believe mam'zelle, I never – ' and she burst
into tears.

But her mother heard evil notes behind the tears, where
there were none. She felt that she was herself to blame
and suffered from an inward terror: it was necessary, she
thought, to remedy everything, even though it was against
her maternal instinct 'to rise to pedagogic and reasonable
measures'. She resolved not to yield to compassion. She decided to wait until the tears, which wounded her deeply, came
to an end.

And she sat down on the bed, gazing quietly and vacantly at
the edge of the bookshelf. There came from her the odour of
costly perfume. When the child grew quiet, she began to
question her again. Zhenya, her eyes brimming with tears,
stared out of the window and whimpered. Ice was coming
down, probably with the sound of ice breaking. A star was glimmering. And there was the darkness of the empty night, cold,
clear-cut, lustreless. Zhenya looked away from the window.

In her mother's voice she heard the menace of impatience. The French governess stood against the wall, all gravity and concentrated pedagogy. Her hand with an adjutant's gesture lay on the ribbon of her watch. Once more Zhenya turned towards the stars and Kama river. She made up her mind. In spite of the cold, in spite of the ice. She . . . plunged. She lost herself in her words, her terrible and inaccurate words, and told her mother about the *thing*. Her mother let her speak to the end only because she was astounded by the warmth with which the child coloured her confession. Everything became clear from the first word. No; from the moment when the child swallowed a deep gulp of air before she began her story. The mother listened happily, full of love and tenderness for this thin little body. She wanted to throw herself on her daughter's neck and burst into tears. But . . . pedagogy; she rose from the bed and lifted the counterpane. She called her daughter to her and began to stroke her head slowly, slowly, tenderly.

'You've been a good girl . . .' the words tumbled out of her mouth. Noisily she went to the window and turned away from them.

Zhenya did not see the French governess. Her tears – her mother – filled the room. 'Who makes the bed?'

The question was senseless. The girl trembled. She was sorry for Grusha. Then unknown words, in familiar French, came to her ears: they were spoken in a severe tone. And then once more in a quite different voice:

'Zhenitchka, my child, go into the dining-room, I shall be there in a minute. I shall tell you about the beautiful dacha we have taken for you in the summer – for us and your father in the summer.'

The lamps became familiar again, as in winter, at home, with the Luvers – warm, zealous, faithful. Her mother's sable moved playfully over the blue woollen tablecloth. '*Won but delayed at Blagodat wait end Passion Week unless*' – impossible to read the rest, the end of the telegram was folded. Zhenya sat down on the edge of the divan, tired and happy. She sat down modestly and comfortably, just as six months later in the corridor of the school in Ekaterinburg she sat on the edge of a cold yellow bench and when she had finished her oral examination in the

Russian language and received the highest marks she knew that she 'could enter'.

The next morning her mother told her what to do when *this thing* happened to her, it was nothing, she mustn't be afraid, it would happen again. She mentioned nothing by name and explained nothing, but added that from now on she herself would prepare her daughter's lessons, because she was not going away again.

The French governess was removed on the grounds of negligence after spending only a few months in the family. When the carriage was ordered for her and she was going down the steps, she met the doctor at the turning as he was coming up. He replied to her greeting coldly, saying nothing at all about her departure; she guessed that he knew everything; she scowled and shrugged her shoulders.

The maid was waiting for the doctor at the door, and therefore in the hall, where Zhenya was standing, the murmur of footsteps and the murmur of ringing flagstones echoed longer than usual in the air. Thus there was impressed upon her memory the history of her early puberty: the shrill echo of the chirping streets in the morning, hesitating on the steps, crisply penetrating into the house; the French governess, the maid and the doctor, the two criminals and the one who was initiated, cleansed, made immune by the light, by the freshness of air and the resonance of footsteps.

The warm April sun was shining. 'Feet, feet, wipe your feet!' from end to end echoed the bright and empty corridor. The furs were removed for the summer. The rooms were clear and transfigured, they sighed with relief and with sweetness. All that day, all that long day which wearily drew out its long length, without end, in all the corners in all the rooms, in the glass sloping against the wall,* in mirrors, in tumblers full of water, in the blue air of the garden, the bird-cherry tree insatiably and unquenchably winked and preened itself, laugh-

* The outer panes of glass from double windows are removed during the summer and were sometimes left standing against the wall. *Translator's Note.*

ing and raging while the honeysuckle foamed and choked itself. The tedious conversations of the courtyards lasted all day: they announced that the night was dethroned and all day long they repeated incessantly in *roulades* that acted like a sleeping-draught that there would be no more evening and they would let no one sleep. 'Feet, feet!' – but they burnt as they came in, drunk with air, with the sound in the ears, and therefore they failed to understand clearly what was being said and strove to finish the meal as quickly as they could, so that after moving their chairs with a tremendous noise, they could run back once more into this day, which was breaking impetuously on the time reserved for dinner, into this day, in which the tree drying in the sun gave forth its exiguous chant and the blue sky chattered piercingly and the earth shone greasily, as though melting. The frontier between the house and the courtyard vanished. The rag could not wash away all the traces of footprints. The floors were covered with a dry and brilliant dust, and crackled.

Her father had brought sweets and miracles. The house was marvellously pleasant. With a moist rustle gemstones announced their appearance from the tissue-paper which gradually assumed their colour and became more and more transparent as layer after layer of the white paper, as soft as gauze, was removed. Some of the stones resembled drops of almond milk, others resembled splashes of blue water-colour, still others were like solidified tears of cheese. Some were blind, sleepy, full of dreams; others sparkled gaily with the sparkle of the frozen juice of blood oranges. No one desired to touch them. They were perfect as they were, as they emerged from the froth of paper which secreted them, like a plum secreting its lustreless juice.

The father was unusually gentle with the children and often accompanied their mother into the town. They would return together, and they appeared to be happy. But the important thing was that they were both quiet and gentle and even-tempered, and when at odd moments their mother gazed into the eyes of the father with an air of playful reproach, it was as though she was deriving a sense of peace from his small and ugly eyes, and then pouring it out again from her own eyes, which were large and beautiful, on her children and those who were near her.

Once her parents rose very late. Then, no one knows why, they decided to take lunch on the steamer which lay off the landing-stage, and they took the children with them. They let Seryozha taste the cold beer. They enjoyed themselves so much that they went to have lunch on the steamer again. The children did not recognize their parents. What had happened? The daughter was blissfully, perplexedly happy, and it seemed to her that life would always be as it was then. They did not grieve when they learned that they were not going to the dacha that summer. Their father left shortly afterwards. Three huge yellow travelling trunks, with durable metal rims, appeared at the house.

3

The train was leaving late at night. Mr Luvers had gone over a month earlier and wrote that the flat was ready. Several *izvozchiks* were driving down to the station at a trot. They knew they were near the station by the colour of the pavement. The pavement was black and the street-lamps lashed at the brown railway. Meanwhile from the viaduct a view opened upon Kama river, while under them rattled and ran a soot-black pit, heavy with gravity and terror. It ran off, swift as lightning, until finally in the far distance it took fright, trembled and went gliding among the twinkling beads of distant signals.

The wind rose. The silhouettes of houses and fences flew upwards like chaff from a sieve; they twirled and their ends frayed in the friable air. There was the smell of potatoes. Their *izvozchik* edged away from the line of rocking baskets and carriage-backs in front of him, and began to outstrip them. From a distance they recognized the cart which was carrying their luggage; they ran alongside; Ulyasha shouted something to her mistress from the cart, but whatever she said was lost in the rattle of wheels, and she trembled and jolted, and her voice jolted.

The girl perceived no sorrow in the novelty of all these night sounds and darkness and the freshness of air. Far in the distance there was something mysterious and black. Beyond the dockside warehouse lights were dangling and the town rinsed them in water from the shore and from ships. Then many more appeared, swarming in black clusters, greasily, blind like maggots. On Lyubimovsky wharf, the funnels, the roofs of the warehouses and the decks were a sober blue. Barges stared at the stars. 'This is a rat-hole,' Zhenya thought. White porters surrounded them. Seryozha was the first to jump down. He glanced round and was extremely surprised when he noticed that the cart with their luggage was already there – the horse threw back her head, her collar rose, she reared up like a cock, she pressed on the back of the cart and began to move backwards. But throughout the drive Seryozha was preoccupied with the thought of how far the cart would remain behind them.

The boy, intoxicated with the prospect of the journey, stood there in his white school shirt. The journey was a novelty for them both, and already he knew and loved those words: depot, loco, siding, through-carriage, and the blending of sounds: 'class' had a sour-sweet taste in his mouth. His sister was also enthusiastic at all this, but in her own way, without the boyish love of method which characterized the enthusiasm of her brother.

Suddenly, as though from under the ground, their mother appeared. She ordered the children to be taken to the buffet. From there, threading her way proudly through the crowds, she went straight to the man who was called, as loudly and threateningly as possible, for the first time, 'the stationmaster' – a name which was to be mentioned often in different places, with variations and among different crowds.

They were overcome by yawning. They sat at one of the windows which were so dusty, so starchy and so vast that they appeared to be institutions of bottle-glass, where it was impossible to remain with a hat on one's head. The girl saw: behind the glass not a street but another room, only more solemn and morose than the one in the decanter before her; and into this room steam-engines moved slowly and came to a pause, bringing the darkness with them; but when they had left the room, it turned out that it was not a room, for there was the sky behind the columns and on the other side, a small hill and wooden houses and there were people walking about, fading into the distance; where perhaps cocks were now crowing and not long ago the water-carrier left pools of water . . .

It was a provincial railway station without the glow and hurly-burly of the capital, with people who arrived in good time from the town shrouded in darkness, with long waiting and silence and settlers who slept on the floor among hunting dogs, baggage, machines wrapped up in bast matting and uncovered bicycles.

The children lay on the upper berth. The boy fell asleep at once. The train was still standing in the station. Day was beginning to dawn, and gradually the girl realized that the carriage was clean, dark blue, cool. And gradually she realized . . . but she was already sleep.

He was a very fat man. He read the newspaper and swayed from side to side. As soon as you looked at him, the swaying became obvious – everything in the carriage was flooded and impregnated with it, as with sunshine. Zhenya regarded him from above with the lazy precision with which one thinks about things or looks at things when one is fresh and wholly awake and when one lies in bed only because one is waiting, because the decision to get up will come of its own accord, without assistance, clear and unconstrained like the other thoughts. She watched the fat man and thought, how did he come to be in their compartment and how did he manage to be already washed and dressed? She had no idea of the time. She had only just wakened, therefore it was morning. She examined him, but he could not see her: her upper berth was inclined deep against the wall. Also, he did not see her because he only rarely glanced from his newspaper, up, sideways, crosswise – and when he lifted his head towards her bed, their eyes did not meet and either he saw only the mattress or else . . . but she quickly tucked them under herself and pulled on her scanty stockings. Mama was in the corner over there. She was already dressed and reading a book, Zhenya decided reflectively as she studied the glances of the tubby man. But Seryozha was not beneath her? Where was he? And she yawned sweetly and stretched herself. The terrible heat – she had realized it only that very moment, and from above she turned and peered at the small window which was at half mast. 'But where is the earth?' she exclaimed in her heart.

What she saw was beyond description. A forest of clamorous hazel trees, into which they were poured by the serpentine train, became the sea, became the world, became anything you pleased, everything. The forest ran on, clean and murmuring, down, down the broad slopes, and growing smaller, thickening and becoming misty, it fell steeply, almost entirely black. And what rose on the other side of the void resembled something huge, all curls and circles, a yellow-green storm-cloud plunged in thought and stupefied by torpor. Zhenya held her breath, and at once perceived the speed of that limitless and all forgetful air, and at once realized that the huge cloud was some country, some place bearing a sonorous and mountainous name, like a thunderstorm tossing in all directions and flung into the valley, with rocks and with sand; and the hazel trees did nothing but whisper it and whisper it; here, there, and away over there; nothing else.

'Is it the Urals?' she asked of the whole compartment, leaning forward.

For the rest of the journey she never took her eyes away from the window in the corridor. She clung to the window and was continually leaning out. She was greedy. She discovered that it was more pleasant to look backward than to look forward. Majestic acquaintances dimmed and disappeared into the distance. A short separation from them, in the course of which, accompanied by the vertical roar of the grinding chains and a draught of fresh air which made her neck grow cold, a new wonder was presented right in front of her nose; and again she searched for them. The mountainous panorama extended and kept on growing. Some became black, others became refreshed, some were shadowy, others were growing dark. They came together and separated, they ascended and climbed down. All this moved slowly in a sort of circle like the rotation of stars, with the prudent caution of giants anxious for the preservation of the earth, on the edge of catastrophe. These complex progressions were ruled by a level and powerful

echo inaccessible to human ears and all-seeing. It watched them
with an eagle eye, dark and silent; it was inspecting them. In
this way the Urals are built, built and rebuilt.

For a moment she returned to the compartment, screwing up
her eyes against the harsh light. Mama was smiling and talking
to the strange gentleman. Seryozha was fidgeting on the
crimson plush and clinging to a leather wall-strap. Mama spat
the last seed into the palm of her hand, swept up the ones which
had fallen on her dress and inclining nimbly and impetuously
threw all the rubbish under the seat. Contrary to their expecta-
tions the fat man possessed a husky, cracked voice. He
evidently suffered from shortness of breath. Mama introduced
him to Zhenya and he offered her a mandarin. He was amusing
and probably kind, and while talking he was continually lifting
a plump hand to his mouth. His voice troubled him, and becoming suddenly short of wind, it often came in gasps. It appeared
that he was from Ekaterinburg and he had often travelled
through the Urals, which he knew well; and when he took his
gold watch from his waistcoat pocket and lifted it to his very
nose and began to put it back again, Zhenya noticed that his
fingers were kind. Like all fat people he picked up things with
a movement which suggested that he was giving them away
and his hands throbbed all the time as though proffered for a
kiss, and they swung gently in the air, as though they were
hitting a ball against the floor.

'It will come soon, now.' His eyes squinting, he looked
away from the boy, although he was speaking to him alone and
smiling broadly.

'You know the signpost they talk about, on the frontier of
Asia and Europe, and "Asia" written on it,' Seryozha blurted
out, slipping off his cushion and bolting into the corridor.

Zhenya did not understand any of this, and when the fat man
explained to her what it was, she immediately ran to the same
side of the compartment and looked for the signpost, afraid
that she had already missed it. In her enchanted head 'the
frontier of Asia' assumed the nature of a hallucinatory border-
line, like the iron balustrade placed between the public and a
cage full of pumas, a menacing bar, black like the night, fraught
with danger and evil-smelling. She waited for the signpost as

though she was waiting for the curtain to rise on the first act of a geographical tragedy, about which she had heard rumours from witnesses, triumphantly excited because this had happened to her and because she would soon see it with her own eyes.

But meanwhile what had compelled her to enter the compartment with the older people monotonously continued: the grey alders, past which they had been moving for half an hour were not coming to an end and nature was apparently making no preparations for what soon awaited it. Zhenya became angry with dust-laden, wearisome Europe, which was awkwardly delaying the miracle. And how amazed she was when, as though in reply to Seryozha's furious cry, something which resembled a gravestone flashed past the window, swung sideways and ran away, withdrawing into the alders from the alders racing after it, the long-awaited legendary name! At that moment a multitude of heads, as though in agreement, leaned out of the windows of all the carriages, while clouds of dust, borne down the slope, enlivened the train. And long after the boundary of Asia had been left far behind, one could still see the kerchiefs fluttering on their flying heads, and they looked at one another, and all of them, bearded or shaven, flew in clouds of whirling sand, flying past the dust-laden alders which were Europe a short while ago and were now long since Asia.

4

Life began afresh. Milk was not brought into the house, into the kitchen, by an itinerant milkmaid; it was brought into the house every morning by Ulyasha in two pails; and the white bread was of a special kind, not like that of Perm. Here there were strange sidewalks resembling marble or alabaster, with a wavy white sheen. The flagstones were blinding even in the shadows, like ice-cold suns, greedily engulfing the shadows of well-dressed trees, which spread out, melted on them and liquefied. Here the feeling was quite different when you stepped out in the street, which was wide and luminous, with trees planted along it, as in Paris – Zhenya repeated after her father.

He spoke of this on the first day of their arrival. It was a fine

and spacious day. Her father had had a snack before going to
meet them at the station and took no part in the dinner. His
place at the table was therefore clean and bright, like Ekaterinburg, and he only spread out his serviette and sat sideways and
spoke about things in generalities. He unbuttoned his waistcoat
and his shirt-front curved crisply and vigorously. He said it
was a beautiful European town and rang the bell when it was
necessary to take the dishes away and order something else,
and he rang the bell and continued talking. And along the
unknown paths of the still unknown rooms a noiseless white
maid came to them, a brunette, all starch and flounces, and
he said 'you' to her, and this maid – this new maid smiled at the
mistress and the children, as though they were old acquaintances. And they gave her various instructions about Ulyasha,
who found herself there, in an unknown and probably very
dark kitchen where certainly there was a window which looked
out upon something new: some steeple or other or a street or
birds. And Ulyasha would at once begin to ask questions of the
girl, putting on her worst clothes, so that she could do the
unpacking afterwards; she would ask questions and become
familiar with things and look: in which corner was the stove,
in that one as in Perm, or elsewhere?

The boy learned from his father that it was not a long walk to
school – indeed it was quite near – and they could not avoid
seeing it as they drove past; the father drank up his *narzan*
water, swallowed and continued:

'Is it possible I didn't show it to you? You don't see it from
here, from the kitchen probably.' (He weighed it in his mind.)
'But only the roof . . .'

He drank some more *narzan* and rang the bell.

The kitchen was cool and bright, exactly, as it now seemed to
the girl, as she had imagined it in the dining-room – a kitchen-
range with tiles painted blue and white, and there were two
windows in the place where she had expected them: Ulyasha
threw something on her bare arms, the room became full of
childish voices, people were walking along the roof of the
school and the topmost scaffolding protruded.

'Yes, it's being repaired,' father said, when they came in one
after another, noisily thrusting their way into the dining-room

through the already known but still unexplored corridor, which she would have to visit again on the following day, after unpacking her exercise books and hanging up her face flannel and finishing a thousand things.

'Wonderful butter,' mother said, sitting down.

They went into the classroom they had already visited, still wearing their hats as they entered.

'Why should it be Asia?' she thought aloud.

But Seryozha did not understand what he would understand perfectly at another time, for until now they had lived and thought in unison. He rushed up to the map hanging on the wall and moved his hand downwards along the Ural mountains, looking at his sister, smitten, so it seemed to him, by his argument.

'They agreed to trace a natural frontier, that's all!'

And she remembered the noon of that same day, already so far away. It was unbelievable that a day which had contained all this – this day, now in Ekaterinburg, and still here – had not yet come to an end. At the thought of all that had fled past, preserving its breathless order, into the predestined distance, she experienced a sensation of amazing exhaustion, the sensation which the body experiences in the evening after a laborious day. As though she had taken part in the implanting and displacement of all this burden of loveliness, and had strained herself. And for some reason convinced that it existed, her Urals, *over there*, she turned and ran across the dining-room into the kitchen where there was less crockery, but where there was still the wonderful iced butter on the damp maple-leaves and the excited mineral water.

The school was being repaired and the air, like linen on the teeth of the sempstress, was ripped by shrill martins and down below – she leaned out of the window – a carriage gleamed in front of the open coachhouse and sparks flew up from a grinding-wheel and there was the smell of food which had been eaten, a finer and more interesting smell than when it was being served, a long-lasting melancholy smell, as in a book. She forgot why she had been running and did not notice that her Urals were not in Ekaterinburg, but she did notice how it was growing dark in the back streets of Ekaterinburg and how

they were singing below, underneath, while they were working
at their simple tasks (probably washing the floors and spreading
bast with hot hands) and how they were splashing the water
from the kitchen pails and how, although they were splashing
downstairs, how quiet it was everywhere. And how the tap
babbled, and how: 'Well, young lady'; but she still avoided
the new girl and had no wish to hear her – and how – she
pursued her thoughts to the end – everyone beneath them
knew and indeed said: 'There are people in number two now.'

Ulyasha entered the kitchen.

The children slept soundly during their first night, and they
woke up: Seryozha in Ekaterinburg, Zhenya in Asia, and once
more it occurred to her how vast and strange it was. Flakes of
alabaster were playing lightly on the ceiling.

This began while it was yet summer. She was told she would
be going to school. This was in no way unpleasant. But they
told it to her. She did not call the tutor into the schoolroom,
where the sunlight clung so closely to the colour-wash wall
that the evening succeeded in tearing off the adhesive day only
with bloodshed. She did not call him when, accompanied by
her mother, he went there to make the acquaintance of 'his
future pupil'. It was not she who gave him the absurd name
of Dikikh. Nor was it she who wished that henceforward the
soldiers would always be taught at noon, wheezing, stern,
perspiring like the convulsions of a scarlet stopcock before
the breakdown of the water supply; and that their thigh-boots
would be squeezed by lilac-coloured stormclouds which knew
more about guns and wheels than their white shirts, white
tents and officers whiter still. Was it she who wished that now
there would always be two things: a small basin and a serviette,
which combined together like the carbon rods of an arc lamp
and evoked a third thing which momentarily evaporated: the
idea of death, like those signboards at the barber's where it
first occurred to her? And was it with her consent that the red
turnpikes, on which it was written, 'No loitering!' assumed
the position of a local and forbidden secret, and that the
Chinese became intimately terrible, closely related to Zhenya
and horrifying? But, of course, not everything lay heavy on
her soul. There were pleasant things too, like her approaching

entry into the school. But all this was told to her. Life ceased to be a poetical caprice; it fermented around her like a harsh and shadowed fable – in so far as it became prose and was transformed into fact. Stubbornly, painfully and lustrelessly, as though in a state of perpetual recovery from intoxication, elements of trivial existence entered into her awakening spirit. They sank deep within her, real, solid, cold: like sleepy pewter spoons. Here, deep down, the pewter began to melt and clot and fuse into fixed ideas.

Luigi Pirandello

DESTRUCTION OF THE MAN

TRANSLATED BY
FREDERICK MAY

LUIGI PIRANDELLO

Born in Agrigento 1867; died in Rome 1936. Italian dramatist (*Six Characters in Search of an Author*, *Enrico IV*) and a prolific short story writer. 'Destruction of the Man' (1921) is from the fifth volume of the series *Novelle per un anno*.

DESTRUCTION OF THE MAN

ALL I should like to know is whether the Examining Magistrate sincerely believes that he's found one single reason which is in itself sufficient to explain – in some measure, at least – why the defendant committed (and I use his own term) *premeditated* murder? Should murder be proved, of course, it would be a *double* murder charge that would have to go to the jury, for the murdered woman was about to bring to a happy conclusion her final month of pregnancy.

We know that Nicola Petix has retreated behind a barrier of impenetrable silence. Not only did he refuse to answer any of the questions put to him by the police, after he was arrested; not only did he preserve silence when brought up before the Examining Magistrate, who tried time and again, using one approach after another, to get him to speak; not only did he refuse to answer *his* questions, but he also declined to give any assistance to the counsel assigned by the court to undertake his defence, since he had indicated his unwillingness himself to instruct counsel.

It seems to me that some explanation should be provided for so stubborn a silence.

They say that, while he's been in prison on remand, Petix has shown all the callous indifference and unmindfulness of a cat which has just slaughtered a mouse or a bird, and which is now happily sunning itself.

It's perfectly obvious, however, that such a rumour is quite obnoxious to the Examining Magistrate, if he's seeking to establish premeditation, and intends to provide evidence to support that contention. You see, to accept such a notion would be to accept the implication that Petix carried out his crime *with all the unawareness of the nature of what he was doing that is characteristic of an animal.* Animals are incapable of premeditation. If they lie in wait for their prey, their lurking in ambush is an instinctive and natural aspect of their completely natural urge to hunt. It doesn't turn them into thieves or murderers. As far as the owner of the chickens concerned, the fox is a chicken-thief; but, as far as the fox himself is concerned, he's not a thief – he's hungry; and when he's hungry, he grabs hold of a chicken and eats it. And after he's eaten it . . . goodbye! He doesn't give it another thought.

Now, Petix isn't an animal. We must, therefore, see whether this indifference of his is real. Because, if it *is* real, then we must also take this indifference into account, in the same way as his stubborn silence. To my manner of thinking, it's the completely natural consequence of that silence. Both seem confirmed by his explicit rejection of defending counsel.

I have no desire, however, to anticipate the jury's verdict, nor, for the moment, do I wish to put forward my own view of the case.

Let me return to what I was discussing with the Examining Magistrate.

If the Examining Magistrate believes that Petix should be punished with all the vigour that the Law provides, because, as far as he's concerned, he's neither a violent lunatic, and so properly comparable to a savage beast, nor a madman who, for no reason whatsoever, killed a woman only a few weeks before she was due to give birth to a child, what can possibly be the motive for this crime? This *premeditated murder*?

A secret passion for the woman? No. I think that possibility is easily ruled out. If the young barrister they've given him to defend him will very kindly show the jury the photograph of the poor dead woman for a moment. Signora Porrella was forty-seven years of age and must, at the time of her death – whatever else she may have looked like – have borne not the slightest resemblance to a woman.

I remember seeing her myself only a few days before the crime. Towards the end of October, it must have been. Walking along the street, arm in arm with her husband. It was early evening. Her husband, you will recall, is a man of fifty. Slightly shorter than his wife. Still, not without his proper share of middle-age spread, Signor Porella. And proud of it. Out for a stroll, along the Viale Nomentano, despite the wind, which was whirling the dead leaves about in warm, noisty gusts.

On my word of honour – yes, I do assure you, there was something provocative about the sight of those two, out walking on a day like that, with all that wind, amidst all those dead, swirling leaves. Two tiny figures dwarfed by the naked plane trees, that seemed to brandish the harsh intricacy of their branches in that stormy sky.

They walked in step. Their feet hit the ground in the same way. Seriously. As if they had a task to perform. A duty laid upon them.

Perhaps they thought that that walk of theirs was absolutely essential, now that her pregnancy was in its final stages. Prescribed by the doctor; recommended by all her friends and neighbours.

Rather annoying for them, maybe. Yes! But they saw it as perfectly natural that that wind should blow up like that, and that it should get stronger every minute, furiously hurling those curled-up leaves hither and thither, without ever succeeding in sweeping them out of the way. Neither did they see anything strange in those naked plane trees there – they'd put forth their leaves in due season, and in due season they'd shed them. Naked they would now remain till the coming spring. Nothing unusual, either, about that stray dog. And the fact that, at every gust of wind which assailed his nostrils with fascinating smells, he would stop at almost every single one of those plane trees, exasperatedly cock a leg against the trunk, and then merely squirt out a few miserable drops; after having frenziedly chased round and round himself in search of his own backside.

I give you my solemn assurance that not only I, but every single person walking along that street that day, thought it quite incredible that that man – such a small man – could possibly feel as satisfied as he looked. I mean, taking his wife out for a stroll in that condition. What was even more incredible was that his wife should let him take her. She seemed most obstinately determined to be cruel to herself, and the more resigned to making that intolerable effort she appeared, the more cruel to herself she seemed. What it must have cost her! She was staggering with every step, panting away, and her eyes were glazed and staring in a spasm of – well, it wasn't because of that far-from-human effort she was being called

upon to make. No, it was because she was terribly afraid that
she wouldn't succeed in bringing to full term that obscene
encumbrance in her slumping belly. It's true, of course, that
from time to time she would lower her ashen lids over her
eyes. But it wasn't so much from shame that she lowered them,
as from the feeling of irritation she got, seeing herself compelled
to sense other people *projecting* shame at her. Everyone who
looked at her, and saw her in that condition. At her age. A
shapeless and worn-out old hag, still being used for something
that – well, they ought to have stopped that sort of thing long
ago. As a matter of fact, walking along there, arm in arm with
her husband, she could quite easily have given his arm a tiny
squeeze and given a jolt to his little world of self-satisfaction.
All too often and all too obviously, he would disappear into
that world, wallowing in the knowledge that he – fifty, bald,
and diminutive – was the author of that huge affliction she was
trundling around. She didn't give him a jolt, because she was,
yes, she was rather pleased that he should have the nerve to
show her off like this. That he should feel so self-satisfied, while
she felt so ashamed of it all.

In my mind's eye I can still see her, suddenly caught from
behind by a more than usually violent gust of wind. She'd stop
short on those thick, stumpy legs of hers, which the wind,
thrusting her frock hard against them, threw into obscene
relief, while simultaneously bellying her out in front like a
balloon. With her only free hand, she didn't know what to deal
with first. Should she push down that balloon in front, before
it . . . ? Well, any minute now the whole world would see what
she had on underneath! Or should she clutch at the brim of her
old mauve velvet hat, with its melancholy black feathers, in
which the wind had stirred up a desperate and foolish desire
to fly?

Let's get to the point, however.

I would urge you, should you ever have the time, to go along
to the Via Alessandria, and take a look at the huge, rambling old
house, in which Signor and Signora Porrella lived. Nicola
Petix lived there too, in two small rooms on the floor below.

There are thousands of houses just like it, all hideous in the
same way. It's as if they'd been branded with the hallmark of the

highest common vulgarity of the time in which they'd been thrown up in such furious haste – in the expectation (later recognized to be erroneous) that there'd be an abundant and immediate flood of His Majesty's subjects rushing to Rome upon the declaration of that city as the third capital of the Kingdom.

So many private fortunes, not only of the newly rich, but of many men of illustrious and ancient families, even. And all the loans made by banks to speculative builders, who seemed, year after year, to be in the grip of an almost fanatical frenzy, were swallowed up in an enormous wave of bankruptcy. People still remember it very vividly.

And so we saw houses going up where formerly there had been the extensive grounds of patrician houses, magnificent villas, and, on the other side of the river, orchards and meadows. Houses, houses, houses. Isolated units, scattered along hardly defined streets, miles from anywhere. So many of them were destined suddenly to be left unfinished – newly constructed ruins – run up as far as the fourth floor, then left to rot, roofless and with the window-openings still gaping emptily. Higher up, the remnants of the scaffolding, just abandoned when work stopped, stuck into holes in the raw, unfinished walls. Flooring left uncompleted, and now all blackened and rotted by the rain. There were other isolated buildings, too, buildings that were already completed, doomed now to remain deserted. Whole streets of them. Whole areas of them. Streets and areas through which not a soul passed. And in the silence of month succeeding month the grass began to sprout again along the edges of the pavement, up against the walls. And then, slender, tenderness itself, shuddering at every breath of wind, it resumed its sway over the whole stone-faced street.

A number of these houses, which had been equipped with all modern conveniences with the aim of attracting the better-off sort of tenant, were later thrown open to an invasion of working-class people – principally in order to make *something* out of them. As you'll readily imagine, these people very quickly made havoc of what they found. So much so that, when, as the years went by, there really *did* develop a housing shortage

in Rome, the new owners thought it best, all things considered,
to do nothing about their property. Yes, a housing shortage –
prematurely feared in the first place, and cautiously remedied
later. Because of that awful shaking-up earlier, people were
terribly afraid now of putting up any new buildings. As I've
already said, the new owners – who'd acquired the property
from the banks that had financed the bankrupt builders – having
worked out what they'd have to spend on putting things to
rights and getting their houses into a fit state to rent them to
tenants who would be willing to pay a higher rent, thought
it best to leave things as they were. To go on happily in the
same old way, with the steps all chipped away, the walls
obscenely spattered with filth, the shutters hanging askew on
their broken hinges, the window-panes smashed, and the windows themselves garlanded with filthy, patched rags, stretched
out on lines to dry.

Every now and again, however, a lower middle-class family
(or a better-class one that had come down in the world) would
seek refuge in one of these large, miserable houses. It's become
more common nowadays: a clerk and his family; a schoolteacher and his – coming to live among the tenants I've just
referred to, all busy finishing off the work of destruction of the
walls, doors, and floors. They'd come because they hadn't been
able to find anywhere else, or because they were desperately
poor, or because they just wanted to economize on rent. It
was a case of conquering your disgust at all that filth and – even
worse – having to mix with. . . . Oh, my God! Yes, he's my
neighbour, all right! True enough! I don't deny it! But – Well,
he's got so little fondness for cleanliness and the ordinary
decencies of civilized living, that you've no desire to get too
near him. Moreoever, I'm not denying that the feeling's
mutual. As a matter of fact, all newcomers are looked at in a
pretty surly way at first. It's only gradually, and only if they've
shown willing that they. . . . Yes, if they've wanted people to
look more favourably on them, they've had to resign themselves to a number of liberties which have been taken rather
than granted.

Now, when the crime occurred, the Porrellas had been living
in the house in the Via Alessandria for the past fifteen years,

more or less, and Nicola Petix for about ten. But, while *they* had for some time enjoyed the favour of all the most long-established inmates, Petix on the other hand had always attracted the strongest antipathy, on account of the contempt with which he looked on everybody, from the inefficient caretaker up. Never a word for anyone. Not even a nod, by way of greeting.

Still, as I said a little while ago, let's get to the point. A fact's like a sack, though – when it's empty it won't stand up.

As the Examining Magistrate will very soon become aware when, as it seems he intends to do, he tries to make his 'sack' stand up, without first of all filling it with all those reasons and experiences which most certainly determined its existence, and of which he has, it may well be, not the faintest idea.

Petix's father was an engineer who had emigrated to America many years before and who died there. He'd amassed a pretty large sum of money over there, working at his profession, and left it all to another son, two years older than Petix, and an engineer himself, on condition that he paid his younger brother a few hundred lire every month for the rest of his life. It was more a kind of alms bestowed upon him than anything the young man was rightfully entitled to, because he'd already 'gobbled-up', as his father's will put it, 'all that was legitimately his, in a life of shameful idleness'.

Before we go any further let me ask that we consider this 'idleness' not only from the point of view of the father, but also, for a moment or so, from his. To tell the truth, Petix was up at a number of universities for many, many years, moving on from one group of subjects to another. From Medicine to Law, from Law to Mathematics, from Mathematics to Letters and Philosophy. It's true, of course, that he never sat any examinations, but only because he never for one moment dreamt of being a doctor or a lawyer, a mathematician, or a man of letters. Bluntly, Petix has never wanted to be anything, but that doesn't mean to say that he's spent his time in idleness, or that that idleness has been shameful. He's spent his time in contemplation, studying in his own way the things that happen in life and the customs of man.

And the fruit of this contemplation has been infinite boredom

– a completely insupportable boredom, not only with me, but also with life itself.

Do we do a thing merely in order to do a thing? Either we must remain completely absorbed in the thing that's to be done – be inside it, like a blind man, without ever looking out – or else we must assign some sort of purpose to it. What purpose? Merely that of doing it? Good God, why, yes, of course! That's the way life's lived. This thing today, something else tomorrow. It might even be the same thing every day. According to your inclination, or what you're capable of; according to your intentions or according to your feeling and instincts. It's the way life's lived.

The trouble arises when you want to see from the outside what the purpose is of all those inclinations, capacities, intentions, feelings, and instincts that you've obeyed inside yourself, simply because you've got them and can feel them. And precisely because you do try and find it outside yourself, you don't find it at all. . . . Just as you'll always find nothingness outside yourself.

Nicola Petix very soon arrived at a knowledge of this nothingness, which must, of course, be the quintessence of *all* philosophy.

Being forced every day to see the hundred or so tenants of that large, filthy, gloomy house – people who lived merely in order to live, without knowing anything about living, other than that tiny fragment which they seemed condemned to live out every day. Every day the same old things. Well, very soon he began to get terribly irritated by it all. A frenzied intolerance swept over him. Every day he got more and more enraged by it.

Particularly unbearable were the sight and din of the countless small children who swarmed all over the courtyard and up and down the stairs. He couldn't even put his head out of the window and look out into the courtyard, without seeing four or five of them in a row, squatting down to pot, chewing away all the time at a rotten apple or a crust of bread. Or, there on the cobbled path, where half the cobbles had come loose, and where water (if it was in fact water) stood about in stagnant pools, three little boys down on their hands and knees, studying a little girl who was having a pee, and trying to see how she managed it and where it came out. She didn't care in the slightest. There she was – solemn, ignorant, and with one eye bandaged. And the way they'd spit at one another! And all that kicking and scratching! Tearing one another's hair! And all the shrieking that led to! Their mothers would join in as well, yelling from every window of the whole five floors in the house. Oh, look! Right in the middle of it all, there's the little school-marm, with that run-down-looking little face of hers, and her hair tumbling on to her shoulders and down her back, coming through the courtyard carrying a large bouquet of flowers, which she's just been given by her fiancé, who's there, smiling, beside her.

Petix felt very tempted to rush over to his chest of drawers, take out his revolver and shoot that little schoolmistress – such and so great were the indignation and fury that those flowers and that smile on her fiancé's face provoked in him! The flattering hopes of love, in the middle of that sickening obscenity, that filthy proliferation of children. And soon she too would be busy increasing their number.

I would now ask you to remember that every day for the past ten years Nicola Petix, living there in that house, had been a member of the audience for Signora Porrella's unfailing sequence of pregnancies. She would reach the seventh or eighth month, having gone through all the refinements of vomiting, suffering, and trepidation, and then miscarry. And every time she'd nearly die. In the nineteen years she'd been married, that carcass of a woman had had fifteen miscarriages.

The most terrifying thing as far as Nicola Petix was concerned was this: he'd never been able to understand what it was in those two people that made them want a child so stubbornly and with such blind ferocity. Tearing away at themselves like that!

Perhaps it was because, eighteen years ago, at the time of her first pregnancy, the woman had prepared a layette for the baby she was expecting. There wasn't a thing she hadn't thought of; swaddling clothes, bonnets, little shirts, bibs, long day-dresses with pom-poms on the strings, woollen bootees – still waiting to be used, and now all yellow and dried-up, stiff and starched, like so many tiny corpses.

For the past ten years there'd been a kind of implied wager between the women of the tenement, who spent their time spawning brats at an incredible rate, and Nicola Petix, who loathed with every fibre of his being their filthy proliferation of children. *They* were busy maintaining that *this time* Signora Porrella would have her baby, while he said, 'No, she won't even bring it off this time'. And the more care they lavished on the belly of that woman as it grew from month to month, the more attentive they were, the more anxious for her well-being, the more they recommended her to do this, that, and the other, the more he felt his vexation, his frenzy, his fury growing within him, as he saw her getting larger and larger with each succeeding month. In the last days of every one of her pregnancies – so over-excited was his imagination – he would gradually come to see the whole of that vast house as an enormous belly, caught in the desperate travail of the gestation of the man who was destined to be born. It was no longer a question for him of Signora Porrella's imminent confinement. Oh, yes! That would mean defeat for him. It was a question of the man, the man whom all those women were willing to be born from the belly of that woman: such a man as can be born from the brute necessity of the two sexes when they're coupled!

Well, it was that man whom Petix wanted to destroy, once he was sure that that sixteenth pregnancy of hers was going to come at last to a successful conclusion. *That* man. Not one man among many, but one man in whom all men were summed up. And he was going to revenge himself on that one man for all the others, the hundreds and hundreds he had to watch swarming around, little brutes who lived merely in order to live, without knowing anything about living, except for that tiny fragment which they seemed condemned every day to get through. Every day the same old thing.

It all happened a few days after that occasion when I chanced to see Signor and Signora Porrella walking along the Viale Nomentano amidst the swirling gusts of dead leaves. Walking in step. Their feet hitting the ground in the same way. Seriously. As if they had a task to perform. A duty laid upon them.

The goal of their daily walk was a large stone on the other

side of the Barrier, where the lane, after turning again once you're past Sant' Agnese – you remember, it narrows a bit, and then drops down towards the valley of the Aniene. Every day, seated on that stone, they'd rest for about half an hour from their long, slow walk. Signor Porrella would look over at the gloomy bridge, thinking no doubt that the ancient Romans had passed that way. Signora Porrella would follow with her eyes the movements of some old woman rummaging for edible greenstuff among the grass on the slope that runs along the riverside. The river makes a brief appearance here, after emerging from under the bridge. Or else she'd study her hands, slowly twisting her rings round her stubby fingers.

Even that day they were quite determined to reach their usual objective, despite the fact that the river, as a result of the recent heavy rain, was in flood and had broken its banks, so that it was encroaching threateningly on the slope leading down to it. As a matter of fact, it had almost risen as far as that stone of theirs. Despite the fact, too, that they could see in the distance their fellow-tenant, Nicola Petix, seated on their stone, just as if he were waiting for them. He was all hunched-up and drawn into himself like some huge owl.

They stopped for a moment or so when they caught sight of him, rather bewildered. Should they go and sit somewhere else or should they turn back? But the very fact that he just *sat* there, seeming somehow to warn them – radiating distrust and hostility – well, it made them decide to go on and to go up to him. Because it seemed to them irrational to allow the unlooked-for presence of that man. And the fact that it seemed obvious that he'd come there especially to meet them. Well, it couldn't mean anything terribly serious, as far as they were concerned. Not so serious as to make them give up their usual little rest. After all, the pregnant woman had special need of that rest.

Petix said nothing. Everything happened in an instant. Almost *quietly*. As the woman came up to the stone to sit down, he seized her by the arm and with one tug dragged her to the edge of the flooding river. Then he gave her a shove that sent her flying into the river, where she was drowned.

Robert Musil

GRIGIA

TRANSLATED BY
EITHNE WILKINS AND
ERNST KAISER

ROBERT MUSIL

Born in Klagenfurt 1880; died in Geneva 1942. Austrian novelist:
Young Törless (1906) and *The Man Without Qualities*, unfinished at
his death. 'Grigia' (1923) derives from Musil's experience as an
Austrian officer on the Italian front in 1915.

GRIGIA

THERE is a time in life when everything perceptibly slows down, as though one's life were hesitating to go on or trying to change its course. It may be that at this time one is more liable to disaster.

Homo had an ailing little son. After this illness had dragged on for a year, without being dangerous, yet also without improving, the doctor prescribed a long stay at a spa; but Homo could not bring himself to accompany his wife and child. It seemed to him it would mean being separated too long from himself, from his books, his plans, and his life. He felt his reluctance to be sheer selfishness, but perhaps it was rather more a sort of self-dissolution, for he had never before been apart from his wife for even as much as a whole day; he had loved her very much and still did love her very much, but through the child's coming this love had become frangible, like a stone that water has seeped into, gradually disintegrating it. Homo was very astonished by this new quality his life had acquired, this frangibility, for to the best of his knowledge and belief nothing of the love itself had ever been lost, and during all the time occupied with preparations for their departure he could not imagine how he was to spend the approaching summer alone. He simply felt intense repugnance at the thought of spas and mountain resorts.

So he remained alone at home, and on the second day he received a letter inviting him to join a company that was about to re-open the old Venetian gold-mines in the Val Fersena. The letter was from a certain Mozart Amadeo Hoffingott, whom he had met while travelling some years previously and with whom he had, during those few days, struck up a friendship.

Yet not the slightest doubt occurred to him whether the project was a sound one. He sent off two telegrams, one to tell his wife that he was, after all, leaving instantly and would send his address, the other accepting the proposal that he should join the company as its geologist and perhaps even invest a fairly large sum in the re-opening of the mines.

In P., a prosperous, compact little Italian town in the midst of mulberry-groves and vineyards, he joined Hoffingott, a tall, handsome, swarthy man of his own age who was always enormously active. He now learnt that the company was backed by immense American funds, and the project was to be carried out in great style. First of all a reconnaissance party was to go up the valley. It was to consist of the two of them and three other partners. Horses were bought, instruments were due to arrive any day, and workmen were being engaged.

Homo did not stay in the inn, but – he did not quite know why – in the house of an Italian acquaintance of Hoffingott's. There he was struck by three things. The beautiful mahogany beds were indescribably cool and soft. The wallpaper had an indescribably bewildering, maze-like pattern, at once banal and very strange. And there was a cane rocking-chair. Sitting in that chair, rocking and gazing at the wallpaper, one seemed to turn into a mere tangle of rising and falling tendrils that would grow within a couple of seconds from nothingness to their full size and then as rapidly disappear into themselves again.

In the streets the air was a blend of snow and the South. It was the middle of May. In the evening the place was lit by big arc-lights that hung from wires stretched across from house to house, so high that the streets below were like ravines of deep blue gloom, and there one picked one's way along, while away up in the universe there was a spinning and hissing of white suns. By day one looked out over vineyards and woods. It was still all red, yellow, and green after the winter, and since the trees did not lose their leaves, the fading growth and the new were interlaced as in graveyard wreaths. Little red, blue, and pink villas still stood out very vividly among the trees, like scattered cubes inanimately manifesting to every eye some strange morphological law of which they themselves knew nothing. But higher up the woods were dark, and the mountain was called Selvot. Above the woods there was pasture-land, now still covered with snow, the broad, smooth, wavy lines of it running across the neighbouring mountains and up the steep little side-valley where the expedition was to go. When men came down from these mountains to sell milk and buy polenta, they sometimes brought great lumps of rock-crystal or amethyst, which was said to grow as profusely in many crevices up there as in other places flowers grow in the field, and these uncannily beautiful fairy-tale objects still further intensified his impression that behind the outward appearance of this district, this appearance that had the flickering remoteness and familiarity the stars sometimes have at night, there was hidden something that he yearningly awaited. When they rode into the mountain valley, passing Sant' Orsola at six o'clock, by a little stone bridge across a mountain rivulet overhung with bushes there were, if not a hundred, at least certainly a score of nightingales singing. It was broad daylight.

When they were well in the valley, they came to a fantastic place. It hung on the slope of a hill. The bridle-path that had brought them now began sheerly to leap from one huge flat boulder to the next, and flowing away from it, like streams meandering downhill, were a few short, steep lanes disappearing into the meadows. Standing on the bridle-path, one saw only forlorn and ramshackle cottages; but if one looked upward from the meadows below it was as though one had been transported back into a prehistoric lake-village built on piles, for the front of each house was supported on tall beams, and the privies floated out to one side of them like litters on four slender poles as tall as trees. Nor was the surrounding landscape without its oddities. It was a more than semicircular wall of high, craggy mountains sweeping down steeply into a crater in the centre of which was a smaller wooded cone, and the whole thing was like a gigantic empty pudding-mould with a little piece cut out of it by a deep-running brook, so that there it yawned wide open against the high flank of the slope on which the village hung. Below the snow-line there were corries, where a few deer strayed in the scrub, and in the woods crowning the round hill in the centre the blackcock were already displaying. The meadows on the sunny side were flowered with yellow, blue, and white stars, as big as thalers emptied out of a sack. But if one climbed another hundred feet or so beyond the village, one came to a small plateau covered with ploughed fields, meadows, hay-barns and a sprinkle of houses, with a little church, on a bastion that jutted over the valley, gazing out over the world that on fine days lay far beyond the valley like the sea beyond the mouth of a river: one could scarcely tell what was still the golden-yellow distance of the blessed plain and where the vague cloud-floors of the sky had begun.

It was a fine life they led there. All day one was up in the mountains, working at old blocked mine-shafts, or driving new ones into the mountainside, or down at the mouth of the valley where a wide road was to be built: and always one was in gigantic air that was already soft, pregnant with the imminent melting of the snow. They poured out money among the people and held sway like gods. They had something for them all to do, men and women alike. The men they organized into working parties and sent them up the mountains, where they had to spend the week; the women they used as porters, sending them in columns up the almost impassable mountainside, bringing provisions and spare parts. The stone schoolhouse was turned into a depot where their stores were kept and whence they were distributed. There a commanding male voice rapped out orders, summoning one by one the women who stood waiting and chattering, and the big basket on each woman's back would be loaded until her knees gave and the veins in her neck swelled. When one of those pretty young women had been loaded up, her eyes stared and her lips hung open; then she took her place in the column and, at a sign, these now silent beasts of burden slowly began to set one foot before the other up the long, winding track into the heights. But it was a rare and precious burden that they bore, bread, meat, and wine, and there was no need to be too scrupulous about the tools either, so that besides their wages a good deal that was useful found its way to their own households, and therefore they carried the loads willingly and even thanked the men who had brought these blessings into the mountains. And it was wonderful to feel: here one was not, as everywhere else in the world, scrutinized to see what sort of human being one was – whether one was reliable, powerful and to be feared, or delicate and beautiful – but whatever sort of human being one was, and no matter what one's ideas about life and the world were, here one met with love because one had brought blessings. Love ran ahead like a herald, love was made ready everywhere like a bed freshly made up for the guest, and each living being bore gifts of welcome in their eyes. The women could let that be freely seen, but sometimes as one passed a meadow there might be an old peasant there, waving his scythe like Death in person.

There were, indeed, peculiar people living at the head of this valley. Their forefathers had come here from Germany, to work in the mines, in the times when the bishops of Trent were mighty, and they were still like some ancient weathered German boulder flung down in the Italian landscape. They had partly kept and partly forgotten their old way of life, and what they had kept of it they themselves probably no longer understood. In the spring the mountain torrents wrenched away the earth from under them, so that there were houses that had once stood on a hill and were now on the brink of an abyss; but nobody lifted a finger to contend with the danger, and by a reverse process the new age was drifting into their houses, casting up all sorts of dreadful rubbish. One came across cheap, shiny cupboards, oleographs, and humorous postcards. But sometimes too there would be a saucepan that their forebears might well have used in Luther's time. For they were Protestants; but even though it was doubtless no more than this dogged clinging to their beliefs that had prevented their being Italianized, they were certainly not good Christians. Since they were poor, almost all the men left their wives shortly after marrying and went to America for years on end; when they came back, they brought with them a little money they had saved, the habits learned in urban brothels, and the irreligion, but not the acuity, of civilization.

Right at the beginning Homo heard a story that interested him extraordinarily. Not long before – it might have been some fifteen years previously – a peasant who had been away for a long time came home from America and bedded with his wife again. For a while they rejoiced because they were re-united, and they lived without a care until the last of his cash had melted away. Then, when the rest of his savings, which had been supposed to come from America, still failed to arrive, the peasant girded himself up and – as all the peasants in this district did – went out to earn a living as a pedlar, while his wife continued to look after the unprofitable smallholding. But he did not come back. Instead, a few days later, on a smallholding some distance from the first, the peasant returned from America, reminded his wife how long it had been, exactly to the day, asked to be given a meal exactly the same as that they had had on the day he left, remembered all about the cow that no longer existed, and got on decently with the children sent him by Heaven during the years when he was away. This peasant too, after a period of relaxation and good living, set off with pedlar's wares and did not return. This happened a third and a fourth time in the district, until it was realized that this was a swindler who had worked with the men over there and questioned them thoroughly about their life at home. Somewhere he was arrested and imprisoned, and none of the women saw him again. This, so the story went, they all were sorry about, for each of them would have liked to have him for a few days more and to have compared him with her memories, in order not to have to admit she had been made a fool of; for each of them claimed to have noticed something that did not quite correspond to what she remembered, but none of them was sufficiently sure of it to raise the matter and make difficulties for the husband who had returned to claim his rights.

That was what these women were like. Their legs were concealed by brown woollen skirts with deep borders of red, blue or orange, and the kerchiefs they wore on their heads and crossed over the breast were cheap printed cotton things with a factory-made pattern, yet somehow, too, something about the colours or the way they wore these kerchiefs suggested bygone centuries. There was something here that was much older than any known peasant costume; perhaps it was only a gaze, one that had come down through the ages and arrived very late, faint now and already dim, and yet one felt it clearly, meeting one's own gaze as one looked at them. They wore shoes that were like primitive dug-out canoes, and because the tracks were so bad they had knife-sharp iron blades fitted into the soles, and in their blue or brown stockings they walked on these as the women walk in Japan. When they had to wait, they sat down, not on the edge of the path, but right on the flat earth of the path itself, pulling up their knees like Negroes. And when, as sometimes happened, they rode up the mountains on their donkeys, they did not sit on their skirts, but rode astride like men, their thighs insensitive to the sharp wooden edges of the baggage-saddles, their legs again raised indecorously high and the whole upper part of the body faintly swinging with the animal's movement.

And they had, besides, a bewilderingly frank friendliness and kindliness. 'Do you come in,' they would say, with all the dignity of great ladies, if one knocked at their rustic doors. Or if one stood chatting with them for a while in the open air, one of them might suddenly ask with extreme courtesy and reserve: 'Shall I not hold your coat for you?' Once, when Homo said to a charming fourteen-year-old girl: 'Come in the hay' – simply because 'the hay' suddenly seemed as natural to him as fodder is to cattle – the childish face under the pointed, ancestral kerchief showed not the slightest dismay: there was only a mirthful puffing and flashing, a tipping this way and that on the rocking shoe-boats, and almost a collapse on to her little bottom, with her rake still on her shoulder, the whole perform-ance conveying, with winsome clumsiness, comic-opera astonishment at the man's intensity of desire.

Another time he asked a tall, Valkyrie-like peasant woman: 'Well, and are you still a virgin?' and chucked her under the chin – this time, too, merely because such jests need a touch of virile emphasis.

But she let her chin rest quietly on his hand and answered solemnly: 'Yes, of course . . .'

Homo was taken aback. 'You're still a virgin!' he repeated, and laughed.

She giggled.

'Tell me!' he said, drawing closer and playfully shaking her chin.

Then she blew into his face and laughed. 'Was once, of course!'

'If I come to see you, what can I have?' he went on with his cross-examination.

'Whatever you want.'

'Everything I want?'

'Everything.'

'Really everything?'

'Everything! Everything!' and her passion was so brilliantly and passionately acted, that the theatrical quality of it, up here, nearly 5,000 feet above sea-level, left him quite bewildered.

After this he could not rid himself of the feeling that this life, which was brighter and more highly spiced than any life he had led before, was no longer part of reality, but a play floating in the air.

Meanwhile summer had come. When he had received the first letter and recognized his ailing little boy's childish handwriting, the shock of happiness and secret possession had flashed right through him, down to the soles of his feet. Their knowing where he was seemed to give everything tremendous solidity. He was here: oh, now everything was known and he had no more need to explain anything. All white and mauve, green and brown, there were the meadows around him. He was no phantom. A fairy-tale wood of ancient larches, feathery with new green, spread over an emerald slope. Under the moss there might be living crystals, mauve and white. The stream in the midst of the wood somewhere ran over a boulder, falling so that it looked like a big silver comb. He no longer answered his wife's letters. Here, amid the secrets of Nature, their belonging together was only one secret more. There was a tender scarlet flower, one that existed in no other man's world, only in his, and thus God had ordered things, wholly as a wonder. There was a place in the body that was kept hidden away, and no one might see it lest he should die: only one man. At this moment it seemed to him as wonderfully senseless and unpractical as only profound religious feeling can be. And only now did he realize what he had done in cutting himself off for this summer and letting himself drift on his own tide, this tide that had taken control of him. Among the trees with their arsenic-green beards he sank down on one knee and spread out his arms, a thing he had never done before in all his life, and it was as though in this moment someone lifted him out of his own embrace. He felt his beloved's hand in his, her voice sounded in his ear, and it was as though even now his whole body were answering to a touch, as though he were being cast in the mould of some other body. But he had invalidated his life. His heart had grown humble before his beloved, and poor as a mendicant; only a little more, and vows and tears would have poured from his very soul. And yet it was certain that he would not turn back, and strangely there was associated with his agitation an image of the meadows in flower round about these woods, and despite all longing for the future a feeling that here, amid anemones, forget-me-not, orchids, gentian, and the glorious greenish-brown sorrel, he would lie dead. He lay down and stretched out on the moss. 'How am I to take you across with me?' he asked himself. And his body felt strangely tired, was like a rigid face relaxing into a smile.

Here he was, having always thought he was living in reality – but was there anything more unreal than that one human being should for him be different from all other human beings? – that among innumerable bodies there was one on which his inmost existence was almost as dependent as on his own body? – whose hunger and fatigue, hearing and seeing, were linked with his own? As the child grew older, this had grown – as the secrets of the soil grow into a sapling – into earthly cares and comforts. He loved his child, but just as the boy would outlive them, so too the boy had earlier killed the other-worldly part of them. And suddenly he flushed hot with a new certainty. He was not a man inclined to religious belief, but at this moment he was illumined within. Thoughts cast as little light as smoky candles in this great radiance of emotion that he experienced; it was all simply one glorious word blazing with the light of youth: Reunion. He was taking her with him for all eternity, and in the moment when he yielded to this thought, the little blemishes that the years had wrought in his beloved were taken from her and all was, eternally, the first day of all. Every worldly consideration vanished, and every possibility of tedium and of unfaithfulness, for no one will sacrifice eternity for the sake of a quarter of an hour's frivolity.

And for the first time he experienced love beyond all doubt as a heavenly sacrament. He recognized the Providence that had guided his life into this solitude and felt the ground with its gold and jewels beneath his feet no longer as an earthly treasure, but as an enchanted world ordained for him alone.

From this day onward he was released from a bondage, as though rid of a stiff knee or a heavy rucksack. It was the bondage of wanting to be alive, the horror of dying. It did not happen to him as he had always thought it would, when in the fullness of one's strength one seems to see one's end approaching, so that one drinks more deeply of life, savours it more intensely. It was merely that he felt no longer involved, felt himself buoyed up by a glorious lightness that made him supreme lord of his own existence.

Although the mining operations had not progressed according to plan it was indeed a gold-digger's life they were leading. A lad had stolen wine, and that was a crime against the community, the punishment of which could count on general approval. The lad was brought in with his wrists bound. Mozart Amadeo Hoffingott gave orders that he should constitute a warning to others by being tied upright to a tree for a day and a night. But when the foreman came with the rope, in jest portentously swinging it and then hanging it over a nail, the lad began to tremble all over in the belief that he was about to be hanged. And it was always just the same – although this was hard to explain – when horses arrived, either fresh horses from beyond the valley or some that had been brought down for a few days' rest: they would stand about on the meadow, or lie down, but would always group themselves somehow, apparently at random, in a perspective, so that it looked as if it were done according to some secretly agreed aesthetic principle, just like that memory of the little green, blue, and pink houses at the foot of Mount Selvot. But if they were up above, standing around all night tethered in some high corrie in the mountains, three or four at a time tied to a felled tree, and one had started out in the moonlight at three in the morning and now came past the place at half-past four, they would all look round to see who was passing, and in the insubstantial dawn light one felt oneself to be a thought in some very slow-thinking mind. Since there was some thieving, and various other risks as well, all the dogs in the district had been bought up to serve as guards. The patrols brought them along in whole packs, two or three led on one rope, collarless. By now there were as many dogs as men in the place, and one might well wonder which was actually entitled to feel he was master in his own house on this earth and which was only adopted as a domestic companion. There were pure-bred gun-dogs among them, Venetian setters such as a few people in this district still kept, and snappy mongrels like spiteful little monkeys. They too would stand about in groups that had formed without anyone's knowing why, and which kept firmly together, but from time to time the members of a group would attack each other furiously. Some were half starved, some refused to eat. One little white dog snapped at the cook's hand as he was putting down a plate of meat and soup for it, and bit one finger off.

At half-past four in the morning it was already broad day-light, though the sun was not yet up. When one passed the grazing-land high up on the mountain, the cattle were still half asleep. In big, dim, white, stony shapes they lay with their legs drawn in under them, their hindquarters drooping a little to one side. They did not look at the passer-by, nor after him, but imperturbably kept their faces turned towards the expected light, and their monotonously, slowly moving jaws seemed to be praying. Walking through the circle of them was like traversing some twilit, lofty sphere of existence, and when one looked back at them from above, the line formed by the spine, the hind legs, and the curving tail made them seem like a scattering of treble-signs.

There was plenty of incident. For instance, a man might break his leg, and two others would carry him into camp on their crossed arms. Or suddenly the shout of: 'Take co-ver!' would ring out, and everyone would run for cover because a great rock was being dynamited for the building of the road. Once, at such a moment, a shower swept a few flickers of moisture over the grass. In the shelter of a bush on the far side of the stream there was a fire burning, forgotten in the excitement, though only a few minutes earlier it had been very

important: standing near it, the only watcher left, was a young
birch tree. And still dangling by one leg from this birch was
the black pig. The fire, the birch, and the pig were now alone.
The pig had squealed even while one man was merely leading
it along on a rope, talking to it, urging it to come on. Then it
squealed all the louder as it saw two other men come delightedly
running towards it. It was frantic at being seized by the ears
and unceremoniously dragged forward. It straddled all four
legs in resistance, but the pain in its ears forced it to make little
jumps onward. Finally, at the other end of the bridge, someone
had grabbed a hatchet and struck it on the forehead with the
blade. From that moment on everything went more quietly.
Both forelegs buckled at the same instant, and the little pig
did not scream again until the knife was actually in its throat.
There was a shrieking, twitching blare, which sank down into
a death-rattle that was no more than a pathetic snore. All these
were things Homo saw for the first time in his life.

When dusk fell, they all gathered in the little vicarage, where
they had rented a room to serve as their mess. Admittedly the
meat, which came the long way up the mountain only twice a
week, was often going off, and not infrequently one had a touch
of food-poisoning. But still all of them came here as soon as
it was dark, stumbling along the invisible tracks with their
little lanterns. For what caused them more suffering than food-
poisoning was melancholy and boredom, even though everything was so beautiful. They swilled it away with wine. After
an hour a cloud of sadness and ragtime hung over the room.
The gramophone went round and round, like a gilded hurdy-
gurdy trundling over a soft meadow spattered with wonderful
stars. They no longer talked to each other. They merely talked.
What should they have said to each other, a literary man of
independent means, a business man, a former inspector of
prisons, a mining engineer, and a retired major? They com-
municated in sign-language – and this even though they used
words: words of discomfort, of relative comfort, of home-
sickness – it was an animal language. Often they would argue
with superfluous intensity about some question that concerned
none of them, and would reach the point of insulting each
other, and the next day seconds would be passing to and fro.

Then it would turn out that nobody had meant a word of it. They had only done it to kill time, and even if none of them had ever really known anything of the world, each of them felt he had behaved as uncouthly as a butcher, and this filled them with resentment against each other.

It was that standard psychic unit which is Europe. It was idleness as undefined as at other times their occupation was. It was a longing for wife, child, home comforts. And interspersed with this, ever and again, there was a gramophone. 'Rosa, we're going to Lódź, Lódź, Lódź. . . .' or: 'Whate'er befall I still recall. . . .' It was an astral emanation of powder and gauze, a mist of far-off variety shows and European sexuality. Indecent jokes exploded into guffaws, each joke, it seemed, beginning: 'You know the one about the Jew in the train. . . .' Only once somebody asked: 'How far is it to Babylon?' And then everyone fell silent, and the major put on the 'Tosca' record and, as it was about to start, said mournfully: 'Once I wanted to marry Geraldine Farrar.' Then her voice came through the horn, out into the room, and this woman's voice that all these drunken men were marvelling at seemed to step into a lift, and the next instant the lift was flashing away up to the top with her, arriving nowhere, coming down again, bouncing in the air. Her skirts billowed out with the movement, with this up and down, this long lying close to, clinging tightly to, one note, and again there was the rise and fall, and with it all this streaming away as if for ever, and yet again and yet again and again this being seized by yet another spasm, and again a streaming out: a voluptuous ecstasy. Homo felt it was that naked voluptuousness which is distributed throughout all the things there are in cities, a lust no longer distinguishable from manslaughter, or jealousy, or business, or motor-car racing – ah, it was no longer lust, it was a craving for adventure – no, it was not a craving for adventure either, it was a knife slashing down out of the sky, a destroying angel, angelic madness – the war?

From one of the many long fly-papers trailing from the ceiling a fly had dropped in front of him and was lying on its back, poisoned, in the middle of one of those pools that the light of the paraffin-lamps made in the scarcely perceptible

wrinkles in the oilcloth – pools with all that sadness of very
early spring, as if a strong wind had swept over them after
rain. The fly made a few efforts, each weaker than the last, to
turn over, and from time to time a second fly that was feeding
on the oilcloth ran to see how it was getting on. Homo also
kept a careful watch – the flies were a great nuisance here. But
when death came, the dying fly folded its six little legs together,
to a point, and kept them straight up like that, and then it died
in its pale spot of light on the oilcloth as in a graveyard of
stillness that could not be measured in inches or decibels, and
which was nevertheless there. Someone was just saying:
'They say someone's worked out that all the Rothschilds put
together haven't enough money to pay for a third-class ticket
to the moon.'

Homo murmured to himself: '. . . Kill, and yet feel the
presence of God? . . . Feel the presence of God and yet kill?'
And with a flick of his forefinger he sent the fly right into the
face of the major sitting opposite, which caused another
incident and thus kept them occupied until the next evening.

By then he had already known Grigia for some time, and
perhaps the major knew her too. Her name was Lene Maria
Lenzi. That sounded like Selvot and Gronleit or Malga
Mendana, had a ring as of amethyst crystals and of flowers,
but he preferred to call her Grigia, pronounced Greeja, after
the cow she had, which she called Grigia, Grey One. At such
times she would be sitting at the edge of her meadow, in her
mauve-brown skirt and dotted kerchief, the toes of her
wooden clogs sticking up into the air, her hands clasped over
her bright apron, and she would look as naturally lovely as
a slender little poisonous mushroom, while now and then she
called out to the cow grazing down the hillside. There were
actually only two things she called: 'Come a-here!' and:
'Come a-up!' when the cow strayed too far. But if her cries
were unavailing, there would follow an indignant: 'Hey, you
devil, come a-*here*!', and in the last resort she herself would go
hurtling down the hillside like a flung stone, the next best piece
of stick in her hand, to be aimed at the Grey One as soon as she
was within throwing distance. Since, however, the cow Grigia
had a distinct taste for straying valley-wards, the whole of this

operation would be repeated with the regularity of pendulum-clockwork that is constantly dropping lower and constantly being wound higher again. Because this was so paradisically senseless, he teased her by calling her Grigia herself. He could not conceal from himself that his heart beat faster when from a distance he caught sight of her sitting there; that is the way the heart beats when one suddenly walks into the smell of pine-needles or into the spicy air rising from the floor of woods where a great many mushrooms grow. In this feeling there was always a residual dread of Nature. And one must not believe that Nature is anything but highly unnatural: she is earthy, edgy, poisonous, and inhuman at all points where man does not impose his will upon her. Probably it was just this that fascinated him in this peasant woman, and the other half of it was inexhaustible amazement that she did so much resemble a woman. One would, after all, be equally amazed, going through the woods, to encounter a lady balancing a tea-cup.

'Do come in,' she too had said, the first time he had knocked at her door. She was standing by the hearth, with a pot on the fire, and since she could not leave it, she made a courteous gesture towards the bench. After a while she wiped her hand on her apron, smiling, and held it out to her visitors: it was a well-formed hand, as velvety-rough as the finest sandpaper or as garden soil trickling between the fingers. And the face that went with the hand was a faintly mocking face, with delicate, graceful bones that one saw best in profile, and a mouth that he noticed very particularly. This mouth was curved like a Cupid's bow, yet it was also compressed as happens when one gulps, and this gave it, with its subtlety, a determined roughness, and to this roughness again a little trace of merriment, which was perfectly in keeping with the wooden shoes that the slight figure grew up out of as out of wild roots. . . . They had come to arrange some matter or other, and when they left, the smile was there again, and the hand rested in his perhaps a moment longer than when they had come. These impressions, which would have been so insignificant in town, out there in this solitude amounted to a shock, as though a tree had moved its branches in a way not to be explained by any stirring of the wind or a bird's taking flight.

A short time later he had become a peasant woman's lover. This change that had taken place in him much occupied his mind, for beyond doubt it was not something he had done, but something that had happened to him.

When he came the second time, Grigia at once sat down on the bench beside him, and when – to see how far he could already go – he put his hand on her lap and said: 'You are the beauty of them all', she let his hand rest on her thigh and merely laid her own upon it. With that they were pledged to each other. And now he kissed her to set the seal upon it, and after the kiss she smacked her lips with a sound like that smack of satisfaction with which lips sometimes let go of the rim of a glass after greedily drinking from it. He was indeed slightly startled by this indecorum and was not offended when she rejected any further advances; he did not know why, he knew nothing at all of the customs and dangers of this place, and, though curious, let himself be put off for another day. 'In the hay,' Grigia had said, and when he was already in the doorway, saying goodbye, she said: 'Goodbye till soon,' and smiled at him.

Even on his way home he realized he was already happy about what had happened: it was like a hot drink suddenly beginning to take effect after an interval. The notion of going to the hay-barn with her – opening a heavy wooden door, pulling it to after one, and the darkness increasing with each degree that it closes, until one is crouching on the floor of a brown perpendicular darkness – delighted him as though he were a child about to play a trick. He remembered the kisses and felt the smack of them as though a magic band had been laid around his head. Picturing what was to be, he could not help thinking of the way peasants eat: they chew slowly, smacking their lips, relishing every mouthful to the full. And it is the same with the way they dance, step after step. Probably it was the same with everything else. His legs stiffened with excitement at these thoughts, as though his shoes were already sticking in the earth. The women lower their eyelids and keep their faces quite stiff, a defensive mask, so as not to be disturbed by one's curiosity. They let scarcely a moan escape them. Motionless as beetles feigning death, they concentrate all their attention on what is going on within them.

And so too it was. With the rim of her clog Grigia scraped together into a pile the scrap of winter hay that was still there, and smiled for the last time when she bent to the hem of her skirt like a lady adjusting her garter.

It was all just as simple and just as magical as the thing about the horses, the cows, and the dead pig. When they were behind the beam, and heavy boots came thumping along the stony path outside, pounding by and fading into the distance, his blood pulsed in his throat; but Grigia seemed to know even at the third footstep whether the footsteps were coming this way or not. And she talked a magical language. A nose she called a neb, and legs she called shanks. An apron was for her a napron. Once when he threatened not to come again, she laughed and said: 'I'll bell thee!' And he did not know whether he was disconcerted or glad of it. She must have noticed that, for she asked: 'Does it rue thee? Does it rue thee much?' Such words were like the patterns of the aprons and kerchiefs and the coloured border at the top of the stocking, already somewhat assimilated to the present because of having come so far, but still mysterious visitants. Her mouth was full of them, and when he kissed it he never knew whether he loved this woman or whether a miracle was being worked upon him and Grigia was only part of a mission linking him ever more closely with his beloved in eternity. Once Grigia said outright: 'Thou'rt thinking other things, I can tell by thy look', and when he tried to pretend it was not so, she said: 'Ah, all that's but glozing.' He asked her what that meant, but she would not explain, and he racked his brains over it for a long time before it occurred to him that she meant he was glossing something over. Or did she mean something still more mysterious?

One may feel such things intensely or not. One may have principles, in which case it is all only an aesthetic joke that one accepts in passing. Or one has no principles, or perhaps they have slackened somewhat, as was the case with Homo when he set out on his journey, and then it may happen that these manifestations of an alien life take possession of whatever has become masterless. Yet they did not give him a new self, a self for sheer happiness become ambitious and earth-bound; they merely lodged, in irrelevantly lovely patches, within the

airy outlines of his body. Something about it all made Homo
sure that he was soon to die, only he did not yet know how or
when. His old life had lost all strength; it was like a butterfly
growing feebler as autumn draws on.

Sometimes he talked to Grigia about this. She had a way of
her own of asking about it: as respectful as if it were something
entrusted to her, and quite without self-seeking. She seemed
to regard it as quite in order that beyond the mountains there
were people he loved more than her, whom he loved with his
whole soul. And he did not feel this love growing less; it was
growing stronger, being ever renewed. It did not grow dim,
but the more deeply coloured it became, the more it lost any
power to decide anything for him in reality or to prevent his
doing anything. It was weightless and free of all earthly
attachment in that strange and wonderful way known only to
one who has had to reckon up with his life and who henceforth
may wait only for death. However healthy he had been before,
at this time something within him rose up and was straight,
like a lame man who suddenly throws away his crutches and
walks on his own.

This became strongest of all when it came to hay-making
time. The hay was already mown and dried and only had to
be bound and fetched in, up from the mountain meadows.
Homo watched it from the nearest height, which was like
being high in a swing, flying free above it all. The girl – quite
alone in the meadow, a polka-dotted doll under the enormous
glass bell of the sky – was doing all sorts of things in her
efforts to make a huge bundle. She knelt down in it, pulling
the hay towards her with both arms. Very sensually she lay on
her belly across the bale and reached underneath it. She turned
over on her side and stretched out one arm as far as she could.
She climbed up it on one knee, then on both. There was
something of the dor-beetle about her, Homo thought – the
scarab, of course. At last she thrust her whole body under the
bale, now bound with a rope, and slowly raised it on high.
The bundle was much bigger than the bright, slender little
human animal that was carrying it – or was that not Grigia?

When, in search of her, Homo walked along the long row
of hay-stooks that the peasant women had set up on the level

part of the hillside, they were resting. He could scarcely believe his eyes, for they were lying on their hillocks of hay like Michelangelo's statues in the Medici chapel in Florence, one arm raised to support the head, and the body reposing as in flowing water. And when they spoke with him and had to spit, they did so with much art: with three fingers they would twitch out a handful of hay, spit into the hollow, and then stop it up again. One might be tempted to laugh; only if one mixed with them, as Homo did when he was in search of Grigia, one might just as easily start in sudden fright at this crude dignity. But Grigia was seldom among them, and when at last he found her, she would perhaps be crouching in a potato-field, laughing at him. He knew she had nothing on but two petticoats and that the dry earth that was running through her slim rough fingers was also touching her body. But the thought of it was no longer strange to him. By now his inner being had become curiously familiar with the touch of earth, and perhaps indeed it was not at the time of the hay-harvest at all that he met her in that field: in this life he was leading there was no longer any certainty about time or place.

The hay-barns were filled. Through the chinks between the boards a silvery light poured in. The hay poured out green light. Under the door was a wide gold border.

The hay smelt sour – like the negro drinks that are made of fermented fruits and human saliva. One had only to remember that one was living among savages here, and the next instant one was intoxicated by the heat of this confined space filled to the roof with fermenting hay.

Hay bears one up in all positions. One can stand in it up to the knees, at once unsure of one's footing and all too firmly held fast. One can lie in it as in the Hand of God, and would gladly wallow in God's Hand like a little dog or a little pig. One may lie obliquely, or almost upright like a saint ascending to heaven in a green cloud.

Those were bridal days and ascension days.

But one time Grigia declared it could not go on. He could not bring her to say why. The sharpness round the mouth and the little furrow plumb between the eyes, which before had appeared only with the effort of deciding which would

be the nicest barn for their next meeting, now boded ill
weather somewhere in the offing. Were they being talked
about? But the other women, who did perhaps notice something, were always smiling as over a thing one is glad to see.
There was nothing to be got out of Grigia. She made excuses
and was more rarely to be found, and she watched her words
as carefully as any mistrustful farmer.

Once Homo met with a bad omen. His puttees had come
undone and he was standing by a hedge winding them on
again, when a peasant woman went by and said in a friendly
way: 'Let thy stockings be – it won't be long till nightfall.'
That was near Grigia's cottage. When he told Grigia, she made
a scornful face and said: 'People will talk, and brooks will
run', but she swallowed hard, and her thoughts were elsewhere. Then he suddenly remembered a woman he had seen
up here, whose bony face was like an Aztec's and who spent
all her time sitting at her door, her black hair loose, hanging
down below her shoulders, and with three healthy, round-
cheeked children around her. Grigia and he unthinkingly
passed by her every day, yet this was the only one of the local
women whom he did not know, and oddly enough he had
never asked about her either, although he was struck by her
appearance: it was almost as though the healthiness of her
children and the illness manifest in her face were impressions
that always cancelled each other out. In his present mood he
suddenly felt quite sure it was from here that the disturbing
element must have come. He asked who she was, but Grigia
crossly shrugged her shoulders and merely exclaimed: 'She
doesn't know what she says! With her it's a word here and a
word over the mountains!' And she made a swift, energetic
gesture, tapping her brow, as though she must instantly
devalue anything that woman might have said.

Since Grigia could not be persuaded to come again into any
of the hay-barns around the village, Homo proposed going
higher up the mountain with her. She was reluctant, and when
at last she yielded, she said, in a tone that afterwards struck
Homo as equivocal: 'Well, then, if go we must.'

It was a beautiful morning that once again embraced the
whole world; far beyond, there lay the sea of clouds and of

mankind. Grigia was anxious to avoid passing any dwelling, and even when they were well away from the village she, who had always been delightfully reckless in all arrangements to do with their love-making, showed concern lest they should be seen by watchful eyes. Then he grew impatient and it occurred to him that they had just passed an old mineshaft that his own people had soon given up trying to put back into use. There he drove Grigia in.

As he turned to look back for the last time, there was snow on a mountain-peak and below it, golden in the sun, a little field of corn-stooks, with the white and blue sky over it all.

Grigia made another remark that seemed strangely pointed. Noticing his backward glance, she said tenderly, 'Better leave the blue alone in the sky, so it'll keep fine'. But he forgot to ask what she meant by this, for they were already intent on groping their way further into darkness, which seemed to be closing around them.

Grigia went ahead, and when after a while the passage opened out into a small chamber, they stopped there and embraced. The ground underfoot seemed pleasantly dry and they lay down without Homo's feeling any of the civilized man's need to investigate it first by the light of a match. Once again Grigia trickled through him like soft, dry earth, and he felt her tensing in the dark, growing stiff with her pleasure. Then they lay side by side, without any urge to speak, gazing towards the little far-off rectangle beyond which daylight blazed white. And within him then Homo experienced over again his climb to this place, saw himself meeting Grigia beyond the village, then climbing, turning, and climbing, saw her blue stockings up to the orange border under the knee, her loose-hipped gait in those merry clogs, he saw them stopping outside the cavern, saw the landscape with the little golden field, and all at once in the brightness of the entrance beheld the image of her husband.

He had never before thought of this man, who was in the company's employ. Now he saw the sharp poacher's face with the dark, cunning eyes of a hunter, and suddenly remembered too the only time he had heard him speak: it was after creeping into an old mine-shaft where nobody else had dared to go, and the man's words were: 'I got into one fix after another. It's getting back that's hard.'

Swiftly Homo reached for his pistol, but at the same instant Lene Maria Lenzi's husband vanished and the darkness all around was as thick as a wall. He groped his way to the entrance, with Grigia clutching his sleeve. But he realized at once that the rock that had been rolled across the entrance was much heavier than anything he could shift unaided. And now too he knew why her husband had left them so much time: he himself needed time to make his plan and get a tree-trunk for a lever.

Grigia knelt by the rock, pleading and raging. It was repulsive in its futility. She swore that she had never done anything wrong and would never again do anything wrong. She squealed like a pig and rushed at the rock senselessly, like a maddened horse. In the end Homo came to feel that this was only in accordance with Nature, but he himself, a civilized man, at first could not overcome his incredulity, could not face the fact that something irrevocable had really happened. He leaned against the rocky wall, his hands in his pockets, and listened to Grigia.

Later he recognized his destiny. As in a dream he felt it descending upon him once again, through days, through weeks, through months, in the way sleep must begin when it will last a very long time. Gently he put one arm round Grigia and drew her back. He lay down beside her and waited for something. Previously he would perhaps have thought that in such a prison, with no escape, love must be sharp as teeth; but he quite forgot to think about Grigia. She had slipped away from him, or perhaps he from her, even though he could still feel her shoulder touching his. His whole life had slipped away from him, just so far that he could still tell it was there, but without being able to lay his hand upon it.

For hours they did not stir. Days might have passed, and nights. Hunger and thirst lay behind them, like one eventful stage of the journey, and they grew steadily weaker, lighter, and more shut into themselves. Their half-consciousness was wide seas, their waking small islands. Once he started up, with glaring awareness, into one such small waking: Grigia was

gone. Some certainty told him that it must have been only a
moment earlier. He smiled . . . telling him nothing of the way
out . . . meaning to leave him behind, as proof for her husband
. . .! He raised himself up on his elbow and looked about him.
So he too discovered a faint, glimmering streak. He crawled
a little nearer, deeper into the passage – they had always been
looking in the other direction. Then he realized there was a
narrow crevice there, which probably led out, obliquely, into
the open air. Grigia had slender bones, yet even he, if he made
an immense effort, might perhaps be able to worm his way
through. It was a way out. But at this moment he was perhaps
already too weak to return to life, or he had no wish to, or he
had lost consciousness.

At this same hour, all efforts having proved unavailing and
the futility of the undertaking having been recognized,
Mozart Amadeo Hoffingott, down in the valley, gave orders
for work to cease.

Isaac Babel

THE STORY OF MY DOVECOT

TRANSLATED BY
WALTER MORISON

ISAAC BABEL

Born in Odessa 1894; believed to have died in 1941 in a concentration camp in Siberia. Russian short story writer whose main subjects are the Jewish community of Odessa and his service in a revolutionary Cossack regiment (*Red Cavalry*). 'The Story of My Dovecot' (1925) refers to the 1905 Odessa pogrom; and the story is continued in a companion piece, 'First Love'.

THE STORY OF MY DOVECOT

To M. GORKY

WHEN I was a kid I longed for a dovecot. Never in all my life have I wanted a thing more. But not till I was nine did father promise the wherewithal to buy the wood to make one and three pairs of pigeons to stock it with. It was then 1904, and I was studying for the entrance exam to the preparatory class of the secondary school at Nikolayev in the Province of Kherson, where my people were at that time living. This province of course no longer exists, and our town has been incorporated in the Odessa Region.

I was only nine, and I was scared stiff of the exams. In both subjects, Russian language and arithmetic, I couldn't afford to get less than top marks. At our secondary school the *numerus clausus* was stiff: a mere five per cent. So that out of forty boys only two that were Jews would get into the preparatory class. The teachers used to put cunning questions to Jewish boys; no one else was asked such devilish questions. So when father promised to buy the pigeons he demanded top marks with distinction in both subjects. He absolutely tortured me to death. I fell into a state of permanent daydream, into an endless, despairing, childish reverie. I went to the exam deep in this dream, and nevertheless did better than everybody else.

I had a knack for book-learning. Even though they asked cunning questions, the teachers could not rob me of my intelligence and my avid memory. I was good at learning, and got top marks in both subjects. But then everything went wrong. Khariton Efrussi, the corn-dealer who exported wheat to Marseille, slipped someone a 500-rouble bribe. My mark was changed from A to A minus, and Efrussi Junior went to the secondary school instead of me. Father took it very badly. From the time I was six he had been cramming me with every scrap of learning he could, and that A minus drove him to despair. He wanted to beat Efrussi up, or at least bribe two

longshoremen to beat Efrussi up, but mother talked him out
of the idea, and I started studying for the second exam the
following year, the one for the lowest class. Behind my back
my people got the teacher to take me in one year through the
preparatory and first-year course simultaneously, and conscious
of the family's despair I got three whole books by heart. These
were Smirnovsky's *Russian Grammar*, Yevtushevsky's *Problems*,
and Putsykovich's *Manual of Early Russian History*. Children no
longer cram from these books, but I learned them by heart
line upon line, and the following year in the Russian exam
Karavayev gave me an unrivalled A plus.

This Karavayev was a red-faced, irritable fellow, a graduate
of Moscow University. He was hardly more than thirty. Crimson glowed in his manly cheeks as it does in the cheeks of
peasant children. A wart sat perched on one cheek, and from
it there sprouted a tuft of ash-coloured cat's whiskers. At the
exam, besides Karavayev, there was the Assistant Curator
Pyatnitsky, who was reckoned a big noise in the school and
throughout the province. When the Assistant Curator asked
me about Peter the Great, a feeling of complete oblivion came
over me, an awareness that the end was near: an abyss seemed
to yawn before me, an arid abyss lined with exultation and
despair.

About Peter the Great I knew things by heart from Putsykovich's book and Pushkin's verses. Sobbing, I recited these
verses, while the faces before me suddenly turned upside
down, were shuffled as a pack of cards is shuffled. This card-
shuffling went on, and meanwhile, shivering, jerking my back
straight, galloping headlong, I was shouting Pushkin's stanzas
at the top of my voice. On and on I yelled them, and no one
broke into my crazy mouthings. Through a crimson blindness,
through the sense of absolute freedom that had filled me, I
was aware of nothing but Pyatnitsky's old face with its silver-
touched beard bent towards me. He didn't interrupt me, and
merely said to Karavayev, who was rejoicing for my sake
and Pushkin's:

'What a people,' the old man whispered, 'those little Jews
of yours! There's a devil in them!'

And when at last I could shout no more, he said:

'Very well, run along, my little friend.'

I went out from the classroom into the corridor, and there, leaning against a wall that needed a coat of whitewash, I began to awake from my trance. About me Russian boys were playing, the school bell hung not far away above the stairs, the caretaker was snoozing on a chair with a broken seat. I looked at the caretaker, and gradually woke up. Boys were creeping towards me from all sides. They wanted to give me a jab, or perhaps just have a game, but Pyatnitsky suddenly loomed up in the corridor. As he passed me he halted for a moment, the frock-coat flowing down his back in a slow heavy wave. I discerned embarrassment in that large, fleshy, upper-class back, and got closer to the old man.

'Children,' he said to the boys, 'don't touch this lad.' And he laid a fat hand tenderly on my shoulder.

'My little friend,' he went on, turning me towards him, 'tell your father that you are admitted to the first class.'

On his chest a great star flashed, and decorations jingled in his lapel. His great black uniformed body started to move away on its stiff legs. Hemmed in by the shadowy walls, moving between them as a barge moves through a deep canal, it disappeared in the doorway of the headmaster's study. The little servingman took in a tray of tea, clinking solemnly, and I ran home to the shop.

In the shop a peasant customer, tortured by doubt, sat scratching himself. When he saw me my father stopped trying to help the peasant make up his mind, and without a moment's hesitation believed everything I had to say. Calling to the assistant to start shutting up shop, he dashed out into Cathedral Street to buy me a school cap with a badge on it. My poor mother had her work cut out getting me away from the crazy fellow. She was pale at that moment; she was experiencing destiny. She kept smoothing me, and pushing me away as though she hated me. She said there was always a notice in the paper about those who had been admitted to the school, and that God would punish us, and that folk would laugh at us if we bought a school cap too soon. My mother was pale; she was experiencing destiny through my eyes. She looked at me with bitter compassion as one might look at a little cripple boy, because she alone knew what a family ours was for misfortunes.

All the men in our family were trusting by nature, and quick to ill-considered actions. We were unlucky in everything we undertook. My grandfather had been a rabbi somewhere in the Belaya Tserkov region. He had been thrown out for blasphemy, and for another forty years he lived noisily and sparsely, teaching foreign languages. In his eightieth year he started going off his head. My Uncle Leo, my father's brother, had studied at the Talmudic Academy in Volozhin. In 1892 he ran away to avoid doing military service, eloping with the daughter of someone serving in the commissariat in the Kiev military district. Uncle Leo took this woman to California, to Los Angeles, and there he abandoned her, and died in a house of ill-fame among Negroes and Malays. After his death the American police sent us a heritage from Los Angeles, a large trunk bound with brown iron hoops. In this trunk there were dumbbells, locks of women's hair, uncle's talith, horsewhips with gilt handles, scented tea in boxes trimmed with imitation pearls. Of all the family there remained only crazy Uncle Simon-Wolf, who lived in Odessa, my father, and I. But my father had faith in people, and he used to put them off with the transports of first love. People could not forgive him for this, and used to play him false. So my father believed that his life was guided by an evil fate, an inexplicable being that pursued him, a being in every respect unlike him. And so I alone of all our family was left to my mother. Like all Jews I was short, weakly, and had headaches from studying. My mother saw all this. She had never been dazzled by her husband's pauper pride, by his incomprehensible belief that our family would one day be richer and more powerful than all others on earth. She desired no success for us, was scared of buying a school jacket too soon, and all she would consent to was that I should have my photo taken.

On 20 September 1905 a list of those admitted to the first class was hung up at the school. In the list my name figured too. All our kith and kin kept going to look at this paper, and even Shoyl, my grand-uncle went along. I loved that boastful old man, for he sold fish at the market. His fat hands were

moist, covered with fish-scales, and smelt of worlds chill and
beautiful. Shoyl also differed from ordinary folk in the lying
stories he used to tell about the Polish Rising of 1861. Years
ago Shoyl had been a tavern-keeper at Skvira. He had seen
Nicholas I's soldiers shooting Count Godlevski and other
Polish insurgents. But perhaps he hadn't. *Now* I know that
Shoyl was just an old ignoramus and a simple-minded liar,
but his cock-and-bull stories I have never forgotten: they were
good stories. Well now, even silly old Shoyl went along to the
school to read the list with my name on it, and that evening
he danced and pranced at our pauper ball.

My father got up the ball to celebrate my success, and asked
all his pals – grain-dealers, real-estate brokers, and the travelling
salesmen who sold agricultural machinery in our parts. These
salesmen would sell a machine to anyone. Peasants and
landowners went in fear of them: you couldn't break loose
without buying something or other. Of all Jews, salesmen are
the widest-awake and the jolliest. At our party they sang
Hasidic songs consisting of three words only but which took an
awful long time to sing, songs performed with endless comical
intonations. The beauty of these intonations may only be
recognized by those who have had the good fortune to spend
Passover with the Hasidim or who have visited their noisy
Volhynian synagogues. Besides the salesmen, old Lieberman,
who had taught me the Torah and ancient Hebrew honoured
us with his presence. In our circle he was known as Monsieur
Lieberman. He drank more Bessarabian wine than he should
have. The ends of the traditional silk tassels poked out from
beneath his waistcoat, and in ancient Hebrew he proposed my
health. In this toast the old man congratulated my parents
and said that I had vanquished all my foes in single combat:
I had vanquished the Russian boys with their fat cheeks, and
I had vanquished the sons of our own vulgar parvenus. So too
in ancient times David King of Judah had overcome Goliath,
and just as I had triumphed over Goliath, so too would our
people by the strength of their intellect conquer the foes who
had encircled us and were thirsting for our blood. Monsieur
Lieberman started to weep as he said this, drank more wine
as he wept, and shouted '*Vivat!*' The guests formed a circle

and danced an old-fashioned quadrille with him in the middle, just as at a wedding in a little Jewish town. Everyone was happy at our ball. Even mother took a sip of vodka, though she neither liked the stuff nor understood how anyone else could – because of this she considered all Russians cracked, and just couldn't imagine how women managed with Russian husbands.

But our happy days came later. For mother they came when of a morning, before I set off for school, she would start making me sandwiches; when we went shopping to buy my school things – pencil-box, money-box, satchel, new books in cardboard bindings, and exercise books in shiny covers. No one in the world has a keener feeling for new things than children have. Children shudder at the smell of newness as a dog does when it scents a hare, experiencing the madness which later, when we grow up, is called inspiration. And mother acquired this pure and childish sense of the ownership of new things. It took us a whole month to get used to the pencil-box, to the morning twilight as I drank my tea on the corner of the large, brightly-lit table and packed my books in my satchel. It took us a month to grow accustomed to our happiness, and it was only after the first half-term that I remembered about the pigeons.

I had everything ready for them: one rouble fifty and a dovecot made from a box by Grandfather Shoyl as we called him. The dovecot was painted brown. It had nests for twelve pairs of pigeons, carved strips on the roof, and a special grating that I had devised to facilitate the capture of strange birds. All was in readiness. On Sunday, 20 October, I set out for the bird market, but unexpected obstacles arose in my path.

The events I am relating, that is to say my admission to the first class at the secondary school, occurred in the autumn of 1905. The Emperor Nicholas was then bestowing a constitution on the Russian people. Orators in shabby overcoats were clambering on to tall kerbstones and haranguing the people. At night shots had been heard in the streets, and so mother didn't want me to go to the bird market. From early morning on 20 October the boys next door were flying a kite right by the police station, and our water-carrier, abandoning all his buckets, was walking about the streets with a red face and brilliantined hair. Then we saw baker Kalistov's sons drag a leather vaulting-horse out into the street and start doing gym in the middle of the roadway. No one tried to stop them: Semernikov the policeman even kept inciting them to jump higher. Semernikov was girt with a silk belt his wife had made him, and his boots had been polished that day as they had never been polished before. Out of his customary uniform, the policeman frightened my mother more than anything else. Because of him she didn't want me to go out, but I sneaked out by the back way and ran to the bird market, which in our town was behind the station.

At the bird market Ivan Nikodimych, the pigeon-fancier, sat in his customary place. Apart from pigeons, he had rabbits for sale too, and a peacock. The peacock, spreading its tail, sat on a perch moving a passionless head from side to side. To its paw was tied a twisted cord, and the other end of the cord was caught beneath one leg of Ivan Nikodimych's wicker-chair. The moment I got there I bought from the old man a pair of cherry-coloured pigeons with luscious tousled tails, and a pair of crowned pigeons, and put them away in a bag on my chest under my shirt. After these purchases I had only forty kopecks left, and for this price the old man was not prepared to let me have a male and female pigeon of the Kryukov breed. What I liked about Kryukov pigeons was their short, knobbly, good-natured beaks. Forty kopecks was the proper price, but the fancier insisted on haggling, averting from me a yellow face scorched by the unsociable passions of bird-snarers. At the end of our bargaining, seeing that there were no other customers, Ivan Nikodimych beckoned me closer. All went as I wished, and all went badly.

Towards twelve o'clock, or perhaps a bit later, a man in felt boots passed across the square. He was stepping lightly on swollen feet, and in his worn-out face lively eyes glittered.

'Ivan Nikodimych,' he said as he walked past the bird-fancier, 'pack up your gear. In town the Jerusalem aristocrats are being granted a constitution. On Fish Street Grandfather Babel has been constitutioned to death.'

He said this and walked lightly on between the cages like a barefoot ploughman walking along the edge of a field.

'They shouldn't,' murmured Ivan Nikodimych in his wake. 'They shouldn't!' he cried more sternly. He started collecting his rabbits and his peacock, and shoved the Kryukov pigeons at me for forty kopecks. I hid them in my bosom and watched the people running away from the bird market. The peacock on Ivan Nikodimych's shoulder was last of all to depart. It sat there like the sun in a raw autumnal sky; it sat as July sits on a pink riverbank, a white-hot July in the long cool grass. No one was left in the market, and not far off shots were rattling. Then I ran to the station, cut across a square that had gone topsy-turvy, and flew down an empty lane of trampled yellow earth. At the end of the lane, in a little wheeled armchair, sat the legless Makarenko, who rode about town in his wheel-chair selling cigarettes from a tray. The boys in our street used to buy smokes from him, children loved him, I dashed towards him down the lane.

'Makarenko,' I gasped, panting from my run, and I stroked the legless one's shoulder, 'have you seen Shoyl?'

The cripple did not reply. A light seemed to be shining through his coarse face built up of red fat, clenched fists, chunks of iron. He was fidgeting on his chair in his excitement, while his wife Kate, presenting a wadded behind, was sorting out some things scattered on the ground.

'How far have you counted?' asked the legless man, and moved his whole bulk away from the woman, as though aware in advance that her answers would be unbearable.

'Fourteen pairs of leggings,' said Kate, still bending over, 'six undersheets. Now I'm a-counting the bonnets.'

'Bonnets!' cried Makarenko, with a choking sound like a sob; 'it's clear, Catherine, that God has picked on me, that I must answer for all. People are carting off whole rolls of cloth, people have everything they should, and we're stuck with bonnets.'

And indeed a woman with a beautiful burning face ran past us down the lane. She was clutching an armful of fezes in one arm and a piece of cloth in the other, and in a voice of joyful despair she was yelling for her children, who had strayed. A

silk dress and a blue blouse fluttered after her as she flew, and
she paid no attention to Makarenko, who was rolling his chair
in pursuit of her. The legless man couldn't catch up. His
wheels clattered as he turned the handles for all he was worth.

'Little lady,' he cried in a deafening voice, 'where did you
get that striped stuff?'

But the woman with the fluttering dress was gone. Round
the corner to meet her leaped a rickety cart in which a peasant
lad stood upright.

'Where've they all run to?' asked the lad, raising a red rein
above the nags jerking in their collars.

'Everybody's on Cathedral Street,' said Makarenko plead-
ingly, 'everybody's there, sonny. Anything you happen to
pick up, bring it along to me. I'll give you a good price.'

The lad bent down over the front of the cart and whipped
up his piebald nags. Tossing their filthy croups like calves, the
horses shot off at a gallop. The yellow lane was once more
yellow and empty. Then the legless man turned his quenched
eyes upon me.

'God's picked on me, I reckon,' he said lifelessly; 'I'm a
son of man, I reckon.'

And he stretched a hand spotted with leprosy towards
me.

'What's that you've got in your sack?' he demanded, and
took the bag that had been warming my heart.

With his fat hand the cripple fumbled among the tumbler
pigeons and dragged to light a cherry-coloured she-bird.
Jerking back its feet, the bird lay still on his palm.

'Pigeons,' said Makarenko, and squeaking his wheels he
rode right up to me. 'Damned pigeons,' he repeated, and
struck me on the cheek.

He dealt me a flying blow with the hand that was clutching
the bird. Kate's wadded back seemed to turn upside down, and
I fell to the ground in my new overcoat.

'Their spawn must be wiped out,' said Kate straightening
up over the bonnets. 'I can't a-bear their spawn, nor their
stinking menfolk.'

She said more things about our spawn, but I heard nothing
of it. I lay on the ground, and the guts of the crushed bird

trickled down from my temple. They flowed down my cheek, winding this way and that, splashing, blinding me. The tender pigeon-guts slid down over my forehead, and I closed my solitary unstopped-up eye so as not to see the world that spread out before me. This world was tiny, and it was awful. A stone lay just before my eyes, a little stone so chipped as to resemble the face of an old woman with a large jaw. A piece of string lay not far away, and a bunch of feathers that still breathed. My world was tiny, and it was awful. I closed my eyes so as not to see it, and pressed myself tight into the ground that lay beneath me in soothing dumbness. This trampled earth in no way resembled real life, waiting for exams in real life. Somewhere far away Woe rode across it on a great steed, but the noise of the hoofbeats grew weaker and died away, and silence, the bitter silence that sometimes overwhelms children in their sorrow, suddenly deleted the boundary between my body and the earth that was moving nowhither. The earth smelled of raw depths, of the tomb, of flowers. I smelled its smell and started crying, unafraid. I was walking along an unknown street set on either side with white boxes, walking in a get-up of bloodstained feathers, alone between the pavements swept clean as on Sunday, weeping bitterly, fully and happily as I never wept again in all my life. Wires that had grown white hummed above my head, a watchdog trotted in front, in the lane on one side a young peasant in a waistcoat was smashing a window-frame in the house of Khariton Efrussi. He was smashing it with a wooden mallet, striking out with his whole body. Sighing, he smiled all around with the amiable grin of drunkenness, sweat, and spiritual power. The whole street was filled with a splitting, a snapping, the song of flying wood. The peasant's whole existence consisted in bending over, sweating, shouting queer words in some unknown, non-Russian language. He shouted the words and sang, shot out his blue eyes; till in the street there appeared a procession bearing the Cross and moving from the Municipal Building. Old men bore aloft the portrait of the neatly-combed Tsar, banners with graveyard saints swayed above their heads, inflamed old women flew on in front. Seeing the procession, the peasant pressed his mallet to his chest and dashed off in pursuit of the banners, while I, waiting till the tail-end of the procession had passed, made my furtive way home. The house was empty. Its white doors were open, the grass by the dovecot had been trampled down. Only Kuzma was still in the yard. Kuzma the yardman was sitting in the shed laying out the dead Shoyl.

'The wind bears you about like an evil wood-chip,' said the old man when he saw me. 'You've been away ages. And now look what they've done to granddad.'

Kuzma wheezed, turned away from me, and started pulling a fish out of a rent in grandfather's trousers. Two pike perch had been stuck into grandfather: one into the rent in his trousers, the other into his mouth. And while grandfather was dead, one of the fish was still alive, and struggling.

'They've done grandfather in, but nobody else,' said Kuzma, tossing the fish to the cat. 'He cursed them all good and proper, a wonderful damning and blasting it was. You might fetch a couple of pennies to put on his eyes.'

But then, at ten years of age, I didn't know what need the dead had of pennies.

'Kuzma,' I whispered, 'save us.'

And I went over to the yardman, hugged his crooked old back with one shoulder higher than the other, and over this back I saw grandfather. Shoyl lay in the sawdust, his chest squashed in, his beard twisted upwards, battered shoes on his bare feet. His feet, thrown wide apart, were dirty, lilac-coloured, dead. Kuzma was fussing over him. He tied the dead man's jaws and kept glancing over the body to see what else he could do. He fussed as though over a newly-purchased garment, and only cooled down when he had given the dead man's beard a good combing.

'He cursed the lot of 'em right and left,' he said, smiling, and cast a loving look over the corpse. 'If Tartars had crossed his path he'd have sent them packing, but Russians came, and their women with them, Rooski women. Russians just can't bring themselves to forgive. I know what Rooskis are.'

The yardman spread some more sawdust beneath the body, threw off his carpenter's apron, and took me by the hand.

'Let's go to father,' he mumbled, squeezing my hand tighter

and tighter. 'Your father has been searching for you since morning, sure as fate you was dead.'

And so with Kuzma I went to the house of the tax-inspector, where my parents, escaping the pogrom, had sought refuge.

Ivan Bunin

SUNSTROKE

TRANSLATED BY
MICHAEL GLENNY

IVAN BUNIN

Born in Voronezh 1870; died in Paris 1953. Russian writer, in exile after 1919. Stories: *The Grammar of Love* (1915), *The Gentleman from San Francisco* (1916). 'Sunstroke' was written in France in 1925.

SUNSTROKE

AFTER dinner they went out of the hot, brightly-lit dining saloon on to the deck and stood at the railing. She shut her eyes, laid her hand palm outward on her cheek, laughed a charming, natural laugh – everything about this little woman was charming – and said: 'I'm completely drunk. . . . In fact I'm quite out of my mind. Where have you come from? Three hours ago I wasn't even aware of your existence. I don't even know where you came on board. Was it at Samara? Anyway, who cares – I like you. Is this my head spinning or is the ship turning?'

Ahead lay darkness and lights. Out of the darkness a strong, warm wind blew into their faces as the lights flashed past to one side: with the helm hard over in the flashy Volga style the steamer was making a sweeping curve as it approached a small jetty.

The lieutenant took her hand, lifted it to his lips. The hand, small and strong, smelt of suntan. Half elated, half afraid, his heart gave a jump at the thought of how strong and brown her whole body must be under this light, plain linen dress after a whole month of lying under a southern sun on the hot sea sand (she had told him that she had come from Anapa). The lieutenant murmured:

'Let's get off . . .'

'Where?' she asked in surprise.

'At this landing.'

'Why?'

He said nothing. Again she laid the back of her hand to her hot cheek.

'You're mad . . .'

'Let's get off,' he repeated obstinately. 'I beg you . . .'

'All right, if you like,' she said, turning away.

As it swung inshore the steamer hit the dimly-lit jetty with a gentle thud and they almost fell over each other. The end of a hawser flew overhead, the ship went astern, there was a noisy thrashing of water, the gangplank clattered. . . . The lieutenant dashed to fetch their luggage.

A minute later they passed the sleepy ticket office, walked out and got into a dusty cab that stood hub-deep in the sand. The uphill climb, past the occasional crooked lamp-post and along a road soft with dust, seemed interminable. But at last they were at the top and were rattling along a roadway; then there was a square, the town hall, the fire-station, the warmth and the smells of a country town on a summer night. . . . The driver stopped outside a lighted porch; within its open doors rose an old, steep wooden staircase. A surly, unshaven old porter in a pink Russian shirt and a frock-coat picked up their luggage and tottered off ahead of them. They walked into a large but extremely stuffy room, roasting with the accumulated heat of a day's sunshine, white curtains drawn over its windows and two unlit candles on the dressing-table. As soon as they were in the room and the porter had shut the door, the lieutenant flung himself at her with such passion, they kissed each other in such a suffocating frenzy that they were to remember that moment for years to come: never in their lives had either of them known anything like it.

At ten o'clock next morning – a hot, cheerful, sunny morning full of the sound of church bells, with a market in the square in front of the hotel redolent of hay and tar and all the complex mixture of smells typical of a Russian country town – the little woman went away, still nameless, as she had never told him who she was but had jokingly called herself the beautiful stranger. They did not sleep much, but when she emerged from behind the screen beside the bed having washed and dressed in five minutes she was as fresh as a seventeen-year-old. Was she embarrassed? Hardly. She was as natural and gay as before and – already being sensible.

'No, my dear,' she had said when he had begged her that they should travel on together. 'No, you must stay here until the next steamer. If we went on together everything would be spoiled. And that would upset me very much. I promise you I'm not the sort of woman you must think I am. Nothing even faintly like this has ever happened to me before and never will again. It is just as if an eclipse had passed over me ... or rather as if we had both caught a touch of sunstroke ...'

Somehow the lieutenant found himself cheerfully agreeing with her. In light-hearted mood he drove her to the jetty, just in time to catch a pink-painted steamer of the 'Samolyot' line, kissed her on deck in front of everybody and just managed to jump on to the gangplank as it was being pulled back.

He was still as gay and carefree when he returned to the hotel. Already, though, there was a change. Without her the room was somehow quite different from the way it had seemed when she had been there. It was full of her, yet empty. Strange – it still smelled of her good English eau-de-cologne, her half-finished cup was still on the tray, yet she was gone. ... And the lieutenant's heart was gripped by such a sudden pang of tenderness that he hurriedly lit a cigarette and paced up and down the room a few times, slapping his boot-top with his swagger cane.

'Extraordinary!' he said aloud, laughing and feeling tears starting to his eyes. '"I promise you I'm not at all the sort of woman you must think I am. ..." And now she's gone. ... Ridiculous woman!'

The screen had been moved away, the bed was still unmade. He found it quite unbearable to look at that bed. He hid it with the screen, shut the window so that he would not hear the babble of the market-place and the creak of wheels, lowered the crumpled white curtains and sat on the divan. ... So his brief encounter was over and she was gone. By now she must be far away, probably sitting in the white glassed-in saloon or on deck watching the vast river glistening in the sunlight, the passing rafts, the yellow sandbanks, the shimmering expanse of water and sky, the immensity of the Volga. ... Goodbye, and for ever, for eternity. ... How could they ever meet again? 'I couldn't,' he thought, 'I just couldn't turn up in that town where she lives – with her husband, her three-year-old daughter, her family and the rest of her everyday life!' He thought of that town as a town in some way special, forbidden, and the thought of how she would have to go on living her lonely life there, perhaps often thinking of him, remembering their chance, transient encounter – this thought, that he would never see her again, bewildered and crushed him. No, it was impossible! It would be too stupid, too unnatural, too improbable! And he felt such pain at the futility of the rest of his life being spent without her that he was seized with horror and despair.

'What the hell!' he thought as he stood up, started to pace the room again and tried not to look at the bed behind the screen. 'What's the matter with me? It's not the first time, after all . . . anyway – what was so special about her and what actually happened? She was right, it really was something like sunstroke. The problem is now, though, how I'm going to spend a whole day here in this dreary hole without her?'

His memory of her was still total, down to the smallest detail. He remembered the perfume of her suntan and her linen dress, her strong body, the simple, bright, cheerful sound of her voice. . . . He could still sense, with remarkable force, the pleasure he had just experienced from her splendid body, but now another and quite new sensation was uppermost – a strange incomprehensible feeling which had simply not been there while they had been together, which he had never even suspected in himself yesterday when he had struck up what had seemed no more than an amusing acquaintance – and now there was no one, no one he could tell about it. 'And the worst of it is,' he thought, 'I shall never be able to tell her! What am I to do, how am I to live through this interminable day with all these memories, with this unrelieved agony, in this God-forsaken little town on the Volga, the same glittering Volga on which she was carried away by that pink steamer?'

He had to find some escape, do something, amuse himself, go somewhere. Firmly he put on his cap, picked up his swagger-stick, set off rapidly, spurs clinking, down the deserted corridor and ran down the steep staircase to the main entrance. Yes, but where should he go? Outside the front door stood a cab whose young driver, in a smart frock-coat, was calmly smoking a cheroot, and obviously waiting for somebody. The lieutenant stared at him in bewildered astonishment: how could anyone calmly sit like that on the box smoking, and be so simple, carefree and unconcerned? 'I suppose I'm the only person in this whole town who's so fearfully unhappy,' he thought as he set off towards the market.

The market was starting to pack up. Unthinking, he walked through fresh manure between the carts, past waggonloads of cucumbers, past new pots and pans as peasant women sitting on the ground competed for his attention, picked up bowls and tapped them, making them ring to show how sound they were. The farmers deafened him as they shouted 'Lovely cucumbers, sir!' It was all so stupid, so absurd that he fled from the market into the cathedral where the singing was loud, cheerful and firm, as if conscious of a duty done. Then he went for a long walk, going round and round the small, hot and unkempt little park on the cliff-top above the limitless, steely-bright expanse of the river. . . . His epaulettes and his tunic buttons had grown too hot to touch. The inside of the head-band of his cap was damp with sweat, his face burning. . . . Back at the hotel it was a relief to walk into the large, cool and empty ground-floor dining-room, a relief to take off his cap and sit down at a table beside the open window through which, although it was hot, there blew a draught of air. He ordered a plate of iced soup. All was well with the world, it was a place full of boundless happiness and great joy; even in this dull, unfamiliar little town and in this antiquated country hotel there was that joy, yet despite it all his heart was breaking. He drank several glasses of vodka, nibbling pickled gherkins between mouthfuls and feeling that he would die the next day without hesitation if only by some miracle she could be brought back, if he could spend just this one day with her – spend it simply to tell her and somehow prove to her, persuade her how agonizingly, how rapturously he loved her. . . . Why must he prove it? Why persuade her? He did not know why, but his need was stronger than life itself.

'My nerves are in shreds!' he said as he poured his fifth glass of vodka.

He drank a whole carafe, hoping to stupefy himself, stun himself, hoping that this state of painful exaltation would finally pass. But instead it grew worse.

He pushed his soup away, ordered some black coffee and started to smoke, thinking intently – what was he to do now, how was he to throw off this sudden, unexpected love? But, as he was all too keenly aware, there was no getting rid of it. Suddenly he jumped to his feet again, picked up his cap and swagger-stick, asked where the post office was and hurried off there with the wording of a telegram already in his head: 'Henceforth my whole life is in your hands forever, until death.' But when he reached the old thick-walled building that housed the post and telegraph office, he stopped in horror: he knew the town where she lived, knew that she had a husband and a three-year-old daughter, but he knew neither her surname nor her christian name. Several times he had asked her yesterday at dinner and in the hotel and each time she had laughed and said: 'But why do you have to know who I am? I'm Marya Morevna, the queen from over the water. . . . The beautiful stranger, if you like. . . . Isn't that enough?'

On the corner beside the post office was a photographer's shop-window. For a long time he stared at a large portrait of some army officer with extravagant epaulettes, a low forehead, gorgeous side-whiskers and a massive chest covered with medals. . . . How idiotic, how ridiculous, how terrible all the drab, humdrum things of everyday life are when your heart has been broken – for he realized now that his heart was broken – by a touch of that terrible 'sunstroke', by love, by happiness too great to be borne. He glanced at a newly-married couple – the young man in a long frock-coat and white tie, hair cut *en brosse*, standing rigidly at attention arm in arm with a girl in her wedding veil; he shifted his glance to the portrait of a pretty, eager girl with a student's cap perched on one side of her head. . . . Then, wracked with envy at all these unknown carefree people, he glared down the street.

'Where can I go? What can I do?' The leaden, insoluble question weighed on his mind. The street was completely deserted. The houses were all alike, white two-storeyed merchants' houses with large gardens, apparently completely empty. A thick white dust covered the roadway. Everything was dazzling, everything was smothered in hot, fiery, glorious yet somehow meaningless sunshine. In the distance the street climbed to a humpbacked rise and then dissolved into a horizon that was pure, cloudless and grey with a tinge of violet. There was something southern about it, something reminiscent of Sevastopol, Kerch ... Anapa. This was especially unbearable. Head down, screwing up his eyes from the glare, staring hard at his feet the lieutenant plodded back, tripping, stumbling, one spur catching against the other.

He returned to the hotel as exhausted as if he had finished a long march somewhere in Turkestan or the Sahara. Gathering what remained of his strength he went into his large, empty room. The room had been tidied, cleared of the last traces of her – only a single forgotten hairpin lay on the bedside table. He took off his tunic and looked at himself in the mirror: his face – a typical officer's face, dark with suntan, with a moustache bleached white by the sun and bluish whites of the eyes that looked even whiter against his tan – now had a disturbed, mad look and there was something boyish and deeply unhappy about his thin white shirt with its high, starched collar. He lay down on the bed, resting his dusty boots on the footboard. The windows were open, the curtains down, and now and again a faint breeze puffed them out, wafting into the room the hot breath of sweltering iron roofs and that whole luminescent world of the Volga country that was now totally empty, silent and deserted. He lay there with his hands clasped behind his head and stared hard into space ahead of him. Then he clenched his teeth and closed his eyelids as he felt tears rolling from under them down his cheeks – until at last he fell asleep. When he opened his eyes again, the reddish-yellow light of the evening sun was shining through the curtains. The wind had dropped, the room was as hot and airless as an oven. Today and the day before came back to him as though they had been ten years ago.

Unhurriedly he got up, unhurriedly washed, drew back the curtains, rang and sent for a samovar and his bill. He spent a long time drinking tea with lemon. Then he ordered a cab, had his luggage taken down and as he sat down on the cab's faded brown seat he gave the porter five whole roubles.

'I think it was me that brought you here, sir,' said the cabby cheerfully as he reached for the reins.

As they drove down towards the jetty the blue summer night had already settled over the Volga, countless coloured lights were scattered along the river and there were the masthead lights of the approaching steamer.

'Right on time,' said the driver ingratiatingly.

The lieutenant gave him five roubles too, bought a ticket, walked out along the landing-stage. As yesterday, there was a gentle thud against its piles and a faint sense of dizziness as it shook underfoot, then came the flying hawser, the sound of the water boiling and thrashing under the paddle-wheels as the ship went slowly astern. . . . And there was something extraordinarily welcoming, something good about this crowded steamer, lit up and smelling of cooking.

A minute later they were sailing away upstream, in the same direction that she had been carried away that morning.

Far ahead the rich summer afterglow was fading, its innumerable colours gently, dimly reflected in the river as an occasional ripple shimmered in the distance beneath it, beneath that glow, and the lights in the surrounding darkness drifted further and further astern.

The lieutenant sat down under an awning on deck, feeling ten years older.

Thomas Mann

DISORDER AND EARLY SORROW

TRANSLATED BY
H. T. LOWE PORTER

THOMAS MANN

Born in Lübeck 1875; died in Zürich 1955. The leading German novelist of his time, from *Buddenbrooks* (1901) to *Confessions of Felix Krull, Confidence Man* (1954): including notably *The Magic Mountain* and *Doctor Faustus*. 'Disorder and Early Sorrow' is a tale of the year 1925, when Mann and his family were living in Munich.

DISORDER AND EARLY SORROW

THE principal dish at dinner had been croquettes made of turnip greens. So there follows a trifle, concocted out of one of those dessert powders we use nowadays, that taste like almond soap. Xaver, the youthful manservant, in his outgrown striped jacket, white woollen gloves, and yellow sandals, hands it round, and the 'big folk' take this opportunity to remind their father, tactfully, that company is coming today.

The 'big folk' are two, Ingrid and Bert. Ingrid is brown-eyed, eighteen, and perfectly delightful. She is on the eve of her exams, and will probably pass them, if only because she knows how to wind masters, and even headmasters, round her finger. She does not, however, mean to use her certificate once she gets it; having leanings towards the stage, on the ground of her ingratiating smile, her equally ingratiating voice, and a marked and irresistible talent for burlesque. Bert is blond and seventeen. He intends to get done with school somehow, anyhow, and fling himself into the arms of life. He will be a dancer, or a cabaret actor, possibly even a waiter – but not a waiter anywhere else save at the Cairo, the night-club, whither he has once already taken flight, at five in the morning, and been brought back crestfallen. Bert bears a strong resemblance to the youthful manservant Xaver Kleinsgutl, of about the same age as himself; not because he looks common – in features he is strikingly like his father, Professor Cornelius – but by reason of an approximation of types, due in its turn to far-reaching compromises in matters of dress and bearing generally. Both lads wear their heavy hair very long on top, with a cursory parting in the middle, and give their heads the same character-istic toss to throw it off the forehead. When one of them leaves the house, by the garden gate, bareheaded in all weathers, in a blouse rakishly girt with a leather strap, and sheers off bent well over with his head on one side; or else mounts his push-bike – Xaver makes free with his employers, of both sexes, or even, in acutely irresponsible mood, with the Professor's own –

Dr Cornelius from his bedroom window cannot, for the life of him, tell whether he is looking at his son or his servant. Both, he thinks, look like young moujiks. And both are impassioned cigarette-smokers, though Bert has not the means to compete with Xaver, who smokes as many as thirty a day, of a brand named after a popular cinema star. The big folk call their father and mother the 'old folk' – not behind their backs, but as a form of address and in all affection: 'Hullo, old folks,' they will say; though Cornelius is only forty-seven years old and his wife eight years younger. And the Professor's parents, who lead in his household the humble and hesitant life of the really old, are on the big folk's lips the 'ancients'. As for the 'little folk', Ellie and Snapper, who take their meals upstairs with blue-faced Ann – so-called because of her prevailing facial hue – Ellie and Snapper follow their mother's example and address their father by his first name, Abel. Unutterably comic it sounds, in its pert, confiding familiarity; particularly on the lips, in the sweet accents, of the five-year-old Eleanor, who is the image of Frau Cornelius's baby pictures and whom the Professor loves above everything else in the world.

'Darling old thing,' says Ingrid affably, laying her large but shapely hand on his, as he presides in proper middle-class style over the family table, with her on his left and the mother opposite: 'Parent mine, may I ever so gently jog your memory, for you probably have forgotten: this is the afternoon we were to have our little jollification, our turkey-trot with eats to match. You haven't a thing to do but just bear up and not funk it; everything will be over by nine o'clock.'

'Oh – ah!' says Cornelius, his face falling. 'Good!' he goes on, and nods his head to show himself in harmony with the inevitable. 'I only meant – is this really the day? Thursday, yes. How time flies! Well, what time are they coming?'

'Half past four they'll be dropping in, I should say,' answers Ingrid, to whom her brother leaves the major role in all dealings with the father. Upstairs, while he is resting, he will hear scarcely anything, and from seven to eight he takes his walk. He can slip out by the terrace if he likes.

'Tut!' says Cornelius deprecatingly, as who should say: 'You exaggerate.' But Bert puts in: 'It's the one evening in the week Wanja doesn't have to play. Any other night he'd have to leave by half past six, which would be painful for all concerned.'

Wanja is Ivan Herzl, the celebrated young leading man at the Stadttheater. Bert and Ingrid are on intimate terms with him, they often visit him in his dressing-room and have tea. He is an artist of the modern school, who stands on the stage in strange and, to the Professor's mind, utterly affected dancing attitudes, and shrieks lamentably. To a professor of history, all highly repugnant; but Bert has entirely succumbed to Herzl's influence, blackens the lower rim of his eyelids – despite painful but fruitless scenes with the father – and with youthful carelessness of the ancestral anguish declares that not only will he take Herzl for his model if he becomes a dancer, but in case he turns out to be a waiter at the Cairo he means to walk precisely thus.

Cornelius slightly raises his brows and makes his son a little bow – indicative of the unassumingness and self-abnegation that befits his age. You could not call it a mocking bow or suggestive in any special sense. Bert may refer it to himself or equally to his so talented friend.

'Who else is coming?' next inquires the master of the house. They mention various people, names all more or less familiar, from the city, from the suburban colony, from Ingrid's school. They still have some telephoning to do, they say. They have to phone Max. This is Max Hergesell, an engineering student; Ingrid utters his name in the nasal drawl which according to her is the traditional intonation of all the Hergesells. She goes on to parody it in the most abandonedly funny and lifelike way, and the parents laugh until they nearly choke over the wretched trifle. For even in these times when something funny happens people have to laugh.

From time to time the telephone bell rings in the Professor's study, and the big folk run across, knowing it is their affair. Many people had to give up their telephones the last time the price rose, but so far the Corneliuses have been able to keep theirs, just as they have kept their villa, which was built before the war, by dint of the salary Cornelius draws as professor of history – a million marks, and more or less adequate to the chances and changes of post-war life. The house is comfortable, even elegant, though sadly in need of repairs that cannot

be made for lack of materials, and at present disfigured by
iron stoves with long pipes. Even so, it is still the proper
setting of the upper middle class, though they themselves look
odd enough in it, with their worn and turned clothing, and
altered way of life. The children, of course, know nothing
else; to them it is normal and regular, they belong by birth to
the 'villa proletariat'. The problem of clothing troubles them
not at all. They and their like have evolved a costume to fit the
time, by poverty out of taste for innovation: in summer it
consists of scarcely more than a belted linen smock and sandals.
The middle-class parents find things rather more difficult.

The big folk's table-napkins hang over their chair-backs, they
talk with their friends over the telephone. These friends are the
invited guests who have rung up to accept or decline or
arrange; and the conversation is carried on in the jargon of the
clan, full of slang and high spirits, of which the old folk
understand hardly a word. These consult together meantime
about the hospitality to be offered to the impending guests.
The Professor displays a middle-class ambitiousness: he wants
to serve a sweet – or something that looks like a sweet – after
the Italian salad and brown-bread sandwiches. But Frau
Cornelius says that would be going too far. The guests would
not expect it, she is sure – and the big folk, returning once
more to their trifle, agree with her.

The mother of the family is of the same general type as
Ingrid, though not so tall. She is languid; the fantastic difficulties of the housekeeping have broken and worn her. She
really ought to go and take a cure, but feels incapable; the floor
is always swaying under her feet, and everything seems upside
down. She speaks of what is uppermost in her mind: the eggs,
they simply must be bought today. Six thousand marks apiece
they are, and just so many are to be had on this one day of the
week at one single shop fifteen minutes' journey away. Whatever else they do, the big folk must go and fetch them immediately after luncheon, with Danny, their neighbour's son,
who will soon be calling for them; and Xaver Kleinsgutl will
don civilian garb and attend his young master and mistress.
For no single household is allowed more than five eggs a
week; therefore the young people will enter the shop singly,

one after another, under assumed names, and thus wring twenty eggs from the shopkeeper for the Cornelius family. This enterprise is the sporting event of the week for all participants, not excepting the moujik Kleinsgutl, and most of all for Ingrid and Bert, who delight in misleading and mystifying their fellow-men and would revel in the performance even if it did not achieve one single egg. They adore impersonating fictitious characters; they love to sit in a bus and carry on long lifelike conversations in a dialect which they otherwise never speak, the most commonplace dialogue about politics and people and the price of food, while the whole bus listens open-mouthed to this incredibly ordinary prattle, though with a dark suspicion all the while that something is wrong somewhere. The conversation waxes ever more shameless, it enters into revolting detail about these people who do not exist. Ingrid can make her voice sound ever so common and twittering and shrill as she impersonates a shop-girl with an illegitimate child, said child being a son with sadistic tendencies, who lately out in the country treated a cow with such unnatural cruelty that no Christian could have borne to see it. Bert nearly explodes at her twittering, but restrains himself and displays a grisly sympathy; he and the unhappy shop-girl entering into a long, stupid, depraved and shuddery conversation over the particular morbid cruelty involved; until an old gentleman opposite, sitting with his ticket folded between his index finger and his seal ring, can bear it no more and makes public protest against the nature of the themes these young folk are discussing with such particularity. He uses the Greek plural: 'themata'. Whereat Ingrid pretends to be dissolving in tears, and Bert behaves as though his wrath against the old gentleman was with difficulty being held in check and would probably burst out before long. He clenches his fists, he gnashes his teeth, he shakes from head to foot; and the unhappy old gentleman, whose intentions had been of the best, hastily leaves the bus at the next stop.

Such are the diversions of the big folk. The telephone plays a prominent part in them: they ring up any and everybody – members of government, opera singers, dignitaries of the Church – in the character of shop assistants, or perhaps as Lord or Lady Dolittle. They are only with difficulty persuaded that they have the wrong number. Once they emptied their parents' card-tray and distributed its contents among the neighbours' letter-boxes, wantonly, yet not without enough impish sense of the fitness of things to make it highly upsetting, God only knowing why certain people should have called where they did.

Xaver comes in to clear away, tossing the hair out of his eyes. Now that he has taken off his gloves you can see the yellow chain-ring on his left hand. And as the Professor finishes his watery eight-thousand-mark beer and lights a cigarette, the little folk can be heard scrambling down the stair, coming, by established custom, for their after-dinner call on Father and Mother. They storm the dining-room, after a struggle with the latch, clutched by both pairs of little hands at once; their clumsy small feet twinkle over the carpet, in red felt slippers with the socks falling down on them. With prattle and shout-ings each makes for his own place: Snapper to Mother, to climb on her lap, boast of all he has eaten, and thump his fat little tum; Ellie to her Abel, so much hers because she is so very much his; because she consciously luxuriates in the deep tenderness – like all deep feeling, concealing a melancholy strain – with which he holds her small form embraced; in the love in his eyes as he kisses her little fairy hand or the sweet brow with its delicate tracery of tiny blue veins.

The little folk look like each other, with the strong undefined likeness of brother and sister. In clothing and hair-cut they are twins. Yet they are sharply distinguished after all, and quite on sex lines. It is a little Adam and a little Eve. Not only is Snapper the sturdier and more compact, he appears consciously to emphasize his four-year-old masculinity in speech, manner and carriage, lifting his shoulders and letting the little arms hang down quite like a young American athlete, drawing down his mouth when he talks and seeking to give his voice a gruff and forthright ring. But all this masculinity is the result of effort rather than natively his. Born and brought up in these desolate, distracted times, he has been endowed by them with an unstable and hypersensitive nervous system and suffers greatly under life's disharmonies. He is prone to sudden anger and outbursts of bitter tears, stamping his feet at every trifle;

for this reason he is his mother's special nursling and care. His round, round eyes are chestnut brown and already inclined to squint, so that he will need glasses in the near future. His little nose is long, the mouth small – the father's nose and mouth they are, more plainly than ever since the Professor shaved his pointed beard and goes smooth-faced. The pointed beard had become impossible – even professors must make some concession to the changing times.

But the little daughter sits on her father's knee, his Eleonorchen, his little Eve, so much more gracious a little being, so much sweeter-faced than her brother – and he holds his cigarette away from her while she fingers his glasses with her dainty wee hands. The lenses are divided for reading and distance, and each day they tease her curiosity afresh.

At bottom he suspects that his wife's partiality may have a firmer basis than his own: that Snapper's refractory masculinity perhaps is solider stuff than his own little girl's more explicit charm and grace. But the heart will not be commanded, that he knows; and once and for all his heart belongs to the little one, as it has since the day she came, since the first time he saw her. Almost always when he holds her in his arms he remembers that first time: remembers the sunny room in the Women's Hospital, where Ellie first saw the light, twelve years after Bert was born. He remembers how he drew near, the mother smiling the while, and cautiously put aside the canopy of the diminutive bed that stood beside the large one. There lay the little miracle among the pillows: so well formed, so encompassed, as it were, with the harmony of sweet proportions, with little hands that even then, though so much tinier, were beautiful as now; with wide-open eyes blue as the sky and brighter than the sunshine – and almost in that very second he felt himself captured and held fast. This was love at first sight, love everlasting: a feeling unknown, unhoped for, unexpected – insofar as it could be a matter of conscious awareness; it took entire possession of him, and he understood, with joyous amazement, that this was for life.

But he understood more. He knows, does Dr Cornelius, that there is something not quite right about this feeling, so unaware, so undreamed of, so involuntary. He has a shrewd suspicion that it is not by accident it has so utterly mastered him and bound itself up with his existence; that he had – even subconsciously – been preparing for it, or, more precisely, been prepared for it. There is, in short, something in him which at a given moment was ready to issue in such a feeling; and this something, highly extraordinary to relate, is his essence and quality as a professor of history. Dr Cornelius, however, does not actually say this, even to himself; he merely realizes it, at odd times, and smiles a private smile. He knows that history professors do not love history because it is something that comes to pass, but only because it is something that *has* come to pass; that they hate a revolution like the present one because they feel it is lawless, incoherent, irrelevant – in a word, unhistoric; that their hearts belong to the coherent, disciplined, historic past. For the temper of timelessness, the temper of eternity – thus the scholar communes with himself when he takes his walk by the river before supper – that temper broods over the past; and it is a temper much better suited to the nervous system of a history professor than are the excesses of the present. The past is immortalized; that is to say, it is dead; and death is the root of all godliness and all abiding significance. Dr Cornelius, walking alone in the dark, has a profound insight into this truth. It is this conservative instinct of his, his sense of the eternal, that has found in his love for his little daughter a way to save itself from the wounding inflicted by the times. For father love, and a little child on its mother's breast – are not these timeless, and thus very, very holy and beautiful? Yet Cornelius, pondering there in the dark, descries something not perfectly right and good in his love. Theoretically, in the interests of science, he admits it to himself. There is something ulterior about it, in the nature of it; that something is hostility, hostility against the history of today, which is still in the making and thus not history at all, on behalf of the genuine history that has already happened – that is to say, death. Yes, passing strange though all this is, yet it is true; true in a sense, that is. His devotion to this priceless little morsel of life and new growth has something to do with death, it clings to death as against life; and that is neither right nor beautiful – in a sense. Though only the most fanatical asceticism could be capable on,

no other ground than such casual scientific perception, of
tearing this purest and most precious of feelings out of his
heart.

He holds his darling on his lap and her slim rosy legs hang
down. He raises his brows as he talks to her, tenderly, with a
half-teasing note of respect, and listens enchanted to her high,
sweet little voice calling him Abel. He exchanges a look with
the mother, who is caressing her Snapper and reading him a
gentle lecture. He must be more reasonable, he must learn self-
control; today again, under the manifold exasperations of life,
he has given way to rage and behaved like a howling dervish.
Cornelius casts a mistrustful glance at the big folk now and
then, too; he thinks it not unlikely they are not unaware of those
scientific preoccupations of his evening walks. If such be the
case they do not show it. They stand there leaning their arms
on their chair-backs and with a benevolence not untinctured
with irony look on at the parental happiness.

The children's frocks are of a heavy, brick-red stuff, embroidered in modern 'arty' style. They once belonged to Ingrid
and Bert and are precisely alike, save that little knickers come
out beneath Snapper's smock. And both have their hair bobbed.
Snapper's is a streaky blond, inclined to turn dark. It is bristly
and sticky and looks for all the world like a droll, badly fitting
wig. But Ellie's is chestnut brown, glossy and fine as silk, as
pleasing as her whole little personality. It covers her ears – and
these ears are not a pair, one of them being the right size, the
other distinctly too large. Her father will sometimes uncover
this little abnormality and exclaim over it as though he had
never noticed it before, which both makes Ellie giggle and
covers her with shame. Her eyes are now golden brown, set
far apart and with sweet gleams in them – such a clear and
lovely look! The brows above are blond; the nose still un-
formed, with thick nostrils and almost circular holes; the
mouth large and expressive, with a beautifully arching and
mobile upper lip. When she laughs, dimples come in her
cheeks and she shows her teeth like loosely strung pearls. So far
she has lost but one tooth, which her father gently twisted out
with his handkerchief after it had grown very wobbling.
During this small operation she had paled and trembled very

much. Her cheeks have the softness proper to her years, but they are not chubby; indeed, they are rather concave, due to her facial structure, with its somewhat prominent jaw. On one, close to the soft fall of her hair, is a downy freckle.

Ellie is not too well pleased with her looks – a sign that already she troubles about such things. Sadly she thinks it is best to admit it once for all, her face is 'homely'; though the rest of her, 'on the other hand', is not bad at all. She loves expressions like 'on the other hand'; they sound choice and grown-up to her, and she likes to string them together, one after the other: 'very likely', 'probably', 'after all'. Snapper is self-critical too, though more in the moral sphere: he suffers from remorse for his attacks of rage and considers himself a tremendous sinner. He is quite certain that heaven is not for such as he; he is sure to go to 'the bad place' when he dies, and no persuasions will convince him to the contrary – as that God sees the heart and gladly makes allowances. Obstinately he shakes his head, with the comic, crooked little peruke, and vows there is no place for him in heaven. When he has a cold he is immediately quite choked with mucus; rattles and rumbles from top to toe if you even look at him; his tempera-ture flies up at once and he simply puffs. Nursy is pessimistic on the score of his constitution: such fat-blooded children as he might get a stroke any minute. Once she even thought she saw the moment at hand. Snapper had been in one of his berserker rages, and in the ensuing fit of penitence stood himself in the corner with his back to the room. Suddenly Nursy noticed that his face had gone all blue, far bluer, even, than her own. She raised the alarm, crying out that the child's all too rich blood had at length brought him to his final hour; and Snapper, to his vast astonishment, found himself, so far from being rebuked for evil-doing, encompassed in tenderness and anxiety – until it turned out that his colour was not caused by apoplexy but by the distempering on the nursery wall, which had come off on his tear-wet face.

Nursy has come downstairs too, and stands by the door, sleek-haired, owl-eyed, with her hands folded over her white apron, and a severely dignified manner born of her limited intelligence. She is very proud of the care and training she gives her nurslings and declares that they are 'enveloping wonderfully'. She has had seventeen suppurated teeth lately removed from her jaws and been measured for a set of symmetrical yellow ones in dark rubber gums; these now embellish her peasant face. She is obsessed with the strange conviction that these teeth of hers are the subject of general conversation, that, as it were, the sparrows on the housetops chatter of them. 'Everybody knows I've had a false set put in,' she will say; 'there has been a great deal of foolish talk about them.' She is much given to dark hints and veiled innuendo: speaks, for instance, of a certain Dr Bleifuss, whom every child knows, and 'there are even some in the house who pretend to be him'. All one can do with talk like this is charitably to pass it over in silence. But she teaches the children nursery rhymes: gems like:

> Puff, puff, here comes the train!
> Puff, puff, toot, toot,
> Away it goes again.

Or that gastronomical jingle, so suited, in its sparseness, to the times, and yet seemingly with a blitheness of its own:

> Monday we begin the week,
> Tuesday there's a bone to pick.
> Wednesday we're half way through,
> Thursday what a great to-do!
> Friday we eat what fish we're able,
> Saturday we dance round the table.
> Sunday brings us pork and greens –
> Here's a feast for kings and queens!

Also a certain four-line stanza with a romantic appeal, unutterable and unuttered:

> Open the gate, open the gate
> And let the carriage drive in.
> Who is it in the carriage sits?
> A lordly sir with golden hair.

Or, finally that ballad about golden-haired Marianne who sat on a, sat on a, sat on a stone, and combed out her, combed out her, combed out her hair; and about bloodthirsty Rudolph, who pulled out a, pulled out a, pulled out a knife – and his ensuing direful end. Ellie enunciates all these ballads charmingly, with her mobile little lips, and sings them in her sweet little voice – much better than Snapper. She does everything better than he does, and he pays her honest admiration and homage and obeys her in all things except when visited by one of his attacks. Sometimes she teaches him, instructs him upon the birds in the picture-book and tells him their proper names: 'This is a chaffinch, Buddy, this is a bullfinch, this is a cowfinch.' He has to repeat them after her. She gives him medical instruction too, teaches him the names of diseases, such as infammation of the lungs, infammation of the blood, infammation of the air. If he does not pay attention and cannot say the words after her, she stands him in the corner. Once she even boxed his ears, but was so ashamed that she stood herself in the corner for a long time. Yes, they are fast friends, two souls with but a single thought, and have all their adventures in common. They come home from a walk and relate as with one voice that they have seen two moollies and a teenty-weenty baby calf. They are on familiar terms with the kitchen, which consists of Xaver and the ladies Hinterhofer, two sisters once of the lower middle class who, in these evil days, are reduced to living '*au pair*' as the phrase goes and officiating as cook and housemaid for their board and keep. The little ones have a feeling that Xaver and the Hinterhofers are on much the same footing with their father and mother as they are themselves. At least sometimes, when they have been scolded, they go downstairs and announce that the master and mistress are cross. But playing with the servants lacks charm compared with the joys of playing upstairs. The kitchen could never rise to the height of the games their father can invent. For instance, there is 'four gentlemen taking a walk'. When they play it Abel will crook his knees until he is the same height with themselves and go walking with them, hand in hand. They never get enough of this sport; they could walk round and round the dining-room a whole day on end, five gentlemen in all, counting the diminished Abel.

Then there is the thrilling cushion game. One of the children, usually Ellie, seats herself, unbeknownst to Abel, in his seat at table. Still as a mouse she awaits his coming. He draws near with his head in the air, descanting in loud, clear tones upon the surpassing comfort of his chair; and sits down on top of Ellie. 'What's this, what's this?' says he. And bounces about, deaf to the smothered giggles exploding behind him. 'Why have they put a cushion in my chair? And what a queer, hard, awkward-shaped cushion it is!' he goes on. 'Frightfully uncomfortable to sit on!' And keeps pushing and bouncing about more and more on the astonishing cushion and clutching behind him into the rapturous giggling and squeaking, until at last he turns round, and the game ends with a magnificent climax of discovery and recognition. They might go through all this a hundred times without diminishing by an iota its power to thrill.

Today is no time for such joys. The imminent festivity disturbs the atmosphere, and besides there is work to be done, and, above all, the eggs to be got. Ellie has just time to recite 'Puff, puff', and Cornelius to discover that her ears are not mates, when they are interrupted by the arrival of Danny, come to fetch Bert and Ingrid. Xaver, meantime, has exchanged his striped livery for an ordinary coat, in which he looks rather rough-and-ready, though as brisk and attractive as ever. So then Nursy and the children ascend to the upper regions, the Professor withdraws to his study to read, as always after dinner, and his wife bends her energies upon the sandwiches and salad that must be prepared. And she has another errand as well. Before the young people arrive she has to take her shopping-basket and dash into town on her bicycle, to turn into provisions a sum of money she has in hand, which she dares not keep lest it lose all value.

Cornelius reads, leaning back in his chair, with his cigar between his middle and index fingers. First he reads Macaulay on the origin of the English public debt at the end of the seventeenth century; then an article in a French periodical on the rapid increase in the Spanish debt towards the end of the sixteenth. Both these for his lecture on the morrow. He intends to compare the astonishing prosperity which accompanied the phenomenon in England with its fatal effects a hundred years earlier in Spain, and to analyse the ethical and psychological grounds of the difference in results. For that will give him a chance to refer back from the England of William III, which is the actual subject in hand, to the time of Philip II and the Counter-Reformation, which is his own special field. He has already written a valuable work on this period; it is much cited and got him his professorship. While his cigar burns down and gets strong, he excogitates a few pensive sentences in a key of gentle melancholy, to be delivered before his class next day: about the practically hopeless struggle carried on by the belated Philip against the whole trend of history: against the new, the kingdom-disrupting power of the Germanic ideal of freedom and individual liberty. And about the persistent, futile struggle of the aristocracy, condemned by God and rejected of man, against the forces of progress and change. He savours his sentences; keeps on polishing them while he puts back the books he has been using; then goes upstairs for the usual pause in his day's work, the hour with drawn blinds and closed eyes, which he so imperatively needs. But today, he recalls, he will rest under disturbed conditions, amid the bustle of preparations for the feast. He smiles to find his heart giving a mild flutter at the thought. Disjointed phrases on the theme of black-clad Philip and his times mingle with a confused consciousness that they will soon be dancing down below. For five minutes or so he falls asleep.

As he lies and rests he can hear the sound of the garden gate and the repeated ringing at the bell. Each time a little pang goes through him, of excitement and suspense, at the thought that the young people have begun to fill the floor below. And each time he smiles at himself again – though even his smile is slightly nervous, if tinged with the pleasurable anticipations people always feel before a party. At half past four – it is already dark – he gets up and washes at the wash-stand. The basin has been out of repair for two years. It is supposed to tip, but has broken away from its socket on one side and cannot be mended because there is nobody to mend it; neither replaced because no shop can supply another. So it has to be hung up above the vent and emptied by lifting in both hands and pouring out the water. Cornelius shakes his head over this basin, as he does several times a day – whenever, in fact, he has occasion to use it.

He finishes his toilet with care, standing under the ceiling light to polish his glasses till they shine. Then he goes downstairs.

On his way to the dining-room he hears the gramophone already going, and the sound of voices. He puts on a polite, society air; at his tongue's end is the phrase he means to utter: 'Pray don't let me disturb you,' as he passes directly into the dining-room for his tea. 'Pray don't let me disturb you' – it seems to him precisely the *mot juste;* towards the guests cordial and considerate, for himself a very bulwark.

The lower floor is lighted up, all the bulbs in the chandelier are burning save one that has burned out. Cornelius pauses on a lower step and surveys the entrance hall. It looks pleasant and cosy in the bright light, with its copy of Marées over the brick chimney-piece, its wainscoted walls – wainscoted in soft wood – and red-carpeted floor, where the guests stand in groups, chatting, each with his tea-cup and slice of bread and butter spread with anchovy paste. There is a festal haze, faint scents of hair and clothing and human breath come to him across the room, it is all characteristic and familiar and highly evocative. The door into the dressing-room is open, guests are still arriving.

A large group of people is rather bewildering at first sight. The Professor takes in only the general scene. He does not see Ingrid, who is standing just at the foot of the steps, in a dark silk frock with a pleated collar falling softly over the shoulders, and bare arms. She smiles up at him, nodding and showing her lovely teeth.

'Rested?' she asks, for his private ear. With a quite unwarranted start he recognizes her, and she presents some of her friends.

'May I introduce Herr Zuber?' she says. 'And this is Fräulein Plaichinger.'

Herr Zuber is insignificant. But Fräulein Plaichinger is a perfect Germania, blonde and voluptuous, arrayed in floating draperies. She has a snub nose, and answers the Professor's salutation in the high, shrill pipe so many stout women have.

'Delighted to meet you,' he says. 'How nice of you to come! A classmate of Ingrid's, I suppose?'

And Herr Zuber is a golfing partner of Ingrid's. He is in business; he works in his uncle's brewery. Cornelius makes a few jokes about the thinness of the beer and professes to believe that Herr Zuber could easily do something about the quality if he would. 'But pray don't let me disturb you,' he goes on, and turns towards the dining-room.

'There comes Max,' says Ingrid. 'Max, you sweep, what do you mean by rolling up at this time of day?' For such is the way they talk to each other, offensively to an older ear; of social forms, of hospitable warmth, there is no faintest trace. They all call each other by their first names.

A young man comes up to them out of the dressing-room and makes his bow; he has an expanse of white shirt-front and a little black string tie. He is pretty as a picture, dark, with rosy cheeks, clean-shaven of course, but with just a sketch of side-whisker. Not a ridiculous or flashy beauty, not like a gipsy fiddler, but just charming to look at, in a winning, well-bred way, with kind dark eyes. He even wears his dinner-jacket a little awkwardly.

'Please don't scold me, Cornelia,' he says; 'it's the idiotic lectures.' And Ingrid presents him to her father as Herr Hergesell.

Well, and so this is Herr Hergesell. He knows his manners, does Herr Hergesell, and thanks the master of the house quite ingratiatingly for his invitation as they shake hands. 'I certainly seem to have missed the bus,' says he jocosely. 'Of course I have lectures today up to four o'clock; I would have; and after that I had to go home to change.' Then he talks about his pumps, with which he has just been struggling in the dressing-room.

'I brought them with me in a bag,' he goes on. 'Mustn't tramp all over the carpet in our brogues – it's not done. Well, I was ass enough not to fetch along a shoe-horn, and I find I simply can't get in! What a sell! They are the tightest I've ever had, the numbers don't tell you a thing, and all the leather today is just cast iron. It's not leather at all. My poor finger' – he confidingly displays a reddened digit and once more characterizes the whole thing as a 'sell', and a putrid sell into the bargain. He really does talk just as Ingrid said he did, with a peculiar nasal drawl, not affectedly in the least, but merely because that is the way of all the Hergesells.

Dr Cornelius says it is very careless of them not to keep a shoe-horn in the cloak-room and displays proper sympathy with the mangled finger. 'But now you *really* must not let me disturb you any longer,' he goes on. '*Auf wiedersehen!*' And he crosses the hall into the dining-room.

There are guests there too, drinking tea; the family table is pulled out. But the Professor goes at once to his own little upholstered corner with the electric light bulb above it – the nook where he usually drinks his tea. His wife is sitting there talking with Bert and two other young men, one of them Herzl, whom Cornelius knows and greets; the other a typical 'Wandervogel' named Möller, a youth who obviously neither owns nor cares to own the correct evening dress of the middle classes (in fact, there is no such thing any more), nor to ape the manners of a gentleman (and, in fact, there is no such thing any more either). He has a wilderness of hair, horn spectacles, and a long neck, and wears golf stockings and a belted blouse. His regular occupation, the Professor learns, is banking, but he is by way of being an amateur folklorist and collects folk songs from all localities and in all languages. He sings them, too, and at Ingrid's command has brought his guitar; it is hanging in the dressing-room in an oilcloth case. Herzl, the actor, is small and slight, but he has a strong growth of black beard, as you can tell by the thick coat of powder on his cheeks. His eyes are larger than life, with a deep and melancholy glow. He has put on rouge besides the powder – those dull carmine highlights on the cheeks can be nothing but a cosmetic. 'Queer,' thinks the Professor. 'You would think a man would be one thing or the other – not melancholic and use face paint at the same time. It's a psychological contradiction. How can a melancholy man rouge? But here we have a perfect illustration of the abnormality of the artist soul-form. It can make possible a contradiction like this – perhaps it even consists in the contradiction. All very interesting – and no reason whatever for not being polite to him. Politeness is a primitive convention – and legitimate. . . . Do take some lemon, Herr Hofschauspieler!'

Court actors and court theatres – there are no such things any more, really. But Herzl relishes the sound of the title, notwith-standing he is a revolutionary artist. This must be another contradiction inherent in his soul-form; so, at least, the Professor assumes and he is probably right. The flattery he is guilty of is a sort of atonement for his previous hard thoughts about the rouge.

'Thank you so much – it's really too good of you, sir,' says Herzl, quite embarrassed. He is so overcome that he almost stammers; only his perfect enunciation saves him. His whole bearing towards his hostess and the master of the house is exaggeratedly polite. It is almost as though he had a bad conscience in respect of his rouge; as though an inward compulsion had driven him to put it on, but now, seeing it through the Professor's eyes, he disapproves of it himself, and thinks, by an air of humility towards the whole of unrouged society, to mitigate its effect.

They drink their tea and chat: about Möller's folk-songs, about Basque folk-songs and Spanish folk-songs; from which they pass to the new production of *Don Carlos* at the Stadt-theater, in which Herzl plays the title-role. He talks about his own rendering of the part and says he hopes his conception of the character has unity. They go on to criticize the rest of the cast, the setting, and the production as a whole; and Cornelius is struck, rather painfully, to find the conversation tending towards his own special province, back to Spain and the Counter-Reformation. He has done nothing at all to give it this turn, he is perfectly innocent, and hopes it does not look as though he had sought an occasion to play the professor. He wonders, and falls silent, feeling relieved when the little folk come up to the table. Ellie and Snapper have on their blue velvet Sunday frocks; they are permitted to partake in the festivities up to bed-time. They look shy and large-eyed as they say how-do-you-do to the strangers and, under pressure, repeat their names and ages. Herr Möller does nothing but gaze at them solemnly, but Herzl is simply ravished. He rolls his eyes up to heaven and puts his hands over his mouth; he positively blesses them. It all, no doubt, comes from his heart, but he is so addicted to theatrical methods of making an impression and getting an effect that both words and behaviour ring frightfully false. And even his enthusiasm for the little folk looks too much like part of his general craving to make up for the rouge on his cheeks.

The tea-table has meanwhile emptied of guests, and dancing is going on in the hall. The children run off, the Professor prepares to retire. 'Go and enjoy yourselves,' he says to Möller and Herzl, who have sprung from their chairs as he rises from his. They shake hands and he withdraws into his study, his peaceful kingdom, where he lets down the blinds, turns on the desk lamp, and sits down to his work.

It is work which can be done, if necessary, under disturbed conditions: nothing but a few letters and a few notes. Of course, Cornelius's mind wanders. Vague impressions float through it: Herr Hergesell's refractory pumps, the high pipe in that plump body of the Plaichinger female. As he writes, or leans back in his chair and stares into space, his thoughts go back to Herr Möller's collection of Basque folk-songs, to Herzl's posings and humility, to 'his' Carlos and the court of Philip II. There is something strange, he thinks about conversations. They are so ductile, they will flow of their own accord in the direction of one's dominating interest. Often and often he has seen this happen. And while he is thinking, he is listening to the sounds next door – rather subdued he finds them. He hears only voices, no sound of footsteps. The dancers do not glide or circle round the room; they merely walk about over the carpet, which does not hamper their movements in the least. Their way of holding each other is quite different and strange, and they move to the strains of the gramophone, to the weird music of the new world. He concentrates on the music and makes out that it is a jazz-band record, with various percussion instruments and the clack and clatter of castanets, which, however, are not even faintly suggestive of Spain, but merely jazz like the rest. No, not Spain. . . . His thoughts are back at their old round.

Half an hour goes by. It occurs to him it would be no more than friendly to go and contribute a box of cigarettes to the festivities next door. Too bad to ask the young people to smoke their own – though they have probably never thought of it. He goes into the empty dining-room and takes a box from his

supply in the cupboard: not the best ones, nor yet the brand
he himself prefers, but a certain long, thin kind he is not averse
to getting rid of – after all, they are nothing but youngsters. He
takes the box into the hall, holds it up with a smile, and deposits
it on the mantelshelf. After which he gives a look round and
returns to his own room.

There comes a lull in dance and music. The guests stand
about the room in groups or round the table at the window or
are seated in a circle by the fireplace. Even the built-in stairs,
with their worn velvet carpet, are crowded with young folk as
in an amphitheatre: Max Hergesell is there, leaning back with
one elbow on the step above and gesticulating with his free
hand as he talks to the shrill, voluptuous Plaichinger. The
floor of the hall is nearly empty, save just in the centre: there,
directly beneath the chandelier, the two little ones in their
blue velvet frocks clutch each other in an awkward embrace
and twirl silently round and round, oblivious of all else.
Cornelius, as he passes, strokes their hair, with a friendly word;
it does not distract them from their small solemn preoccupation.
But at his own door he turns to glance round and sees young
Hergesell push himself off the stair by his elbow – probably because he noticed the Professor. He comes down into the arena,
takes Ellie out of her brother's arms, and dances with her
himself. It looks very comic, without the music, and he
crouches down just as Cornelius does when he goes walking
with the four gentlemen, holding the fluttered Ellie as though
she were grown up, and taking little 'shimmying' steps. Everybody watches with huge enjoyment, the gramophone is put
on again, dancing becomes general. The Professor stands and
looks, with his hand on the door-knob. He nods and laughs;
when he finally shuts himself into his study the mechanical
smile still lingers on his lips.

Again he turns over pages by his desk lamp, takes notes,
attends to a few simple matters. After a while he notices that the
guests have forsaken the entrance hall for his wife's drawing-
room, into which there is a door from his own study as well.
He hears their voices and the sounds of a guitar being tuned.
Herr Möller, it seems, is to sing – and does so. He twangs the
strings of his instrument and sings in a powerful bass a ballad

in a strange tongue, possibly Swedish. The Professor does not succeed in identifying it, though he listens attentively to the end after which there is great applause. The sound is deadened by the portière that hangs over the dividing door. The young bank-clerk begins another song. Cornelius goes softly in.

It is half-dark in the drawing-room; the only light is from the shaded standard lamp, beneath which Möller sits, on the divan, with his legs crossed, picking his strings. His audience is grouped easily about; as there are not enough seats, some stand, and more, among them many young ladies, are simply sitting on the floor with their hands clasped round their knees or even with their legs stretched out before them. Hergesell sits thus, in his dinner jacket, next the piano, with Fräulein Plaichinger beside him. Frau Cornelius is holding both children on her lap as she sits in her easy-chair opposite the singer. Snapper, the Boeotian, begins to talk loud and clear in the middle of the song and has to be intimidated with hushings and finger-shakings. Never, never would Ellie allow herself to be guilty of such conduct. She sits there daintily erect and still on her mother's knee. The Professor tries to catch her eye and exchange a private signal with his little girl; but she does not see him. Neither does she seem to be looking at the singer. Her gaze is directed lower down.

Möller sings the 'joli tambour':

> *Sire, mon roi, donnez-moi votre*
> *fille –*

They are all enchanted. 'How good!' Hergesell is heard to say, in the odd, nasally condescending Hergesell tone. The next one is a beggar ballad, to a tune composed by young Möller himself; it elicits a storm of applause:

> Gipsy lassie a-goin' to the fair,
> Huzza!
> Gipsy laddie a-goin' to be
>   there –
> Huzza, diddlety umpty dido!

Laughter and high spirits, sheer reckless hilarity, reigns after this jovial ballad. 'Frightfully good!' Hergesell comments again, as before. Follows another popular song, this time a Hungarian one; Möller sings it in its own outlandish tongue, and most effectively. The Professor applauds with ostentation. It warms his heart and does him good, this outcropping of artistic, historic, and cultural elements all amongst the shimmying. He goes up to young Möller and congratulates him, talks about the songs and their sources, and Möller promises to lend him a certain annotated book of folk-songs. Cornelius is the more cordial because all the time, as fathers do, he has been comparing the parts and achievements of this young stranger with those of his own son, and being gnawed by envy and chagrin. This young Möller, he is thinking, is a capable bank-clerk (though about Möller's capacity he knows nothing whatever) and has this special gift besides, which must have taken talent and energy to cultivate. 'And here is my poor Bert, who knows nothing and can do nothing and thinks of nothing except playing the clown, without even talent for that!' He tries to be just; he tells himself that, after all, Bert has innate refinement; that probably there is a good deal more to him than there is to the successful Möller; that perhaps he has even something of the poet in him, and his dancing and table-waiting are due to mere boyish folly and the distraught times. But paternal envy and pessimism win the upper hand; when Möller begins another song, Dr Cornelius goes back to his room.

He works as before, with divided attention, at this and that, while it gets on for seven o'clock. Then he remembers a letter he may just as well write, a short letter and not very important, but letter-writing is wonderful for the way it takes up the time, and it is almost half past when he has finished. At half past eight the Italian salad will be served; so now is the prescribed moment for the Professor to go out into the wintry darkness to post his letters and take his daily quantum of fresh air and exercise. They are dancing again, and he will have to pass through the hall to get his hat and coat; but they are used to him now, he need not stop and beg them not to be disturbed. He lays away his papers, takes up the letters he has written, and goes out. But he sees his wife sitting near the door of his room and pauses a little by her easy-chair.

She is watching the dancing. Now and then the big folk or some of their guests stop to speak to her; the party is at its height, and there are more onlookers than these two: blue-faced Ann is standing at the bottom of the stairs, in all the dignity of her limitations. She is waiting for the children, who simply cannot get their fill of these unwonted festivities, and watching over Snapper, lest his all too rich blood be churned to the danger-point by too much twirling round. And not only the nursery but the kitchen takes an interest: Xaver and the two ladies Hinterhofer are standing by the pantry door looking on with relish. Fräulein Walburga, the elder of the two sunken sisters (the culinary section – she objects to being called a cook), is a whimsical, good-natured sort, brown-eyed, wearing glasses with thick circular lenses; the nose-piece is wound with a bit of rag to keep it from pressing on her nose. Fräulein Cecilia is younger, though not so precisely young either. Her bearing is as self-assertive as usual, this being her way of sustaining her dignity as a former member of the middle class. For Fräulein Cecilia feels acutely her descent into the ranks of domestic service. She positively declines to wear a cap or other badge of servitude, and her hardest trial is on the Wednesday evening when she has to serve the dinner while Xaver has his afternoon out. She hands the dishes with averted face and elevated nose – a fallen queen; and so distressing is it to behold her degradation that one evening when the little folk happened to be at table and saw her they both with one accord burst into tears. Such anguish is unknown to young Xaver. He enjoys serving and does it with an ease born of practice as well as talent, for he was once a 'piccolo'. But otherwise he is a thorough-paced good-for-nothing and windbag – with quite distinct traits of character of his own, as his long-suffering employers are always ready to concede, but perfectly impossible and a bag of wind for all that. One must just take him as he is, they think, and not expect figs from thistles. He is the child and product of the disrupted times, a perfect specimen of his generation, follower of the revolution, Bolshevist sympathizer. The Professor's name for him is the 'minute-man', because he is always to be counted on in any sudden crisis, if only it address his sense of humour or love of novelty, and will display therein amazing readiness and resource. But he utterly lacks a sense of duty and can as little be trained to the performance of the daily round and common task as some kinds of dog can be taught to jump over a stick. It goes so plainly against the grain that criticism is disarmed. One becomes resigned. On grounds that appealed to him as unusual and amusing he would be ready to turn out of his bed at any hour of the night. But he simply cannot get up before eight in the morning, he cannot do it, he will not jump over the stick. Yet all day long the evidence of this free and untrammelled existence, the sound of his mouth-organ, his joyous whistle, or his raucous but expressive voice lifted in song, rises to the hearing of the world above-stairs; and the smoke of his cigarettes fills the pantry. While the Hinterhofer ladies work he stands and looks on. Of a morning while the Professor is breakfasting, he tears the leaf off the study calendar – but does not lift a finger to dust the room. Dr Cornelius has often told him to leave the calendar alone, for he tends to tear off two leaves at a time and thus add to the general confusion. But young Xaver appears to find joy in this activity, and will not be deprived of it.

Again, he is fond of children, a winning trait. He will throw himself into games with the little folk in the garden, make and mend their toys with great ingenuity, even read aloud from their books – and very droll it sounds in his thick-lipped pronunciation. With his whole soul he loves the cinema; after an evening spent there he inclines to melancholy and yearning and talking to himself. Vague hopes stir in him that some day he may make his fortune in that gay world and belong to it by rights – hopes based on his shock of hair and his physical agility and daring. He likes to climb the ash tree in the front garden, mounting branch by branch to the very top and frightening everybody to death who sees him. Once there he lights a cigarette and smokes it as he sways to and fro, keeping a look-out for a cinema director who might chance to come along and engage him.

If he changed his striped jacket for mufti, he might easily dance with the others and no one would notice the difference. For the big folk's friends are rather anomalous in their clothing: evening dress is worn by a few, but it is by no means the rule.

There is quite a sprinkling of guests, both male and female, in the same general style as Möller the ballad-singer. The Professor is familiar with the circumstances of most of this young generation he is watching as he stands beside his wife's chair; he has heard them spoken of by name. They are students at the high school or at the School of Applied Art; they lead, at least the masculine portion, that precarious and scrambling existence which is purely the product of the time. There is a tall, pale, spindling youth, the son of a dentist, who lives by speculation. From all the Professor hears, he is a perfect Aladdin. He keeps a car, treats his friends to champagne suppers, and showers presents upon them on every occasion, costly little trifles in mother-of-pearl and gold. So today he has brought gifts to the young givers of the feast: for Bert a gold lead-pencil, and for Ingrid a pair of earrings of barbaric size, great gold circlets that fortunately do not have to go through the little ear-lobe, but are fastened over it by means of a clip. The big folk come laughing to their parents to display these trophies; and the parents shake their heads even while they admire – Aladdin bowing over and over from afar.

The young people appear to be absorbed in their dancing – if the performance they are carrying out with so much still concentration can be called dancing. They stride across the carpet, slowly, according to some unfathomable prescript, strangely embraced; in the newest attitude, tummy advanced and shoulders high, waggling the hips. They do not get tired, because nobody could. There is no such thing as heightened colour or heaving bosoms. Two girls may dance together or two young men – it is all the same. They move to the exotic strains of the gramophone, played with the loudest needles to procure the maximum of sound: shimmies, foxtrots, one-steps, double foxes, African shimmies, Java dances and Creole polkas, the wild musky melodies follow one another, now furious, now languishing, a monotonous Negro programme in unfamiliar rhythm, to a clacking, clashing, and strumming orchestral accompaniment.

'What is that record?' Cornelius inquires of Ingrid, as she passes by him in the arms of the pale young speculator, with reference to the piece then playing, whose alternate languors and furies he finds comparatively pleasing and showing a certain resourcefulness in detail.

'*Prince of Pappenheim:* "Console thee, dearest child,"' she answers, and smiles pleasantly back at him with her white teeth.

The cigarette smoke wreathes beneath the chandelier. The air is blue with a festal haze compact of sweet and thrilling ingredients that stir the blood with memories of green-sick pains and are particularly poignant to those whose youth – like the Professor's own – has been over-sensitive. . . . The little folk are still on the floor. They are allowed to stop up until eight, so great is their delight in the party. The guests have got used to their presence; in their own way, they have their place in the doings of the evening. They have separated, anyhow: Snapper revolves all alone in the middle of the carpet, in his little blue velvet smock, while Ellie is running after one of the dancing couples, trying to hold the man fast by his coat. It is Max Hergesell and Fräulein Plaichinger. They dance well, it is a pleasure to watch them. One has to admit that these mad modern dances, when the right people dance them, are not so bad after all – they have something quite taking. Young Hergesell is a capital leader, dances according to rule, yet with individuality. So it looks. With what aplomb can he walk backwards – when space permits! And he knows how to be graceful standing still in a crowd. And his partner supports him well, being unsuspectedly lithe and buoyant, as fat people often are. They look at each other, they are talking, paying no heed to Ellie, though others are smiling to see the child's persistence. Dr Cornelius tries to catch up his little sweetheart as she passes and draw her to him. But Ellie eludes him, almost peevishly; her dear Abel is nothing to her now. She braces her little arms against his chest and turns her face away with a persecuted look. Then escapes to follow her fancy once more.

The Professor feels an involuntary twinge. Uppermost in his heart is hatred for this party, with its power to intoxicate and estrange his darling child. His love for her – that not quite disinterested, not quite unexceptionable love of his – is easily wounded. He wears a mechanical smile, but his eyes have clouded, and he stares fixedly at a point in the carpet, between the dancers' feet.

'The children ought to go to bed,' he tells his wife. But she pleads for another quarter of an hour; she has promised already, and they do love it so! He smiles again and shakes his head, stands so a moment and then goes across to the cloak-room, which is full of coats and hats and scarves and overshoes. He has trouble in rummaging out his own coat and Max Hergesell comes out of the hall, wiping his brow.

'Going out, sir?' he asks, in Hergesellian accents, dutifully helping the older man on with his coat. 'Silly business this, with my pumps,' he says. 'They pinch like hell. The brutes are simply too tight for me, quite apart from the bad leather. They press just here on the ball of my great toe' – he stands on one foot and holds the other in his hand – 'it's simply unbearable. There's nothing for it but to take them off; my brogues will have to do the business. . . . Oh, let me help you, sir.'

'Thanks,' says Cornelius. 'Don't trouble. Get rid of your own tormentors. . . . Oh, thanks very much!' For Hergesell has gone on one knee to snap the fasteners of his snow-boots.

Once more the Professor expresses his gratitude; he is pleased and touched by so much sincere respect and youthful readiness to serve. 'Go and enjoy yourself,' he counsels. 'Change your shoes and make up for what you have been suffering. Nobody can dance in shoes that pinch. Goodbye, I must be off to get a breath of fresh air.'

'I'm going to dance with Ellie now,' calls Hergesell after him. 'She'll be a first-rate dancer when she grows up, and that I'll swear to.'

'Think so?' Cornelius answers, already half out. 'Well, you are a connoisseur, I'm sure. Don't get curvature of the spine with stooping.'

He nods again and goes. 'Fine lad,' he thinks as he shuts the door. 'Student of engineering. Knows what he's bound for, got a good clear head, and so well set up and pleasant too.' And again paternal envy rises as he compares his poor Bert's status with this young man's, which he puts in the rosiest light that his son's may look the darker. Thus he sets out on his evening walk.

He goes up the avenue, crosses the bridge, and walks along the bank on the other side as far as the next bridge but one. The air is wet and cold, with a little snow now and then. He turns up his coat-collar and slips the crook of his cane over the arm behind his back. Now and then he ventilates his lungs with a long deep breath of the night air. As usual when he walks, his mind reverts to his professional preoccupations, he thinks about his lectures and the things he means to say tomorrow about Philip's struggle against the Germanic revolution, things steeped in melancholy and penetratingly just. Above all just, he thinks. For in one's dealings with the young it behoves one to display the scientific spirit, to exhibit the principles of enlightenment – not only for purposes of mental discipline, but on the human and individual side, in order not to wound them or indirectly offend their political sensibilities; particularly in these days, when there is so much tinder in the air, opinions are so frightfully split up and chaotic, and you may so easily incur attacks from one party or the other, or even give rise to scandal, by taking sides on a point of history. 'And taking sides is unhistoric anyhow,' so he muses. 'Only justice, only impartiality is historic.' And could not, properly considered, be otherwise. . . . For justice can have nothing of youthful fire and blithe, fresh, loyal conviction. It is by nature melancholy. And, being so, has secret affinity with the lost cause and the forlorn hope rather than with the fresh and blithe and loyal – perhaps this affinity is its very essence and without it it would not exist at all! . . . 'And is there then no such thing as justice?' the Professor asks himself, and ponders the question so deeply that he absently posts his letters in the next box and turns round to go home. This thought of his is unsettling and disturbing to the scientific mind – but is it not after all itself scientific, psychological, conscientious, and therefore to be accepted without prejudice, no matter how upsetting? In the midst of which musings Dr Cornelius finds himself back at his own door.

On the outer threshhold stands Xaver, and seems to be looking for him.

'Herr Professor,' says Xaver, tossing back his hair, 'go upstairs to Ellie straight off. She's in a bad way.'

'What's the matter?' asks Cornelius in alarm. 'Is she ill?'

'No-o, not to say ill,' answers Xaver. 'She's just in a bad way and crying fit to bust her little heart. It's along o' that chap with the shirt-front that danced with her – Herr Hergesell. She couldn't be got to go upstairs peaceably, not at no price at all, and she's b'en crying bucketfuls.'

'Nonsense,' says the Professor, who has entered and is tossing off his things in the cloak-room. He says no more; opens the glass door and without a glance at the guests turns swiftly to the stairs. Takes them two at a time, crosses the upper hall and the small room leading into the nursery. Xaver follows at his heels, but stops at the nursery door.

A bright light still burns within, showing the gay frieze that runs all round the room, the large row of shelves heaped with a confusion of toys, the rocking-horse on his swaying platform, with red-varnished nostrils and raised hoofs. On the linoleum lie other toys – building blocks, railway trains, a little trumpet. The two white cribs stand not far apart, Ellie's in the window corner, Snapper's out in the room.

Snapper is asleep. He has said his prayers in loud, ringing tones, prompted by Nurse, and gone off at once into vehement, profound, and rosy slumber – from which a cannon-ball fired at close range could not rouse him. He lies with both fists flung back on the pillows on either side of the tousled head with its funny crooked little slumber-tossed wig.

A circle of females surrounds Ellie's bed: not only blue-faced Ann is there, but the Hinterhofer ladies too, talking to each other and to her. They make way as the Professor comes up and reveal the child sitting all pale among her pillows, sobbing and weeping more bitterly than he has ever seen her sob and weep in her life. Her lovely little hands lie on the coverlet in front of her, the nightgown with its narrow lace border has slipped down from her shoulder – such a thin, birdlike little shoulder – and the sweet head Cornelius loves so well, set on the neck like a flower on its stalk, her head is on one side, with the eyes rolled up to the corner between wall and ceiling above her head. For there she seems to envisage the anguish of her heart and even to nod to it – either on purpose or because her head wobbles as her body is shaken with the violence of her sobs. Her eyes rain down tears. The bow-shaped lips are parted, like a little *mater dolorosa*'s, and from them issue long, low wails that in nothing resemble the unnecessary and exasperating shrieks of a naughty child, but rise from the deep extremity of her heart and wake in the Professor's own a sympathy that is well-nigh intolerable. He has never seen his darling so before. His feelings find immediate vent in an attack on the ladies Hinterhofer.

'What about the supper?' he asks sharply. 'There must be a great deal to do. Is my wife being left to do it alone?'

For the acute sensibilities of the former middle class this is quite enough. The ladies withdraw in righteous indignation, and Xaver Kleingutl jeers at them as they pass out. Having been born to low life instead of achieving it, he never loses a chance to mock at their fallen state.

'Childie, childie,' murmurs Cornelius, and sitting down by the crib enfolds the anguished Ellie in his arms. 'What is the trouble with my darling?'

She bedews his face with her tears.

'Abel . . . Abel . . .' she stammers between sobs. 'Why – isn't Max – my brother? Max ought to be – my brother!'

Alas, alas! What mischance is this? Is this what the party has wrought, with its fatal atmosphere? Cornelius glances helplessly up at blue-faced Ann standing there in all the dignity of her limitations with her hands before her on her apron. She purses up her mouth and makes a long face. 'It's pretty young,' she says, 'for the female instincts to be showing up.'

'Hold your tongue,' snaps Cornelius, in his agony. He has this much to be thankful for, that Ellie does not turn from him now; she does not push him away as she did downstairs, but clings to him in her need, while she reiterates her absurd, bewildered prayer that Max might be her brother, or with a fresh burst of desire demands to be taken downstairs so that he can dance with her again. But Max, of course, is dancing with Fräulein Plaichinger, that behemoth who is his rightful partner and has every claim upon him; whereas Ellie – never, thinks the Professor, his heart torn with the violence of his pity, never has she looked so tiny and birdlike as now, when she nestles to him shaken with sobs and all unaware of what is happening in her little soul. No, she does not know. She does not comprehend that her suffering is on account of Fräulein Plaichinger, fat, overgrown, and utterly within her rights in dancing with Max Hergesell, whereas Ellie may only do it once, by way of a joke, although she is incomparably the more charming of the two. Yet it would be quite mad to reproach young Hergesell with the state of affairs or to make fantastic demands upon him. No, Ellie's suffering is without help or healing and must be covered up. Yet just as it is without understanding, so it is also without restraint – and that is what makes it so horribly painful. Xaver and blue-faced Ann do not feel this pain, it does not affect them – either because of native callousness or because they accept it as the way of nature. But the Professor's fatherly heart is quite torn by it, and by a distressful horror of this passion, so hopeless and so absurd.

Of no avail to hold forth to poor Ellie on the subject of the perfectly good little brother she already has. She only casts a distraught and scornful glance over at the other crib, where Snapper lies vehemently slumbering, and with fresh tears calls again for Max. Of no avail either the promise of a long, long walk tomorrow, all five gentlemen, round and round the dining-room table; or a dramatic description of the thrilling cushion games they will play. No, she will listen to none of all this, nor to lying down and going to sleep. She will not sleep, she will sit bolt upright and suffer. . . . But on a sudden they stop and listen, Abel and Ellie; listen to something miraculous that is coming to pass, that is approaching by strides, two strides, to the nursery door, that now overwhelmingly appears . . .

It is Xaver's work, not a doubt of that. He has not remained by the door where he stood to gloat over the ejection of the Hinterhofers. No, he has bestirred himself, taken a notion; likewise steps to carry it out. Downstairs he has gone, twitched Herr Hergesell's sleeve, and made a thick-lipped request. So here they both are. Xaver, having done his part, remains by the door; but Max Hergesell comes up to Ellie's crib; in his dinner-jacket, with his sketchy side-whisker and charming black eyes; obviously quite pleased with his role of swan knight and fairy prince, as one who should say: 'See, here am I, now all losses are restored and sorrows end.'

Cornelius is almost as much overcome as Ellie herself.

'Just look,' he says feebly, 'look who's here. This is uncommonly good of you, Herr Hergesell.'

'Not a bit of it,' says Hergesell. 'Why shouldn't I come to say good night to my fair partner?'

And he approaches the bars of the crib, behind which Ellie sits struck mute. She smiles blissfully through her tears. A funny, high little note that is half a sigh of relief comes from her lips, then she looks dumbly up at her swan knight with her golden-brown eyes – tear-swollen though they are, so much more beautiful than the fat Plaichinger's. She does not put up her arms. Her joy, like her grief, is without understanding; but she does not do that. The lovely little hands lie quiet on the coverlet, and Max Hergesell stands with his arms leaning over the rail as on a balcony.

'And now,' he says smartly, 'she need not "sit the livelong night and weep upon her bed"!' He looks at the Professor to make sure he is receiving due credit for the quotation. 'Ha ha!' he laughs, 'she's beginning young. "Console thee, dearest child!" Never mind, you're all right! Just as you are you'll be wonderful! You've only got to grow up. ... And you'll lie down and go to sleep like a good girl, now I've come to say good night? And not cry any more, little Lorelei?'

Ellie looks up at him, transfigured. One birdlike shoulder is bare; the Professor draws the lace-trimmed nighty over it. There comes into his mind a sentimental story he once read about a dying child who longs to see a clown he had once, with unforgettable ecstasy, beheld in a circus. And they bring the clown to the bedside marvellously arrayed, embroidered before and behind with silver butterflies; and the child dies happy. Max Hergesell is not embroidered, and Ellie, thank God, is not going to die, she has only 'been in a bad way'. But, after all, the effect is the same. Young Hergesell leans over the bars of the crib and rattles on, more for the father's ear than the child's, but Ellie does not know that – and the father's feelings towards him are a most singular mixture of thankfulness, embarrassment, and hatred.

'Good night, little Lorelei,' says Hergesell, and gives her his hand through the bars. Her pretty, soft, white little hand is swallowed up in the grasp of his big, strong, red one. 'Sleep well,' he says, 'and sweet dreams! But don't dream about me – God forbid! Not at your age – ha ha!' And then the fairy clown's visit is at an end. Cornelius accompanies him to the door. 'No, no, positively, no thanks called for, don't mention it,' he large-heartedly protests; and Xaver goes downstairs with him, to help serve the Italian salad.

But Dr Cornelius returns to Ellie, who is now lying down, with her cheek pressed into her flat little pillow.

'Well, wasn't that lovely?' he says as he smooths the covers. She nods, with one last little sob. For a quarter of an hour he sits beside her and watches while she falls asleep in her turn, beside the little brother who found the right way so much earlier than she. Her silky brown hair takes the enchanting fall it always does when she sleeps; deep, deep lie the lashes over the eyes that late so abundantly poured forth their sorrow; the angelic mouth with its bowed upper lip is peacefully relaxed and a little open. Only now and then comes a belated catch in her slow breathing.

And her small hands, like pink and white flowers, lie so quietly, one on the coverlet, the others on the pillow by her face – Dr Cornelius, gazing, feels his heart melt with tenderness as with strong wine.

'How good,' he thinks, 'that she breathes in oblivion with every breath she draws! That in childhood each night is a deep, wide gulf between one day and the next. Tomorrow, beyond all doubt, young Hergesell will be a pale shadow, powerless to darken her little heart. Tomorrow, forgetful of all but present joy, she will walk with Abel and Snapper, all five gentlemen, round and round the table, will play the ever-thrilling cushion game.'

Heaven be praised for that!

Colette

THE CAPTAIN

TRANSLATED BY
ENID McLEOD

COLETTE (SIDONIE-GABRIELLE)

Born at Saint-Sauveur-en-Puisaye (Yonne) 1873; died in Paris 1954. Novelist and memorialist of childhood, animals, the music-hall and her own emancipation. The novels include the series devoted to 'Claudine', *Chéri*, *The Cat* and *Gigi*. 'The Captain', dealing with her father, is from the volume mainly about her mother, *Sido* (1929).

THE CAPTAIN

IT seems strange to me, now, that I knew him so little. My attention, my fervent admiration, were all for Sido and only fitfully strayed from her. It was just the same with my father. His eyes dwelt on Sido. On thinking it over I believe that she did not know him well either. She was content with a few broad and clumsy truths: his love for her was boundless – it was in trying to enrich her that he lost her fortune – she loved him with an unwavering love, treating him lightly in everyday matters but respecting all his decisions.

All that was so glaringly obvious that it prevented us, except at moments, from perceiving his character as a man. When I was a child, what in fact did I know of him? That he was wonderfully skilful at building me 'cockchafers' houses' with glazed windows and doors, and boats too. That he sang. That he handed out to us – and hid too – coloured pencils, white paper, rosewood rulers, gold dust, and big, white sealing-wafers which I ate by the fistful. That he swam with his one leg faster and better than his rivals with all four limbs.

But I knew also that, outwardly at least, he took little interest in his children. 'Outwardly', I say. Since those days I have pondered much on the curious shyness of fathers in their relations with their children. Mine was never at ease with my mother's two eldest children by her first marriage – a girl with her head always full of romantic visions of heroes, so lost in legends that she was hardly present, and a boy who looked haughty but was secretly affectionate. He was naïve enough to believe that you can conquer a child with presents. He refused to recognize in his son, the 'lazzarone' as my mother called him, his own carefree musical extravagances. I was the one he set most store by, and I was still quite small when he began to appeal to my critical sense. Later on, thank goodness, I proved less precocious, but I well remember how severe a judge I was at ten years old.

'Listen to this,' my father would say, and I would listen,

very sternly. Perhaps it would be a purple passage of oratorical prose, or an ode in flowing verse, with a great parade of rhythm and rhyme, resounding as a mountain storm.

'Well?' my father would ask. 'I really believe that this time. . . . Go on, say!'

I would toss my head with its fair plaits, a forehead too high to look amiable, and a little marble of a chin, and let fall my censure: 'Too many adjectives, as usual!'

At that my father exploded, thundering abuse on me: I was dust, vermin, a conceited louse. But the vermin, unperturbed, went on: 'I told you the same thing last week, about the *Ode à Paul Bert*. Too many adjectives!'

No doubt he laughed at me behind my back, and I dare say he felt proud of me too. But at the moment we glared at each other as equals, already on a fraternal footing. There can be no doubt that it is his influence I am under when music or a display of dancing – not words, never words – move me to tears. And it was he, longing to express himself, who inspired my first fumbling attempts to write, and earned for me that most biting, and assuredly most useful praise from my husband. 'Can it be that I've married the last of the lyric poets?'

Nowadays I am wise enough, and proud enough too, to distinguish what in me is my father's lyricism, and what my mother's humour and spontaneity, all mingled and super-imposed; and to rejoice in a dichotomy in which there is nothing and no one to blush for on either side.

Yes, all we four children certainly made my father un-comfortable. How can it be otherwise in families where the father, though almost past the age for passion, remains in love with his mate? All his life long we had disturbed the tête-à-tête of which he had dreamed. Sometimes a pedagogic turn of mind can draw a father closer to his children. In the absence of affection, which is much rarer than is generally admitted, the vainglorious pleasure of teaching may bind a man to his sons. But Jules-Joseph Colette, though a cultivated man, made no parade of any learning. He had at first enjoyed shining for 'Her', but as his love increased, he came to abandon even his desire to dazzle Sido.

I could go straight to the corner of our garden where the

snowdrops bloomed. And I could paint from memory the climbing rose, and the trellis that supported it, as well as the hole in the wall and the worn flagstone. But I can only see my father's face vaguely and intermittently. He is clear enough sitting in the big, rep-covered armchair. The two oval mirrors of his open pince-nez gleam on his chest, and the red line of his peculiar lower lip, like a rolled rim, protrudes a little beneath the moustache which joins his beard. In that position he is fixed for ever.

But elsewhere he is a wandering, floating figure, full of gaps, obscured by clouds and only visible in patches. I can always see his white hands, particularly since I've begun to hold my thumb bent out awkwardly, as he did, and found my hands crumpling and rolling and destroying paper with explosive rage, just as his hands used to. And talking of anger! But I won't enlarge on my own rages which I inherit from him. One has only to go to Saint-Sauveur, and see the state to which my father reduced the marble chimney-piece there, with two kicks from his one foot.

I disentangle those things in me that come from my father, and those that are my mother's share. Captain Colette never kissed children; his daughter maintains that a kiss destroys their bloom. But if he did not often kiss me, at least he tossed me in the air, right up to the ceiling, which I warded off with both hands and knees, shrieking with delight. He had great muscular strength, controlled and dissimulated like a cat's, and no doubt it was maintained by a frugality which disconcerted our good neighbours in Lower Burgundy: bread, coffee, lots of sugar, half a glass of wine, any amount of tomatoes, and aubergines. When he was past seventy he consented to take a little meat, as a remedy. And sedentary though his life was, this southerner, with his satiny white skin, never put on flesh.

'Italian! Knife-man!' were the names my mother used to call him, when she was displeased with him, or when this faithful lover of hers suddenly revealed his outrageous jealousy. And it is a fact that, though he may never have killed anyone, my father always carried in his pocket a dagger whose horn handle concealed a spring. He despised firearms.

When he worked himself up into one of those sham southern

rages, he would give vent to growls and high-sounding oaths
to which we paid not the slightest attention. But how I trembled, on one occasion, at the melodious tone of his voice in
genuine fury! I was eleven at the time.

My mysterious half-sister had recently married by her own
choice, so unwisely and unhappily that she had nothing left to
hope for but death. She swallowed some kind of tablets and a
neighbour came to tell my mother. In twenty-odd years my
father and sister had never grown fond of each other. But at
the sight of Sido suffering, without raising his voice and in the
most honeyed tones, my father said:

'Go and tell *my* daughter's husband, tell Doctor R., that if
he does not save that child, by evening he will have ceased to
live.'

The suavity of his voice thrilled me. It was a wonderful
sound, full and musical as the song of an angry sea. If it had
not been for Sido's grief, I should have run dancing back to
the garden, cheerfully hoping for the richly deserved death of
Doctor R.

He was not only misunderstood, but unappreciated. 'That
incorrigible gaiety of yours!' my mother would exclaim, not
in reproach but astonishment. She thought he was gay because
he sang. But I who whistle whenever I am sad, and turn the
pulsations of fever, or the syllables of a name that torments me,
into endless variations on a theme, could wish she had understood that pity is the supreme insult. My father and I have no
use for pity; our nature rejects it. And now the thought of my
father tortures me, because I know that he possessed a virtue
more precious than any facile charms: that of knowing full well
why he was sad, and never revealing it.

It is true that he often made us laugh, that he told a good
tale, embroidering recklessly when he got into the swing of
it, and that melody bubbled out of him; but did I ever see him
gay? Wherever he went, his song preceded and protected him.
'*Golden sunbeams, balmy breezes* . . .' he would carol as he
walked down our deserted street, so that 'She' should not
guess, when she heard him coming, that Laroche, the Lamberts'
farmer, was impudently refusing to pay his rent, and that one

of this same Lambert's creatures had advanced my father – at
seven per cent interest for six months – a sum he could not do
without.

> By what enchantment, say, didst thou my heart beguile?
> When now I thee behold, methinks it was thy smile.

Who in the world could have believed that this baritone,
still nimble with the aid of crutch and stick, is projecting his
song like a smoke-screen in front of him, so as to detract
attention from himself? He sings in the hope that perhaps
today 'She' will forget to ask him if he has been able to borrow
a hundred louis on the security of his disabled officer's pension.
When he sings, Sido listens to him in spite of herself, and does
not interrupt him.

> This is the trysting-place of dames and knights,
> Who gather here within this charming glade,
> To pass their days in tasting the delights (*twice*)
> Of sparkling wine and love beneath the shade!
> (*three times*).

If, when he comes to the *grupetto*, the final long-drawn
organ note with a few high staccato notes added for fun, he
throws his voice right up against the walls of the rue de
l'Hospice, my mother will appear on the doorstep, scandalized
but laughing:

'Oh, Colette! In the street!' and after that he has only to
fire off two or three everyday ribaldries at one of the neighbouring young women, and Sido will pucker those sparse
Mona Lisa eyebrows of hers and banish from her mind the
painful refrain that never passes her lips: 'We shall have to
sell the Forge . . . sell the Forge . . . Heavens, must we sell the
Forge, as well as the Mées, the Choslins, and the Lamberts?'

Gay indeed, what real reason had he to be gay? Just as in
his youth he had desired to die gloriously in public, now he
needed to live surrounded by warm approval. Reduced now to
his village and his family, his whole being absorbed by the
great love that bounded his horizon, he was most himself with
strangers and distant friends. One of his old comrades-in-arms,
Colonel Godchot, who is still alive, has kept Captain Colette's
letters and repeats sayings of his. For this man who talked so

readily was strangely silent about one thing: he never related his military exploits. It was Captain Fournès and private Lefèvre, both of the First Zouaves, who repeated to Colonel Godchot some of my father's 'sayings' at the time of the war with Italy in 1859. My father, then twenty-nine years old, fell before Melegnano, his left thigh shot away. Fournès and Lefèvre dashed forward and carried him back, asking: 'Where would you like us to put you, Captain?'

'In the middle of the square, under the colours!'

He never told any of his family of those words, never spoke of that hour when he hoped to die, in the midst of the tumult and surrounded by the love of his men. Nor did he ever tell any of us how he had lain alongside 'his old Marshal' (Mac-Mahon). In talking to me he never referred to the one long illness I had. But now, twenty years after his death, I find that his letters are full of my name, and of the 'little one's' illness.

Too late, too late! That is always the cry of children, of the negligent and the ungrateful. Not that I consider myself more guilty than any other 'child', on the contrary. But while he was alive, ought I not to have seen through his humorous dignity and his feigned frivolity? Were we not worthy, he and I, of a mutual effort to know each other better?

He was a poet and a townsman. The country, where my mother seemed to draw sustenance from the sap of all growing things, and to take on new life whenever in stooping she touched the earth, blighted my father, who behaved as though he were in exile there.

We were sometimes scandalized by the sociability which urged him into village politics and local councils, made him stand for the district council and attracted him to those assemblies and regional committees where the human voice provokes an answering human roar. Most unfairly, we felt vaguely vexed with him for not being sufficiently like the rest of us, whose joy it was to be far from the madding crowd.

I realize now that he was trying to please us when he used to organize 'country picnics', as townsfolk do. The old blue victoria transported the family, with the dogs and eatables, to the banks of some pool – Moutiers, Chassaing, or the lovely little forest lake of Guillemette which belonged to us. My father was so much imbued with the 'Sunday feeling', that urban need to celebrate one day out of seven, that he provided himself with fishing-rods and camp-stools.

On arrival at the pool he would adopt a jovial mood quite different from his weekday jovial mood. He uncorked the bottle of wine gaily, allowed himself an hour's fishing, read, and took a short nap, while the rest of us, light-footed woodlanders that we were, used to scouring the countryside without a carriage, were as bored as could be, sighing, as we ate cold chicken, for our accustomed snacks of new bread, garlic, and cheese. The open forest, the pool, and the wide sky filled my father with enthusiasm, but only as a noble spectacle. The more he called to mind *the blue Titaresius and the silver gulf*, the more taciturn did we become – the two boys and I, that is – for we were already accustomed to express our worship of the woods by silence alone.

Only my mother, sitting beside the pool, between her husband and her children, seemed to derive a melancholy pleasure from counting her dear ones as they lay about her on the fine, reedy grass, purple with heather. Far from the importunate sound of doorbells, from the anxious, unpaid tradesmen, and insinuating voices, there she was with her achievement and her torment – with the exception of her faithless elder daughter – enclosed within a perfect circle of birches and oaks. Flurries of wind in the treetops passed over the circular clearing, rarely rippling the water. Domes of pinky mushrooms broke through the light silver-grey soil where the heather thrived, and my mother talked about the things that she and I loved best.

She told of the wild boars of bygone winters, of the wolves still known to exist in Puysaie and Forterre, and of the lean summer wolf which once followed the victoria for five hours. 'If only I had known what to give him to eat! I dare say he would have eaten bread. Every time we came to a slope he would sit down to let the carriage keep fifty yards ahead. The scent of him made the mare mad, so much so that it was nearly she who attacked him.'

'Weren't you frightened?'

'Frightened? No, not of that poor, big, grey wolf, thirsty

and famished under a leaden sun. Besides, I was with my first
husband. It was my first husband, too, who saw the fox
drowning its fleas one day when he was out shooting. Holding
on to a bunch of weeds with its teeth, it lowered itself backwards into the water very, very gradually until it was in right
up to its muzzle.'

Innocent tales and maternal instructions, such as the swallow,
the mother-hare, and the she-cat also impart to their young.
Delightful stories of which my father retained only the words
'my first husband', at which he would bend on Sido that grey-
blue gaze of his whose meaning no one could ever fathom. In
any case, what did the fox and the lily of the valley, the ripe
berry and the insect, matter to him? He liked them in books,
and told us their learned names, but passed them by out of
doors without recognizing them. He would praise any full-
blown flower as a 'rose', pronouncing the o short, in the
Provençal way, and squeezing as he spoke an invisible 'roz'
between his thumb and forefinger.

Dusk descended at last on our Sunday-in-the-country. By
then our number had often dropped from five to three: my
father, my mother, and I. The circular rampart of darkling
woods had swallowed up those two lanky, bony lads, my
brothers.

'We shall catch them up on the road home,' my father
would say.

But my mother shook her head: her boys never returned
except by cross-country paths and swampy blue meadows;
and then, cutting across sand-pits and bramble-patches, they
would jump over the wall at the bottom of the garden. She
was resigned to the prospect of finding them at home, bleeding
a little and a little ragged. She gathered up from the grass the
remains of the meal, a few freshly-picked mushrooms, the
empty tit's nest, the springy, cellular sponge made by a colony
of wasps, the bunch of wild flowers, some pebbles bearing the
imprint of fossilized ammonites, and the 'little one's' wide-
brimmed hat, while my father, still agile, jumped with a hop
like a wader's back into the victoria.

It was my mother who patted the black mare, offering her
yellowed teeth tender shoots, and wiped the paws of the

paddling dog. I never saw my father touch a horse. No curiosity ever impelled him to look at a cat or give his attention to a dog. And no dog ever obeyed him.

'Go on, get in!' his beautiful voice would order Moffino. But the dog remained where he was by the step of the carriage, wagging his tail coldly and looking at my mother.

'Get in, you brute! What are you waiting for?' my father repeated. 'I'm waiting for the *command*,' the dog seemed to reply.

'Go on, jump!' I would call to him; and there was never any need to tell him twice.

'That's very odd,' my mother would remark, to which my father retorted: 'It merely proves what a stupid creature the dog is.' But the rest of us did not believe a word of that, and at heart my father felt secretly humiliated.

Great bunches of yellow broom fanned out like a peacock's tail behind us in the hood of the old victoria. As we approached the village, my father would resume his defensive humming, and no doubt we looked very happy, since to look happy was the highest compliment we paid each other. But was not everything about us, the gathering dusk, the wisps of smoke trailing across the sky, and the first flickering star, as grave and restless as ourselves? And in our midst a man, banished from the elements that had once sustained him, brooded bitterly.

Yes, bitterly; I am sure of that now. It takes time for the absent to assume their true shape in our thoughts. After death they take on a firmer outline and then cease to change. 'So that's the real you? Now I see, I'd never understood you.' It is never too late, since now I have fathomed what formerly my youth hid from me: my brilliant, cheerful father harboured the profound sadness of those who have lost a limb. We were hardly aware that one of his legs was missing, amputated just below the hip. What should we have said if we had suddenly seen him walking like everyone else?

Even my mother had never known him other than supported by crutches, agile though he was and radiant with the arrogance of one in love. But she knew nothing, apart from his military exploits, of the man he was before he met her, the Saint-Cyr cadet who danced so well, the lieutenant tough as what in my native province we call a *bois-debout* – the ancient chopping-block, made of a roundel of close-grained oak that defies the axe. When she followed him with her eyes she had no idea that this cripple had once been able to run to meet every danger. And now, bitterly, his spirit still soared, while he remained sitting beside Sido with a sweet song on his lips.

Sido and his love for her were all that he had been able to keep. For him, all that surrounded them – the village, the fields, and the woods – was but a desert. He supposed that life went on for his distant friends and comrades. Once he returned from a trip to Paris with moist eyes because Davout d'Auerstaedt, Grand Chancellor of the Legion of Honour, had removed his red ribbon in order to replace it by a rosette.

'Couldn't you have asked me for it, old chap?'

'I never asked for the ribbon either,' my father answered lightly.

But his voice, when he described the scene to us, was husky. What was the source of his emotion? He wore the rosette, amply displayed in his button-hole, sitting up very straight in our old carriage with his arm lying on the cross-bar of his crutch. He would start showing off on the outskirts of the village, for the benefit of the first passers-by at Gerbaude. Was he dreaming of his old comrades in the division who marched without crutches and rode by on horseback, of Février and Désandré, and Fournès who had saved his life and still tactfully addressed him as 'my Captain'? Had he a vision of learned societies, of politics perhaps, and platforms, and all their dazzling symbols; a vision of masculine joys?

'You're so human!' my mother would sometimes say to him, with a note of indefinable suspicion in her voice. And so as not to wound him too much, she would add: 'You know what I mean, you always put your hand out to see if it's raining.'

His anecdotes were inclined to be ribald, but my mother's presence was enough to check the Toulon or Africa story on his lips. And although her own speech was piquant, she modestly toned it down in front of him. But sometimes when she was not thinking, she got carried away by a familiar rhythm and surprised herself quietly singing bugle calls whose words had been handed down unaltered from the imperial to the republican armies.

'Now we needn't feel embarrassed any longer,' remarked my father from behind the outspread sheets of *Le Temps*.

'Oh,' gasped my mother, 'I only hope the child didn't hear.'

'Oh, the child, it doesn't matter about her,' retorted my father. And he would fasten on his chosen one that extraordinary, challenging, grey-blue gaze of his, which revealed his secrets to no one, though sometimes admitting that such secrets existed.

When I am alone I try to imitate that look of my father's. Sometimes I succeed fairly well, especially when I use it to face up to some hidden hurt, which proves how efficacious insult can be against something that has you in its power, and how great is the pleasure of standing up to a tyrant: 'You may cause my death in the end, but I shall take as long as possible over it, never fear.'

'Oh, the child, it doesn't matter about her.' Well, that was frank enough, and what a challenge to his one and only love! All the same he liked me for certain characteristics in which, had he seen me more clearly, he might have recognized himself. Little by little he was losing the gift of observation and the power of comparison. I was not more than thirteen when I noticed that my father was ceasing to see, in the physical sense of the word, his Sido herself.

'Another new dress?' he would exclaim with surprise. 'Bless my soul, Madam!'

Taken aback, Sido would round on him in earnest: 'New? Oh come now, Colette, where are your eyes?' With two fingers she would take hold of the worn silk of a 'Sunday best' embroidered with jet. 'I've had it three years, Colette! D'you hear what I say? It's three years old! And there's life in it yet!' she added quickly, with a note of pride in her voice. 'Dyed navy blue . . .'

But he was no longer listening to her. He had already jealously rejoined her in some favourite spot, where she wore a chignon with Victorian side-curls, and a bodice with tulle ruching and a heart-shaped opening at the neck. As he grew older he could not even bear her to look tired or to be ill.

'Keep on now, keep on!' he would urge her, as though she were a horse that only he had the right to overwork. And she kept on.

I never surprised them in a passionate embrace. Who had imposed such reserve on them? Sido, most assuredly. My father would have had no such scruples about it. Always on the alert where she was concerned, he used to listen for her quick step, and bar her way:

'Pay up, or I won't let you pass!' he would order, pointing to the smooth patch of cheek above his beard. Pausing in her flight, she would 'pay' with a kiss as swift as a sting, and speed on her way, irritated if my brothers or I had seen her 'paying'.

Only once, on a summer day, when my mother was removing the coffee-tray from the table, did I see my father, instead of exacting the familiar toll, bend his greying head and bearded lips over my mother's hand with a devotion so ardent and ageless that Sido, speechless and as crimson with confusion as I, turned away without a word. I was still a child and none too pure-minded, being exercised as one is at thirteen by all those matters concerning which ignorance is a burden and discovery humiliating. It did me good to behold, and every now and again to remember afresh, that perfect picture of love: the head of a man already old, bent in a kiss of complete self-surrender on a graceful, wrinkled little hand, worn with work.

For a long time he was terrified lest she should die before he did. This is a thought common to lovers and truly devoted married people, a cruel hope that excludes any idea of pity. Before my father's death, Sido used to talk of him to me:

'I mustn't die before him, I simply must not. Can't you imagine how, if I let myself die, he'd try to kill himself, and fail? I know him,' she said, with the air of a young girl. She mused for a while, her eyes on the little street of Châtillon-Coligny, or the enclosed square of our garden. 'There's less chance of that with me, you see. I'm only a woman, and once past a certain age, a woman practically never dies of her own free will. Besides, I've got you as well and he hasn't.'

For she knew everything, even to those preferences that one never mentions. Far from being any support to us, my father was merely one of the cluster that clung round her and hung on to her arms.

She fell ill and he sat often near the bed. 'When are you going to get well? What day, what time do you think it will be? Don't you dare not to recover! I should soon put an end to my life!' She could not bear this masculine attitude, so threatening and pitiless in its demands. In her effort to escape, she turned her head from side to side on her pillow, as she was to do later when she was shaking off the last ties.

'My goodness, Colette, you're making me so hot!' she complained. 'You fill the whole room. A man's always out of place at a woman's bedside. Go out of doors! Go and see if the grocer's got any oranges for me. Go and ask Monsieur Rosimond to lend me the *Revue des Deux Mondes*. But go slowly, because it's thundery, otherwise you'll come back in a sweat!'

Thrusting his crutch up under his armpit, he did as she bade.

'D'you see?' said my mother, when he had gone, 'd'you notice how all the stuffing goes out of him when I'm ill?'

As he passed beneath her window he would clear his throat so that she could hear him:

> I think of thee, I see thee, I adore thee,
> At every moment, always, everywhere,
> My thoughts are of thee when the sun is rising,
> And when I close my eyes thy face is there.

'D'you hear him? D'you hear him?' she would say feverishly. Then her sense of mischief got the upper hand, making her whole face suddenly younger, and leaning out of bed she would say: 'Would you like to know what your father is? I'll tell you. Your father is the modern Orpheus!'

She recovered, as she always did. But when they removed one of her breasts and, four years later, the other, my father became terribly mistrustful of her, even though each time she recovered again. When a fish-bone stuck in her throat, making her cough so violently that her face turned scarlet and her eyes filled with tears, my father brought his fist down on the table, shivering his plate to fragments and bellowing: 'Stop it, I say!'

She was not misled by this, and she soothed him with compassionate tact, and comic remarks, and fluttering glances.

The words 'fluttering glance' always come to my lips when I am thinking of her. Hesitation, the desire to say something tender, and the need to tell a lie, all made her flutter her eyelids while her grey eyes glanced rapidly in all directions. This confusion, and the vain attempt of those eyes to escape from a man's gaze, blue-grey as new-cut lead, was all that was revealed to me of the passion which bound Sido and the Captain throughout their lives.

One day, ten years ago, at the suggestion of a friend I called at the house of Madame B., whose professional business is with 'spirits'. That is her word for what remains, in the air about us, of the departed, particularly of those who were closely bound to us by ties of blood and love. It must not be thought that I cherish any particular belief, nor even that I take special pleasure in the company of those privileged persons who are gifted with second sight. It is merely my curiosity, always the same, which impels me to go and see, indiscriminately and one after the other, Madame B., the 'woman-with-the-candle', the dog-who-can-count, the rose-bush with edible fruit, the doctor who adds human blood to my human blood, and I don't know what else. If ever I lose that curiosity you may as well bury me, for I shall have ceased to exist. One of my latest imprudences was concerned with the big hymenoptera of blue steel which abounds in Provence from July to August, when the sunflowers are in bloom. Vexed at not knowing the name of this steel-clad warrior, I kept asking myself: 'Has he or has he not got a sting? Is he merely a magnificent but sabreless samurai?' It is a great relief to have this uncertainty removed. A funny little disfigurement on the middle joint of one of my fingers is proof that the blue warrior is not only superbly armed, but quick on the draw.

At Madame B.'s I was agreeably surprised to find a modern, sunlit apartment. Birds were singing in a cage in the window, and children laughing in the next room. A pleasant, plump woman with white hair assured me that she had no need either of dim lights or a sinister setting. All she wanted was a moment of meditation, with my hand held between both of hers.

'Are there any questions you would like to put to me?' she

asked. I realized then that I was quite without any eagerness or desire for another world of any kind, or indeed any excessive wishes, and the only question I could think of was the commonplace: 'So you see the dead, do you? What do they look like?'

'Like the living,' Madame B. answered briskly. 'Behind you, for instance ...'

Behind me was the sunlit window and the cage of green canaries.

'... behind you the "spirit" of an old man is sitting. He has a spreading, untrimmed beard, nearly white, and rather long grey hair, brushed back. His eyebrows – my word, what eyebrows, extraordinarily bushy – and as for the eyes under them! They're small, but so brilliant one can hardly endure their gaze. Have you any idea who it might be?'

'Yes, indeed I have.'

'In any case he's a spirit in very good circumstances.'

'?'

'In very good circumstances in the spirit world. He's very much taken up with you. ... Don't you believe it?'

'I rather doubt it.'

'Well he is. He's very much taken up with you *at present*.'

'Why at present?'

'Because you represent what he would so much have liked to be when he was on earth. You are exactly what he longed to be. But he himself was never able.'

I shall not mention here the other portraits which Madame B. painted for me. Every one of them was remarkable, in my eyes, for some detail so striking and private that I was enchanted as though by a harmless and inexplicable piece of sorcery. Of one 'spirit' in whom I could not but recognize, feature by feature, my elder half-brother, she said compassionately: 'I've never seen a dead person so sad!'

'But,' I asked her, vaguely jealous, 'don't you see an old woman who might be my mother?'

Madame B.'s kind glance wandered all round me. 'No, I can't say I do,' she finally answered, adding quickly, as if to comfort me, 'Perhaps she's resting. That does happen sometimes. Are you the only child left?'

'I still have one brother.'

'That's it!' exclaimed Madame B., kindly. 'No doubt she's busy with him. A spirit can't be everywhere at once you know.'

I did not know. During the same visit I learned that intercourse with the departed is not hampered by daylight or everyday fun. 'They're like the living,' asserts Madame B., serene in her faith. Why not? Like the living except that they are dead. Dead – that's all. That was why she was astonished to see in my elder brother a dead person 'so sad'. But doubtless she was seeing him, through the transparent veil of my subconscious, as I had seen him when he was as though battered with blows by his last painful journey, careworn still and utterly exhausted, most sad indeed.

As for my father ... 'You are exactly what he longed to be, and in his lifetime he was never able.' There indeed is something for me to brood upon, something to touch my heart. I can still see, on one of the highest shelves of the library, a row of volumes bound in boards, with black linen spines. The firmness of the boards, so smoothly covered in marbled paper, bore witness to my father's manual dexterity. But the titles, handwritten in Gothic lettering, never tempted me, more especially since the black-rimmed labels bore no author's name. I quote from memory: *My Campaigns, The Lessons of '70, The Geodesy of Geodesies, Elegant Algebra, Marshal Mac-Mahon seen by a Fellow-Soldier, From Village to Parliament, Zouave Songs* (in verse) ... I forget the rest.

When my father died, the library became a bedroom and the books left their shelves.

'Just come and see,' my elder brother called one day. In his silent way, he was moving the books himself, sorting and opening them in search of a smell of damp-stained paper, of that embalmed mildew from which a vanished childhood rises up, or the pressed petal of a tulip still marbled like a tree-agate.

'Just come and see!'

The dozen volumes bound in boards revealed to us their secret, a secret so long disdained by us, accessible though it was. Two hundred, three hundred, one hundred and fifty pages to a volume; beautiful, cream-laid paper, or thick 'foolscap' carefully trimmed, hundreds and hundreds of blank pages. Imaginary works, the mirage of a writer's career.

There were so many of these virgin pages, spared through timidity or listlessness, that we never saw the end of them. My brother wrote his prescriptions on them, my mother covered her pots of jam with them, her granddaughters tore out the leaves for scribbling, but we never exhausted those cream-laid notebooks, his invisible 'works'. All the same my mother exerted herself to that end with a sort of fever of destruction: 'You don't mean to say there are still some left? I must have some for cutlet-frills. I must have some to line my little drawers with . . .' And this not in mockery but out of piercing regret and the painful desire to blot out this proof of incapacity.

At the time when I was beginning to write, I too drew on this spiritual legacy. Was that where I got my extravagant taste for writing on smooth sheets of fine paper, without the least regard for economy? I dared to cover with my large round hand-writing the invisible cursive script, perceptible to only one person in the world like a shining tracery which carried to a triumphant conclusion the single page lovingly completed and signed, the page that bore the dedication:

> TO MY DEAR SOUL,
> HER FAITHFUL HUSBAND:
> JULES-JOSEPH COLETTE

Cora Sandel

ALBERTA

TRANSLATED BY
ELIZABETH ROKKAN

CORA SANDEL

Born in Oslo 1880; living in Sweden since 1922. Norwegian novelist. 'Alberta' is from *Alberta and Freedom* (1931), the second volume of a trilogy, in which Cora Sandel draws on her experience as a painter in Paris before the First World War.

ALBERTA

THE furnishings were the depressing kind in brown-painted wood that seem inevitable in all administration. The light was poor and grey. There was a smell of poverty.

From old habit, perhaps from atavism, Alberta looked furtively about her on the way in and squeezed herself quickly through the door. Taking everything into consideration from childhood onwards, she was once more embarked on one of the small back ways of life. Once right in, such notions fell away as if she were throwing off a burdensome old garment. She was quite simply herself, and felt relieved. A failure, a little on the side-lines of life – yes. But so were the other people who came here. Nobody expected her to be any different, nobody was any more successful than herself. On the contrary, a quiet acknowledgement of life's difficulties, of the fact that it consists of alternatives, was in the air. The low-voiced people who gathered here recognized in each other reliable individuals, who gave guarantees, and they exchanged glances full of understanding and little smiles. No one needed to brace himself to persuade the others of facts.

The bench under the window was Alberta's habitual seat. She was away from the light, could see all who came in, and right into the little window where a bald head with grey bristling moustaches and spectacles appeared from time to time. The head directed its spectacles towards one or another of those waiting, mentioned a sum with a not unfriendly '*ça va?*' to follow. The person concerned would get up and go forward.

Taking everything into consideration, it was an obliging head. It looked at one seriously, but without disapproval. It was the same to everyone, to the lady who nervously and surreptitiously took a ring out of her handbag, to the woman fumbling with trifles in a knot of cloth. It listened to what people had to say and went to the trouble of giving explanations. Not all heads in windows did that.

She could trust it. When, for instance, it said '*Quarante francs,*

ça va?' Alberta made no objection. She took its infallibility
for granted in such matters, considering besides that if she
did not get an enormous sum, no enormous sum would be
demanded of her when it was time to come back again. And
all the little things she had been given at her confirmation or
which had been Mama's, the brooches, the rings, the necklace,
the watch, had disappeared into the unknown – the enormous,
grey complex of buildings that surrounded her and filled the
quartier.

What is property? In the final instance a piece of paper,
which renews your admittance to life for a while, a ticket to
it, so to speak. If your luck is in you celebrate it with a brief
reunion with something you thought you owned once. Round
the corner, in the rue de Regard, there was a door, a mysterious
place, where a sparse gathering, silent as a congregation
awaiting the miracle, sat on benches in rows. It was there.
There you bought dearly the illusion of owning your property
for a while. Putting it in was almost a more cheerful business
than taking it out, for you could never really afford the latter.

Money in your pocket makes your step light. It is a sort of
credential, giving one again the right to exist and look people
in the eyes, to do things that increase one's well-being and
self-respect: to ask them about prices, choose foodstuffs, take
them home and eat them, pay debts, smarten oneself up. On
the way across the courtyard Alberta reacted as she usually
did when she saw the word '*Matelas*' above a door: Thank
God I've not sunk as low as the mattress yet. I haven't one,
but even so. . . . She also noted with satisfaction that she had
no intention of turning the corner into the rue St Placide and
borrowing more money on the basis of her receipt. She was
not as depraved as all that.

The municipal guard in the gateway twirled his moustache
and smiled at Alberta as she passed. He did so out of good
nature. Alberta did not misinterpret it either, but smiled back
at him.

It was an evening in July following a completely still day.
The heat outside beat down on her sickeningly and suffocat-
ingly. The sun had gone from the street, but the asphalt gave
off heavy, accumulated warmth. Thick with the reek of fatigue,

dust, petrol and food, the air hung immovable between the walls.

Under the café awnings people were crowded round the small round marble tables. Blue syphons, golden, red or emerald liquids shone dully, sugar dripped glutinously into turbid absinthe, glasses and coolers were hazed over by quickly melting ice. The sight of a lump of ice sliding cool and smooth down into a vermouth reminded Alberta of a seal she had once seen at a circus. It had had a little rubber bath-tub to flop in and out of. It was immediately succeeded by another image, which floated up from hidden depths and remained for a second behind her eyes: a few small houses, half buried in snow under a grey sky, uninhabited, ice-cold.

Alongside the pavement the last fruit and vegetable barrows were moving slowly along under the impatient *'Avançons, messieursdames, avançons,'* of a policeman. A reek of decay, of things stored too long and slightly fermented, followed in their wake.

It was summer again, exhausted and cheapened, unaired and a little dirty, as it so quickly becomes in the paved streets. It breathes freely in parks and quiet residential districts; there, full of dark, melancholy sweetness it lets itself be surprised, but it yawns on the asphalt, trampled and soiled. Trees appear as if dying, animals and people half die. Alberta knew all about it, she had experienced it many times. For the first time she felt her courage flag on seeing it.

Slowly she wandered upwards, looked critically at the fruit barrows, studied the menu outside Léon's Restaurant, but left again. It was not the moment for extravagance, even though she had the rent, that nightmare of all the impecunious, in her pocket.

'Liesel!'

With her back towards Alberta, loaded with paper bags and parcels, Liesel was standing beside a late barrow, choosing from amongst the day's last squashed peaches. She started and looked up, her eyes wide in surprise, and collected the things she was carrying into one hand in order to give her hat a shove. It appeared to be losing its balance on top of her coiled-up hair. 'Albertchen! *Wie geht's?* It's close this evening, *aber so, nicht wahr?* That one and that one and that one, *ach nein*, not that one, it's rotten, but that one and that one.' Liesel picked and chose outspokenly from among the peaches. The fruitseller, a coarsely built woman with honest eyes and skin like copper, muttered something to the effect that if the customers were to take matters into their own hands trade would soon take a turn for the worse, then suddenly changed her mind and laughed: '*Enfin*, it's the end of the day, and Madame is charming. Here you are, over a pound, *ma petite*.' She handed Liesel the bag and winked at Alberta: 'Her husband's fortunate, he has a thrifty housekeeper and a charming *amie*, he'll have a good dessert this evening. And you, *ma petite dame*? A pound for you too, *n'est-cepas*?'

She filled another bag quickly. 'There, thirty centimes. They were fifty. I'm honest, I admit you couldn't offer them to the President of the Republic, but they are good, they are juicy, believe you me. You'll be satisfied.' Holding the coin Alberta handed her tightly between her teeth, she fumbled in her bag for change, and then wandered on with her barrow. 'Good evening, *mesdames, bonne chance*.'

Liesel blushed her pale blush. 'Did you hear what she said, Albertchen? It's just as if they can tell.'

'They say that sort of thing to anyone who's pretty, Liesel.'

'They can tell,' insisted Liesel. 'But they like it. Here it's the way it ought to be, not wrong as it is elsewhere. She saw very well that I had no ring. Look, not a single rotten one. I always got rotten ones before. *Am* I pretty, Albertchen?'

Timidly, with a shy little smile, Liesel produced this decisive question. At the same time she stopped, loaded Alberta with her bags, drew out her hatpins and stuck them in again differently, brushed dust off her dress. And Alberta, who knew what it was all about, and honestly thought Liesel was pretty besides, nodded in confirmation: 'Yes, of course you are.'

There was no doubt as to where Liesel was going. The days were past when she was on her way to Alberta's, or on her way home to light the spirit stove. Feeling a little flat, a little left behind and out of things, Alberta thought: Liesel might ask how I am. But Liesel said: 'I was looking at the hats in the window on the other side of the street. You know, the place where they're all the same price, four ninety-five. But they're so boring, Albertchen, so *bürgerlich*. The ones we put together ourselves look better, more artistic, *nicht wahr*? There's one in Bon Marché – Marushka said she'd help me with it. It only needs a flower or two, *fertig*. But fourteen francs just for the form, *unmöglich*. Especially now. I've done something very reckless, Albertchen.'

'You're always doing something reckless.' The words came out of Alberta's mouth unintentionally, from fatigue, half-teasingly. She regretted them instantly. Liesel's face seemed to fall for a second. At any rate she said in a thin little voice: 'It's true, I *am* reckless. Not a month goes by but I'm in torture – but in *torture*. And yet it's been no more than two so far.'

Faces she had watched turn miserable here on Montparnasse, disappear and turn up again even more miserable – or simply disappear, paraded before Alberta. Indifferent, casual words from street corners and cafés rang in her ears: 'Mm – yes – things went badly for her, you understand – she got pregnant.'

Cold alarm for Liesel gripped her. Then she thought: After all, it's Eliel, Eliel's decent and kind. And simultaneously Liesel said firmly and with intensity: 'I've only done what I had to do. It's as natural as being alive. I'm in *love* with him, Albertchen, I'm in *love* with Eliel. You see how mad I am to say it out loud in the street.'

Liesel's little confession was completely drowned by the traffic, a lorry thundering past making it as inaudible as a sigh in an avalanche. Nobody had heard it besides Alberta. Nevertheless Liesel looked about her fearfully and ascertained with relief: 'No one we know, *Gott sei Dank*.'

It was a fact that the most incredible things, truth and untruth in confusion, leaked out from Montparnasse to the rest of the world, finding and causing alarm to unsuspecting relatives, even as far away as America, giving rise to turmoil and catastrophe. It probably would not take long for a rumour to reach Liesel's cabinet-sized family. They were quite obviously unsuited to receive news of this kind.

'They think you ought to be married *und so weiter*,' said

Liesel, as if Alberta had spoken aloud. 'They might decide to come, and disturb Eliel.'

And Eliel must not be disturbed. He was so gifted. Someone was supposed to have used the word genius once at the Versailles. Besides, he was ill-suited to dramatic conflict, it was quite unthinkable that he should be involved in any such thing. Liesel emphasized still further the gravity of the case: 'No one knows besides yourself, Albertchen, no one, and you will be careful, won't you?'

'Of course I shall, Liesel.' Alberta was not the kind of person to give anyone away. Keeping silent was one of the things she really knew how to do. It offended her a little to have it enjoined on her. Coldly she asked, 'Where have you been?'

Liesel smiled her new, disingenuous smile: 'I told you I'd done something reckless – yet again.'

Alberta looked her up and down. She was wearing her eternal black. The dust showed up terribly on it in summer. Altogether it was ill-suited to the time of year, and Liesel was perspiring, pale with the heat. Alberta noticed that it had been cut down still more, the sleeves only reached to the elbow. Her hat was the faded violet one from last year, enormous, as fashion had then demanded, with small red roses round it. Liesel's bags clearly contained food from the barrows. But from her little finger there dangled a light little package.

'You're looking at my dress, Albertchen. Should I have left the sleeves alone?'

'No, no. What's *that*, Liesel?'

'You'll never guess.'

'Something from Bon Marché?'

'*Gar nicht, gar nicht.*'

'Then I don't know.' Alberta was suddenly tired of the joke. The money she had in her pocket no longer had any effect on her; she felt superfluous and futile. But beside her Liesel was saying: 'I *want* to be beautiful, Albertchen, I want to be beautiful now. I want to be ...' She looked round inquiringly and found a word that expressed her thought: '*Troublante. Troublante*, like the Parisian women. You can laugh, *aber* ...'

'*Troublante* is the right word. That's what we want to be. It's just that we're not properly equipped.'

'There, you see. Albertchen!' Liesel's voice assumed a confidential tone. 'I've just come from *"Cent Mille Chemises"* – *Hunderttausend Chemisen*. I've bought a frilly nightie, *ganz allerliebst*, nineteen francs ninety-five.'

Liesel nodded in the direction of the little package. But Alberta, who knew no better than that Liesel's wardrobe cried out for other replacements, and who was in addition short-sighted and stupid, exclaimed from an honest heart: 'Have you become a millionaire or completely mad?'

'Mad, Albertchen, mad, not a millionaire. I haven't the rent for the fifteenth, but still . . .' A shadow passed over Liesel's face, then she suddenly exclaimed: 'It can't be helped, Albertchen!'

Her voice became still more confidential, filled with fervent, repressed emotion: 'I'm going to stay with him all night, for the first time. I'm not going to get dressed and go home again. We shall sleep together and wake together. It'll be more proper, more natural, won't it? I've wanted it all the time. One *wants* it, Albertchen.'

The tram to Fontenay aux Roses came into view at the bottom of the street, and Liesel set off for the tram stop at top speed. 'I *must* catch it. He *never* eats a proper *déjeuner*, only sardines *und so was*. I *must* get hold of a chop before they close out there. I've got the mayonnaise and ham and Brie and fruit here. You'll come out soon, won't you, Albertchen? Just imagine, he hopes to sell the group – the small, patinated one. Then we'll go away to St Jean du Doigt – as long as Potter or Marushka don't decided on the same place. He wants to make sketches of me in plastolin, he says I resemble a Cranach, that I've given him an idea! For a large figure, Albertchen!' In all her busyness Liesel found time to look up at Alberta significantly. Her life was no longer uninteresting, she was everything, she was a Muse. She had the right to ask for a little assistance with nondescript everyday matters. 'Oh, would you mind taking a coupon for me, please?'

Alberta took the coupon, and Liesel mounted the congested tramcar, hot and flustered, her hat awry. Struggling to protect herself and her packages she stood in the crush on the platform, jostled back and forth, out of breath and radiant. Her breast rose and fell, her lips glowed as if painted. A couple of youths with cigarettes stuck in the corners of their mouths nodded at each other, and exchanged complimentary remarks: 'She's charming, *la petite*, very charming – if only it was worth the trouble of paying court to her.'

It was clear to everyone that it was not worth the trouble. A motherly old soul made room for her: 'Here you are, *ma petite dame*, you can stand more easily here with everything you've got to carry. I know what it's like to take the tramcar at this time of day, when one has done one's shopping.'

Liesel became even more radiant, in happy connivance with the whole world. She looked down with emotion at Alberta, left alone and probably looking a little pathetic. Just as the tramcar started to move, Liesel had an impulse. She leaned out and whispered at the last minute: 'You should find someone, Albertchen – Marushka is right – you should . . .'

Her final words were swallowed up by the noise. Liesel was gone.

Up in her room Alberta gasped in the enclosed atmosphere that met her. Quickly and roughly as if in desperation she tore off her clothes, threw them on to the bed and rubbed herself down with a sponge. Then she lighted the spirit stove, sat down naked among her clothes and sucked peach after peach.

At first she thought about nothing at all, keeping hateful thoughts successfully at a distance. They can resemble greedy birds round carrion. They circle round you in narrower and narrower rings. You throw them off, they return once more. Finally they alight on you, flapping their dark wings and hooting in your ears. They tear at your heart with their sharp beaks, and your heart writhes in pain, and sometimes stops.

For the time being Alberta had sufficient food. After the peaches came the eternal eggs. She stuffed bread into her mouth while she waited for them to boil, then ate and cleared away, threw a kimono round herself and opened the door out on to the stairs, leaving it wide open.

The staircase windows were open on to the minute court-yard, deep as a well. It was dinner-time and the house was quiet. The sound of forks could be heard from downstairs in Monsieur's and Madame's apartment and the clink of dishes from the kitchen. Looking over the banisters she could see Jean and the new *garçon* going downstairs for their meal. They buttoned up their waistcoats on the way and smoothed down their hair with their fingers.

She sniffed towards the draught which she hoped would come. But the heavy, dead air did not move. Nothing moved, nothing could be heard, but the light scattered sounds of cutlery and the muffled noise of the street. Nevertheless Alberta paced between the window and the door as if on guard, listening, prepared to turn the key in the lock instantly.

She was used to the summer emptiness of the upper storeys and knew its dangers and advantages. These depended to a certain extent on the menservants, whose rooms were also up in the roof. But here there was only respectable Jean trudging round. She had nothing to fear from that quarter, nor from the couple farther down the corridor.

But the unexpected can happen.

She remembered an evening last year, heavy, suffocating, with peals of thunder far away. The demands of the body for fresh air, dammed up in her summer after summer, had all of a sudden become unbearable. Carelessly she had thrown the door wide open and stood on a chair, naked under the kimono, with her head out of the skylight, inhaling through every pore the small puffs of wind that moved now and again across the rooftops. The countless rows of yellow chimneys were pallid beneath the gathering storm. To the south, above Vanves and Malakoff, the metallic sky exploded in flash after flash of lightning, and an occasional violent gust of wind promised release. She seemed to feel how her blood drank the air in her lungs and flowed on, giving life to the dry network of veins. The draught played with the light material of the kimono, fluttering it momentarily. She was bathed in air, inside and out, and mind and body expanded to receive it. On a corner of the boulevard she could see the dry curled-up leaves, which the exhausted city trees strew about themselves

at the height of summer, swarming along the pavement,
all in the same direction, like scattered Lilliputian armies in
flight. The whine of the trains at Montparnasse cut through
the air.

Then her heart gave a jump as she realized that she was not
alone. She looked down, and there the man stood, fat, bearded,
in shirt and trousers, his chest bare, and dark with animal hair.
In the sick, thundery twilight he looked unreal, especially as
he did not speak, only stared at her. Alberta did not speak
either. Dumb and tense she climbed down off her chair, and
drove him out backwards in mutual silence, while her brain
hammered with the realization: We're alone up here – it's a
long way down – he'll get to the door first – if he shuts it, no
one will hear us.

He did not shut it. As silently as he had come, he disappeared
again, in slippers or his stockinged feet. A lock that turned
quietly out in the darkness was the only indication that he had
actually been there.

He had been neither a vision nor a rapist. Alberta saw him
again the next day on the stairs, a commonplace traveller in a
top hat and waterproof. An ordinary man, who lived cheaply
on top floors and sought cheap pleasures, led astray by the
open door and the woman in scanty attire inside. It might have
been worse.

Other memories from the top floors of other hotels lay
stored up in her memory, uglier, more dangerous. She did
not like meddling with them. And this last incident had been
almost the most vexatious. The fact that she could not leave
the door open on a suffocating evening unpunished, because
she was everyman's booty, a woman, had left her bitter.

She walked a little way down the stairs and looked out of
the low window. Now they had finished eating down there,
only the clinking from the kitchen could be heard. At the
bottom of the courtyard's depressing shaft someone was squatting, playing with the hotel cat. It was lying on its side, half on
its back, striking out lazily with its paws. It was Jean sitting
there. He had just hosed down the yard. A ring of small black
puddles had been left round him in the depressions in the
asphalt.

Someone was coming up the stairs, and Alberta drifted in again, shutting the door. She could go out walking, as was her custom, or she could go down and sit on the boulevard. She was free to do so, it was a harmless, cheap evening's entertainment, shared by thousands, by large sections of the population. The melancholy summer evening in the city, she had admittance to that: to its dying, sickly green light lingering in the window-panes high up, the suffocating atmosphere with its sudden puffs of fresher air which slap feebly at the café awnings, chase the dust upwards and die away again; to its gasp for tranquillity, which is drowned in the clamour of gramophones and the clanging of tramcars. Tired, low-voiced or silent people sit on the benches. If they tilt their heads backwards they can see the sky, thin, clear as glass, far too light, pitched to hang whole and free above a scented landscape, drawn taut in bits and pieces above desert formations of stone and cement. Even the trees along the pavement look foreign and irrelevant, as if picked up from a Noah's Ark and set out in rows, artificial, unnaturally dark.

Alberta had experienced it summer after summer. It is then that the lonely cannot withstand their loneliness any longer, but come out from their hiding-places, and walk quietly down the street as if they had a route and a purpose. It is then that poor, elderly women get something impracticable and out-of-date from their drawers, something that suited them once, put it on and go out in it, guilty and uneasy, a little wry in the face.

There were evenings when a compulsion, an inner necessity, made Alberta seek out precisely this; when, with a kind of appetite, she inhaled the heaviness of the atmosphere, all it carried with it besides the reek of the day: human frugality, fatigue, resignation, unsatisfied longing. Something in her was nourished by it, and began to put out painful shoots. But it had to happen in freedom and according to her own choice, not as the only way out. It easily acquired a tinge of necessity and of touching bottom against which she had to be on her guard. It could be worse alone with herself down there than anywhere else.

Should she go to see Liesel? Look out for her when she

came from her evening class? Ignore her slightly tired surprise and force an entrance to her sooty, narrow balcony, barely separated from the neighbours by a low trellis? Comfort herself with the thought that even if Liesel might perhaps have preferred to go to bed, she was at any rate sitting on her balcony enjoying this asset, a thing she seldom dared do when she was alone, because she would be accosted and pursued across the trellis?

No. That had come to an end. Liesel was with Eliel. She was no longer the rather lonely girl, who trailed her painting things and her long, black dress around between Colarossi's, the banks of the Seine and the Luxembourg Gardens, returning home untidy, dusty, dirty with paint and ravenously hungry, and who would explain despondently: 'There were four of them watching today. I can't do anything if someone's watching. Everything was different when I got there – now I've spoiled it again. I'll never be any good – my life is not interesting.'

Ever since a day last winter, when Eliel had taken her hand in his, lifted it towards the light, inspected it from every angle and asked if he might model it – 'It's so unusually beautiful and full of character' – Liesel had gone through the usual stages in the correct order, sitting for a hand, for the head, for a shoulder, for everything, sewing on buttons and making coffee, collapsing like an empty rind, and blossoming like a rose; and had now invested half her rent money in a frilly nightdress. And all of it without Alberta really being aware of what was going on. Now Alberta was left by the wayside, while the others drove on with everything settled and a final 'You should find someone too.'

Find someone! Alberta stood up and walked restlessly about the room. Women repeated it in every tone of voice, wherever she happened to be. From old Mrs Weyer in the little town at home, who had patted her on the shoulder and repeated 'A good husband, a good husband . . .', to Marushka who smiled introspectively at her memories and said: 'Why live as you do, *mes enfants*? To what purpose? Love gives happiness – what would life be without love? – I'd wither up and die, I admit it frankly,' and to Alphonsine, whose green

eyes studied her through and through, and who stated quietly
'*Il vous manque une affection, Mademoiselle.*'

But Alberta remembered Liesel on one occasion last winter,
when Marushka had yet again been giving her variation on
the theme. It had suddenly struck Liesel. She had heard it
many times before, but now it struck her. Her eyes had become
big and shining, like those of a child who has been given the
answer to decisive questions. Something had happened to
Liesel at that moment. Perhaps it was then that she had
changed course and gradually steered towards Eliel, who had
been tacking round her for a long time, allowing him to
approach, as if testing him.

Then the Swedish girl had come – the one thing after the
other.

'A good friend – two arms round you at the end of the day –
that is what I wish for you, Mademoiselle.'

Alphonsine again. Her reflective and divergent answer to
some comment Alberta had made about unsuccessful attempts
to work, the incompetence from which she had suffered. No one
could, like her, strike down into one's daydreams and light
on what they were really about, whether one admitted it to
oneself or not. She did not carry on insidious propaganda
like the married women at home, who knew no rest until the
whole world was caught in the trap in which they found
themselves: food and servant worries, gynaecological troubles,
Nurse Jullum the midwife like an official executioner in the
background. She did not share Marushka's attitude either;
Marushka, who glided from one affair to another incredibly
easily and insouciantly, banishing all scruples by the device
of trusting in her lucky star.

Alphonsine brought out one's weaknesses, holding them
up to the light for an instant. She would shake her head seriously in denial, if one day Alberta were to broach the question,
expose her wretchedness, and say: 'Who, Alphonsine? Who?
The man in the street, who says *Tu viens*? The hotel guest who
tries to get into one's room? The fairly good-looking fellow
who wanders about the studios looking for love, gratis, and
whom almost anybody can have once or twice? Or the kind of
person from whom mind and body shrink, one with catarrh,

one with an obstinate will deep down in those cautious eyes?'
She would say: 'But there are others, Mademoiselle.'

'Not for me,' said Alberta bitterly, out loud. She continued
her train of thought: 'Tenderness? What about tenderness,
Alphonsine? When you have lived next door to all kinds of
people, and the walls are thin, you begin to find it a little
difficult to believe in that. At first you are frightened, thinking
of madness or confined animals, finally you understand.
Groans, struggle, a smothered bellow in the darkness, a heavy
silence as if death had supervened, the snoring. The snoring!
Or women's tears, streams of bitter, upbraiding words. What
happened to tenderness? It must have been lost on the way?'

Alphonsine would probably smile a melancholy smile and
know better. And rightly so.

Alberta was sitting on her bed in the dark, her arms round
her knees and her chin resting on them. Suddenly she got
down, found a light, and dressed herself feverishly. Now the
evil had reached her heart, anxiety gripped it. That vague
anxiety for life as it reveals itself step by step; anxiety that in
spite of everything it might slip through her fingers unused.

She ran downstairs, bought the evening papers, *Le Rire*,
more cigarettes, even an expensive literary monthly, drank a
vermouth at the zinc counter in the building next door, wasted
a lot of money in great haste.

Cesare Pavese

WEDDING TRIP

TRANSLATED BY
A. E. MURCH

CESARE PAVESE

Born at Santo Stefano Belbo (Piedmont) 1908; died by suicide,
Turin 1950. Novelist of the young generation in the North Italian
towns and the Piedmontese villages. The outstanding works are
the novel *The Moon and the Bonfire* (1950) and his diary for 1935–50,
This Business of Living. 'Wedding Trip', written in 1936, is one of
a number of stories found in manuscript after his death.

WEDDING TRIP

Now that I, shattered and full of remorse, have learned how foolish it is to reject reality for the sake of idle fancies, how presumptuous to receive when one has nothing to give in return, now – Cilia is dead. Though I am resigned to my present life of drudgery and ignominy, I sometimes think how gladly I would adapt myself to her ways, if only those days could return. But perhaps that is just another of my fancies. I treated Cilia badly when I was young, when nothing should have made me irritable; no doubt I should have gone on ill-treating her, out of bitterness and the disquiet of an unhappy conscience. For instance, I am still not sure, after all these years, whether I really loved her. Certainly I mourn for her; I find her in the background of my inmost thoughts; never a day passes in which I do not shrink painfully away from my memories of those two years, and I despise myself because I let her die. I grieve for her youth, even more for my own loneliness, but – and this is what really counts – did I truly love her? Not, at any rate, with the sincere, steady love a man should have for his wife.

The fact is, I owed her too much, and all I gave her in return was a blind suspicion of her motives. As it happens, I am by nature superficial and did not probe more deeply into such dark waters. At the time I was content to treat the matter with my instinctive diffidence and refused to give weight or substance to certain sordid thoughts that, had they taken root in my mind, would have sickened me of the whole affair. However, several times I did ask myself: 'And why did Cilia marry me?' I do not know whether it was due to a sense of my own importance, or to profound ineptitude, but the fact remains that it puzzled me.

There was no doubt that Cilia married me, not I her. Oh! Those depressing evenings I endured in her company – wandering restlessly through the streets, squeezing her arm, pretending to be free and easy, suggesting as a joke that we should jump in the river together. Such ideas didn't bother me – I was used to them – but they upset her, made her anxious to help me; so much so that she offered me, out of her wages as a shop-assistant, a little money to live on while I looked for a better job. I did not want money. I told her that to be with her in the evenings was enough for me, as long as she didn't go away and take a job somewhere else. So we drifted along. I began to tell myself, sentimentally, that what I needed was someone nice to live with; I spent too much time roaming the streets; a loving wife would know how to contrive a little home for me, and just by going into it I should be happy again, no matter how weary and miserable the day had made me.

I tried to tell myself that even alone I managed to muddle along quite well, but I knew this was no argument. 'Two people together can help each other,' said Cilia, 'and take care of one another. If they're a little in love, George, that's enough.' I was tired and disheartened, those evenings; Cilia was a dear and very much in earnest, with the fine coat she had made herself and her little broken handbag. Why not give her the joy she wanted? What other girl would suit me better? She knew what it was to work hard and be short of money; she was an orphan, of working-class parents; I was sure that she was more eager and sincere than I.

On impulse I told her that if she would accept me, uncouth and lazy as I was, I would marry her. I felt content, soothed by the warmth of my good deed and proud to discover I had that much courage. I said to Cilia: 'I'll teach you French!' She responded with a smile in her gentle eyes as she clung tightly to my arm.

2

In those days I thought I was sincere, and once again I explained to Cilia how poor I was. I warned her that I hardly ever had a full day's work and didn't know what it was to get a pay-packet. The college where I taught French paid me by the hour. One day I told her that if she wanted to get on in the world she ought to look for some other man. Cilia looked troubled and offered to keep on with her job. 'You know very well that isn't what I want,' I muttered. Having settled things thus, we married.

It made no particular difference to my life. Already, in the past, Cilia had sometimes spent evenings with me in my room. Lovemaking was no novelty. We took two furnished rooms; the bedroom had a wide, sunny window, and there we placed the little table with my books.

Cilia, though, became a different woman. I, for my part, had been afraid that, once married, she would grow vulgar and slovenly – as I imagined her mother had been – but instead I found her more particular, more considerate towards me. She was always clean and neat, and kept everything in perfect order. Even the simple meals she prepared for me in the kitchen had the cordiality and solace of those hands and that smile. Her smile, especially, was transfigured. It was no longer the half-timid, half-teasing smile of a shop-girl on the spree, but the gentle flowering of an inner joy, utterly content and eager to please, a serene light on her thin young face. I felt a twinge of jealousy at this sign of a happiness I did not always share. 'She's married me and she's enjoying it,' I thought.

Only when I woke up in the morning was my heart at peace. I would turn my head against hers in our warm bed and lie close beside her as she slept (or was pretending to), my breath ruffling her hair. Then Cilia, with a drowsy smile, would put her arms around me. How different from the days when I woke alone, cold and disheartened, to stare at the first gleam of dawn!

Cilia loved me. Once she was out of bed, she found fresh joys in everything she did as she moved around our room, dressing herself, opening the windows, stealing a cautious glance at me. If I settled myself at the little table, she walked quietly so as not to disturb me; if I went out, her eyes followed me to the door; when I came home she sprang up quickly to greet me.

There were days when I did not want to go home at all. It irritated me to think I should inevitably find her there, waiting for me, even though she learned to pretend she took no special interest; I should sit beside her, tell her more or less the same things, or probably nothing at all. We should look at one another with distaste and a smile. It would be the same tomorrow and the next day, and always. Such thoughts entrapped me whenever the day was foggy and the sun looked grey. If, on the other hand, there was a lovely day when the air was clear and the sun blazed down on my head, or a perfume in the wind enfolded and enraptured me, I would linger in the streets, wishing that I still lived alone, free to stroll around till midnight and get a meal of some sort at the pub on the corner of the street. I had always been a lonely man, and it seemed to me to count for a great deal that I was not unfaithful to Cilia.

She, waiting for me at home, began to take in sewing, to earn a little. A neighbour gave her work, a certain Amalia, a woman of thirty or so, who once invited us to dinner. She lived alone in the room below ours, and gradually fell into the habit of bringing the work upstairs to Cilia so that they could pass the afternoon together. Her face was disfigured by a frightful scar – when she was a little girl she had pulled a boiling saucepan down on her head. Her two sorrowful, timid eyes, full of longing, flinched away when anyone looked at her, as if their humility could excuse the distortion of her features. She was a good girl. I remarked to Cilia that Amalia seemed to me like her elder sister. One day, for a joke, I said: 'If I should run away and leave you, one fine day, would you go and live with her?' 'She's had such bad luck all her life. I wouldn't mind if you wanted to make love to her!' Cilia teased me. Amalia called me 'Sir' and was shy in my presence. Cilia thought this was madly funny. I found it rather flattering.

3

It was a bad thing for me that I regarded my scanty intellectual attainments as a substitute for a regular trade. It lay at the root of so many of my wrong ideas and evil actions. But my education could have proved a good means of communion with Cilia, if only I had been more consistent. Cilia was very quick, anxious to learn everything I knew myself because, loving me so much, she could not bear to feel unworthy of me. She wanted to understand my every thought. And – who knows? – if I could have given her this simple pleasure I might have learned, in the quiet intimacy of our joint occupation, what a fine person she really was, how real and beautiful our life together, and perhaps Cilia would still be alive at my side, with her lovely smile that in two years I froze from her lips.

I started off enthusiastically, as I always do. Cilia's education consisted of a few back numbers of serial novels, the news in the daily papers, and a hard, precocious experience of life itself. What was I to teach her? She very much wanted to learn French and indeed, Heaven knows how, she managed to piece together scraps of it by searching through my dictionaries when she was left alone at home. But I aspired to something better than that and wanted to teach her to read properly, to appreciate the finest books. I kept a few of them – my treasures – on the little table. I tried to explain to her the finer points of novels and poems, and Cilia did her best to follow me. No one excels me in recognizing the beauty, the 'rightness' of a thought or a story, and explaining it in glowing terms. I put a great deal of effort into making her feel the freshness of ancient pages, the truth of sentiments expressed long before she and I were born, how varied, how glorious, life had been for so many men at so many different periods. Cilia would listen with close attention, asking questions that I often found embarrassing. Sometimes as we strolled in the streets or sat eating our supper in silence, she would tell me in her candid voice of certain doubts she had, and once when I replied without conviction or with impatience – I don't remember which – she burst out laughing.

I remember that my first present to her, as her husband, was a book, *The Daughter of the Sea*. I gave it to her a month after our wedding, when we started reading lessons. Until then I had not bought her anything – nothing for the house, no new clothes – because we were too poor. Cilia was delighted and made a new cover for the book, but she never read it.

Now and then, when we had managed to save enough, we went to a cinema, and there Cilia really enjoyed herself. An additional attraction, for her, was that she could snuggle up close to me, and now and then ask me for explanations that she could understand. She never let Amalia come to the cinema with us, though one day the poor girl asked if she could. She explained to me that we got to know each other best of all in a cinema, and in that blessed darkness we had to be alone together.

Amalia came to our place more and more often. This, and my well-deserved disappointments, soon made me first neglect our reading lessons, and finally stop them altogether. Then, if I was in a good mood, I amused myself by joking with the two girls, and Amalia lost a little of her shyness. One evening, as I came home very late from the college with my nerves on edge, she came and stared me full in the face, with a gleam of reproof and suspicion in her timid glance. I felt more disgusted than ever by the frightful scar on her face, and spitefully I tried to make out what her features had been before they were destroyed. I remarked to Cilia, when we were alone, that Amalia as a child must have been very like her.

'Poor thing,' said Cilia. 'She spends every penny she earns trying to get cured. She hopes that then she'll find a husband.'

'But don't all women know how to get a husband?'

'I've already found mine,' Cilia smiled.

'Suppose what happened to Amalia had happened to you?' I sneered.

Cilia came close to me. 'Wouldn't you want me any more?'

'No.'

'But what's upset you this evening? Don't you like Amalia to come up here? She gives me work and helps me . . .'

What had got into me – and I couldn't get rid of it – was the thought that Cilia was just another Amalia. I felt disgusted and furious with both of them. My eyes were hard as I stared at Cilia, and the tender look she gave me only made me pity her, irritating me still more. On my way home I had met a husband with two dirty brats clinging round his neck, and behind him a thin worn-out little woman, his wife. I imagined what Cilia would look like when she was old and ugly, and the thought clutched me by the throat.

Outside, the stars were shining. Cilia looked at me in silence. 'I'm going for a walk,' I told her with a bitter smile, and I went out.

4

I had no friends and I realized, now and then, that Cilia was my whole life. As I walked the streets I thought about us and felt troubled that I did not earn enough to repay her by keeping her in comfort, so that I needn't feel ashamed when I went home. I never wasted a penny – I did not even smoke – and, proud of that, I considered my thoughts were at least my own. But what could I make of those thoughts? On my way home I looked at people and wondered how so many of them had managed to succeed in life. Desperately I longed for changes, for something fresh and exciting.

I used to hang around the railway station, thrilled by the smoke and the bustle. For me, good fortune has always meant adventure in far-away places – a liner crossing the ocean, arrival at some exotic port, the clang of metal, shrill, foreign voices – I dreamed of it all the time. One evening I stopped short, terrified by the sudden realization that if I didn't hurry up and travel somewhere with Cilia while she was still young and in love with me, I should never go at all. A fading wife and a squalling child would, for ever, prevent me. 'If only we really had money,' I thought again. 'You can do anything with money.'

'Good fortune must be deserved,' I told myself. 'Shoulder every load that life may bring. I am married but I do not want a child. Is that why I'm so wretched? Should I be luckier if I had a son?'

To live always wrapped up in oneself is a depressing thing, because a brain that is habitually secretive does not hesitate to follow incredibly stupid trains of thought that mortify the man who thinks them. This was the only origin of the doubts that plagued me.

Sometimes my longing for far-away places filled my mind even in bed. If, on a still and windless night, I suddenly caught the wild sound of a train whistle in the distance, I would start up from Cilia's side with all my dreams re-awakened.

One afternoon, when I was passing the station without even stopping, a face I knew suddenly appeared in front of me and gave a cry of greeting. Malagigi: I hadn't seen him for ten years. We shook hands and stood there exchanging courtesies. He was no longer the ugly, spiteful ink-spotted little devil I knew at school, always playing jokes in the lavatory, but I recognized that grin of his at once. 'Malagigi! Still alive, then?'

'Alive, and a qualified accountant.' His voice had changed. It was a man speaking to me now.

'Are you off somewhere, too?' he asked. 'Guess where I'm going!' As he spoke he picked up a fine leather suitcase that toned perfectly with his smart new raincoat and the elegance of his tie. Gripping my wrist he went on: 'Come to the train with me. I'm going to Genoa.'

'I'm in a hurry.'

'Then I leave for China!'

'No!'

'It's true. Can't a man go to China? What have you got against China? Instead of talking like that, wish me luck! Perhaps I may stay out there.'

'But what's your job?'

'I'm going to China. Come and see me off.'

'No, I really can't spare the time.'

'Then come and have coffee with me, to say goodbye. You're the last man I shall talk to, here.'

We had coffee there in the station, at the counter, while Malagigi, full of excitement, told me in fits and starts all about himself and his prospects. He was not married. He'd fathered a baby, but luckily it died. He had left school after I did, without finishing. He thought of me once, when he had to take an exam a second time. He'd gained his education in the battle of life. Now all the big firms had offered him a job. And he spoke four languages. And they were sending him to China.

I said again that I was in a hurry (though it was not true), and managed to get away from him, feeling crushed and overwhelmed. I reached home still upset by the chance meeting, my thoughts in a turmoil. How could he rise from such a drab boyhood to the audacious height of a future like that? Not that I envied Malagigi, or even liked him; but to see, un- expectedly superimposed on his grey background, which had been mine too, his present colourful and assured existence, such as I could glimpse only in dreams, was torment to me.

Our room was empty, because now Cilia often went downstairs to work in our neighbour's room. I stayed there a while, brooding in the soft darkness lit only by the little blue glow of the gas-jet under the saucepan bubbling gently on the stove.

5

I passed many evenings thus, alone in the room, waiting for Cilia, pacing up and down or lying on the bed, absorbed in that silent emptiness as the dusk slowly deepened into dark. Subdued or distant noises – the shouts of children, the bustle of the street, the cries of birds – reached me only faintly. Cilia soon realized that I didn't want to be bothered with her when I came home, and she would put her head out of Amalia's room, still sewing, to hear me pass and call to me. I didn't care whether she heard me or not, but if she did I would say something or other. Once I asked Amalia, quite seriously, why she didn't come up to our room any more, where there was plenty of light. Amalia said nothing; Cilia looked away and her face grew red.

One night, for something to say, I told her about Malagigi and made her laugh gaily at that funny little man. Then I added: 'Fancy him making a fortune and going to China! I wish it had been me!'

'I should like it, too,' Cilia sighed, 'if we went to China.'

I gave a wry grin. 'In a photograph, perhaps, if we sent one to Malagigi.'

'Why not one for ourselves?' she said. 'Oh, George, we haven't ever had a photograph of us together.'

'No money.'

'Do let's have a photograph.'

'But we oughtn't to afford it. We're together day and night, and anyway I don't like photographs.'

'We are married and we have no record of it. Let's have just one!'

I did not reply.

'It wouldn't cost much. I'll pay for it.'

'Get it done with Amalia.'

Next morning Cilia lay with her face to the wall, her hair over her eyes. She would not take any notice of me, or even look at me. I caressed her a little, then realized she was resisting me, so I jumped out of bed in a rage. Cilia got up, too, washed her face and gave me some coffee, her manner quiet and cautious, her eyes downcast. I went away without speaking to her.

An hour later I came back again. 'How much is there in the savings book?' I shouted. Cilia looked at me in surprise. She was sitting on the stool, unhappy and bewildered.

'I don't know. You've got it. About 300 lire, I think.'

'Nearly three hundred and sixteen. Here it is.' I flung the roll of notes on the table. 'Spend it as you like. Let's have a high old time! It's all yours.'

Cilia stood up and came over to face me. 'Why have you done this, George?'

'Because I'm a fool. Listen! I'd rather not talk about it. When money is in your pocket it doesn't count any more. D'you still want that photograph?'

'But, George, I want you to be happy.'

'I am happy.'

'I do love you so much.'

'I love you, too.' I took her by the arm, sat down, and pulled her on my knee. 'Put your head here, on my shoulder.' My voice was indulgent and intimate. Cilia said nothing and leaned her cheek against mine. 'When shall we go?' I asked.

'It doesn't matter,' she whispered.

'Then listen!' I held the back of her neck and smiled at her. Cilia, still trembling, threw her arms around my shoulders and tried to kiss me.

'Darling!' I said. 'Let's make plans. We have three hundred lire. Let's drop everything and go on a little trip. Quickly! Now! If we think it over we'll change our minds. Don't tell anyone about it, not even Amalia. We'll only be away a day. It will be the honeymoon we didn't have.'

'George, why wouldn't you take me away then? You said it was a silly idea then.'

'Yes, but this isn't a honeymoon. You see, now we know each other. We're good friends. Nobody knows we're going. And, besides, we need a holiday. Don't you?'

'Of course, George. I'm so happy. Where shall we go?'

'I don't know, but we'll go at once. Would you like us to go to the sea? To Genoa?'

6

Once we were on the train, I showed a certain preoccupation. As we started, Cilia was almost beside herself with delight, held my hand and tried to make me talk. Then, finding me moody and unresponsive, she quickly understood and settled down quietly, looking out of the window with a happy smile. I remained silent, staring into nothingness, listening to the rhythmic throb of the wheels on the rails as it vibrated through my whole body. There were other people in the carriage, but I scarcely noticed them. Fields and hills were flashing past. Cilia, sitting opposite and leaning on the window-pane, seemed to be listening to something, too, but now and then she glanced swiftly in my direction and tried to smile. So she spied on me, at a distance.

When we arrived it was dark, and at last we found somewhere to stay, in a large, silent hotel, hidden among the trees of a deserted avenue, after going up and down an eternity of tortuous streets, making inquiries. It was a grey, cold night, that made me want to stride along with my nose in the air. Instead, Cilia, tired to death, was dragging on my arm and I was only too glad to find somewhere to sit down. We had wandered through so many brightly-lit streets, so many dark alleys that brought our hearts into our mouths, but we had never reached the sea. No one took any notice of us. We looked like any couple out for a stroll, except for our tendency to step off the pavements and Cilia's anxious glances at the houses and passers-by.

That hotel would do for us; nothing elegant about it. A bony young fellow with his sleeves rolled up was eating at a white table. We were received by a tall, fierce-looking woman wearing a coral necklace. I was glad to sit down. Walking with

Cilia never left me free to absorb myself in what I saw, or in myself. Preoccupied and ill at ease, I nevertheless had to keep her beside me and answer her, at least with gestures. Now, all I wanted – and how I wanted it – was to look around and get to know in my heart of hearts this unknown city. That was precisely why I had come.

We waited downstairs to order supper, without even going upstairs to see our room or discussing terms. I was attracted by that young fellow with his auburn whiskers and his vague, lonely manner. On his forearm was a faded tattoo mark, and as he went away he picked up a patched blue jacket.

It was midnight when we had our supper. At our little table, Cilia laughed a great deal at the disdainful air of the landlady. 'She thinks we're only just married,' she faltered. Then, her weary eyes full of tenderness, she asked me: 'And are we really?' as she stroked my hand.

We inquired about places in the neighbourhood. The harbour was only a hundred yards away, at the end of the avenue. 'Let's go and see it for a minute,' said Cilia. She was fit to drop, but she wanted to take that little walk with me.

We came to the railings of a terrace and caught our breath. The night was calm but dark, and the street-lamps floundered in the cold black abyss that lay before us. I said nothing, and my heart leapt as I breathed the smell of it, wild and free. Cilia looked around her and pointed out to me a line of lights, their reflection quivering in the water. Was it a ship? A breakwater? We could hear waves splashing gently in the darkness. 'Tomorrow,' she breathed ecstatically. 'Tomorrow we'll see it all.'

As we made our way back to our hotel, Cilia clung tightly to my side. 'How tired I am! George, it's lovely! Tomorrow! I'm so happy! Are you happy, too?' and she rubbed her cheek against my shoulder.

I did not feel like that. I was walking with clenched jaws, taking deep breaths and letting the wind caress me. I felt restless, remote from Cilia, alone in the world. Halfway up the stairs I said to her: 'I don't want to go to bed yet. You go on up. I'll go for another little stroll and come back.'

7

That time, too, it was the same. How I hurt Cilia! Even now, when I think of her in bed as dawn is breaking, I am filled with a desolate remorse for the way I treated her. Yet I couldn't help it! I always did everything like a fool, a man in a dream, and I did not realize the sort of man I was until the end, when even remorse was useless. Now I can glimpse the truth. I become so engrossed in solitude that it deadens all my sense of human relationships and makes me incapable of tolerating or respond-ing to any tenderness. Cilia, for me, was not an obstacle: she simply did not exist. If I had only understood this! If I had had any idea of how much harm I was doing to myself by cutting myself off from her in this way, I should have turned to her with intense gratitude and cherished her presence as my only salvation.

But is the sight of another's suffering ever enough to open a man's eyes? Instead, it takes the sweat of agony, the bitter pain that comes as we awake, lives with us as we walk the streets, lies beside us through sleepless nights, always raw and pitiless, covering us with shame.

Dawn broke wet and cloudy. The avenue was still deserted as I wandered back to the hotel. I saw Cilia and the landlady quarrelling on the stairs, both in their night clothes. Cilia was crying. The landlady, in a dressing-gown, gave a shriek as I went in. Cilia stood motionless, leaning on the handrail. Her face was white with shock, her hair and her clothes in wild disorder.

'Here he is!'

'Whatever's going on here, at this time in the morning?' I asked harshly.

The landlady, clutching her bosom, started shouting that she had been disturbed in the middle of the night because of a missing husband; there had been tears, handkerchiefs ripped to shreds, telephone calls, police inquiries. Was that the way to behave? Where did I come from?

I was so weary I could hardly stand. I gave her a listless glance of disgust. Cilia had not moved. She stood there breathing deeply through her open mouth, her face red and distorted. 'Cilia,' I cried, 'haven't you been to sleep?'

She did not reply. She just stood there, motionless, making no attempt to wipe away the tears that streamed from her eyes. Her hands were clasped at her waist, tearing at her handkerchief.

'I went for a walk,' I said in a hollow voice. 'I stopped by the harbour.' The landlady seemed about to interrupt me, then shrugged her shoulders. 'Anyway, I'm alive, and dying for the want of sleep. Let me throw myself on the bed.'

I slept until two, heavily as a drunkard, then I awoke with a start. The light in the room was dim, but I could hear noises in the street. Instinctively I did not move. Cilia was there, sitting in a corner, looking at me, staring at the walls, examining her fingers, jumping up now and then. After a while I whispered cautiously: 'Cilia, are you watching me?' Swiftly she raised her eyes. The shattered look I had seen earlier now seemed engraved on her face. She moved her lips to speak, but no sound came.

'Cilia, a husband shouldn't be watched,' I said in a playful voice like a child's. 'Have you had anything to eat today?' The poor girl shook her head. I jumped out of bed and looked at the clock. 'The train goes at half past three,' I cried. 'Come on, Cilia, hurry! Let's try to look happy in front of the landlady.' She did not move, so I went over and pulled her up by her cheeks.

'Listen,' I went on. 'Is it because of last night?' Her eyes filled with tears. 'I could have lied, said I had got lost, smoothed things over. I didn't do that, because I hate lies. Cheer up! I have always liked to be alone. Still, even I,' and I felt her give a start, 'even I haven't enjoyed myself much at Genoa. Yet I'm not crying.'

Isaac Bashevis Singer

THE OLD MAN

TRANSLATED BY
NORBERT GUTERMAN AND
ELAINE GOTTLIEB

ISAAC BASHEVIS SINGER

Born in Radzymin (Poland) 1904; living in America since 1935.
Hebrew and Yiddish novelist and short-story writer: *Satan in
Goray, The Magician of Lublin, Gimpel the Fool*. 'The Old Man' was
published in Warsaw in 1933.

THE OLD MAN

I

A T the beginning of the Great War, Chaim Sachar of Kroch-
malna Street in Warsaw was a rich man. Having put aside
dowries of a thousand roubles each for his daughters, he was
about to rent a new apartment, large enough to include a
Torah-studying son-in-law. There would also have to be
additional room for his ninety-year-old father, Reb Moshe
Ber, a Turisk hassid, who had recently come to live with him
in Warsaw.

But two years later, Chaim Sachar's apartment was almost
empty. No one knew where his two sons, young giants, who
had been sent to the front, had been buried. His wife and two
daughters had died of typhus. He had accompanied their bodies
to the cemetery, reciting the memorial prayer for the three of
them, pre-empting the most desirable place at the prayer stand
in the synagogue, and inviting the enmity of other mourners,
who accused him of taking unfair advantage of his multiple
bereavement.

After the German occupation of Warsaw, Chaim Sachar, a
tall, broad man of sixty who traded in live geese, locked his
store. He sold his furniture by the piece, in order to buy frozen
potatoes and mouldy dried peas, and prepared gritty blackish
noodles for himself and his father, who had survived the
grandchildren.

Although Chaim Sachar had not for many months been
near a live fowl, his large caftan was still covered with goose
down, his great broad-brimmed hat glistened with fat, and his
heavy, snub-toed boots were stained with slaughterhouse
blood. Two small eyes, starved and frightened, peered from
beneath his dishevelled eyebrows; the red rims about his eyes
were reminiscent of the time when he could wash down a dish
of fried liver and hard-boiled eggs with a pint of vodka every
morning after prayer. Now, all day long, he wandered through

the market place, inhaling butchershop odours and those from restaurants, sniffing like a dog, and occasionally napping on porters' carts. With the refuse he had collected in a basket, he fed his kitchen stove at night; then, rolling the sleeves over his hairy arms, he would grate turnips on a grater. His father, meanwhile, sat warming himself at the open kitchen door, even though it was midsummer. An open Mishna treatise lay across his knees, and he complained constantly of hunger.

As though it were all his son's fault, the old man would mutter angrily, 'I can't stand it much longer ... this gnawing ...'

Without looking up from his book, a treatise on impurity, he would indicate the pit of his stomach and resume his mumbling in which the word 'impure' recurred like a refrain. Although his eyes were a murky blue, like the eyes of a blind man, he needed no glasses, still retained some of his teeth, yellow and crooked as rusty nails, and awoke each day on the side on which he had fallen asleep. He was disturbed only by his rupture, which nevertheless did not keep him from plodding through the streets of Warsaw with the help of his pointed stick, his 'horse', as he called it. At every synagogue he would tell stories about wars, about evil spirits, and of the old days of cheap and abundant living when people dried sheepskins in cellars and drank spirits directly from the barrel through a straw. In return, Reb Moshe Ber was treated to raw carrots, slices of radish, and turnips. Finishing them in no time, he would then, with a trembling hand, pluck each crumb from his thinning beard – still not white – and speak of Hungary, where, more than seventy years before, he had lived in his father-in-law's house. 'Right after prayer, we were served a large decanter of wine and a side of veal. And with the soup there were hard-boiled eggs and crunchy noodles.'

Hollow-cheeked men in rags, with ropes about their loins, stood about him, bent forward, mouths watering, digesting each of his words, the whites of their eyes greedily showing, as if the old man actually sat there eating. Young yeshiva students, faces emaciated from fasts, eyes shifty and restless as those of madmen, nervously twisted their long earlocks around their fingers, grimacing, as though to suppress stomach aches, repeating ecstatically, 'That was the time. A man had his share of heaven and earth. But now we have nothing.'

For many months Reb Moshe Ber shuffled about searching for a bit of food; then, one night in late summer, on returning home, he found Chaim Sachar, his first-born, lying in bed, sick, barefoot, and without his caftan. Chaim Sachar's face was as red as though he had been to a steam bath, and his beard was crumpled in a knot. A neighbour woman came in, touched his forehead, and chanted, 'Woe is me, it's that sickness. He must go to the hospital.'

Next morning the black ambulance reappeared in the court-yard. Chaim Sachar was taken to the hospital; his apartment was sprayed with carbolic acid; and his father was led to the disinfection centre, where they gave him a long white robe and shoes with wooden soles. The guards, who knew him well, gave him double portions of bread under the table and treated him to cigarettes. The Sukkoth holiday had passed by the time the old man, his shaven chin concealed beneath a kerchief, was allowed to leave the disinfection centre. His son had died long before, and Reb Moshe Ber said the memorial prayer, *kaddish*, for him. Now alone in the apartment, he had to feed his stove with paper and wood shavings from garbage cans. In the ashes he baked rotten potatoes, which he carried in his scarf, and in an iron pot he brewed chicory. He kept house, made his own candles by kneading bits of wax and suet around wicks, laundered his shirt beneath the kitchen tap, and hung it to dry on a piece of string. He set the mousetraps each night and drowned the mice each morning. When he went out he never forgot to fasten the heavy padlock on the door. No one had to pay rent in Warsaw at that time. Moreover, he wore his son's boots and trousers. His old acquaintances in the Houses of Study envied him. 'He lives like a king!' they said, 'He has inherited his son's fortune!'

The winter was difficult. There was no coal, and since several tiles were missing from the stove, the apartment was filled with black smoke each time the old man made a fire. A crust of blue ice and snow covered the window panes by November, making the rooms constantly dark or dusky. Overnight, the water on his night table froze in the pot. No matter how many clothes he piled over him in bed, he never felt warm; his feet remained stiff, and as soon as he began to doze, the entire pile of clothes would fall off, and he would have to climb out naked to make his bed once more. There was no kerosene; even matches were at a premium. Although he recited chapter upon chapter of the Psalms, he could not fall asleep. The wind, freely roaming about the rooms, banged the doors; even the mice left. When he hung up his shirt to dry, it would grow brittle and break like glass. He stopped washing himself; his face became coal black. All day long he would sit in the House of Study, near the red-hot iron stove. On the shelves, the old books lay like piles of rags; tramps stood around the tin-topped tables, nondescript fellows with long matted hair and rags over their swollen feet – men who, having lost all they had in the war, were half-naked or covered only with torn clothes, bags slung over their shoulders. All day long, while orphans recited *kaddish*, women stood in throngs around the Holy Ark, loudly praying for the sick, and filling his ears with their moans and lamentations. The room, dim and stuffy, smelled like a mortuary chamber from the numerous anniversary candles that were burning. Every time Reb Moshe Ber, his head hanging down, fell asleep, he would burn himself on the stove. He had to be escorted home at night, for his shoes were hobnailed, and he was afraid he might slip on the ice. The other tenants in his house had given him up for dead. 'Poor thing – he's gone to pieces.'

One December day, Reb Moshe Ber actually did slip, receiving a hard blow on his right arm. The young man escorting him hoisted Reb Moshe Ber on his back, and carried him home. Placing the old man on his bed without undressing him, the young man ran away as though he had committed a burglary. For two days the old man groaned, called for help, wept, but no one appeared. Several times each day he said his Confession of Sins, praying for death to come quickly, pounding his chest with his left hand. It was quiet outside in the daytime, as though everyone had died; a hazy green twilight came through the windows. At night he heard scratching noises as though a cat were trying to climb the walls; a hollow roar seemed to come repeatedly from underground. In the darkness the old man fancied that his bed stood in the middle of the room and all the windows were open. After sunset on the second day he thought he saw the door open suddenly, admitting a horse with a black sheet on its back. It had a head as long as a donkey's and innumerable eyes. The old man knew at once that this was the Angel of Death. Terrified, he fell from his bed, making such a racket that two neighbours heard it. There was a commotion in the courtyard; a crowd gathered, and an ambulance was summoned. When he came to his senses, Reb Moshe Ber found himself in a dark box, bandaged and covered up. He was sure this was his hearse, and it worried him that he had no heirs to say *kaddish*, and that therefore the peace of his grave would be disturbed. Suddenly he recalled the verses he would have to say to Duma, the Prosecuting Angel, and his bruised, swollen face twisted into a corpse-like smile:

> What man is he that liveth and shall not see death?
> Shall he deliver his soul from the grave?

2

After Passover, Reb Moshe Ber was discharged from the hospital. Completely recovered, he once more had a great appetite but nothing to eat. All his possessions had been stolen; in the apartment only the peeling walls remained. He remembered Jozefow, a little village near the border of Galicia, where for fifty years he had lived and enjoyed great authority in the Turisk hassidic circle, because he had personally known the old rabbi. He inquired about the possibilities of getting there, but those he questioned merely shrugged their shoulders, and each said something different. Some assured him Jozefow had been burned to the ground, wiped out. A wandering beggar, on the other hand, who had visited the region, said that Jozefow was more prosperous than ever, that its inhabitants ate the Sabbath white bread even on week days. But Jozefow was on the Austrian side of the border, and whenever Reb Moshe Ber broached the subject of his trip, men smiled mockingly in their beards and waved their hands. 'Don't be foolish, Reb Moshe Ber. Even a young man couldn't do it.'

But Reb Moshe Ber was hungry. All the turnips, carrots, and watery soups he had eaten in public kitchens had left him with a hollow sensation in his abdomen. All night he would dream of Jozefow knishes stuffed with ground meat and onions, of tasty concoctions of tripe and calf's feet, chicken fat and lean beef. The moment he closed his eyes he would find himself at some wedding or circumcision feast. Large brown rolls were piled up on the long table, and Turisk hassidim in silken caftans with high velvet hats over their skull caps danced, glasses of brandy in their hands, singing:

> What's a poor man
> Cooking for his dinner?
> Borscht and potatoes!
> Borscht and potatoes!
> Faster, faster, hop-hop-hop!

He was the chief organizer of all those parties; he quarrelled with the caterers, scolded the musicians, surpervised every detail, and having no time to eat anything, had to postpone it all for later. His mouth watering, he awoke each morning, bitter that not even in his dream had he tasted those wonderful dishes. His heart pounded; his body was covered with a cold perspiration. The light outside seemed brighter every day, and in the morning rectangular patterns of sunlight would waver on the peeling wall, swirling, as though they mirrored the rushing waves of a river close by. Around the bare hook for a chandelier on the crumbling ceiling, flies hummed. The cool golden glow of dawn illumined the window-panes, and the distorted image of a bird in flight was always reflected in them. Beggars and cripples sang their songs in the courtyard below, playing their fiddles and blowing little brass trumpets. In his shirt, Reb Moshe Ber would crawl down from the one remaining bed, to warm his feet and stomach and to gaze at the barefoot girls in short petticoats who were beating red comforters. In all directions feathers flew, like white blossoms, and there were familiar scents of rotten straw and tar. The old man, straightening his crooked fingers, pricking up his long hairy ears as though to hear distant noises, thought for the thousandth time that if he didn't get out of here this very summer, he never would.

'God will help me,' he would tell himself. 'If he wills it, I'll be eating in a holiday arbour at Jozefow.'

He wasted a lot of time at first by listening to people who told him to get a passport and apply for a visa. After being photographed, he was given a yellow card, and then he had to stand with hordes of others for weeks outside the Austrian consulate on a crooked little street somewhere near the Vistula. They were constantly being cursed in German and punched with the butts of guns by bearded, pipe-smoking soldiers. Women with infants in their arms wept and fainted. It was rumoured that visas were granted only to prostitutes and to men who paid in gold. Reb Moshe Ber, going there every day at sunrise, sat on the ground and nodded over his Beni Issachar treatise, nourishing himself with grated turnips and mouldy red radishes. But since the crowd continued to increase, he decided one day to give it all up. Selling his cotton-padded caftan to a peddler, he bought a loaf of bread, and a bag in which he placed his prayer shawl and phylacteries, as well as a few books for good luck; and planning to cross the border illegally, he set out on foot.

It took him five weeks to get to Ivangorod. During the day, while it was warm, he walked barefoot across the fields, his boots slung over his shoulders, peasant fashion. He fed on unripened grain and slept in barns. German military police often stopped him, scrutinized his Russian passport for a long time, searched him to see that he was not carrying contraband, and then let him go. At various times, as he walked, his intestines popped out of place; he lay on the ground and pushed them back with his hands. In a village near Ivangorod he found a group of Turisk hassidim, most of them young. When they heard where he was going and that he intended to enter Galicia, they gaped at him, blinking, then, after whispering among themselves, they warned him, 'You're taking a chance in times like these. They'll send you to the gallows on the slightest pretext.'

Afraid to converse with him, lest the authorities grow suspicious, they gave him a few marks and got rid of him. A few days later, in that village, people spoke in hushed voices of an old Jew who had been arrested somewhere on the road

and shot by a firing squad. But not only was Reb Moshe alive
by then; he was already on the Austrian side of the border.
For a few marks, a peasant had taken him across, hidden in a
cart under a load of straw. The old man started immediately
for Rajowiec. He fell ill with dysentery there and lay in the
poorhouse for several days. Everyone thought he was dying,
but he recovered gradually.

Now there was no shortage of food. Housewives treated
Reb Moshe Ber to brown buckwheat with milk, and on
Saturdays he even ate cold calf's foot jelly and drank a glass of
brandy. The moment his strength returned, he was off again.
The roads were familiar here. In this region, the peasants still
wore the white linen coats and quadrangular caps with tassels
that they had worn fifty years ago; they had beards and spoke
Ukrainian. In Zamosc the old man was arrested and thrown
into jail with two young peasants. The police confiscated his
bag. He refused gentile food and accepted only bread and
water. Every other day he was summoned by the commandant
who, as though Reb Moshe Ber were deaf, screamed directly
into his ear in a throaty language. Comprehending nothing,
Reb Moshe Ber simply nodded his head and tried to throw
himself at the commandant's feet. This went on until after Rosh
Hashonah; only then did the Zamosc Jews learn that an old
man from abroad was being held in jail. The rabbi and the head
of the community obtained his release by paying the commandant a ransom.

Reb Moshe Ber was invited to stay in Zamosc until after
Yom Kippur, but he would not consider it. He spent the night
there, took some bread, and set out on foot for Bilgorai at
daybreak. Trudging across harvested fields, digging turnips
for food, he refreshed himself in the thick pinewoods with
whitish berries, large, sour and watery, which grow in damp
places and are called Valakhi in the local dialect. A cart gave
him a lift for a mile or so. A few miles from Bilgorai, he was
thrown to the ground by some shepherds who pulled off his
boots and ran away with them.

Reb Moshe Ber continued barefoot, and for this reason did
not reach Bilgorai until late at night. A few tramps, spending
the night in the House of Study, refused to let him in, and he

had to sit on the steps, his weary head on his knees. The
autumnal night was clear and cold; against the dark yellow, dull
glow of the starry sky, a flock of goats, silently absorbed,
peeled bark from the wood that had been piled in the synagogue
courtyard for winter. As though complaining of an unforgettable sorrow, an owl lamented in a womanish voice, falling
silent and then beginning again, over and over. People with
wooden lanterns in their hands came at daybreak to say the
Selichoth prayers. Bringing the old man inside, they placed him
near the stove and covered him with discarded prayer shawls
from the chest. Later in the morning they brought him a heavy
pair of hobnailed, coarse-leathered military boots. The boots
pinched the old man's feet badly, but Reb Moshe Ber determined to observe the Yom Kippur fast at Jozefow, and Yom
Kippur was only one day off.

He left early. There were no more than about four miles to
travel, but he wanted to arrive at dawn, in time for the *Selichoth*
prayers. The moment he had left town, however, his stiff boots
began to cause him such pain that he couldn't take a step. He
had to pull them off and go barefoot. Then there was a down-
pour with thunder and lightning. He sank knee deep in puddles,
kept stumbling, and became smeared with clay and mud. His
feet swelled and bled. He spent the night on a haystack under
the open sky, and it was so cold that he couldn't sleep. In the
neighbouring villages dogs kept barking, and the rain went on
forever. Reb Moshe Ber was sure his end had come. He prayed
God to spare him until the *Nilah* prayer, so that he might reach
heaven purified of all sin. Later, when on the eastern horizon
the edges of clouds began to glow, while the fog grew milky
white, Reb Moshe Ber was infused with new strength and
once again set off for Jozefow.

He reached the Turisk circle at the very moment when the
hassidim had assembled in the customary way, to take brandy
and cake. A few recognized the new arrival at once, and there
was great rejoicing for he had long been thought dead. They
brought him hot tea. He said his prayers quickly, ate a slice of
white bread with honey, gefilte fish made of fresh carp, and
kreplach, and took a few glasses of brandy. Then he was led
to the steam bath. Two respectable citizens accompanied him

to the seventh shelf and personally whipped him with two bundles of new twigs, while the old man wept for joy.

Several times during Yom Kippur he was at the point of fainting, but he observed the fast until it ended. Next morning the Turisk hassidim gave him new clothes and told him to study the Torah. All of them had plenty of money, since they traded with Bosnian and Hungarian soldiers, and sent flour to what had been Galicia in exchange for smuggled tobacco. It was no hardship for them to support Reb Moshe Ber. The Turisk hassidim knew who he was – a hassid who had sat at the table of no less a man than Reb Motele of Chernobel! He had actually been a guest at the famous wonder-rabbi's home!

A few weeks later, the Turisk hassidim, timber merchants, just to shame their sworn enemies, the Sandzer hassidim, collected wood and built a house for Reb Moshe Ber and married him to a spinster, a deaf and dumb girl of about forty.

Exactly nine months later she gave birth to a son – now he had someone to say *kaddish* for him. As though it were a wedding, musicians played at the circumcision ceremony. Well-to-do housewives baked cakes and looked after the mother. The place where the banquet was held, the assembly room of the Turisk circle, smelled of cinnamon, saffron, and the women's best Sabbath dresses. Reb Moshe Ber wore a new satin caftan and a high velvet hat. He danced on the table, and for the first time, mentioned his age:

'And Abraham was a hundred years old,' he recited, 'when his son Isaac was born unto him. And Sarah said: God hath made me laugh so that all who hear will laugh with me.'

He named the boy Isaac.

Ivo Andrić

THE BRIDGE ON THE ŽEPA

TRANSLATED BY
SVETOZAR KOLJEVIĆ

IVO ANDRIĆ

Born in Travnik (Bosnia) 1892. Yugoslav novelist whose principal subject is his native Bosnia in the period of Ottoman rule: *Bosnian Story, Devil's Yard, The Bridge on the Drina*. The historical and symbolist interests of the novels are reflected in 'The Bridge on the Žepa', published in Zagreb in 1947.

THE BRIDGE ON THE ŽEPA

IN the fourth year of his viziership Grand Vizier Jusuf tottered and, victim of a dangerous intrigue, suddenly fell into disfavour. The struggle went on all winter and spring. (It was a wicked, cold spring, stubbornly refusing to let summer shine forth.) The month of May saw Jusuf walk out of prison, in triumph. And life went on, glamorous, quiet, unchanging. But the winter months, in which life and death, fame and ruin were hardly divided by so much as a dagger's blade, had left a trace of something subdued and wistful in the triumphant man. Something unutterable that experienced men who have known suffering keep in themselves like a hidden treasure and that is reflected, now and then, unawares, in a look, a gesture, a word.

Living confined, alone and in disgrace, the vizier remembered more vividly his origin and his native land. For disappointment and pain take the mind back to the past. He remembered his father and mother. (They had both died while he was still a humble assistant of the Sultan's Master of the Horse, and he had their graves edged with stone and marked by white tomb-stones.) He remembered Bosnia and the village of Žepa, from which he had been taken away when he was nine.

It was pleasant in misfortune to think of the distant land and the scattered village, Žepa, where every house told the story of his fame and success in Constantinople and where no one knew or suspected the seamy side of fame or the price of success.

That same summer he had opportunities for talking to people who came from Bosnia. He asked questions, and they told him what things were like. After the uprisings and wars there were disorders, dearth, starvation, and all kinds of disease. He ordered substantial aid to be given to all his people, to everyone still living at Žepa, and at the same time he started an inquiry into what was most needed in the way of public buildings. He learned that there were still four households of Šetkićes and that they were among the most prosperous families in the village, but that the village and all the surrounding country was impoverished, their mosque dilapidated and partly burnt, the fountain gone dry; and, worst of all, there was no bridge over the Žepa. The village was situated on a hill right above the confluence of the Žepa and the Drina, and the only road to Višegrad crossed the Žepa about fifty paces further upstream. Whatever bridge they made of logs, water carried it away. For either the Žepa swelled suddenly like all mountain streams, undermined the bridge, and washed the logs away; or the Drina rose and blocked the Žepa, overflowing into its channel, so that the Žepa rose too and swept the bridge away as if it had never been there. And in winter slippery ice covered the logs, and both men and cattle were in danger of breaking their necks. Were someone to build a bridge there he would do them the greatest service.

The vizier gave six carpets for the mosque and enough money to have a fountain with three pipes erected in front of it. And at the same time he decided to have a bridge built for them.

At that time there was a man living in Constantinople, an Italian master-mason who had built several bridges in the vicinity and so made his reputation. He was engaged by the vizier's treasurer and sent with two of the vizier's men to Bosnia.

There was still snow at Višegrad when they arrived. For several days the surprised townsmen watched the master-mason, bowed and grey, but with a ruddy young face, pacing about the big stone bridge, pounding the mortar from the joints, crumbling it among his fingers and tasting it with his tongue, and measuring the span of the arches with his steps. Then for a few days he kept visiting Banja and its quarry, from which the stone for the Višegrad bridge had come. He brought workers and had the quarry cleared; it had been covered with earth and overgrown with coppice and young pines. They kept digging until they found a wide, deep vein of stone which was denser and whiter than that used for the Višegrad bridge. Then he went down the Drina, as far as the Žepa, and designated the place to ferry the stone. Then one of the vizier's two men went back to Constantinople with the estimate and plans.

The mason remained and waited, but he did not want to

live either at Višegrad or in any of the Christian houses above the Žepa. On a plateau, in the corner formed by the confluence of the Drina and the Žepa, he made a log-cabin – the vizier's man and a Višegrad clerk were his interpreters – and he lodged there. He prepared his own meals. He bought eggs, cream, onions, and dried fruit from peasants. As to meat, people said he never bought any. Most of the time he spent hewing, making sketches, examining various kinds of stone, or watching the course of the Žepa.

One day the clerk who had gone to Constantinople came back with the vizier's approval and the first third of the money needed for the bridge.

Work started. People stood agape wondering what was going on. It did not look like a bridge. First, heavy pine beams were driven into the river bed obliquely across the Žepa, then two rows of stakes were set between them, and everything was wattled together with brushwood and stuffed with clay, like a trench. So the course of the river was diverted and half its bed left dry. The work was just finished when, one day, there was a cloudburst in the mountains, and at once the Žepa became troubled and swollen. On the following night the newly-finished dam gave way in the middle. And when the next day dawned the water had already withdrawn, but the wattle had been broken in many places, the stakes plucked out, the beams bent. Among the workers and peasants there were rumours that the Žepa would not let itself be bridged. But already on the third day the master-mason ordered new stakes to be driven in, deeper than before, and the remaining beams to be straightened and brought into line. And again, from deep down, the rocky river-bed echoed with mallets, workers' noise, and rhythmic blows.

Stone-dressers and masons, from Herzegovina and Dalmatia, arrived only after everything had been finished and ready, and the stone from Banja brought in. Sheds were put up for them, and they chipped stone in front of the sheds, white with stone-dust like millers. The master-mason walked among them, leaning down and measuring their work with a yellow try-square and a leaden plummet on a green thread. Both steep, craggy banks were already cut through when the

money ran out. The workers grumbled and the people murmured that nothing would come of the bridge. Some of those
who came from Constantinople reported rumours that the
vizier had greatly changed. No one knew what was the matter
with him, sickness or worries, but he was more unapproachable
every day, forgetting and giving up the work he had begun
in Constantinople itself. But a few days later one of the vizier's
men came back with the rest of the money, and the building
went on.

A fortnight before St Demetrius's Day, people crossing
the Žepa over the logs, a little upstream from the works,
noticed for the first time that from the dark grey slate on both
banks a white, smooth wall of dressed stone was beginning to
appear, plaited all over with the cobwebs of scaffolding. It
grew every day. But then the first frosts came and the work
was stopped. The stone-dressers went home for the winter,
and the master-mason spent the winter in his log-cabin which
he hardly ever left, bowed all the time over his plans and
calculations. But he often visited the building site. When
spring approached and the ice began to crack, every now and
then, worried, he paced about the scaffolding and the dams;
sometimes even by night, with a link in his hand.

Before St George's Day the masons came back and the work
went on. And just at midsummer the work was finished. The
workers pulled down the scaffolding merrily, and from the
criss-cross of beams and planks the bridge appeared, slender
and white, a single arch spanned between two rocks.

Nothing could have been more difficult to imagine than
such a marvellous structure in this desolate split landscape. It
seemed as if spurts of foam had gushed out from one bank to
the other, and the two spurts had collided, joined into an arch,
and remained like that for a moment, floating above the abyss.
Through the arch, in the background, a stretch of the blue
Drina could be seen, and deep below it the foamy Žepa, now
tamed, gurgled on. It took a long time for the eye to get used
to the arch of well-designed, slender outlines; the arch seemed
to have been arrested in flight, only for a moment, caught on
the rugged dark rocks with their hellebore and clematis, on
the point of taking off again and disappearing.

From the neighbouring villages people bustled to see the bridge. The townsmen of Višegrad and Rogatica also came and admired it, regretting that it was built in such a rocky wilderness and not in their town.

'It isn't easy to give birth to a vizier!' the inhabitants of Žepa would answer, patting with their palms the parapet of the bridge, straight and sharp-edged, as if cut from cheese and not hewn from stone.

While the first travellers, stopping in surprise, were crossing the bridge, the master-mason paid off the workers, loaded and fastened his chests full of instruments and papers, and with the vizier's men set off for Constantinople.

It was only then that townsmen and villagers began to talk about him. Selim, the gipsy, who had brought him things from Višegrad on his horse, and was the only man who had visited his log-cabin, would sit in shops and tell, God knows how many times, everything he knew about the stranger.

'Indeed, he is not a man like other people are. When the work was stopped in winter, sometimes for ten or fifteen days I wouldn't go to see him. But whenever I came everything was in a mess, just as I had left it. In the cold log-cabin he sat with a bear-skin cap on his head, wrapped up to his arm-pits, only his hands showing free, livid with cold, while he chipped at his stones and wrote something down; chipped and wrote. And so all the time. I would load my horse and he would look at me with his green eyes, his eyebrows raised – you'd think he'd devour you. But he never said a word. I have never seen anything like it. And, my friends, you wouldn't believe how hard he was at it for a year and a half, and when he finished his work, he left for Constantinople and we took him across on the ferry, and he hurried off on his horse; but do you think that he turned back one single time to look at us or the bridge? No!'

And the shopkeepers asked more and more questions about the mason and his life, marvelled more and more at what they heard, regretting that they had not watched him more closely when he walked in the streets of Višegrad.

Meanwhile the master-mason went on his journey and, two stages before Constantinople, he fell ill of the plague. In a fever, hardly able to cling on to his horse, he reached the city. He went immediately to the hospital of the Italian Franciscans. And at the same time next day he breathed his last in a monk's arms.

The next morning the vizier had already learned about the mason's death, and the remaining bills and plans of the bridge were brought to him. The mason had received only a quarter of his wages. He had left behind him no debts and no cash, no will and no heirs. The vizier thought it over for a while and ordered one of the remaining three-quarters of the wages to be paid to the hospital and the other two given for the paupers' bread and broth.

As he was giving the orders – it was a quiet morning of late summer – a petition from a young, learned Constantinople mullah was brought to him. The man had been born in Bosnia, wrote smooth verses, and the vizier had sometimes endowed him and helped him. He had heard, he said, of the bridge which the vizier had built in Bosnia and hoped that an inscription would be carved on it, as on any other public edifice, telling the world when it was built and who had built it. As always, his services were at the vizier's disposal and he begged the vizier to deign to accept the enclosed chronogram which he had composed with great difficulty. On the enclosed sheet of stouter paper there was a finely copied chronogram with a red and gold initial:

> When Good Rule and Noble Skill
> Offered each other a friendly hand
> This beautiful bridge was born,
> To the delight of the subjects and Jusuf's pride –
> In both worlds.

Underneath was the vizier's oval seal, divided into two unequal fields; on the larger one was written: *Jusuf Ibrahim – God's true slave*, and on the smaller one was the vizier's motto: *In silence is safety*.

The vizier sat for a long time with the petition, his hands apart, one of his palms pressing the inscription in verse and the other the mason's bills and plans. He spent more and more time lately thinking over petitions and papers.

This summer it was two years since his fall and confinement. At first, after his return to power, he had not noticed any changes in himself. He was in his best years – when the man knows and feels the full value of living; he had triumphed over all his opponents and was more powerful than before; he could measure the height of his power by the depths of his recent fall. But as time went on – instead of forgetting – he was more and more haunted by the thought of prison. And if he sometimes found enough strength to drive away such thoughts, he could not stop his dreams. The prison began to obsess his dreams, and from the dreams of night, like a vague horror, it passed into the waking state and poisoned his days.

He became more sensitive to the objects about him. He was irritated by things which he had not even noticed before. He gave orders to have all the velvet in the palace replaced by bright cloth, soft and smooth, which did not rustle under the touch. He came to hate mother-of-pearl, for it was suggestive of some cold, desolate loneliness. The touch of mother-of-pearl, the mere sight of it, made his teeth go numb and his flesh creep with horror. All furniture and weapons which had mother-of-pearl on them were removed from his rooms.

He began to regard everything with secret but deep mistrust. Without any apparent origin one thought was firmly rooted in his mind: every human action, every word *may* bring evil. And this *possibility* linked itself to everything he heard, saw, said, or thought. The triumphant vizier had come to know the fear of life. So, unawares, he entered the stage which is the first phase of dying, when a man comes to be absorbed more in the shadows of things than in the things themselves.

This evil gnawed at him, tearing him from within; he could not even think of confiding it to anyone; and by the time it had completed its work and burst through the surface, no one would be able to recognize it; people would simply say: death. For people did not suspect how many of the powerful and the great were so silently, invisibly, but quickly dying from within.

This morning the vizier was again weary, not having slept, but calm and cool-headed; his eyelids were heavy, and his face as if frozen in the freshness of the morning. He thought of the foreign mason who had died and of the poor who would eat his earnings. He thought of the distant, mountainous, gloomy land of Bosnia (there had always been gloom in his thoughts of Bosnia!) which even the light of Islam could only partially illuminate and where life, lacking lofty conduct and gentleness, was miserable, niggardly, harsh. And how many such lands there were in Allah's world? How many rivers without a bridge or ford? How many places without drinking water, how many mosques without decoration or beauty?

Before his mind's eye a world appeared, full of various needs, misery, and fear in different shapes.

The small green tiles of the summer house blazed in the sun. The vizier looked down on the mullah's verses, raised his hand slowly, and crossed out twice the whole inscription. He stopped a moment, and then crossed out also the first part of the seal with his name. Only the motto remained: *In silence is safety*. He stopped for a while, faced with the motto, and then raised his hand again and in a resolute stroke wiped that out too.

So the bridge was left nameless, without any sign.

Over there, in Bosnia, it shone in the sun and glistened in the light of the moon, taking men and cattle from one bank to another. Little by little the circle of dug-out earth and scattered things, which surrounds every new erection, disappeared; people carried off and the water swept away broken stakes, the pieces of scaffolding and the rest of the timber, and the rains washed off the traces of stone-dressing. But the country could not accept the bridge and the bridge could not accept the country. Seen from the other side, the bold span of its white arch always looked isolated and lonely and took the traveller by surprise like a strange thought, gone astray and caught among crags, in the wilderness.

The teller of this story was the first man to whom it occurred to examine and find out how it came to be there. This happened one evening when he came back from the mountains and, weary, sat down by its parapet. It was the season of hot summer days and cool nights. When he leaned his back against the stone, it was still warm with the heat of day. The man was sweaty, and a cold wind blew from the Drina; pleasant and strange was the touch of the warm, hewn stone. They understood each other at once. Then he decided to write its history.

Bertolt Brecht

THE UNSEEMLY OLD LADY

TRANSLATED BY
YVONNE KAPP

BERTOLT BRECHT

Born in Augsburg 1898; died in Berlin 1956. German dramatist and founder of the Berliner Ensemble. Plays: *Galileo, Mother Courage, The Caucasian Chalk Circle.* 'The Unseemly Old Lady' is from a collection of verse and sketches, *Tales from the Calendar* (1949).

THE UNSEEMLY OLD LADY

My grandmother was seventy-two years old when my grandfather died. He had a small lithographer's business in a little town in Baden and there he worked with two or three assistants until his death. My grandmother managed the household without a maid, looked after the ramshackle old house and cooked for the menfolk and children.

She was a little thin woman with lively lizard's eyes, though slow of speech. On very scanty means she had reared five of the seven children she had borne. As a result, she had grown smaller with the years.

Her two girls went to America and two of the sons also moved away. Only the youngest, who was delicate, stayed in the little town. He became a printer and set up a family far too large for him.

So after my grandfather died she was alone in the house.

The children wrote each other letters dealing with the problem of what should be done about her. One of them could offer her a home, and the printer wanted to move with his family into her house. But the old woman turned a deaf ear to these proposals and would only accept, from each of her children who could afford it, a small monetary allowance. The lithographer's business, long behind the times, was sold for practically nothing, and there were debts as well.

The children wrote saying that, all the same, she could not live quite alone, but since she entirely ignored this, they gave in and sent her a little money every month. At any rate, they thought, there was always the printer who had stayed in the town.

What was more, he undertook to give his brothers and sisters news of their mother from time to time. The printer's letters to my father, and what my father himself learned on a visit and, two years later, after my grandmother's burial, give me a picture of what went on in those two years.

It seems that, from the start, the printer was disappointed

that my grandmother had declined to take him into the house, which was fairly large and now standing empty. He had four children and lived in three rooms. But in any case the old lady had only very casual relations with him. She invited the children for coffee every Sunday afternoon, and that was about all.

She visited her son once or twice in three months and helped her daughter-in-law with the jam-making. The young woman gathered from some of her remarks that she found the printer's little dwelling too cramped for her. He, in reporting this, could not forbear to add an exclamation mark.

My father wrote asking what the old woman was up to nowadays, to which he replied rather curtly: going to the cinema.

It must be understood that this was not at all the thing; at least, not in her children's eyes. Thirty years ago the cinema was not what it is today. It meant wretched, ill-ventilated premises, often converted from disused skittle-alleys, with garish posters outside displaying the murders and tragedies of passion. Strictly speaking, only adolescents went, or, for the darkness, courting couples. An old woman there by herself would certainly be conspicuous.

And there was another aspect of this cinema-going to be considered. Of course, admission was cheap, but since the pleasure fell more or less into the category of self-indulgence, it represented 'money thrown away'. And to throw money away was not respectable.

Furthermore, not only did my grandmother keep up no regular association with her son in the place, but she neither invited nor visited any of her other acquaintances. She never went to the coffee-parties in the little town. On the other hand, she frequented a cobbler's workshop in a poor and even slightly notorious alley where, especially in the afternoon, all manner of not particularly reputable characters hung about: out-of-work waitresses and itinerant craftsmen. The cobbler was a middle-aged man who had knocked about the world without it leading to anything. It was also said that he drank. In any case, he was no proper associate for my grandmother.

The printer intimated in a letter that he had hinted as much to his mother and had met with a very cool reply. 'He's seen a thing or two,' she answered and that was the end of the conversation. It was not easy to talk to my grandmother about things she did not wish to discuss.

About six months after my grandfather's death the printer wrote to my father saying that their mother now ate at the inn every other day.

That really was news! Grandmother, who all her life had cooked for a dozen people and herself had always eaten up the leavings, now ate at the inn. What had come over her?

Shortly after this, my father made a business trip in the neighbourhood and he visited his mother. She was just about to go out when he turned up. She took off her hat again and gave him a glass of red wine and a biscuit. She seemed in a perfectly equable mood, neither particularly animated nor particularly silent. She asked after us, though not in much detail, and wanted principally to know whether there were cherries for the children. There she was completely her old self. The room was of course scrupulously clean and she looked well.

The only thing that gave an indication of her new life was that she did not want to go with my father to the churchyard to visit her husband's grave. 'You can go by yourself,' she said lightly. 'It's the third on the left in the eleventh row. I've got to go somewhere.'

The printer said afterwards that probably she had had to go to her cobbler. He complained bitterly.

'Here am I, stuck in this hole with my family, and only five hours' badly-paid work, on top of which my asthma's troubling me again, while the house in the main street stands empty.'

My father had taken a room at the inn, but nevertheless expected to be invited by his mother, if only as a matter of form; however, she did not mention it. Yet even when the house had been full, she had always objected to his not staying with them and spending money on an hotel into the bargain.

But she appeared to have finished with family life and to be treading new paths now in the evening of her days. My father, who had his fair share of humour, found her 'pretty sprightly' and told my uncle to let the old woman do what she wanted.

And what did she want to do?

The next thing reported was that she had hired a brake and

taken an excursion on a perfectly ordinary Thursday. A brake was a large, high-sprung, horse-drawn vehicle with a seating capacity for whole families. Very occasionally, when we grand-children had come for a visit, grandfather had hired a brake. Grandmother had always stayed behind. She had refused to come along with a scornful wave of the hand.

And after the brake came the trip to K., a larger town some two hours' distance by train. There was a race-meeting there and it was to the races that my grandmother went.

The printer was now positively alarmed. He wanted to have a doctor called in. My father shook his head as he read the letter, but was against calling in a doctor.

My grandmother had not travelled alone to K. She had taken with her a young girl who, according to the printer's letter, was slightly feeble-minded: the kitchen-maid at the inn where the old lady took her meals every second day.

From now on this 'half-wit' played quite a part.

My grandmother apparently doted on her. She took her to the cinema and to the cobbler – who, incidentally, turned out to be a Social Democrat – and it was rumoured that the two women played cards in the kitchen over a glass of wine.

'Now she's bought the half-wit a hat with roses on it,' wrote the printer in despair. 'And our Anna has no communion dress!'

My uncle's letters became quite hysterical, dealt only with the 'unseemly conduct of our dear mother' and otherwise said nothing. The rest I know from my father.

The innkeeper had whispered to him with a wink: 'Mrs B.'s enjoying herself nowadays, so they say.'

As a matter of fact, even in these last years my grandmother did not live extravagantly in any way. When she did not eat at the inn, she usually took no more than a little egg dish, some coffee and, above all, her beloved biscuits. She did, however, allow herself a cheap red wine, of which she drank a small glass at every meal. She kept the house very clean, and not just the bedroom and kitchen which she used. All the same, without her children's knowledge, she mortgaged it. What she did with the money never came out. She seems to have given it to the cobbler. After her death he moved to another town and was said to have started a fair-sized business in hand-made shoes.

When you come to think of it, she lived two lives in succession. The first one as daughter, wife and mother; the second simply as Mrs B., an unattached person without responsibilities and with modest but sufficient means. The first life lasted some sixty years; the second no more than two.

My father learned that in the last six months she had permitted herself certain liberties unknown to normal people. Thus she might rise in summer at three in the morning and take walks in the deserted streets of the little town, which she had entirely to herself. And, it was generally alleged, when the priest called on her to keep the old woman company in her loneliness, she invited him to the cinema.

She was not at all lonely. A crowd of jolly people forgathered at the cobbler's, it appears, and there was much gossip. She always kept a bottle of her own red wine there and drank her little glassful whilst the others gossiped and inveighed against the town officials. This wine was reserved for her though sometimes she provided stronger drink for the company.

She died quite suddenly on an autumn afternoon, in her bedroom, though not in bed but on an upright chair by the window. She had invited the 'half-wit' to the cinema that evening, so the girl was with her when she died. She was seventy-four years old.

I have seen a photograph of her which was taken for the children and shows her laid out.

What you see is a tiny little face, very wrinkled, and a thin-lipped, wide mouth. Much that is small, but no smallness. She had savoured to the full the long years of servitude and the short years of freedom and consumed the bread of life to the last crumb.

Albert Camus

THE SILENT MEN

TRANSLATED BY
JUSTIN O'BRIEN

ALBERT CAMUS

Born at Mondovi (Algeria) 1913; died in a road accident in France 1960. French novelist, dramatist and essayist associated with the philosophy of 'the absurd': which is sometimes not far from liberal humanism, as in 'The Silent Men' (1957). The novels are *The Outsider, The Plague* and *The Fall*.

THE SILENT MEN

It was the dead of winter and yet a radiant sun was rising over the already active city. At the end of the jetty, sea and sky fused in a single dazzling light. But Yvars did not see them. He was cycling slowly along the boulevards above the harbour. On the fixed pedal of his cycle his crippled leg rested stiffly while the other laboured to cope with the slippery road surface still wet with the night's moisture. Without raising his head, a slight figure astride the saddle, he avoided the rails of the former tram-line, suddenly turned the handlebars to let cars pass him, and occasionally elbowed back into place the bag in which Fernande had put his lunch. At such moments he would think bitterly of the bag's contents. Between the two slices of coarse bread, instead of the Spanish omelet he liked or the beefsteak fried in oil, there was nothing but cheese.

The ride to the shop had never seemed to him so long. To be sure, he was ageing. At forty, though he had remained as slim as a vine shoot, a man's muscles don't warm up so quickly. At times, reading sports commentaries in which a thirty-year-old athlete was referred to as a veteran, he would shrug his shoulders. 'If he's a veteran,' he would say to Fernande, 'then I'm practically in a wheelchair.' Yet he knew that the reporter wasn't altogether wrong. At thirty a man is already beginning to lose his wind without noticing it. At forty he's not yet in a wheelchair, but he's definitely heading in that direction. Wasn't that just why he now avoided looking towards the sea during the ride to the other end of town where the cooper's shop was? When he was twenty he never got tired of watching it, for it used to hold in store a happy week-end on the beach. Despite or because of his lameness, he had always liked swimming. Then the years had passed, there had been Fernande, the birth of the boy, and, to make ends meet, the overtime, at the shop on Saturdays and on various odd jobs for others on Sundays. Little by little he had lost the habit of those violent days that used to satiate him. The deep, clear water, the hot sun, the girls, the physical life – there was no other form of happiness in this country. And that happiness disappeared with youth. Yvars continued to love the sea, but only at the end of the day when the water in the bay became a little darker. The moment was pleasant on the terrace beside his house where he would sit down after work, grateful for his clean shirt that Fernande ironed so well and for the glass of anisette all frosted over. Evening would fall, the sky would become all soft and mellow, the neighbours talking with Yvars would suddenly lower their voices. At those times he didn't know whether he was happy or felt like crying. At least he felt in harmony at such moments, he had nothing to do but wait quietly, without quite knowing for what.

In the morning when he went back to work, on the other hand, he didn't like to look at the sea. Though it was always there to greet him, he refused to see it until evening. This morning he was pedalling along with head down, feeling even heavier than usual; his heart too was heavy. When he had come back from the meeting, the night before, and had announced that they were going back to work, Fernande had gaily said: 'Then the boss is giving you all a rise?' The boss was not giving any rise; the strike had failed. They hadn't managed things right, it had to be admitted. An impetuous walk-out, and the union had been right to back it up only half-heartedly. After all, some fifteen workers hardly counted; the union had to consider the other cooper's shops that hadn't joined in. You couldn't really blame the union. Cooperage, threatened by the building of tankers and tank trucks, was not thriving. Fewer and fewer barrels and large casks were being made; work consisted chiefly in repairing the huge tuns already in existence. Employers saw their business compromised, to be sure, but even so they wanted to maintain a margin of profit and the easiest way still seemed to them to block wages despite the rise in living costs. What can coopers do when cooperage disappears? You don't change trades when you've gone to the trouble of learning one; this one was hard and called for a long apprenticeship. The good cooper, the one who fits his curved staves and tightens them in the fire with an iron hoop, almost hermetically, without caulking

with raffia or oakum, was rare. Yvars knew this and was proud
of it. Changing trades is nothing, but to give up what you know,
your master craftsmanship, is not easy. A fine craft without
employment and you're stuck, you have to resign yourself.
But resignation isn't easy either. It was hard to have one's
mouth shut, not to be able to discuss really, and to take the
same road every morning with an accumulating fatigue, in
order to receive at the end of every week merely what they are
willing to give you, which is less and less adequate.

So they had got angry. Two or three of them had hesitated,
but the anger had spread to them too after the first discussions
with the boss. He had told them flatly, in fact, that they could
take it or leave it. A man doesn't talk like that. 'What's he
expect of us?' Esposito had said. 'That we'll stoop over and
wait to be kicked?' The boss wasn't a bad sort, however. He
had inherited from his father, had grown up in the shop, and
had known almost all the workers for years. Occasionally he
invited them to have a snack in the shop; they would cook
sardines or sausage meat over fires of shavings and, thanks
partly to the wine, he was really very nice. At New Year he
always gave five bottles of vintage wine to each of the men, and
often, when one of them was ill or celebrated an event like
marriage or first communion, he would make a gift of money.
At the birth of his daughter, there had been sugar-coated
almonds for everyone. Two or three times he had invited
Yvars to shoot on his coastal property. He liked his workmen,
no doubt, and often recalled the fact that his father had begun
as an apprentice. But he had never gone to their homes; he
wasn't aware. He thought only of himself because he knew
nothing but himself, and now you could take it or leave it. In
other words, he had become obstinate likewise. But, in his
position, he could allow himself to be.

He had forced the union's hand, and the shop had closed
its doors. 'Don't go to the trouble of picketing,' the boss had
said; 'when the shop's not working, I save money.' That
wasn't true, but it didn't help matters since he was telling them
to their faces that he gave them work out of charity. Esposito
was wild with fury and had told him he wasn't a man. The boss
was hot-blooded and they had to be separated. But, at the same

time, it had made an impression on the workers. Twenty days on strike, the wives sad at home, two or three of them discouraged, and, in the end, the union had advised them to give in on the promise of arbitration and recovery of the lost days through overtime. They had decided to go back to work. Swaggering, of course, and saying that it wasn't all settled, that it would have to be reconsidered. But this morning, with a fatigue that resembled defeat, cheese instead of meat, the illusion was no longer possible. No matter how the sun shone, the sea held forth no more promises. Yvars pressed on his single pedal and with each turn of the wheel it seemed to him he was ageing a little. He couldn't think of the shop, of the fellow workers and the boss he would soon be seeing again without feeling his heart become a trifle heavier. Fernande had been worried: 'What will you men say to him?' 'Nothing.' Yvars had straddled his bicycle, and had shaken his head. He had clenched his teeth; his small, dark, and wrinkled face with its delicate features had become hard. 'We're going back to work. That's enough.' Now he was cycling along, his teeth still clenched, with a sad, dry anger that darkened even the sky itself.

He left the boulevard, and the sea, to attack the moist streets of the old Spanish quarter. They led to an area occupied solely by sheds, junkyards, and garages, where the shop was – a sort of low shed that was faced with stone up to half-way point and then glassed in up to the corrugated metal roof. This shop opened on to the former cooperage, a courtyard surrounded by a covered shed that had been abandoned when the business had enlarged and now served only as a storehouse for worn-out machines and old casks. Beyond the courtyard, separated from it by a sort of path covered with old tiles, the boss's garden began, at the end of which his house stood. Big and ugly, it was nevertheless prepossessing because of the Virginia creeper and the straggling honeysuckle surrounding the outside steps.

Yvars saw at once that the doors of the shop were closed. A group of workmen stood silently in front of them. This was the first time since he had been working here that he had found the doors closed when he arrived. The boss had wanted to emphasize that he had the upper hand. Yvars turned towards the left, parked his bicycle under the lean-to that prolonged the shed on that side, and walked towards the door. From a distance he recognized Esposito, a tall, dark, hairy fellow who worked beside him, Marcou, the union delegate, with his tenor's profile, Saïd, the only Arab in the shop, then all the others who silently watched him approach. But before he had joined them, they all suddenly looked in the direction of the shop doors, which had just begun to open. Ballester, the foreman, appeared in the opening. He opened one of the heavy doors and, turning his back to the workmen, pushed it slowly on its iron rail.

Ballester, who was the oldest of all, disapproved of the strike but had kept silent as soon as Esposito had told him that he was serving the boss's interests. Now he stood near the door, broad and short in his navy-blue jersey, already barefoot (he was the only one besides Saïd who worked barefoot), and he watched them go in one by one with his eyes that were so pale they seemed colourless in his old tanned face, his mouth downcast, under his thick, drooping moustache. They were silent, humiliated by this return of the defeated, furious at their own silence, but the more it was prolonged the less capable they were of breaking it. They went in without looking at Ballester, for they knew he was carrying out an order in making them go in like that, and his bitter and downcast look told them what he was thinking. Yvars, for one, looked at him. Ballester, who liked him, nodded his head without saying a word.

Now they were all in the little locker-room on the right of the entrance: open stalls separated by unpainted boards to which had been attached, on either side, little locked cupboards; the farthest stall from the entrance, up against the walls of the shed, had been transformed into a shower above a gutter hollowed out of the earthen floor. In the centre of the shop could be seen work in various stages, already finished large casks, loose-hooped, waiting for the forcing in the fire, thick benches with a long slot hollowed out in them (and in some of them had been slipped circular wooden bottoms waiting to be planed to a sharp edge), and finally cold fires. Along the wall, on the left of the entrance, the workbenches

extended in a row. In front of them stood piles of staves to be
planed. Against the right wall, not far from the dressing-room,
two large power-saws, thoroughly oiled, strong and silent,
gleamed.

Some time ago, the workshop had become too big for the
handful of men who worked there. This was an advantage
in the hot season, a disadvantage in winter. But today, in this
vast space, the work dropped half-finished, the casks abandoned in every corner with a single hoop holding the base of
the staves spreading at the top like coarse wooden flowers,
the sawdust covering the benches, the tool-boxes, and
machines – everything gave the shop a look of neglect. They
looked at it, dressed now in their old sweaters and their faded
and patched trousers and they hesitated. Ballester was watching
them. 'So,' he said, 'we get started?' One by one, they went
to their posts without saying a word. Ballester went from one
to another, briefly reminding them of the work to be begun or
finished. No one answered. Soon the first hammer resounded
against the iron-tipped wedge sinking a hoop over the convex
part of a barrel, a plane groaned as it hit a knot, and one of the
saws, started up by Esposito, got under way with a great
whirring of blade. Saïd would bring staves on request or
light fires of shavings on which the casks were placed to make
them swell in their corset of iron hoops. When no one called
for him, he stood at a work-bench riveting the big rusty hoops
with heavy hammer blows. The scent of burning shavings
began to fill the shop. Yvars, who was planing and fitting the
staves cut out by Esposito, recognized the old scent and his
heart relaxed somewhat. All were working in silence, but a
warmth, a life was gradually beginning to reawaken in the shop.
Through the broad windows a clean, fresh light began to fill
the shed. The smoke rose bluish in the golden sunlight; Yvars
even heard an insect buzz close to him.

At that moment the door into the former shop opened in
the end wall and M. Lassalle, the boss, stopped on the threshold. Thin and dark, he was scarcely more than thirty. His
white overall hanging open over a tan gabardine suit, he looked
at ease in his body. Despite his very bony face cut like a hatchet,
he generally aroused liking, as do most people who exude

vitality. Yet he seemed somewhat embarrassed as he came through the door. His greeting was less sonorous than usual; in any case, no one answered it. The sound of the hammers hesitated, lost the beat, and resumed even louder. M. Lassalle took a few hesitant steps, then he headed towards little Valery, who had been working with them for only a year. Near the power-saw, a few feet away from Yvars, he was putting a bottom on a big hogshead and the boss watched him. Valery went on working without saying anything. 'Well, my boy,' said M. Lassalle, 'how are things?' The young man suddenly became more awkward in his movements. He glanced at Esposito, who was close to him, picking up a pile of staves in his huge arms to take them to Yvars. Esposito looked at him too while going on with his work, and Valery peered back into his hogshead without answering the boss. Lassalle, rather nonplussed, remained a moment planted in front of the young man, then he shrugged his shoulders and turned towards Marcou. The latter, astride his bench, was giving the finishing touches, with slow, careful strokes, to sharpening the edge of a bottom. 'Hello, Marcou,' Lassalle said in a flatter voice. Marcou did not answer, entirely occupied with taking very thin shavings off his wood. 'What's got into you?' Lassalle asked in a loud voice as he turned towards the other workmen. 'We didn't agree, to be sure. But that doesn't keep us from having to work together. So what's the use of this?' Marcou got up, raised his bottom piece, verified the circular sharp edge with the palm of his hand, squinted his languorous eyes with a look of satisfaction, and, still silent, went towards another workman who was putting together a hogshead. Throughout the whole shop could be heard nothing but the sound of hammers and of the power-saw. 'O.K.,' Lassalle said. 'When you get over this, let me know through Ballester.' Calmly, he walked out of the shop.

Almost immediately afterwards, above the din of the shop, a bell rang out twice. Ballester, who had just sat down to roll a cigarette, got up slowly and went to the door at the end. After he had left, the hammers resounded with less noise; one of the workmen had even stopped when Ballester came back. From the door he said merely: 'The boss wants you, Marcou and Yvars.' Yvars's first impulse was to go and wash his hands, but Marcou grasped him by the arm as he went by and Yvars limped out behind him.

Outside in the courtyard, the light was so clear, so liquid, that Yvars felt it on his face and bare arms. They went up the outside stairs, under the honeysuckle on which a few blossoms were already visible. When they entered the corridor, whose walls were covered with diplomas, they heard a child crying and M. Lassalle's voice saying: 'Put her to bed after lunch. We'll call the doctor if she doesn't get over it.' Then the boss appeared suddenly in the corridor and showed them into the little office they already knew, furnished with imitation rustic furniture and its walls decorated with sports trophies. 'Sit down,' Lassalle said as he took his place behind the desk. They remained standing. 'I called you in because you, Marcou, are the delegate and you, Yvars, my oldest employee after Ballester. I don't want to get back to the discussions, which are now over. I cannot, absolutely not, give you what you ask. The matter has been settled, and we reached the conclusion that work had to be resumed. I see that you are angry with me, and that hurts me, I'm telling you just as I feel it. I merely want to add this: what I can't do today I may perhaps be able to do when business picks up. And if I can do it, I'll do it even before you ask me. Meanwhile, let's try to work together.' He stopped talking, seemed to reflect; then looked up at them. 'Well?' he said. Marcou was looking out of the window. Yvars, his teeth clenched, wanted to speak but couldn't. 'Listen,' said Lassalle, 'you have all closed your minds. You'll get over it. But when you become reasonable again, don't forget what I've just said to you.' He rose, went towards Marcou, and held out his hand. 'Ciao!' he said. Marcou suddenly turned pale, his popular tenor's face hardened and, for a second only, became mean-looking. Then he abruptly turned on his heel and went out. Lassalle, likewise pale, looked at Yvars without holding out his hand. 'Go to hell!' he shouted.

When they went back into the shop, the men were lunching. Ballester had gone out. Marcou simply said: 'Just wind,' and returned to his bench. Esposito stopped biting into his bread to ask what they had answered; Yvars said they hadn't answered anything. Then he went to get his haversack and came back and sat down on his workbench. He was beginning to eat when, not far from him, he noticed Saïd lying on his back in a pile of shavings, his eyes looking vaguely at the windows made blue by a sky that had become less luminous. He asked him if he had already finished. Saïd said he had eaten his figs. Yvars stopped eating. The uneasy feeling that hadn't left him since the interview with Lassalle suddenly disappeared to make room for a pleasant warmth. He broke his bread in two as he got up and, faced with Saïd's refusal, said that everything would be better next week. 'Then it'll be your turn to treat me,' he said. Saïd smiled. Now he bit into the piece of Yvars's sandwich, but in a gingerly way like a man who isn't hungry.

Esposito took an old pot and lighted a little fire of shavings and chips. He heated some coffee that he had brought in a bottle. He said it was a gift to the shop that his grocer had made when he learned of the strike's failure. A mustard jar passed from hand to hand. Each time Esposito poured out the already sugared coffee. Saïd swallowed it with more pleasure than he had taken in eating. Esposito drank the rest of the coffee right from the burning pot, smacking his lips and swearing. At that moment Ballester came in to give the back-to-work signal.

While they were rising and gathering papers and utensils into their haversacks, Ballester came and stood in their midst and said suddenly that it was hard for all, and for him too, but that this was no reason to act like children and that there was no use in sulking. Esposito, the pot in his hand, turned towards him; his long, coarse face had suddenly become flushed. Yvars knew what he was about to say – and what everyone was thinking at the same time – that they were not sulking, that their mouths had been closed, they had to take it or leave it, and that anger and helplessness sometimes hurt so much that you can't even cry out. They were men, after all, and they weren't going to begin smiling and simpering. But Esposito said none of this, his face finally relaxed, and he slapped Ballester's shoulder gently while the others went back to their work. Again the hammers rang out, the big shed filled with the familiar din, with the smell of shavings and of old clothes damp with sweat. The big saw whined and bit into the fresh wood of the stave that Esposito was slowly pushing in front of him. Where the saw bit, damp sawdust spurted out and covered, with something like bread-crumbs, the big hairy hands firmly gripping the wood on each side of the moaning blade. Once the stave was ripped, you could hear only the sound of the motor.

At present Yvars felt only the strain in his back as he leaned over the plane. Generally the fatigue didn't come until later on. He had got out of training during these weeks of inactivity, it was clear. But he thought also of age, which makes manual labour harder when it's not mere precision work. That strain also foreshadowed old age. Wherever the muscles are involved, work eventually becomes hateful, it precedes death, and on evenings following great physical effort sleep itself is like death. The boy wanted to become a schoolteacher, he was right; those who indulge in clichés about manual work don't know what they're talking about.

When Yvars straightened up to catch his breath and also to drive away these evil thoughts, the bell rang out again. It was insistent, but in such a strange way, with stops and imperious starts, that the men interrupted their work. Ballester listened, surprised, then made up his mind and went slowly to the door. He had disappeared for several seconds when the ringing finally ceased. They resumed work. Again the door was flung open and Ballester ran towards the locker-room. He came out wearing canvas shoes and, slipping on his jacket, said to Yvars as he went by: 'The child has had an attack. I'm off to get Germain,' and he ran towards the main door. Dr Germain took care of the shop's health; he lived in this outlying quarter. Yvars repeated the news without commentary. They gathered around him and looked at one another, embarrassed. Nothing could be heard but the motor of the power saw running freely. 'It's perhaps nothing,' one of them said. They went back to their places, the shop filled again with their noises, but they were working slowly, as if waiting for something.

A quarter of an hour later, Ballester came in again, hung up his jacket, and, without saying a word, went out through the little door. On the windows the light was getting dimmer. A little later, in the intervals when the saw was not ripping into the wood, the dull bell of an ambulance could be heard, at first in the distance, then nearer, finally just outside. Then silence. After a moment Ballester came back and everyone went up to him. Esposito had turned off the motor. Ballester said that while undressing in her room the child had suddenly keeled over as if mowed down. 'Did you ever hear anything like it!' Marcou said. Ballester shook his head and gestured vaguely towards the shop; but he looked as if he had had quite a turn. Again the ambulance bell was heard. They were all there, in the silent shop, under the yellow light coming through the glass panels, with their rough, useless hands hanging down along their old sawdust-covered trousers.

The rest of the afternoon dragged. Yvars now felt only his fatigue and his still heavy heart. He would have liked to talk. But he had nothing to say, nor had the others. On their uncommunicative faces could be read merely sorrow and a sort of obstinacy. Sometimes the word 'calamity' took shape in him, but just barely, for it disappeared immediately – as a bubble forms and bursts simultaneously. He wanted to get home, to be with Fernande again, and the boy, on the terrace. As it happened, Ballester announced closing-time. The machines stopped. Without hurrying, they began to put out the fires and to put everything in order on their benches, then they went one by one to the locker-room. Saïd remained behind; he was to clean up the shop and water down the dusty soil. When Yvars reached the locker-room, Esposito, huge and hairy, was already under the shower. His back was turned to them as he soaped himself noisily. Generally, they kidded him about his modesty; the big bear, indeed, obstinately hid his pudenda. But no one seemed to notice on this occasion. Esposito backed out of the shower and wrapped a towel around him like a loincloth. The others took their turns, and Marcou was vigorously slapping his bare sides when they heard the big door roll slowly open on its cast-iron wheel. Lassalle came in.

He was dressed as at the time of his first visit, but his hair was rather dishevelled. He stopped on the threshold, looked at the vast deserted shop, took a few steps, stopped again, and looked towards the locker-room. Esposito, still covered with his loincloth, turned towards him. Naked, embarrassed, he teetered from one foot to the other. Yvars thought that it was up to Marcou to say something. But Marcou remained invisible behind the sheet of water that surrounded him. Esposito grabbed a shirt and was nimbly slipping it on when Lassalle said: 'Good night,' in a rather toneless voice and began to walk towards the little door. When it occurred to Yvars that someone ought to call him, the door had already closed.

Yvars dressed without washing, said good night likewise, but with his whole heart, and they answered with the same warmth. He went out rapidly, got his bicycle, and when he straddled it, he felt the strain in his back again. He was cycling along now in the late afternoon through the trafficky city. He was going fast because he was eager to get back to the old house and the terrace. He would wash in the washhouse before sitting down to look at the sea, which was already accompanying him, darker than in the morning, above the parapet of the boulevard. But the little girl accompanied him too and he couldn't stop thinking of her.

At home, his boy was back from school and reading the picture papers. Fernande asked Yvars whether everything had gone all right. He said nothing, cleaned up in the washhouse, then sat down on the bench against the low wall of the terrace. Mended washing hung above his head and the sky was becoming transparent; over the wall the soft evening sea was visible. Fernande brought the anisette, two glasses, and the jug of cool water. She sat down beside her husband. He told her everything, holding her hand as in the early days of their marriage. When he had finished, he didn't stir, looking towards the sea where already, from one end of the horizon to the other, the twilight was swiftly falling. 'Ah! it's his own fault!' he said. If only he were young again, and Fernande too, they would have gone away, across the sea.

Alain Robbe-Grillet

THE BEACH

TRANSLATED BY
BARBARA WRIGHT

ALAIN ROBBE-GRILLET

Born in Brest 1922. French writer and film-maker, associated with the 'nouveau roman' and the pursuit of objectivity – not usually pursued so directly as in 'The Beach' (1962). The novels include *The Voyeur* and *Into the Labyrinth*. Films: *Last Year at Marienbad* (with Alain Resnais), *Trans-Europ-Express*.

THE BEACH

THREE children are walking along a beach. They move forward, side by side, holding hands. They are roughly the same height, and probably the same age too: about twelve. The one in the middle, though, is a little smaller than the other two.

Apart from these three children, the whole long beach is deserted. It is a fairly wide, even strip of sand, with neither isolated rocks nor pools, and with only the slightest downward slope between the steep cliff, which looks impassable, and the sea.

It is a very fine day. The sun illuminates the yellow sand with a violent, vertical light. There is not a cloud in the sky. Neither is there any wind. The water is blue and calm without the faintest swell from the open sea, although the beach is completely exposed as far as the horizon.

But, at regular intervals, a sudden wave, always the same, originating a few yards away from the shore, suddenly rises and then immediately breaks, always in the same line. And one does not have the impression that the water is flowing and then ebbing; on the contrary, it is as if the whole movement were being accomplished in the same place. The swelling of the water at first produces a slight depression on the shore side, and the wave recedes a little, with a murmur of rolling gravel; then it bursts, and spreads milkily over the slope, but it is merely regaining the ground it has lost. It is only very occasionally that it rises slightly higher and for a moment moistens a few extra inches.

And everything becomes still again; the sea, smooth and blue, stops at exactly the same level on the yellow sand along the beach where, side by side, the three children are walking. They are blond, almost the same colour as the sand: their skin is a little darker, their hair a little lighter. They are all three dressed alike; shorts and shirt, both of a coarse, faded blue linen. They are walking side by side, holding hands, in a straight line, parallel to the sea and parallel to the cliff, almost equidistant from both, a little nearer the water, though. The sun is at the zenith and leaves no shadow at their feet.

In front of them is virgin sand, yellow and smooth from the rock to the water. The children move forward in a straight line, at an even speed, without making the slightest little detour, calm, holding hands. Behind them the sand, barely moist, is marked by the three lines of prints left by their bare feet, three even series of similar and equally spaced footprints, quite deep, unblemished.

The children are looking straight ahead. They don't so much as glance at the tall cliff, on their left, or at the sea, whose little waves are periodically breaking, on the other side. They are even less inclined to turn round and look back at the distance they have come. They continue on their way with even, rapid steps.

*

In front of them is a flock of sea-birds walking along the shore, just at the edge of the waves. They are moving parallel to the children, in the same direction, about a hundred yards away from them. But, as the birds are going much less quickly, the children are catching them up. And while the sea is continually obliterating the traces of their star-shaped feet, the children's footsteps remain clearly inscribed in the barely moist sand, where the three lines of prints continue to lengthen.

The depth of these prints is constant; just less than an inch. They are not deformed; either by a crumbling of the edges, or by too deep an impression of toe or heel. They look as if they have been mechanically punched out of a more mobile, surface-layer of ground.

Their triple line extends thus ever farther, and seems at the same time to narrow, to become slower, to merge into a single line, which divides the shore into two strips along the whole of its length, and ends in a minute mechanical movement at the far end: the alternate fall and rise of six bare feet, almost as if they are marking time.

But as the bare feet move farther away, they get nearer to the birds. Not only are they covering the ground rapidly, but the relative distance separating the two groups is also diminishing far more quickly, compared to the distance already covered. There are soon only a few paces between them . . .

But when the children finally seem just about to catch up with the birds, they suddenly flap their wings and fly off, first one, then two, then ten. . . . And all the white and grey birds in the flock describe a curve over the sea and then come down again on to the sand and start walking again, still in the same direction, just at the edge of the waves, about a hundred yards away.

At this distance, the movements of the water are almost imperceptible, except perhaps through a sudden change of colour, every ten seconds, at the moment when the breaking foam shines in the sun.

*

Taking no notice of the tracks they are carving so precisely in the virgin sand, nor of the little waves on their right, nor of the birds, now flying, now walking, in front of them, the three blond children move forward side by side, with even, rapid steps, holding hands.

Their three sunburnt faces, darker than their hair, are alike. The expression is the same: serious, thoughtful, perhaps a little anxious. Their features, too, are identical, though it is obvious that two of these children are boys and the third a girl. The girl's hair is only slightly longer, slightly more curly, and her limbs just a trifle more slender. But their clothes are exactly the same: shorts and shirt, both of coarse, faded blue linen.

The girl is on the extreme right, nearest the sea. On her left walks the boy who is slightly the smaller of the two. The other boy, nearest the cliff, is the same height as the girl.

In front of them the smooth, yellow sand stretches as far as the eye can see. On their left rises, almost vertically, the wall of brown stone, with no apparent way through it. On their right, motionless and blue all the way to the horizon, the level surface of the sea is fringed with a sudden little wave, which immediately breaks and runs away in white foam.

*

Then, ten seconds later, the swelling water again hollows out the same depression on the shore side, with a murmur of rolling gravel.

The wavelet breaks; the milky foam again runs up the slope, regaining the few inches of lost ground. During the ensuing silence, the chimes of a far distant bell ring out in the calm air.

'There's the bell,' says the smaller of the boys, the one walking in the middle.

But the sound of the gravel being sucked up by the sea drowns the extremely faint ringing. They have to wait till the end of the cycle to catch the few remaining sounds, which are distorted by the distance.

'It's the first bell,' says the bigger boy.

The wavelet breaks, on their right.

When it is calm again, they can no longer hear anything. The three blond children are still walking in the same regular rhythm, all three holding hands. In front of them, a sudden contagion affects the flock of birds, who were only a few paces away; they flap their wings and fly off.

They describe the same curve over the water, and then come down on to the sand and start walking again, still in the same direction, just at the edge of the waves, about a hundred yards away.

*

'Maybe it wasn't the first,' the smaller boy continues, 'if we didn't hear the other, before . . .'

'We'd have heard it the same,' replies the boy next to him.

But this hasn't made them modify their pace; and the same prints, behind them, continue to appear, as they go along, under their six bare feet.

'We weren't so close, before,' says the girl.

After a moment, the bigger of the boys, the one on the cliff side, says:

'We're still a long way off.'

And then all three walk on in silence.

They remain thus silent until the bell, still as indistinct, again rings out in the calm air. The bigger of the boys says then: 'There's the bell.' The others don't answer.

The birds, which they had been on the point of catching up, flap their wings and fly off, first one, then two, then ten . . .

Then the whole flock is once more on the sand, moving along the shore, about a hundred yards in front of the children.

The sea is continually obliterating the star-shaped traces of their feet. The children, on the other hand, who are walking nearer to the cliff, side by side, holding hands, leave deep footprints behind them, whose triple line lengthens parallel to the shore across the very long beach.

On the right, on the side of the level, motionless sea, always in the same place, the same little wave is breaking.

Samuel Beckett

IMAGINATION DEAD IMAGINE

SAMUEL BECKETT

Born in Dublin 1906; living in France since 1938. Novels: *Murphy, Watt, Molloy, Malone Dies*. Plays: *Waiting for Godot, Endgame*. 'Imagination Dead Imagine' (1965) was first published in French and translated by the author into English.

IMAGINATION DEAD IMAGINE

No trace anywhere of life, you say, pah, no difficulty there, imagination not dead yet, yes, dead, good, imagination dead imagine. Islands, waters, azure, verdure, one glimpse and vanished, endlessly, omit. Till all white in the whiteness the rotunda. No way in, go in, measure. Diameter three feet, three feet from ground to summit of the vault. Two diameters at right angles AB CD divide the white ground into two semicircles ACB BDA. Lying on the ground two white bodies, each in its semicircle. White too the vault and the round wall eighteen inches high from which it springs. Go back out, a plain rotunda, all white in the whiteness, go back in, rap, solid throughout, a ring as in the imagination the ring of bone. The light that makes all so white no visible source, all shines with the same white shine, ground, wall, vault, bodies, no shadow. Strong heat, surfaces hot but not burning to the touch, bodies sweating. Go back out, move back, the little fabric vanishes, ascend, it vanishes, all white in the whiteness, descend, go back in. Emptiness, silence, heat, whiteness, wait, the light goes down, all grows dark together, ground, wall, vault, bodies, say twenty seconds, all the greys, the light goes out, all vanishes. At the same time the temperature goes down, to reach its minimum, say freezing-point, at the same instant that the black is reached, which may seem strange. Wait, more or less long, light and heat come back, all grows white and hot together, ground, wall, vault, bodies, say twenty seconds, all the greys, till the initial level is reached whence the fall began. More or less long, for there may intervene, experience shows, between end of fall and beginning of rise, pauses of varying length, from the fraction of the second to what would have seemed, in other times, other places, an eternity. Same remark for the other pause, between end of rise and beginning of fall. The extremes, as long as they last, are perfectly stable, which in the case of the temperature may seem strange, in the beginning. It is possible too, experience shows, for rise and fall to stop short at any point and mark a pause, more or less long, before resuming, or reversing, the rise now fall, the fall rise, these in their turn to be completed, or to stop short and mark a pause, more or less long, before resuming, or again reversing, and so on, till finally one or the other extreme is reached. Such variations of rise and fall, combining in countless rhythms, commonly attend the passage from white and heat to black and cold, and vice versa. The extremes alone are stable as is stressed by the vibration to be observed when a pause occurs at some intermediate stage, no matter what its level and duration. Then all vibrates, ground, wall, vault, bodies, ashen or leaden or between the two, as may be. But on the whole, experience shows, such uncertain passage is not common. And most often, when the light begins to fail, and along with it the heat, the movement continues unbroken until, in the space of some twenty seconds, pitch black is reached and at the same instant say freezing-point. Same remark for the reverse movement, towards heat and whiteness. Next most frequent is the fall or rise with pauses of varying length in these feverish greys, without at any moment reversal of the movement. But whatever its uncertainties the return sooner or later to a temporary calm seems assured, for the moment, in the black dark or the great whiteness, with attendant temperature, world still proof against enduring tumult. Rediscovered miraculously after what absence in perfect voids it is no longer quite the same, from this point of view, but there is no other. Externally all is as before and the sighting of the little fabric quite as much a matter of chance, its whiteness merging in the surrounding whiteness. But go in and now briefer lulls and never twice the same storm. Light and heat remain linked as though supplied by the same source of which still no trace. Still on the ground, bent in three, the head against the wall at B, the arse against the wall at A, the knees against the wall between B and C, the feet against the wall between C and A, that is to say inscribed in the semicircle ACB, merging in the white ground were it not for the long hair of strangely imperfect whiteness, the white body of a woman finally. Similarly inscribed in the other semicircle, against the wall his head at A, his arse at B, his knees between A and D, his feet between

D and B, the partner. On their right sides therefore both and
back to back head to arse. Hold a mirror to their lips, it mists.
With their left hands they hold their left legs a little below the
knee, with their right hands their left arms a little above the
elbow. In this agitated light, its great white calm now so rare
and brief, inspection is not easy. Sweat and mirror notwith-
standing they might well pass for inanimate but for the left
eyes which at incalculable intervals suddenly open wide and
gaze in unblinking exposure long beyond what is humanly
possible. Piercing pale blue the effect is striking, in the
beginning. Never the two gazes together except once, when
the beginning of one overlapped the end of the other, for
about ten seconds. Neither fat nor thin, big nor small, the bodies
seem whole and in fairly good condition, to judge by the
surfaces exposed to view. The faces too, assuming the two
sides of a piece, seem to want nothing essential. Between their
absolute stillness and the convulsive light the contrast is
striking, in the beginning, for one who still remembers having
been struck by the contrary. It is clear however, from a
thousand little signs too long to imagine, that they are not
sleeping. Only murmur ah, no more, in this silence, and at
the same instant for the eye of prey the infinitesimal shudder
instantaneously suppressed. Leave them there, sweating and
icy, there is better elsewhere. No, life ends and no, there is
nothing elsewhere, and no question now of ever finding again
that white speck lost in whiteness, to see if they still lie still
in the stress of that storm, or of a worse storm, or in the black
dark for good, or the great whiteness unchanging, and if not
what they are doing.

MORE ABOUT PENGUINS

Penguin Book News, which appears every month, contains details of all the new books issued by Penguins as they are published. From time to time it is supplemented by *Penguins in Print,* which is a complete list of all books published by Penguins which are in print. (There are well over three thousand of these.)

A specimen copy of *Penguin Book News* will be sent to you free on request, and you can become a subscriber for the price of the postage – 4s. for a year's issues (including the complete lists). Just write to Dept EP, Penguin Books Ltd, Harmondsworth, Middlesex, enclosing a cheque or postal order, and your name will be added to the mailing list.

Note: *Penguin Book News* and *Penguins in Print* are not available in the U.S.A. or Canada

THE PENGUIN BOOK OF ENGLISH
SHORT STORIES

Edited by Christopher Dolley

Some of the stories in this collection – such as Wells's 'The Country of the Blind' and Joyce's 'The Dead' – are classics; others – like Dickens's 'The Signalman' and Lawrence's 'Fanny and Annie' – are less well known. But all of them – whether funny, tragic, wry or fantastic – show their authors at their concise best. Which makes this representative collection, at the least, ferociously entertaining.

THE PENGUIN BOOK OF FRENCH
SHORT STORIES

Edited by Edward Marielle

Many unusual stories are included in this representative and highly entertaining volume, including two from medieval times – the anonymous *The Return of the Crusader* and Margaret of Navarre's *The Substitute*. The authors range from Voltaire, the Marquis de Sade and Alfred de Vigny to Anatole France, Guy de Maupassant, Colette, Albert Camus and Alain Robbe-Grillet.

THE PENGUIN BOOK OF ITALIAN
SHORT STORIES

Edited by Guido Waldman

The Italians have been producing short stories since the Middle Ages and most of the great prose writers of this century and the last – Verga, Pirandello, Svevo, Moravia, Pavese – have written brilliantly in this form.
This selection represents the best of the tradition from Boccaccio and his contemporaries to the present day. It provides readers with as vivid and as lively a portrait of Italy and the Italians as is ever likely to be composed within so compact a framework.